"FEAR NOT,"
DAMIAN SAID VERY SOFTLY.

"I swear that you will know me very, very well, and quickly so," he added.

Kat felt a shivering inside. "You will be sorry, sir, if you marry me!"

"Pray, lady! I am sorry at this moment! But we will wed. And if you are capable of being demure and quiet and well-behaved, we will have an easy enough time of it. And if not . . ."

"I am not demure and I am not well-behaved! This is my castle and my inheritance, and I—" She broke off because he was striding toward her purposefully, menacingly. "My lord, I am warning you—"

"And I am warning you, my lady. You've two seconds to march up those stairs and prepare for our wedding. Else I will take you there myself."

"Nay, my lord, you will not!" Then she gasped in astonishment as she felt his rough knight's hands on her soft flesh as he ruthlessly swept her up into his arms.

SHANNON DRAKE

DAMSEL IN DISTRESS

AVON BOOKS ◆ NEW YORK

DAMSEL IN DISTRESS is an original publication of Avon Books. This work has never before appeared in book form. This work is a novel. Any similarity to actual persons or events is purely coincidental.

AVON BOOKS
A division of
The Hearst Corporation
1350 Avenue of the Americas
New York, New York 10019

First Avon Books Printing: March 1992

AVON TRADEMARK REG. U.S. PAT. OFF. AND IN OTHER COUNTRIES, MARCA REGISTRADA, HECHO EN U.S.A.

Printed in the U.S.A.

RA 10 9 8 7 6 5 4 3 2 1

Prologue

Legends

Summer 1180
In the Reign of King Henry II
The Forest

She loved to come to the forest. It was beautiful here. Nowhere else was the world so radiantly colored. There were the deep brown and black hues of the earth and the various shades of green—the kelly-green of the grasses that grew from the rich turf; the lighter bursts of color from the brush; the deep, cool, secretive, enchanting dark green of the copses, where tall branches shadowed the sun and made a realm of fantasy and wonder. And when the boughs of the trees did give way, there was the sky. Sometimes shimmering with sunlight, a splash of blue. Sometimes shaded over with iron-gray storm clouds. And on those days, the wind would howl and moan, and the branches would lie low, as if they bowed to that greater, godlike power.

Then there were days when fog rolled in, soft, gray, swirling, adding to the mystery and magic to be found there. She loved to come.

Perhaps it was her father who first gave her the magic.

For she was a child of privilege through him, and when he was home, resting from his duty, his fealty to the King, he brought her here.

She hadn't known at first that she could come because she was a child of privilege. She only knew that her father was wonderful and good. He had sea-green eyes and platinum-blond hair, and he was tall and shining and wonderful. The King thought so, too, and that was why he was so often called away. But when he came back home, he brought her here, to the King's forest.

She rode a horse today: no little pony, but a full-sized mare. Her father said she could because she had become so fine a horsewoman. It was a special day. She was dressed in a very adult fashion, her hair neatly braided and coiled into loops on each side of her head, her mode of dress exquisite. She wore an underdress of deep rich green, to rival the forest, with long, sweeping sleeves that came to an elegant point below her wrist. Her ivory tunic offset the very deep color of the green.

And she carried a quiver of arrows on her back, her bow slung over her shoulder. She had never told her father that she really had no desire to aim at something as beautiful as a deer. She was too happy to be able to come hunting with him. And though a deer might be beautiful, she knew full well that it would help to feed their household of so very many in the long winter months to come.

Aye, it began as such a wonderful day! There were no other barons with them. They came, she and her father, with her cousin Little Rob and two of her father's pages, since they would need help bringing back a kill. Rob was thirteen, five years her elder, but he still liked to tease and taunt her, and he did so mightily that day. He bowed and laughed, and called her the Lady Greensleeves, and she warned him that he was sounding very much like a little devil. He still teased her mercilessly. She didn't mind. She was able to retort to him quickly, no matter what his taunt, and she could see her father, riding ahead, smiling as she and Rob chatted their way through the forest. It was really no way to come upon a deer. But her father didn't mind. They had all day. And it was beautiful, and cool. There was a light breeze. The trees rustled. Birds chirped and cried, and the radiant heat of the sun could just be felt beneath the canopy of green.

Curiously, she felt that she knew something was going to happen, long before it did. There was just something . . . some sudden stillness in the air, something that warned her, almost as if she were a special princess, and there really were forest gods at her beck and call.

Magical, fantastic, charming . . .

Nay, what seized her was none of these. It was fear, swift and horrible. Something awful was going to happen. She wanted to go no farther into the woods.

Before she could cry out, before she could warn anyone, they burst upon the tragic scene.

They were not alone in the forest. Just ahead of them was a party of noblemen. Three men, riding huge, well-groomed horses, dressed in the finest wools and linens and fur-trimmed cloaks. Their horses, too, were decked in finery, the colors of the one man, yellow and deep blue, blazoned on the blanket beneath his saddle.

The riders were attended by several squires, less splendid than the nobles, in simpler garb, but clearly one with them.

Nobles and squires were all circled around a tree. A doe lay near death at the base of that tree. Her huge brown eyes remained open. The blood pulsed swiftly from her chest, where an arrow shaft protruded.

Death would come to the doe swiftly. It had been a good, clean kill.

It wasn't the sight of the doe that disturbed her, even though she felt sad to see such a beautiful creature die.

What frightened her was the way the party of noblemen encircled the men who stood by the doe.

There were just two of them. And they were certainly not noble. They were both dressed in coarse brown tunics. One did not even have hose to warm his very skinny calves. Their faces were both smudged, as if they slept in dirt, or as close as they could to the ashes from a fire. Their brown hair was long, in the Saxon fashion. The older man wore a beard, while the younger man was just growing whiskers.

Both looked terrified.

"What is this? What happens here?" her father began to ask.

But even as her father rode forward, trying to break into their circle, she saw, in a flash of sunlight, the rise and fall of a small hunting axe.

And she heard a scream. An awful, agonized scream.

The circle of men had parted somewhat. She saw the younger man raising the stump of his arm. She saw his hand, disengaged from that arm, lying useless on a rock, blood spurting from it.

"Be glad 'tis nothing more for you, that I have shown mercy!" the nobleman on the horse in the fancy colors called out. "And as for you—" He turned to the older man who was being dragged up to stand upon the rock, as a noose was produced to be slipped about his neck. "You will hang for your thievery!" The nobleman who seemed to be the leader had an evil face.

So did one of his companions, the lad at his side. They appeared to be father and son, like the father and son Saxon pair they seemed so determined to cripple and kill.

The Saxon father didn't say a word in his behalf, but looked in horror at his son lying on the ground, bleeding. There was something helpless in his look. Helpless and fatalistic and far beyond despair.

God in heaven, she was going to be sick. The younger man was in the dirt. Blood gushed from his wound.

And now the noble was ordering his men to throw a rope over the tree.

She heard the roar of her father's voice. "Nay, ye'll not do this—"

"They've broken the law. These Saxon pigs, taking the King's good game from the forest!" the leader of the noblemen told her father. He seemed to know him.

"The King would not have this! Ever!" her father shouted, and he pulled his sword. "Jesu—let them go! Can't you see? They are starving to death. What is one doe?"

"My God, Father!" she cried out. There were so many of them, and only one of her father.

But behind her father, Rob was pulling out his small sword, too.

"Count de Montrain!" the nobleman addressed her father. "Would you die over this offal? Aye, but then you would. You've that Saxon whelp at your heels again, eh? So be it! Die then!"

The nobleman drew his own sword and yelled out to his companions to do the same. At his side, his son instantly drew his weapon, a leer upon his face. Cruelty touched his young eyes. He was eager for the fray.

"Run!" her father commanded, quickly turning to her and Rob.

But Rob would not run. She knew it. And neither would she. If her father would die here, then so would they.

But they were not destined to die.

Even as the massive party bore down on them, the leader suddenly screamed out. His horse reared, and he nearly fell from it, for there was an arrow shaft protruding from his thigh.

Another arrow flew, and another. Two more men were

hit. They ceased their assault, and their horses pranced about in confusion.

"Where the hell—?" the leader shouted.

"There must be an army of bandits!" his son cried.

"Jesu, I'll not die here!" said a third man.

"De Montrain!" the leader warned her father, pointing his sword. "You will pay for this!"

"Nay, de la Ville, I will not!" her father responded. "For the King will hear my side of it!"

The horsemen were suddenly gone, racing from the hail of arrows that rained down upon them.

The older man, with a rope still about his neck, stood on the rock, shivering. The younger man lay on the ground, moaning, holding the stump of his arm.

"Father, the arrows!" she warned in alarm, watching as her father hurried his horse forward, anxious to reach the poor peasants.

"We are safe. I know it," he said softly. And he dismounted from his horse, rushing to remove the rope from around the peasant's neck. The man fell to his knees, shaking, trying to kiss her father's booted feet. "Nay, nay, good fellow," her father protested. He looked almost helplessly at his daughter. "Your sleeve, my love. Rip up some of your sleeve. If the lad continues to bleed, he will die."

She hadn't realized that she had just sat there through it all, horrified, on the verge of tears and probably far worse. Her teeth were chattering. She could scarcely move at first.

Then she found life. She ripped the length of her sleeve from her underdress and managed to dismount from her horse on shaky little legs. She pushed aside Robin and her father when they would have helped her.

Alone, she went to the young man. His blood spilled over her, and she feared that she would swoon.

She didn't. She managed to bind up his arm. His

blood stained the beautiful green material to a dark and rusty red. She met the lad's eyes. "Thank you, my lady, thank you!"

The older man, his father, was behind him then, trying to lift him to his feet. "Bring the deer," her father commanded his pages. "The lad will need the food if he is to live. Is there someone to cauterize that wound?" He asked the older man, using the Saxon's language he had learned from his wife.

"Aye, his mother," said the man.

"Good."

"But my lord," one of the pages said. "It is against the law—"

"These people are starving. King Henry, our lawgiver, might well be known as the justice giver. He would not condemn me. Now the deer is dead. We are alone."

"Alone. Except for someone shooting arrows," Robin reminded his uncle with wide eyes.

"We are safe," her father insisted. "Go! Hurry, now!" he warned the peasants and his pages.

The men were quickly gone. The deer disappeared. Robin opted to ride with the Saxons and the pages, insisting that the injured youth ride before him on his horse.

She was left with her father, alone with him.

And she burst into tears, throwing herself into his arms. "Father, Father, how could those awful men do such a thing!"

Her father sighed deeply, holding her against him. "Well, in truth, there are laws, you see. Laws against hunting here."

"Laws are awful then!"

"Nay, my love. Most laws are good. They protect men. Even the way that we live is good. You see, the peasants and the villeins, people such as this, they work for us, as well as tilling their own little pieces of tenant land. And we protect them within our castle walls. We settle their disputes. We hold court over our serfs, and over our freemen. They serve us. And we—"

"We serve the King," she whispered. "Father, they called these people Saxon pigs. And Rob—they called him a Saxon whelp, and they said it so hatefully!" She began to shiver anew.

Her father sighed deeply. "Well, my love, it has been well over a hundred years since Duke William of Normandy came here to conquer England and become King William. He won his crown well. But in all this time, we still have his people, the Normans, and we still have the English people who were here, the Saxons. Now, in a way, Duke William won. In a way, he did not. His people never ceased to fear the Saxons, and so some of them hate the very people who they vanquished. Some of the Saxons vanquished the Normans in turn." He offered her a tender smile, touching her cheek. "Your mother conquered me, she did. Stole my heart away!"

She tried to smile in turn.

"Laws are not bad things, my dear. Henry has tried to make all the laws for all of the people. He is a good king. A strong king."

She knew the King. He was a handsome man with endless energy. He fought all the time with his wife and sons. He was opinionated and arrogant. He could be determined.

But she had never, never seen him cruel.

Not like the noblemen she'd just encountered.

Hot tears welled in her eyes. She blinked hard.

She looked at her father. "So, the laws are good, as long as we have a good king."

"And good nobles to combat bad nobles."

"What shall happen if we have a king who is not good? And many nobles who are bad?"

Her father, watching her, shuddered suddenly. He held her close. "Then evil will rule the land," he told her starkly. "But my love, bear this in mind—a good strong king keeps a firm hand upon his nobles. Men like those you saw today are not allowed to become too powerful. And there will always be good men. And it will not matter what language they speak, or how they clothe themselves, or from where they come." He looked around himself suddenly, remembering the hidden archer who had saved them all.

The pages rode up once again with Rob, who quickly dismounted from his horse and came to his cousin, for they were very close. He swept his arms around her. "It will be all right, my fair Lady Greensleeves," he told her solemnly. She tried to smile for him. He was looking at her father.

"I will learn to let fly my arrows like that, my lord!"

"I'm sure you will, my young sir!" he agreed. He stood. It was time to take the children from the forest.

"You ride on now, my love. Robin take her. Roc, Reginald, see to their safety. I will catch up with you." He needed a moment alone.

The children mounted their horses. "Go!" he told them, and they rode on.

He stood in the forest, and listened. The wind rustled around him. The air was soft. Still. Yet he was certain that he was still being watched.

"Thank you, my friend, wherever you are!" he called out softly.

There was a sudden burst of sound in the forest. He looked up.

One of de la Ville's men was bearing down on him on horseback. Bursting through the trees, ready to do murder.

His sword was raised high. Aimed at de Montrain's throat.

And there was no time. De Montrain could not reach for his own sword. He could not defend himself. He could scarcely rail against fate.

He could only stand there, bleed, and die.

"Move over, my lord!" he was suddenly commanded. There was a man with him. A man who shoved him when he could not manage to move out of the way of the thundering steed himself.

The man was armed with a sword of his own. A silver sword that gleamed wickedly in the shimmering green light of the day.

The ground thundered. The horseman, with his sword raised high, was smiling.

And oddly enough, he was still smiling as he died.

For though he came upon the young defender with his arm wickedly high and his weapon sharp, his blade was quickly parried. And as the horse rushed forward, de la Ville's man was impaled on the defender's own sword.

Only his eyes showed his surprise and horror as he died.

De Montrain stared at the fallen enemy who would have slain him, then at the man who had saved him.

Nay, not a man fully grown, but a youth, nearing his full maturity perhaps.

He was dark. Aye, hair dark as ebony. He was tall, with proud, handsome features. And he was vaguely familiar.

De Montrain smiled slowly. "You!" he said, surprised.

The youth colored, uneasy at having been discovered. "I know the law," he said quickly. "I couldn't let them hang the old man; I just couldn't let them do it. They were starving, you could see it in their eyes, it was just one doe—"

"My son, you needn't tell me!"

"And then, of course, well, I couldn't let that knave slay you!"

"And rightly grateful I am. But you needn't fear. I will tell Henry the truth—"

"Nay, please! Say nothing."

De Montrain hesitated a moment, then agreed. "Aye, lad, your secret is safe with me. I swear it! However, if you would run around the forest so, I would suggest a disguise of some sort."

The handsome youth bowed gravely, only a slight smile curving his lip. "I shall give it the gravest thought, my lord."

There was a rustling in the bush. The youth stepped back, ready to wield his sword again. Then he eased. "It is your family, returning. God go with you, my lord."

"And with you!" De Montrain called quickly. The lad was already gone, disappeared into the forest.

De Montrain stepped past de la Ville's fallen henchman. He wouldn't have the children see the body, or know that any more danger had come his way. He hurriedly walked forward, eager to greet them.

His saw his daughter, her beautiful eyes lustrous, even in the shadowy green forest, as they touched his. She would not easily forget this day, he thought. Nay, she would not easily forget it.

He tried to smile, and to bow very gallantly to her. "Ah, 'tis my lovely Lady Greensleeves, is it not?" He turned and bowed to his nephew in kind. "Master Robin!"

They both tried to smile in turn.

All three smiles faded.

"Come. Let's go home," he said softly. "This day is over. We must go home."

He mounted his horse, and wearily they started from the forest, a somber party.

Rob paused suddenly, turning back. "I thought I saw you with someone, Uncle."

"Did you?"

"And I thought I knew . . ."

"What?"

"Nothing," Rob said. But his hazel eyes were curiously alight. And he smiled suddenly, a grim, determined smile. "I will learn to shoot my arrows like that! Nay, my lord uncle, I will do better!"

"So shall I!" his daughter vowed. "Oh, Father, so shall I!"

He was uneasy, watching the two earnest young faces.

And most uneasy watching his nephew, for somehow the lad knew. The lad knew exactly what had occurred. Just as he knew the identity of their secret savior.

"The day is over," he said firmly. "We'll talk no more of it. It is done."

In silence, they rode on. Darkness was shrouding the trees. Indeed, the day was over.

But the legends had just begun.

Chapter 1

Summer 1190
In the Reign of King Richard, Coeur de Lion
The Forest

The leader of the small party of bandits crouched tensely behind the barrier of the old oak, watching as the group of noblemen approached.

The leader's eyes narrowed, assessing the strength of the oncoming travelers.

A shivering sensation seemed to steal its way into the leader's heart. The man at the head of the group of well-dressed and richly festooned riders was wearing a tunic that proclaimed the colors of the house of Montjoy, a tunic with a rich yellow-gold background, the Plantagenet lions in one corner to proclaim the Norman relationship to the King, and the field of broadswords in the lower right-hand corner, perhaps to signify that the Montjoy men were knights and fighters, and gained their riches that way, and would continue to hold them so.

Again, that ripple of unease swept along the outlaw leader's spine. Montjoy. A formidable opponent.

But as the bandit had heard, this party of travelers was lightly armed. Montjoy wore no armor. He was clad in silver-gray chausses, trousers and hose combined, leather boots; the family-crested tunic; and a sweeping gray cloak held in place at his shoulder with a jeweled brooch.

13

He wore no hat or cowl, and his hair seemed blacker than a raven's wing beneath the sun, a color that somehow added to his formidable appearance, for despite his lack of armor, he was formidable appearing indeed. He rode a huge black war-horse, an animal incredibly tall and muscled, and atop it, he seemed almost a god, exuding an energy and animal strength as great as that of the beast beneath him.

Montjoy . . .

It shouldn't have been he traveling through the forest here. Word had come that a small guard would be riding through with a wagonload of wheat, wool and coin taken from the poor people of a nearby village as taxes trumped up for the Prince's "protecting" army.

A good king sat on the throne now. At least, a king that the people admired and loved. But that good king had left them. He'd gone off on Crusade.

And already the strong control of his barons and government that Henry II had held was sinking by the wayside. Dukes, counts, earls—they were all becoming little kings unto themselves. Chief among the power grabbers was the King's own brother, Prince John. Richard had scarce left the country but already John's hands were reaching.

The laws were left to the lawless.

But Montjoy . . .

His ability as a knight was legendary. Perhaps they should melt away into the forest now.

"Nay, nay!" the bandit leader mouthed, determined not to be swayed by this man's appearance. Damian Montjoy, Count Clifford, was nothing more than mortal man, no matter how tall and dark and powerful he might appear.

Once again, a shiver snaked along the bandit leader's spine. The man did appear forbidding indeed. No armor padding made the man's shoulders appear so broad, no

plates of steel added to the hard ripple of muscle beneath
the fabric of his clothing. The lines of his face were
hard ones, perhaps handsome in their very ruggedness,
cleanly structured. His cheekbones were high and broad,
his clean-shaven jaw was dead-set firm, with a surprisingly sensual mouth above it. His nose was long and
very straight, and like his high cheekbones, his eyes
were well set apart, dark it seemed today, but the bandit
leader could not see them so well against the glimmer of
sunlight that now rose behind the travelers.

The sunlight caught and shimmered on something else.
Something else created of silver and steel. Montjoy's
sword.

Perhaps this had been a mistake . . .

"Now?" the man to the leader's right queried.

"Nay, nay, not quite yet. Wait. Wait until they are
close, so close that we can see them sweat, and give
them no leave to defend themselves."

And so they waited. One more moment . . .

"Now!" the leader cried. They leaped out from the
shield of the trees, five of them dressed in simple spun-
wool tunics and hose in the colors of the forest, brown
and green, their silver swords flashing the only bright
color about them. They were quite good at their craft,
having learned over the past months to separate many
men from their riches, doing far more with threats than
with any real violence.

The bandit leader, clad in a green cloak and cowl,
faced Montjoy, determined not to display fear.

"Halt, sir! Give over the coin wrested from the people,
and pass in peace!"

Montjoy quickly took in the five who had surrounded
his party. A slow smile of challenge curled his lip. "I
give over nothing that is mine!"

"Give over, my lord, give over!" cried the fatter of
the two friars accompanying him.

Montjoy cast him a contemptuous glare. The bandit leader swiftly decided to use the good friar's fear.

"Surrender the riches you rob from the people. We shall then let you go in peace!"

"I'm not known for being a man of peace," Montjoy retorted. "Nor have I robbed any people."

"Then the blood be on your hands, sir!" cried the bandit leader.

"As you would have it!" Montjoy returned. His sword was suddenly freed from his scabbard. To the bandit leader's astonishment, he sent that sword flying first against the haunches of one friar's horse, and then the other's. Both animals reared, then went flying down the length of the road.

"Hop aboard the wagon, boy!" Montjoy ordered his pale young squire, and the towheaded boy did as he was commanded, leaping for the wagon and the reins.

"No!" shrieked the bandit leader, but it was too late, for Montjoy had sent the flat of his blade against the wagon horse, and that animal, too, bolted, carrying all the riches from the forest.

"God's blood!" swore the bandit leader, turning about with dismay. "Lem, Martin, go! See if you can catch it!" Then the leader turned again, certain that Montjoy would have given chase to the wagon.

He had not.

"Now, lad, you will give over!" Montjoy ordered. "Surrender, or your own blood will be upon your hands!"

"Jesu!" shrilled one of the remaining bandits, stepping forward. He shook, and his fingers trembled around his sword, but he was determined to meet Montjoy for his leader. "Meet my sword, my lord!"

Montjoy did. Without causing a whit of harm to the young man, he swirled his great broadsword from atop his horse, and sent the bandit's blade flying to some far corner of the forest.

Once again, with cold, calculating eyes, Montjoy faced the leader.

The leader's blade rose high. Despite the encumbrance of cloak and cowl, the leader moved agilely in a circle, trying to unseat the nobleman, who now had the advantage of height and power.

And more. Montjoy had unbelievable confidence. A deep, rich laugh riddled the air as his blade swung in a sure arc.

Swords met and clashed. The bandit dug in against the force of power. Montjoy smiled. "A worthy opponent, so I see. Ah, but young! Too young to have learned that supple play cannot always make up for youth and inexperience!"

Once again, Montjoy swung, this time catching the blade on an upward stroke.

And like the sword that had come against Montjoy's before it, the bandit leader's blade went flying into some green oblivion of forest, bracken, and trees.

Retreat could be most noble. The bandit leader had learned that long ago.

Noble, indeed. And now—this very second!—seemed the most noble time ever for retreat.

The bandits knew how to melt into the forest. "Separate!" the leader called to them, and fell into the westward section of the road, running down a trail of dense bracken and bush, certain that, if they went in separate directions, the great Lord Montjoy could not follow them all.

Nay, he could not.

But their scattering did not cause him the least confusion.

He meant to follow the leader.

Just seconds after plowing down the overgrown and near-forgotten trail, the bandit leader heard the heavy sound of the destrier's hooves pounding close behind.

The bandit leader zigged and zagged, surefooted and comfortable with the forest here.

And all to no avail.

Within seconds the horse was there, pounding the ground, breathing down the bandit leader's very neck.

The great horse reared, and the bandit leader pitched forward, rolling quickly to avoid the lethal hooves of the animal. Panting, gasping, the leader tried to rise again, but was cut down quickly with a new assault.

Montjoy!

The man had leaped from the rearing horse.

The bandit, felt the warm, redolent earth, and reached quickly for a handful of dirt and grass, throwing it into Montjoy's face as he approached.

"Fool!" Montjoy roared, adding almost as an afterthought, "and an ignoble and dirty fighter, at that, I daresay!" The dirt did not even give him pause. He was still coming.

Scrambling against the ground in an attempt to either gain footing or find some other weapon to hurtle at the aggressive Montjoy, the bandit cried back in return. "A dirty fighter against a filthy set of monsters keen on destroying this country!" There were no stones or twigs. The bandit's fingers curled around another clump of earth.

But there was no chance to throw it. Montjoy, not blinded at all but ever more furious, moved with a startling ease and agility for a man so well-muscled. Like lightning, he crossed the few feet left between them, and pounced upon his prey himself.

A knight's thighs, solid as rock, wrapped around the bandit's hip. Teeth gritted tight, struggling desperately against the hold, the bandit lashed out, slapping, clawing at Montjoy's face.

Something within Montjoy quickened as he held the bandit. Sheer amazement at his discovery regarding his opponent held him still for a second, and the bandit leader lashed out again with renewed energy, desperate for freedom.

But Montjoy was quick, and ruthless in his determination. Gauntleted hands found the bandit's wrists and forced them tightly together, as if they were locked in prayer. The force and weight were so great that the bandit cried out in pain, trapped for the moment, but still defiant and determined to fight.

"Now, my young cutthroat—" Montjoy began, easing his weight up just a bit.

The bandit found an advantage and bucked upward, struggling fiercely and now trying to kick out with a vengeful fervor.

"Christ's bones!" Montjoy swore. "But you are looking for a serious whipping with an oak stick—"

"Give me a chance with a sword or an arrow—"

"Any further chance, and I'd have had your heart cut squarely from your body. Your chances are all over. Ah, yes! An oak stick, I think." The bandit leader was horrified as Montjoy suddenly leaned close, something akin to a smile curving his lips. "You should be stripped bare, I think, and severely chastised from head to toe."

The leader's eyes widened. Stripped?

"What say you?" Montjoy demanded, and his thumb traced the bandit's chin. It was a sensual movement, and the bandit was horrified to feel a rush of heat at the touch. Dear God, he wouldn't. He might. Did he know that he dealt with a woman?

Ah, yes, the way that he touched her. And the way that it made her feel.

Fury cascaded through her. Against herself, and most certainly, against him. Then a shivering, fierce and desperate, seized hold of her. The bandit's eyes closed. Memories swept over her and the years washed away. So many years. But the forest was the same, green and deep. And a lad lay on the ground, blood gushing from the stump of his arm, punishment for the thievery of a deer, a mouthful of food for the harsh winter to come.

Her eyes flew open, meeting Montjoy's. "I shall kill you! Let me up!"

"Oh, I think not!" His thighs locked around hers tightly. Intimately. Yes, he knew! He spoke in a leisurely fashion now with a husky voice that taunted and teased. "You're nothing but a little thief out here in these woods, and you ought to know that you're interfering with something bigger than you can imagine. You'll learn to stay home and—mind your fields. Or whatever it is that you usually do mind."

"Let go—"

"They hang thieves, you know."

"Let go of me! I'll kill you or you can kill me! But get your hands off me!"

"Hmm." Montjoy seemed to enjoy his dominant position with his legs locked around her. "Once, the Norman laws were truly hard against poaching and thievery. Why," he paused, leaning very close, "once, a poacher might have been blinded and castrated for just such an offense as that you've committed here. Lie still. You wouldn't want me to determine to lop off your manhood, eh?"

His eyes glittered tauntingly. She felt her temper rise, along with a startling degree of heat within her. Her voice seemed to have left her when she first tried to speak.

"Ah, let's see. Where shall I begin? Strip you naked first, I think. And see what there is that one might lop off."

Enraged, she found her voice. "Hang me, and be damned with you—"

"Life is precious, my little thief. I'll not take yours, nor will you take mine!"

"Then let me go!"

"Not on your life!"

The bandit spit cleanly into Montjoy's face.

Montjoy swore. "A thief and a brat! With lessons in manners to be learned."

Lessons in manners! Her fury and her fear suddenly exploding into recklessness, she reached swiftly for the knife that protruded from a small sheath in Montjoy's scabbard. The blade flickered before Montjoy's face.

"I'll have your throat," she cried, triumph ringing plainly in the words. "Now, my great lord, you step back! Take yourself off me, and get yourself to a field to plow! Ah, wait! Perhaps I should strip you naked first. And lop off your manhood!"

The point of the sword was close against Montjoy's throat. So close that it tickled the flesh beneath his jaw. "Up!" the bandit cried.

"Or else?"

She smiled like a cat. The tables were turned. "I'll punish you the way you intended to punish me, my lord. Stand, and pay heed. I shall give you a few lessons in manners. Taught, perhaps, with an oak stick!"

Eyes narrowed dangerously, Montjoy began to rise as he had been ordered.

"There, there! Good lad!" she cried. "Ah, now! Where is a good oak stick when one is needed? I do believe that the big strong knight might find his arrogant manners well repaired with a good switching! Ah! But we need some bare flesh here, I think."

"Take care—you will have what you threaten!" he warned.

"Hmm," she murmured. "You are the one who so seems to enjoy threats!"

"You tempt the very heavens!" Montjoy warned.

"I tempt the heavens? But sir, I hold the blade! Ah, dear! A stick! Upon that bare hide, I think. It is a kindness, surely, to teach lessons in humility. And what could be more humiliating than trudging naked through a forest?" she taunted. Ah, yes, this victory was sweet!

But too soon savored, for even as Montjoy rose and the bandit scrambled up, keeping the knife at Montjoy's throat, Montjoy suddenly defied the blade, his fingers reaching swift as sound to swipe the hilt of the weapon from the bandit.

"Nay!" she cried.

But Montjoy's fingers were vises, nearly crushing her bones. With a second cry, she released the weapon, gasping at the pain, stunned to be weaponless against the dirt once again.

"What, ho!" Montjoy cried. "And now, you see, I hold the blade!"

The tables were indeed turned.

Damn!

Ah, it seemed time to run again, the bandit thought in distress. Running could be such great valor . . .

But running was impossible. Even as the bandit turned to leave, Montjoy reached out. Those powerful fingers curled into the material of her shirt. She was wrenched around, gasping.

"Oh where, oh where, is a good stick when one needs one!" Montjoy moaned mockingly. "Ah, but first! Let's snatch away every stitch of clothing here."

The bandit tried to escape his grasp. The shirt tore.

The flesh beneath Montjoy's fingers was soft and ivory in color. She wasn't just a maid, he determined. She was an exceptional one. No matter how she attempted to deepen her voice, it was soft and feminine.

Thinking her nothing but a girl, he eased his hold somewhat. A mistake. She was a maid, indeed, but a bold and angry one. Any attempt at mercy on his part would be a foolish one. She would kill him now if she got the chance.

He had nearly lost his hold on his captive. He caught

the bandit's arm, and wrenched the defiant soul around with such a force that the bandit fell flat to the forest floor. Gasping, stunned, the bandit tried too late to rise again.

Montjoy straddled her, his thighs a punishing prison once again.

He had wanted to tease her into submission. He had been startled by the sensual pull he had felt toward his captive, and had even thought that the sexual threat might make a more amiable prisoner of her.

But now she threatened them both, and she had to understand her position—and her danger.

He set the knife against her cheek. "Never produce a weapon unless you intend to use it," he warned chillingly.

Suddenly, the bandit was trembling beneath him, teeth gritted for a pretense of bravado. "Don't threaten, my lord! Slice and be done with it!"

Slice, Jesu! The bandit tried to banish from her mind the image of blood dripping from the severed hand . . .

Montjoy touched his chin, wiping away the small drop of blood that had formed there.

Seeing Montjoy's eyes, the bandit was filled with an even greater dread. Blood had been drawn. Here. Now. What revenge would there be? Montjoy would not forgive, or forget.

"Come! Do it! Slay me and be done with it!"

The words were spoken recklessly, the fear behind them well hidden.

The knife flickered briefly in the sunlight through the leaves in the forest canopy above them.

Then it was sheathed.

"Nay, I think too highly of any life to end it so swiftly, but you do need some discipline. Something for a wayward child. A sound thrashing, I daresay. And damn! I've still not found a good oak stick! Alas, though. Something must be done. A knight's hand in lieu of some wretched weapon."

"Don't you dare!" the bandit shrieked. "Oh! Let me up, let me go, you threaten idly—"

"I never threaten idly!" Montjoy declared. "Perhaps your wounded dignity will give fair warning, for dignity can be regained, and life cannot."

"I'll bite you 'til you bleed," the bandit warned.

God's blood! But she did need some lesson!

In truth, Montjoy did not threaten idly, and he had the force to carry out any threat. In a second he was up, twisting the slender bandit around, and in seconds he had one knee beneath him and one knee balanced on the ground and the maid was beneath him, feeling the full force of his hand—and his anger.

She shrieked and swore, fighting, and pulling away at last, stumbling backwards. Free.

No, not free. Montjoy was too quick. He was up, adding insult to injury as he caught hold of a green sleeve and held punishingly tight. "Who are you?" he demanded harshly. "And what are you doing out here in this forest attacking those who pass through it?"

"I am no one! Find yourself another lad to—"

"Lad!" he cried, and then laughed aloud. To her horror, he leaned low against her, the fingers of his one hand creating a bind about her wrists while his left hand moved boldly to her breast. A flush of crimson colored her cheeks.

"You are no lad," he whispered, gently squeezing her soft flesh.

She gritted her teeth, fighting the delicious sensations his touch aroused in her, wishing she could slap the amused grin from his handsome face. "Fine! I am no lad! You have taught your lesson! Let me free from you!"

He shook his head, still touching her. "I will know who you are!"

Montjoy reached out quickly, stripping away the cowl that had shadowed the bandit's face.

He was met with a handful of near golden hair. Beautiful hair, wild hair. Hair that caused his breath to catch, and the blood to quicken within him. Even as he felt the startling contraction of his muscles, he realized that he was staring into a pair of aquamarine eyes that were assuredly the most striking he had ever seen.

Nay! For he had seen eyes like this before.

Once . . .

Hadn't he?

"This is insanity," he muttered. "I must know what you're doing and who you are. If you'll not answer me, I'll take you to my castle—"

Montjoy paused suddenly. But the bandit didn't realize it at first. She was too busy thinking.

To his castle! To be hanged there? By this man? Who taunted her so easily, and brought such a heat to her body, such a flush to her cheeks? Would he find her amusing—and then hang her? Nay, it could not happen, he didn't know what he dealt with, he . . .

He had very suddenly gone silent.

The bandit turned, realizing that Montjoy was looking over her shoulder.

Hope suddenly filled her heart.

Help had arrived. The true prince of the forest had come upon them.

Robin had come. Dressed in hunter's green as she was herself, he stepped into the clearing.

He had grown to be a handsome and well-honed man. He was smaller than Montjoy, not so tall and not so muscled, but his courage did not lack in any way. Boldly he walked toward the knight. The bandit was surprised that he came unprepared. His bow and quiver hung from his back. His eyes were upon Montjoy's, not hers.

"My lord!" Robin called out swiftly, as if he feared

that Montjoy might come against her with some further violence.

She was suddenly very frightened for Robin. She could not let anything happen to him. She did some good as the Lady Greensleeves, but it was Robin's name that the barons feared, and Robin who protected the poor people who were now so dangerously at the whim of the nobility.

"Take heed!" she cried out in warning.

Take heed. Indeed. Robin's eyes flashed to hers. He was furious with her, she realized. He'd never wanted her to be part of any of the real danger. She had tried to tell him again and again. She'd been there that day. She'd seen the blood.

No matter his anger now. He needed to be watching out for Montjoy.

"My lord!" Robin cried again to Montjoy. "I beg you. Let go this too anxious child."

"Child!" she protested. Had Robin lost his senses? Was he expecting some mercy from this rough-hewn Norman knight?

Montjoy watched as she quickly lowered her head, hiding the fear and anger in her eyes. She tried to cover herself again with the cowl. He almost smiled, except that he was puzzled and still furious himself. He would like to set his hands upon her again. What did she think she was doing? Did she imagine that he would forget she was a woman?

She didn't even seem to suspect that he had recognized her.

"Go!" Robin ordered her. She stared from him to Montjoy, certain that Montjoy would make a move to stop her.

But he did not.

She stared at the man in green. "Robin, I cannot leave you—"

"Go!" Robin repeated. "He will let you go, so do so now before he changes his mind. We will settle this, Count Clifford and I."

Montjoy saw her eyes once again. Beautiful, passionate—defiant. Eyes that burned into him, and despised him.

Then she did as Robin had commanded her, turning to run like an agile doe through the forest.

And then they were left alone, the man in the forest-green and the great Lord Montjoy, Count Clifford.

Robin waited. He wanted to be sure that she had gone, that no one remained to hear what passed between him and this knight.

It was Robin who spoke first, sighing, his shoulders hunching. "Jesu, Damian, I am sorry."

Damian watched Robin, the man in green, the outlaw who should have been his sworn enemy. He shook his head angrily. "Robin, what in the name of God are you doing here? Had she not appeared so young, I might well have skewered her through!"

"You know who she is?"

"Perhaps. Tell me, and I will be certain."

Robin shook his head. "I cannot do that! Like this forest, I keep the secrets that I am bade to keep. I hold to my heart many identities for those who choose not to be known. I keep all secrets, just as I will keep what is spoken between us now."

"Ah, but this one might well concern the King."

Robin shook his head. "I swear to you, Damian, I will find out what happened here with her."

"You didn't order her out upon the highway to rob me?"

"Sweet Jesu, no! This was her own doing. And it will not happen again."

"See to it," Damian warned softly. "It seems that you have an obedience problem."

"Not among my men," he said stiffly. Then the slightest smile curved his mouth. "All right. Perhaps among my kin."

"If you've further problems, the lady is not my kin. I will gladly see that she is kept to her place."

"You don't understand," Robin said softly. "We formed a bond that day in the forest. She was there, you see—"

"She plays at this!" Montjoy said angrily. "Dangerous play. She needs no part in it."

"I think that she will remember her encounter with you for some time to come."

"Better an encounter with me than with another man's sword. Get her out of this profession, and quickly."

"You are right, of course. She has brought me news. That was all that she was allowed. She will not be so reckless again. My God, I do so promise," Robin assured him. Then he added urgently. "But now she has seen us together. Do I give away all that I know of you? By all rights, one of us should be slaying the other here. How shall we have parted one another after having met here, friend?"

"Is she aware of our relationship?"

Robin smiled. "Our blood relationship? Or the friendship between two denizens of the forest?"

"Either."

Robin shook his head. "No one would imagine that the great Count Clifford is any kin to a bandit." He paused. "Nor, assuredly, would she ever imagine you to have any sympathy with the people. So—how do we manage to part, both alive and well?"

Damian mulled the problem for a moment. "Ah, I have it! More matter for legend and stories and wagging tongues! We will have had a clash of swords, yet one so even that we parted, leaving the finale for some later date. How does that sound?" As he spoke, he strode toward his mount. The great black horse had awaited him silently in the copse, enjoying the sprigs of rich green grass that grew upon the ground.

Robin smiled slowly. He bowed deeply to Montjoy as Montjoy mounted the destrier. "My lord, you are a match indeed for either prince or king."

"So I hope," Damian said softly, lifting the reins and circling about to address Robin. "I leave to join the King in the Holy Lands soon. Take care then. Take grave care, I beg of you."

"As always. And you, friend, take care that you are not the target of a Saracen blade."

"I will manage well enough, thank you. May England do so well."

Robin walked over to Montjoy's horse, rubbing his palm over the animal's soft nose. "Must you go? It seems that we just begin to hold our own in certain places. They say that some fellow named Hood—Robin Hood, that is—is doing vast damage in the woods. And of late, those who would flaunt the laws set down by the late Henry II, and those who would abuse the poor, especially our Saxon peasantry, are meeting with severe resistance from that curious fellow, the Silver Sword."

Montjoy grimaced. "So there's a name to the fellow now?"

Robin continued to stroke the horse's nose softly. "You know the people, Montjoy. They like to give names to the mysteries in life."

"Do they, now?" Montjoy leaned low, his eyes narrowed severely. "So tell me, then. What of the bandit I met just moments ago? The one who should not be in this forest at all?"

Robin shrugged unhappily. "They whisper that she is called the Lady Greensleeves, what else?" There was a touch of humor to his voice, but then he sighed. "She shouldn't have been in harm's way as you saw—"

"Coming against me? Indeed not!"

"Coming against any man so. But she is quite excellent with her father's sword."

"I could have killed her. Heaven alone knows what other men might have done."

Robin knew. He had seen what men did in the forest, time and time again. "You don't know her," he said softly.

"And pray I will not come to know her! But you are wrong, we do cross paths upon occasion. And that spark of fire is ever in her eyes. Thankfully, she is your concern."

Robin laughed softly. "Her mother was my father's sister. While my mother was your mother's cousin. It seems a pity that my dearest relations cannot be friends."

"'Tis my opinion she should be locked in a tower," Damian said, "and there kept from harm's way. Her father—"

"Her father is gone," Robin reminded Montjoy. "Lost with the same fever that . . ." He paused, then added softly. "The fever that swept away Alyssa. I am sorry, Damian."

"Aye, I am sorry, too." He gritted his teeth against the pain that could still seize him. "And I am heartily sorry for the loss of your cousin's father. He was a good man. A fellow with such integrity is hard to find these days. But as for his daughter . . . she needs discipline. She needs a husband." He shrugged. "Richard will see to it—somewhere along the line."

"She wants no husband. She is independent, and determined on her course here, in the forest. She cherishes her freedom."

"Her freedom will see her neck severed from her head one of these days. Well, it is your concern. Cousin, take care."

Robin smiled slowly and doffed his cap. "To our good

King Richard, and his hasty return!"

"Amen!"

With that last word, the men parted.

And the forest sheltered the secrets spoken between them.

Chapter 2

Summer 1192
The King's Crusade
The March to Jerusalem

"Mark your targets, bowsmen. Aim, fire!" Damian called out, his swirling sword a directive to the fine English bowsmen who had been directed throughout the caravan of Richard's march.

There was no denying by any man—any crowned head of Europe—that Richard, Coeur de Lion, was an exceptional knight, and a brilliant military tactician.

While the Emperor Frederick I of Germany had begun on the Pope's Holy Quest in 1189, Richard of England and Phillip of France had followed along the next year, going first to Sicily, where the two monarchs had spent the winter quarreling. Then they had moved on to Cyprus, where they had conquered. Damian had been with the King then, and when they came to Acre in the Holy Land, and he had been with Richard when his monarch had ordered his troops to take their positions for siege warfare. Richard's leadership was tacitly accepted by all the Crusaders there, and the victory had been stunning. Damian had led his own knights in one of the battles against men who had relieved the garrison, and when no new men or supplies were received, the garrison at last gave up the two-year siege. Richard had forced a surrender.

Damian had been heartily glad of it. Desert fighting was new to him, and to his men. The heat was oppressive, day after day when the sun rose blindingly into the sky, night after night when a sudden chill came to sweep away that dead heat created by the mesmerizing orb.

There was sand everywhere. Sand in his clothing, sand in his boots. So much sand. They were bogged down by it. Even as he slept, he felt the sand in his mouth. The snakes and insects were new and different here, and his men had to learn of just which to beware they laid their heads down at night to try to sleep.

And yet Damian was glad to be there, and whatever his thoughts were of the King, he admired Richard's abilities tremendously and keenly felt that his place was here. He knew that he was a good commander of men, just as Richard was.

Now, as they marched down the coast, determined on the final conquest of Jerusalem, they did so with a solid and well-ruled force of nearly fifty thousand men. Richard's fleet of ships followed them out on the water. Each day, they moved in short stretches, keeping tightly together.

The great Moslem commander and caliph, Saladin, kept troops hounding their inland flank, determined to break up the forces, seeking to and conquer the troops thus. But Richard was well aware of the strategy, and the troops were forbidden to engage in warfare with the harassers.

Richard's ranks remained unbroken.

But as Saladin's Turks launched a strong rear attack against the marching Crusaders, Richard at last gave his commanders a signal to attack. When the prearranged sound of the trumpet blared, Damian was ready. English crossbowmen had been dispersed throughout the ranks through all the long days of travel. Their arrows had kept the Turkish archers at a distance.

Now, the bowsmen heralded a mighty charge. Their arrows flew, and then the Crusader army turned in a massive and organized strike.

Damian let loose with a battle shriek, and then he, like the massive and colorful army of Europeans, set his heels to the flanks of his horse, and enjoined the overwhelming charge against the infidels.

Earth and sand flew beneath the thundering hooves of his mount and within minutes, he and the troop of light cavalry beneath him were bearing down upon a like group of mounted Turks. They were excellent swordsmen— Damian was well aware of their talent, as were his men. And once they had met, horses clashing together, animals shrieking in pain when caught by a blow intended for a man, the cries of the men ceased, and the more awful sounds of war could be heard: the clang of steel; the shuddering as steel fell upon flesh; the moans, and the cries of agony.

Dark faces appeared before Damian time and again. Surrounded, he stood tall in his saddle, using his sword to slash at the sudden multitude of enemies. One by one, they fell back.

Or died.

He had been cut on the forehead, and blood dripped into his eyes. He wiped it away quickly with the back of his hand, not daring to be blinded now for even seconds.

But a cry was going up. A Crusader cry. "After them! After them all!"

"Nay!" Damian commanded. He roared out the order again. "Nay! We are not to scatter! The King's command! We will not scatter, and be mowed down in turn!"

For a moment, he thought that he had lost control. But then the wildness left the eyes of the survivors, and he knew that his calming words had prevailed.

He blinked. The wound in his head was beginning to cause him an awful headache. There was something else he had learned from Richard, though. Never, never betray a weakness. And he was determined that he would not. "Let's see to our own dying and dead men. Allah will see to theirs!"

Later that night, when the battle was over, Damian met with the King and his other commanders in a great war tent spread out over the sand.

It had been an amazing victory. Perhaps seven hundred Crusaders had been lost.

They had cut down seven thousand Turks.

It was a night when congratulations were in order. No king was more supportive of his knights when victory lay in his hands than Richard, and so there was feasting and entertainment.

Saladin's people were not without their dissidents; no army traveled without a scattering of camp women behind.

And that night there was a multitude of rewards for the weary men. Sweet dates abounded along with grapes and the sizzling meat of goats and lambs. Wine flowed freely into the Crusaders' chalices. Musicians played, a discordant combination of European and strange, sad desert melodies.

There were the jugglers, the animal handlers.

And the women.

Ah, the women of Allah.

Dark-skinned beauties who moved to a unique, haunting call within their souls. Dancers who whisked and swayed their hips from side to side.

Dancers with huge almond-colored and almond-shaped eyes, eyes that haunted and beckoned. Eyes that promised the most unusual and exotic pleasures to the senses.

Leaning upon a violet-dyed pillow, Damian closed his eyes for the moment, feeling the pulse around him. The exhilaration of the day passed suddenly from him. He was a Christian knight, and he would die, just as the Templars or others in the Holy Orders of knighthood, for his King and for his God.

But he felt no special venom for these people of Islam. Here in the Holy Lands he had discovered them to be a people fascinated with learning. They were often soft-spoken, and they cared for their sons and daughters as did any men. Like the King, Damian had studied their architecture, and he had learned a great deal from the walled cities and fortresses they had seen. As well as the beautiful tilework and delicate works and moldings within. Sometimes it seemed that these "infidels" were far more civilized than the men of the country he had left behind. In England, all these years after the conquest, Saxon and Norman still fought and struggled, French was spoken at court—by God, the King himself barely spoke English!—and the knights and barons were ready to go to battle over any small stretch of land.

Ah, but land was power. And these were turbulent times. As fair a king as Richard might be, his heart lay with his Angevin possessions, Aquitaine and Tours, not with England. He was King of England—but he was ruler of a far greater empire.

"Damian!"

A soft whisper aroused him, and he looked up. Affa had come down on her knees beside him. She was one of the dancers, and had been a gift to Richard from a sultan near Acre after that city had been taken.

Affa had not seemed to mind. She danced with plea-sure, with a flush to her cheeks, with an excitement. And all the while there was something soft and very feminine about her.

He smiled. She was very beautiful, with her long jet hair and big eyes and voluptuous veils of deep crimson and soft lilac.

"Aye, Affa!"

Her fingers moved across his arm, delicate, like the brush of a butterfly's wings. Soft, seductive. "I will wait for you tonight?"

Why not? Affa and some of the girls who had come here before her had taught him secrets he had not known himself. "Come to me now," he teased her gently, but she shook her head.

"The golden King will call you. I have heard it. He has already left the feasting behind and is seeing his men. Something has happened. Someone has come in from the ships. He is distressed, so they say. Angry. And I have heard that he does penance frequently before the Christian God for the things that he does when he is angry."

"Well, he is not angry with me," Damian assured her, but he rose, his curiosity piqued.

If someone had come from the sea, he might well have brought messages from home. A sudden pang seemed to touch Damian's heart. He was homesick, he realized.

Yet they were so close to Jerusalem! He couldn't wait until they had taken the city.

"Shall I come later?" Affa asked, looking up at him.

"Aye, do . . ." Damian began. Then he paused, wondering just what was going on with Richard. It might be a late night. And his head was still pounding from the headache caused by his wound. Tonight, despite all of Affa's considerable talents, he wanted to sleep alone.

He stroked her cheek. "Nay, sleep tonight, little one. Something must be amiss. I might be very late."

He left her then, and the rest of the revelers who remained in the huge tent upon the sand. Striding out into the night, he looked up at the black velvet sky just in time to see a shooting star. It seemed to fall toward England.

"An omen, my Lord Montjoy," came a soft voice.

Damian spun around, startled. His senses were usually so keen, he could hear the lightest footfall, even on the desert sand.

But he had not heard Ari Abdul come upon him that night.

Like Affa, Ari had been a gift to Richard after the fortress at Acre had fallen and the local sheiks had been determined to salvage what they could of their lives, dignity—and treasure.

He was a curious man, a very old one, Damian was certain, but his olive skin was not nearly as wrinkled as it should have been, nor was he stooped or slow in any way. A slight rim of blue tinged his large dark eyes, hinting at a vast age, but it was more than that bluish-gray tint that seemed to proclaim him old. There was a curious sense of destiny and wisdom about him that could only come from the passage of years. He always seemed a fascinating creature. Despite the heat or dirt that might surround them, he was always dressed in white robes that stayed immaculately clean at all times.

"Good evening, Ari," Damian replied, determined not to be drawn into the man's curious web of enchantment.

"It's a beautiful night, here in the desert," Ari replied. He gazed idly toward the direction the star had taken. "I think you will miss it just a little bit."

"Will I?"

"Yes. You will be going home soon, Lord Montjoy."

"You are mistaken, Ari. I will stay by the King's side. Jerusalem must be taken."

"Jerusalem will be taken. But you will not be here."

Damian wanted to be amused. Instead, he felt a faint and annoying sensation of unease. "Just where will I be?" Damian said, then silently damned himself. Why was he playing along with this game?

Because he'd seen too many things that Ari had said come true, he told himself. The man was a complexity.

He was a Moslem fascinated by the Christian religion. He could add fantastic sums in his head in a matter of seconds. He knew the stars in the sky just as well as he knew the layout of the land, and his talent with herbs and chemistry was amazing. Damian had seen him heal wounds that should have proven fatal to many a Crusader.

Ari bowed deeply, and then smiled. "I will be with you."

Damian sighed. "And just where will I be."

"England. England. Far away where the grass is green. Where the great pillars of rock stand tall at Stonehenge. Where—"

"Ari, I am not going home. Not until Jerusalem is conquered."

"The wedding will be magnificent!"

Damian sighed deeply. He had been betrothed at birth, but she had died in his very arms, and he had no intention of thinking about wedlock again, not for some time.

"Ari—"

The man closed his eyes, and the desert seemed to grow very still. Despite himself, Damian was listening, amazed at what the man could do with his voice, then somewhat transfixed by the cadence of it.

"She will be enchanting, a child of the water. Her eyes will be aquamarine, rippling like the sweetest clear water. Her hair will fall like liquid sunshine, pouring out upon your hands. Her—"

Ari stopped, his eyes popping open as he stared, dismayed, at Damian.

"What? All right, Ari, come on, what?" Damian demanded.

"I see darkness," Ari murmured.

"So do I," Damian muttered. "It's nighttime!"

Ari shook his head. "I see darkness, a great pit of darkness. Only the slightest ripple of red light is there, a fire, dying low. It just touches upon her hair. She is innocent, but . . .

"But betraying you."

"Jesu!" Damian ground out irritably. "You're seeing some wife I do not yet have betraying me in the darkness? Ari, it has been a long day—"

"He is the one in darkness, masked, like a devil in the night. He has swept her up, for there is tumult all around her; she creates it as she moves, passionate for the causes of others. They'll come after her, again and again, seeking more than beauty, seeking fortune and position, and all material things."

"A real damsel in distress," Damian muttered, tiring of the conversation.

"But none can take the greatest treasure. It must be given."

"And what is that?"

"Don't you know?"

"Ari, I know that I have to see the King, and I do not care to keep Richard waiting."

Ari's eyes were closed again. "She is ivory and roses. A scent so sweet, skin so soft. I see her naked, cloaked only in the richness of her hair. I see her upon the darkness of fur; see the curve of her mouth; the liquid beauty of her eyes; the length of her legs; the soft, sweet, supple thighs—"

"Ari, if you can't produce her in the next twenty minutes, I really don't care to hear any more about her," Damian said with a touch of humor. But he was disturbed. Ari was good. Really good. He had almost pictured the woman as Ari spoke.

A dark shuddering swept through him. He found himself furious with this woman who would betray him. He didn't even know her. And he had no intention of wedding any woman at this time.

And still . . .

He had felt the most curious sensation again. As if he knew the girl the Arab described.

He gritted his teeth. He was fighting ghosts in his mind!

"You'll have to take care. Take care of the masked man when the time arrives," Ari warned him.

"Ari—"

"Good night, my great Lord Montjoy," Ari said, bowing deeply.

Then, just as he had come, he silently disappeared into the darkness of the desert night once again.

Damian swore softly, then started out for Richard's tent with long strides.

One of Richard's scribes stood at the entry. "My Lord Montjoy!" the man said tensely. "I was about to come for you."

Damian arched a brow and walked past the man. "I am here now."

"Ah! Montjoy!" the King boomed out.

Something was bothering Richard. He paced the room, still clad in mail beneath a white tunic with a bloodred cross emblazoned on it. Something surely bothered him if he had not changed from his stained battle clothing.

Richard was an impressive king. He was very tall, with a head of golden hair and a handsome, ruggedly chiseled face. His eyes were a soft blue, a color that added a touch of warmth to an otherwise fierce countenance. By nature he was fair-minded, except sometimes in the excesses of war, and when he felt he had been too brutal or cruel in his pursuits, he did extreme homage to God. The King paused suddenly in his pacing, slamming a fist on the table where maps of the region had been strewn, but where now, atop those maps, lay all manner of letters.

Damian waited, watching Richard. The King's anger was not directed at him.

"Aye, Your Grace? What is the problem?"

The anger suddenly seemed to vent from the King, and he sat down hard on a camp chair behind the portable map table and sighed, and then lifted his hands. "Longchamp fell from favor. I set my brother to watch over my country in my absence. After all, if I die, then John shall be King."

"There is your nephew," Damian reminded him. Though Geoffrey, the next eldest Plantagenet brother, was dead, he had a son living in Brittany.

Richard indicated the cross-legged chair across the table from him. Damian sat, waiting for the King to continue.

Richard did so.

"Leave an empire like this to a child?" Richard said, then shook his head. "Politically, that would be a disaster. It would mean war. Civil war. John is not without his followers!"

Damian kept his silence. Of course, John Plantagenet— Lackland, as he was often called, since it seemed that the family goods had all been given away before his birth— did draw in his fair share of support.

In truth, he could no longer be called Lackland. He had been given an heiress, Avisa, as his bride. She had brought him tremendous wealth.

She despised him. He hated her.

No matter. The lands gave him power. And, Damian thought, John was a far more intelligent prince than either of his parents had ever realized. Perhaps he even had some qualities that would make him more fit than Richard to govern England.

The main quality being that he was in England, liked England, and intended to stay in England.

"I mean him to be King," Richard said, then added hastily, "Unless, of course, Queen Berengaria and I should produce an heir to the throne."

"Of course," Damian agreed.

Again, that powerful Plantagenet fist swung and hit the table.

"But not while I'm still alive, damn it! God's blood, Damian, I try and try and try to be fair to that brother of mine! Why does he defy me at every turn?"

"All men like power, Your Grace," Damian said. "Especially those born of kings. Prince John has his virtues. And he has his abilities."

"You would imagine he would steal my crown if he could."

Damian hesitated, then shrugged. He had thought things much better before when William Longchamp had been left regent of England. William had believed in the law.

But Richard had left John with too much power, and William had lost his hold on the government. Now John was holding the power.

A dangerous situation.

"John would take your crown without a second's thought, Your Grace," Damian said bluntly.

Richard nodded. "So my brother has his virtues and his sins. And those must be held in check." Richard hesitated a moment. Then he said quietly, "That's exactly why you're going back to England."

Startled, Damian rose quickly to his feet. "But we are nearly in Jerusalem!"

"Aye, that I know," Richard said flatly.

"I have been one of your most able commanders. I have been hard by your side. I have helped to give you this victory!" Damian told Richard heatedly, his hands braced upon the table as he leaned close to the King.

Richard held his ground.

"Aye, you have often been at my right hand. But the news from England distresses me more and more. Too many nobles are growing far too powerful. They would all be kings unto themselves. John aligns himself with some of these men. It is a dangerous situation. Damian, you have helped me with this battle here against the infidels. Now you must help win another. A different battle."

"Why must it be I?"

"Because Damian Montjoy, Count Clifford, is a respected knight. A man who served my father first, then bowed to the legality that I was his heir, and honored me as King. John knows that you are just. And that you are powerful. You can meet him as a great baron of England. You can carry my authority. And . . ."

Damian gritted his teeth and sank down to his chair again. There would be no further argument. Certainly no argument that he could win. The King's mind was set.

"And?" Damian pressed, his tone still hard.

"You go back as more than one man."

The expression in Damian's silver-gray eyes turned wary.

"What do you mean?"

"I mean that I know that the woods in England are often peopled by outlaws. I mean that I'm not against outlaws, not when they serve my purpose."

"Do you accuse me of being an outlaw, Your Grace?"

"Accuse, never, Damian. What a word. I simply demand that you go back, and preserve my kingdom in my absence. You will be instructed further on all the events that have occurred over the past months. Then you will carry my seal, and my power, and return to place my brother in checkmate upon this weary game he plays!"

"This assumes I have great power," Damian commented. "And the lands and means to sustain it."

Richard stood and walked across the room. "Aye, it does. I did not mean, of course, to send you home without compensation for what I ask."

Damian arched a dour brow. "Um. You will grant me some withered and aging crone who is as wealthy as Midas?"

Richard laughed loudly, his good temper quite suddenly restored. "That is not at all what I had in mind!"

"No wife?" Damian inquired politely. It really made no difference to him. Once he had found the perfect woman. Fate had cast them together.

But then fate had cruelly swept them apart.

Now his marital status meant little to him.

Except for land. And land was power. And Richard was in a bargaining mood.

"I have a lady in mind," Richard said, drumming his fingers on the table. "Not old and withered in the least. Wealthy, incredibly wealthy." He leaned close to Damian. "And in sore need of a husband from my camp—quickly. For in my absence, so it seems, my brother has dangled her before another to gain his support and aid."

"And she is?"

"Young and fair. Some dub her the most beautiful lady in all Christendom. And she is in deep trouble, so it seems, for John will try any trickery against her. The man he intends her for is none other than Raymond de la Ville."

De la Ville. He was famed for his cruelty and debaucheries. Damian hated the man, just as he had hated his father before him.

Who was the woman? Damian felt a growing curiosity.

"A name, Richard," he insisted.

"Katherine, Countess of Ure."

Damian started. Kat de Montrain? Jesu. The mere thought of the woman still heated his temper.

For a moment that anger cooled.

Mentally he calculated the woman's worth. She was tremendously wealthy.

She was more. Much, much more.

Richard had said that he condoned certain outlaws.

Did he know that the very heiress he was busy promising to Damian was out in the woods, causing havoc?

Or could he possibly know that the girl would not be pleased in the least to see Damian, even if he did come to rescue her from some other awful fate.

She was rich and she was beautiful, Richard gave no lie there.

But as a wife . . .

She was willful and headstrong, certainly a problem. Never the chatelaine that Damian would require, obedient and talented in the running of great estates while a knight was about a man's business.

"Well?" Richard demanded.

What did it matter? Damian wondered for one bleak moment. There were women like Affa in the world to fill a man's needs when his heart lay empty. Wives brought property, and Kat de Montrain, Countess of Ure, would do that.

And, he decided dryly, any woman could be tamed.

Any woman at all.

And more so than most women, Kat de Montrain needed to be tamed.

He stood and stretched out his hand. Richard clasped it.

"I am always your servant," he promised Richard.

The King smiled.

"For home then, Montjoy!"

"Aye, Your Grace, I am for home."

He started to leave the King's tent. Richard was bent over his maps once again. "Damian!"

"Aye, Your Grace?"

"If you should see the likes of these outlaws, be they legends or men—you know, this Robin Hood character, or the . . . er, Silver Sword—be sure to give them my best regards. In secret, of course."

Damian nodded. "Aye, Your Grace."

He walked out into the night.

Damn Ari. The man had been right. He was going home.

He inhaled sharply, remembering the Arab seer's words.

Darkness, and betrayal . . .

By Kat de Montrain. The beauty with her aquamarine eyes and swirling, golden-blond hair to defy the very fire of the sun . . .

And anger seized hold of him suddenly. It didn't matter that she barely knew him.

That she despised him.

She was his betrothed, and he would not be betrayed.

Actually, there was a challenge to the arrangement. Maybe he deserved Kat de Montrain.

He smiled slowly. And maybe Kat de Montrain deserved him. Oh, aye. There would be certain compensations here!

Ruefully, he remembered telling Robin that Richard would find Kat a husband.

He had simply not imagined that it might be he!

It was late. He stormed into the tent where many of his men lay sleeping. He could not take them all. Only his closest retainers.

"Home!" he roared, awakening them suddenly. "My friends, we are for home!"

And suddenly, he was anxious.

England awaited him. England, and bandits and princes and traitors . . .

And a woman.

A wife.

Ah, Saladin's best cutthroats could hold little challenge when compared to the other!

Yet who would prove most dangerous? he wondered.

The Prince, the bandits, the traitors . . .

Or the woman, the wife?

Chapter 3

Autumn 1192
In the Reign of King Richard, Coeur de Lion
Castle de Montrain

"Riders, my lady. Coming from the east."

From the herb cellar, in the deepest section of the castle keep, Lady Katherine de Montrain, Countess of Ure—Kat to her friends—looked up at the guard with wary curiosity. She was tempted to leap up and fly along the multitude of stairs to the parapets high above the enclosure of the handsome castle that was her birthright, but then again, she was determined that she would remain calm and serene. As the countess, she was trying very hard to nurture a reputation of being a poised and composed lady, the perfect chatelaine. In keeping with that calling, she had been spending the day in her larders and cellars, seeing to supplies for the coming winter.

Riders, of course, would change all the assessments she had just made. Courtesy demanded that she entertain any nobleman, priest, or pilgrim who came seeking hospitality—any man, or lady, and all of that person's retainers.

And these days, one just never knew who might ride in.

"What colors do they wear?" she inquired.

"It is the Prince who comes, my lady."

"God's blood!" she swore, then quickly gritted her teeth. She had been trying very hard to control her language lately. The Lady Katherine de Montrain should not swear so—not as a common bandit might do.

She glanced quickly to Marie Ostout, her maid and companion. Marie was ten years her senior, a round and determined woman with dark hair, clear blue eyes, and wonderful cherry-red cheeks to enhance them.

Marie never minded when her lady slipped into less than courtly language. She grinned now, wickedly pleased.

"Well, then, there goes the whole of the larder!" Marie commented flatly.

Kat stood quickly, wiping her hands nervously along the plain apron she had slipped over her good linen tunic to keep it clean. It was a beautiful garment, dyed a soft blue, a gown that was gracefully fitted to her breasts and torso, with a long skirt that swept in heavier folds to the floor. The sleeves were wide from the elbow to the wrist, wide and sweeping, and fine embroidery decorated both the neckline and the hems of the sleeves.

In keeping with the fashionable dignity of her position, Kat had her hair neatly plaited, with the plaits drawn into coils at the back of her head. A veil that matched the color of her gown fell over the abundance of her hair, held to her crown within the delicate circle of a finely crafted gold band. All she had to do to greet her company was cast off her apron.

Yet even as she did so, she turned to Marie, the wildness in her eyes belying any pretense of the poised young noblewoman.

"You know the Prince," she said. "He will have friends with him. And they will want to hunt. And the King's forest lies just beyond our doors." She didn't need to say the words aloud. Both women knew that she was longing to find some excuse that could be given to the Prince for her absence. She was anxious to get into the forest.

"There is no choice. You will have to greet the Prince," Marie said simply.

Kat hesitated, then nodded. She doffed the apron at last, nodding to the young guard who had come to inform her of John's coming. "We are ready for the Prince. The bridge is lowered?"

"Aye, lady."

"Then we are ready. Marie, hurry to the kitchens, and see that they are prepared. The Prince and his retainers will surely want to hunt, but we'll greet them first with wine, and perhaps some of those pastries that young Howard makes so very well. Aye, those, and some of the salted fish, I think, and whatever fruit we've managed to obtain. Go on now, quickly. I will be waiting in the main hall."

Marie was clicking her teeth. "Winter comes," she stated flatly. "Give away our fruit now—"

"Marie, Prince John comes our way."

"Prince John the thief comes our way!" Marie snorted.

"All the more I need give him what he seeks before he takes it," Kat muttered. "And hold your tongue. I've heard that he does not deal lightly with those who condemn him."

"And to think England used to be a place where men obeyed the law!"

"Some men still do—"

"Nay, now there's a lie!" Marie stated. "Those who would follow the law have resorted to being against it, and that's a fact."

Kat gripped her by the shoulders, looking deeply into her eyes. "Marie! Within these walls we do not say such things. You know that well! Now help me. Get on to the kitchen and see what aid you can give Howard."

Marie sniffed again, then walked on by Kat, muttering beneath her breath despite any words from her mistress.

"'Tis bad enough when friends come to eat one out of house and home, I daresay. But when the larder must be emptied for the likes of the Prince, well then it is a sorry world."

Kat watched Marie with a mixture of amusement and worry. Then she followed her up the stairs that wound their way to the great hall.

Hers was truly a fine castle—Castle de Montrain, named for her great-grandfather who had come from Normandy with William the Conqueror to subjugate England. William had sent his own architects to help the baron he had chosen to reward for his fine services, and it was both a worthy defensive work, and a very livable one.

The castle was walled and sat within a moat. There were three main towers to the place, one holding armaments and armor and the men to use them, another being a storehouse and granary with guest apartments above them, and the third being the living quarters for the family in attendance, with a great hall on the ground level, just above the cellars for food storage for the family—and for the guests who sought shelter and nourishment on their travels to and fro, for the castle was located in the north of England, close to the old Roman roads travelers used frequently when visiting York or the vicinity.

It had been built at a time when Duke William had just become King William, when the new Norman aristocracy had lived with a certain fear that the old Anglo-Saxon aristocracy might well seek to oust them from their positions of grandeur.

Such an overthrow did not occur, perhaps because the English people lost heart, perhaps because of destiny.

Or perhaps because the Saxons did, in their way, encroach upon the Normans. Kat's great-grandfather had married a dispossessed Saxon's daughter, and their son had married a lady from Anjou. Kat's father had been the only male child of that marriage, and he had married the very beautiful Elysa of Sherwood, a Saxon girl left with no land and little dowry, but a woman still so renowned that many landed lords had vied for her hand.

Kat's father had told her that he had heard her mother singing in the forest. He had paused in his riding and followed the sound of her voice. He had seen her by a stream, stripped of hose and shoes, bathing her toes in the clear running waters. The sound of her voice had tied a silken cord about his heart, and no one could tell him that he could not have her.

Not even the damsel herself.

"It was rough going at first, for she was determined to have no Norman lord," Kat's father had said. And in the telling, Kat's mother had smiled, and added her own version of the story. "I pretended not to know a word of his Norman French. And I made him learn to speak our Saxon English so that he could ask for my hand in person. But then he did so with such great ardor, and so very well! And I was cleanly swept off my feet!"

When their eyes fell upon one another, their love was evident, and Kat had been delighted. She had spun her own fairy tales about singing in the forest while a knight in beautiful shining armor rode by, only to fall desperately in love with her.

But it seemed that a love like her parents' was doomed to be found only in heaven. She had barely reached her teens when the two had died nearly simultaneously, taken by the horror of the yellow fever that ravished the entire area. Kat herself caught the fever but survived it, only to discover that she had been left as the ward of Henry II. Then, within a few years, she found herself under the protection of the new king, Richard, Coeur de Lion. Either because Richard Plantagenet had always

respected his mother, Eleanor, therefore believed that a
woman could manage a castle just as well as any man,
or because he hadn't had any need to bargain her away,
Richard had left her in charge of Castle de Montrain,
believing that he would make no moves regarding her
or her properties without consulting her. And that, Kat
knew well, was far more than any young noblewoman
dared hope. From the stairway she hurried to the front
door of the great hall, a door that opened to a small
covered courtyard that faced the drawbridge to the moat.
The Prince had already crossed over the bridge with his
retainers and servants. He dismounted from his horse as
she watched, and strode the rest of the way to the main
door to the tower keep.

"Lady Katherine! I do hope that I have not come at
an inconvenient time."

She forced a smile to her lips. "Why, Prince John!
There is no inconvenient time to greet a royal guest,
my lord."

"Well and beautifully spoken." John applauded, stripping off his riding gloves. Having reached her, he caught
her hand and gallantly kissed it. She forced herself not
to shudder.

There was nothing really evil about John, she reminded
herself. He was just such a paler version of his brother!
He was not so tall, or so golden. His height was medium,
his hair was a dark sand to brown color, and his eyes
were not as vividly blue as his brother's, rather a
paler, watered-down version. But he was cunning and
quick-witted.

"Well, so come in, Your Grace," Kat murmured,
backing her way into the hall. She looked beyond his
shoulders, trying to ascertain which of his followers had
accompanied him.

First there came Father Donovan, a curious priest if
ever there were one. He was a tall, lean, handsome man

with a startling brightness to his eyes. Though he could rattle out a fiery sermon on the duty of man and how goodness and chastity must rule life, Kat found it difficult to believe that he adhered to any vows of celibacy himself. She did not like the way he watched her.

"My lady," he greeted her, seeming exceptionally amused and cheerful today.

Beyond the priest came Lord Gerald Mortimer, the son of the great Earl Latimer, a youth whose greatest sin seemed to be in his intense desire to have fun at all times and all costs. He had platinum-blond hair and twinkling hazel eyes. He, too, greeted Kat with a wolfish grin, and she became very uneasy, wondering at their true purpose in coming here.

Then the last of John's company left his horse to his squire, coming through the overpass to the keep doorway.

He was taller than the others, more striking than the others—more frightening than the others.

Raymond de la Ville. Evil. Like father, like son.

She hated the man with an intensity that had grown throughout the years. She could never look at him without remembering that long-ago time when she had ridden into the woods with her father.

She could not look at him without seeing the poor peasant lad screaming, falling to the ground. Without seeing blood.

De la Ville . . .

He had neatly clipped dark hair and a well-defined, clean-shaven, square-jawed face. It should have been an attractive face, except that the excesses he lived by already showed too clearly in it.

There was more to the evil about him than her remembrances. The sight of de la Ville could make many women shiver. No knight in the realm had so horrid a reputation.

It was said that he had already killed one wife, and no one knew just how many peasant maids he had ruined, tormented, or killed.

Like the excesses he lived by, his penchant for cruelty was very much alive in his face.

"My Lord de la Ville!" Kat forced herself to say. She was certainly safe enough for the moment. John couldn't let anything bad happen to her while he was a guest in her house. Richard might forgive much, but he would never forgive his brother for letting any harm come to her while he was present. Also, men who might side with Prince John would rise against him if he harmed one of the country's major heiresses, who was Richard's own ward.

But what was this visit then? She had never willingly entertained de la Ville. On the few occasions when he and his men had sought rest or hospitality here, she had defied all propriety, leaving some excuse for her absence and vacating her home while he and his men were present. "Lady Kat . . . ah, Kat is what your friends call you, is it not?" de la Ville said, catching her hand and placing a small kiss upon it.

She withdrew her hand as quickly as she could. "Aye, my lord. It is what my friends call me." She stressed the word *friends*.

De la Ville smiled slightly, pleased by the challenge.

"I intend, my lady, that we should be very good friends."

Her heart seemed to shudder violently as she realized with absolute horror what this visit was all about.

Dear God. She could have been ill right then and there. De la Ville had decided that he wanted her.

Could she ignore the reference? She intended to!

She turned from him without an answer, sweeping into the great hall where already wine had been poured in the appropriate number of goblets and where delicacies for the guests had begun to appear on the long table. "Wine, my lords?" Kat asked them. "Surely you are thirsty from your ride. Has it been a long one?" She offered John a charming smile, trying to remember that she had a role to play, no matter what.

"Not so long. We have been at de la Ville's, and came here hastily from there. But your wine cellar always seems stocked with the very finest, Katherine, and your cooks create the best tasting food. What is it that you have here, something magic?"

"Not at all magic. We're just always pleased to see you, Your Grace, and nothing more."

"Um," John murmured, his eyes on her. For a moment, they were marked with suspicion.

Gerald Mortimer pulled a chair from the banquet table, sat down, and stretched his legs out comfortably before him.

"There's the best hunting in the forest here, too, you know. And with Raymond's place so near . . . why, your properties nearly touch, did you know that, Kat?"

"Oh, aye, I was aware," she murmured. "So are you planning on some hunting?"

Mortimer began to chuckle, swallowing down a large portion of the wine that Kat had just given him. "Oh, aye, we're out for anything that moves, snarls, or runs!"

"Man or beast?" Kat said lightly.

"And woman, perhaps," Father Donovan remarked, every bit as lightly. "Of course, I shall not join the hunt, lady. I'll wait here with you."

"But we'll be back for supper this eve, my lady," John said, setting down his silver goblet. "Supper, and matters of importance. We thought we'd give fair warning."

"They shall be delighted in the kitchen to prepare for your coming," Kat murmured to the Prince, anxious for them to leave. So Donovan was staying. To keep an eye on her?

De la Ville was behind her. She felt his presence with a great unease.

"It will be a day for acquisitions."

"How glad I shall be for you!" Kat said, swirling around. "Something to cheer you. Why, my lord, 'tis what, now? Not a year since your lovely wife left this earth for the promise beyond?"

Anger flashed in his eyes. "Indeed, Isabel is gone now."

"No man should live alone," Father Donovan intoned gravely.

"Amen—and let's be on our way!" John said. He slapped his riding gloves against his thighs. "Tell your people to make pleasing desserts, Katherine, for the meat we will bring back fresh. That is, of course, if the local peasantry hasn't robbed the forest of all good kills!"

"I would imagine not," Kat murmured uneasily.

"I imagine it might well be so!" Gerald Mortimer exclaimed. "Lady Katherine, I cannot believe that you have not heard of all the activity hereabouts. Why, the forest here is alive with outlaws and bandits. Numerous parties traveling through well-known trails have been stopped and stripped of their belongings."

"The tales reach out to all of England," the Prince said irritably, "and I am sure that they are grossly exaggerated. You have heard something of them, have you not, Katherine?"

"I have heard stories, Your Grace."

John moved closer to her, watching her eyes. "These woods must actually breed bandits. There is some man they call Robin Hood. And another with the silly name of the Silver Sword, though perhaps he is dead, for he has not been heard of in some time. Have you heard anything of him?"

"The Silver Sword?" Kat repeated, relieved. She didn't need to lie. "I haven't the least idea of who it might be, Your Grace. I swear, before the Holy Father high above us!"

A fist suddenly swung hard upon the table. "Robin Hood, Silver Sword! They must be rooted out! Hanged before the people. Drawn and quartered."

"And the other. The one they call Greensleeves," Gerald Mortimer said glumly. "I have had my men robbed oft enough while trying to bring some of my tenants' taxes and goods through this forest! 'Tis said that this lad Greensleeves is the eyes and ears of the outlaw Robin Hood."

"Ah, I should like to discover this Greensleeves myself!" de la Ville said. "'Tis said that it is *Lady* Greensleeves, and no lad. If so, I imagine that I could deal with her well."

Chills shot along Kat's spine. "I can see that you quite imagine that you could," she said coolly. "Perhaps, Your Grace," she told the Prince, "you prefer not to hunt in the forest here. We've plenty of meat to entertain you, your party, and even your servants beyond the doors."

"Nonsense! I am the Prince! I will hunt!" John assured her, striding for the door, determined on his course of action.

"As you say, Your Grace," Kat returned.

Gerald Mortimer grinned at her, causing the chair to screech against the floor as he rose, quick to follow John.

Raymond de la Ville stared at her for a long moment, then reached out to touch her cheek.

"It will be a day for acquisitions," he repeated, as if reiterating a promise.

"Happy hunting, my Lord de la Ville," she said coolly, and stepped back.

When they were gone, having caused a mass of confusion as they shouted for their squires, pages, and horses,

Kat turned back to Father Donovan.

"Please, make yourself at home. If the Prince is return-ing this evening, I think I'd like some time to bathe and rest and dress. Will you forgive me if I leave you alone?"

His lip curled. "My lady." He bowed to her. "I will be sitting in the hall, warmed by your fire, and by your mead. Watching and waiting for your return."

She smiled, dropped him a formal curtsy, and left him. She hurried up the spiraling stairway that led to her room high in the tower.

Marie had come there before her. "What are they up to now?" she asked anxiously.

"I have to move quickly, Marie. The Prince has already left with de la Ville and Mortimer. They plan on hunting. Anything that moves. They've left Donovan below in the hall. To see that I can't leave."

"Maybe you shouldn't leave," Marie warned her.

"Nonsense," Kat said. "Of all days, I have to leave! I have to make sure that no man is hunting in the forest, and no poor maid is walking somewhere alone." She paused, shivering fiercely. How odd that de la Ville was here now. De la Ville—he had helped shape her into all that she was.

Maybe it was dangerous to go out now. Had they been suspicious of her? she wondered. She tried to remember every word of the conversation. Nay . . . they did not suspect her. Father Donovan was staying below as a guard just because de la Ville wanted her there this time when he returned.

She had already stripped off her golden circlet and veil. The blue overgown came sliding over her head then, followed by her soft white undertunic. Seeing Kat's intent and that she was half-naked and shivering already, Marie muttered and dove beneath the down ticking of Kat's bed for a bundle tied in cloth. Therein lay a rough wool tunic in deep forest-green and a cape and cowl to match.

In a matter of seconds, Kat had redressed, the great cowl falling well over her face to hide her identity from any man or woman who might come upon her.

"This is awfully dangerous," Marie moaned.

"What will he do?" Kat said recklessly, referring to Prince John. "Hang me?"

"He might well," Marie muttered unhappily.

Kat shook her head. "For one, he will never catch me," she assured Marie.

"You were almost caught once," Marie reminded her warningly. "You told me so yourself."

Kat paused, startled as she felt a distant fear surge into her blood.

Damian Montjoy. Aye, he'd nearly had her! She'd love to give Montjoy one good punch. Right in the jaw. Just one. To pay him back for the awful humiliation in the forest. Nay, perhaps a sound slap to his cheek.

Robin, who had rescued her from the Knave, claimed that Montjoy hadn't recognized her, had, in fact, taken her for a peasant girl! The man infuriated her and frightened her, she had to admit as she recalled the strange way he had made her shiver and then burn when he touched her.

She reminded herself that Damian Montjoy was far, far away, fighting in the Holy Lands with the King. She had nothing to fear.

"I've got to go!" she said quickly to Marie. She kissed her impulsively on the cheek. "I won't be long."

"Will you take your sword?"

Kat shook her head, still remembering that long-ago encounter with Montjoy. Robin had been furious. She had played the bandit in truth several times before, but successfully, all of them. But since her encounter with Montjoy, she knew that Robin would truly disavow any further relationship with her if he caught her carrying arms again. He'd made her promise that her only role in the affairs of the forest would be that of an informant.

"Nay, I'll give a quick warning and be back."

Marie, distressed, still walked with her across the tower bedroom, where they came to what appeared to be mortared stone. But Kat pressed against the third lowest stone to the ground, and the wall itself seemed to shift back, creating a door.

Kat entered into darkness, but she knew her way just as she knew the back of her hand.

The steps spiraled down, and then a tunnel ran through the width of the moat, and into the forest.

The tunnel let out where nature kept its secret, just at the overgrown falls to a wide, bubbling brook. Kat slipped from behind the wall of water and foliage to look back at her castle, smiling with a certain wicked pleasure.

Donovan would still be there, smugly waiting for her to try to pass him.

Her pleasure, however, was short-lived, for with de la Ville in the forest, anything could happen. She turned, and started running through the narrow paths between the trees, seeking the point where she knew she would find one of her cousin's lookouts posted.

She had not traveled far before she heard a heartrending and anguished cry tear through the forest. She paused and heard the cry again. Changing her course slightly, she started to run.

The villagers of Willow Wood were not far beyond. They owed homage to her. Farmers, they tilled the land, raised sheep and cattle, and lived a simple life, loving and fearing God, looking to her for justice.

"I shall skewer de la Ville myself!" she muttered, panting as she raced along. But what would happen if she did come upon some outrageous scene? The Prince would have her dragged away for aiding and abetting outlaws. He could imprison her, and perhaps convince a number of the Norman barons that he was entirely in the right.

She nearly burst out into a clearing but held back, biting her lower lip.

Just ahead were the men who had so recently sat in her hall.

Prince John and Mortimer were to one side.

De la Ville had found some prey. Feminine prey. A young girl.

She couldn't have been more than fifteen, pretty, dressed in rough wool, her face slightly smudged.

Her dark eyes were enormous, and her cheeks had gone pale white. She was as terrified as any young doe hunted down in the forest.

Only does were usually quickly slain. Their terror was brought to an end.

Not so with this girl.

Her hands were tied together. Now he had called to his squire and his page, and the two young men had caught hold of the girl and were wrestling her to the ground for de la Ville.

The girl tried to bite one of them.

De la Ville laughed. Then, when she would have screamed, he slapped her face, hard.

Kat nearly jumped up. She had to go out there! she thought desperately. She had to! The girl was dependent on her. She could stop this outrage.

Or could she? What would the men do if they realized that she had stumbled upon their play? Would they wrestle her to the ground, too? They dare not! She was a countess—

And an outlaw.

She couldn't suddenly jump in among them.

She would give herself away.

Even as she sat, desperately trying to drum up some strategy, the forest was suddenly rent with a bloodcurdling cry. She wasn't sure of the sound at first, only that it seemed like some battle cry.

Then a horseman bore down upon the Prince's party.

The coal-black steed raced with such speed and fury that he nearly seemed to be a blur. The rider was encased in a silver mesh mail that covered his face and head as protection, as well as his torso, neck, shoulders, and arms. A dark gray emblemless tunic lay over the mail. He wore a black cloak that swirled around him, seeming to ride the air like the smoke that followed fire and lightning, rippling in his wake.

His sword rose high toward the heavens, cutting a silver slash across the sky.

De la Ville turned around to meet the threat and saw the rider. Astonishment filled his face at first. Then he realized the deadly intent of the rider. And for once, naked fear burst starkly into his dark eyes.

The rider meant to ask no questions and give no quarter.

De la Ville thrust himself behind his young squire to allow the youth to take the sword blow intended for him.

The rider saw the change in time and seemed to choose not to slay the squire. Perhaps he had never intended to slay de la Ville, but rather to threaten him and demand the release of the girl.

It didn't matter. They would never know. The horseman suddenly sheathed his sword. An expert rider, he managed to maintain his saddle as he reached down to the ground and swept up the peasant girl, placing her before him on the saddle.

The horse reared high, then plunged downward, dust and dirt rising from beneath its hooves. The animal then burst into a gallop, and within seconds, horse, rider, and girl had disappeared into the forest.

For a moment, a stunned silence reigned in the clearing.

Then de la Ville, red-faced and furious, ran forward into the space the horse had just vacated and shouted, "After him!"

"You would have me pursue a bandit?" Prince John demanded coolly. "I think you forget yourself, de la Ville."

Kat could almost hear the grating of de la Ville's teeth.

"Nay, my Prince! I spoke to my squire, to Mortimer, to myself! Never to you, my lord!" De la Ville swept into a low and somewhat mocking bow. "Nay, my lord! I never forget what we are about! Or that I am one of your strongest sword arms!"

John was unperturbed by de la Ville's words. He sighed, leaning low against his saddle. "You'll never find strength, de la Ville, until you find patience—and a proper sense of priorities. So this land is filled with bandits! It can be cleaned out. The forest belongs to the King—to the Prince in his absence. The neighboring land, however—that land which helps these bandits!—can be yours. Think with your head instead of your loins for once, man! There is far greater hunting ahead tonight!"

Kat sat back, breathing hard. Ah, yes, new prey! Her!

And she had to go back, had to play the role.

De la Ville! The man was totally despicable! So cruel to the poor young maiden in the woods . . .

Had the girl really been so swiftly and miraculously rescued? It had not been Robin, Kat was certain, or any of his men. None that she knew.

But once . . .

Aye, once there had been another legend. The one they had asked her about today.

The Silver Sword.

She felt breathless suddenly. The Silver Sword. He had come to life soon after that day when the elder de la Ville had sought to murder her father here. When the hail of arrows had saved them, and sent the de la Villes and their party fleeing!

Who had come here today, then? A ghost? Ghosts did not save maidens in distress. Only flesh-and-blood men on flesh-and-blood horses could do so. Heroes who rode to save the poor and the weak.

A fierce shivering swept through her.

But what of her?

She was neither poor nor weak. What man would save her if the powerful Prince offered her in marriage to de la Ville?

What man would dare come for her?

A lump caught in her throat. Robin. Robin would try to save her . . . no matter what powers came against her.

And betray his cause, his people, himself.

She had to run. Now. Just run away. Give up the castle, give up her life. Hide deep within the forest, and be safe . . .

It was tempting. So tempting.

Nay. She had to beat de la Ville and the Prince at their own games. She was a countess, she couldn't forget that fact. They truly wouldn't dare treat her as they had treated the peasant girl.

She couldn't run. She had to remain the chatelaine. She had to listen and learn, and bring her information to the forest.

She inhaled and exhaled deeply, closed her eyes tightly, and prayed for courage.

Even now, she still had to reach Robin and tell him all that had occurred, and that Prince John, de la Ville, Mortimer, and Donovan would be dining at the castle tonight.

She squared her shoulders. She was Katherine, Countess of Ure.

I am ever determined! she vowed to herself. She would not be afraid of the Prince or de la Ville.

But her teeth were still chattering. Nonsense, she tried to assure herself. De la Ville couldn't touch her. Not tonight—not for days or weeks, even months! A betrothal could take a long, long time, if John was planning on giving her to de la Ville in marriage.

There would be plenty of time to run if and when a betrothal was brought about. She was safe, surely.

But de la Ville meant to have her, her castle, and her land. She was certain of it.

He must know that she would refuse him. That she despised him. Yet he seemed so sure of himself.

Aye . . .

He had something planned.

What?

The question filled her with dread.

What indeed?

Chapter 4

"It was the strangest occurrence! Just when I thought that I must do something—even though I knew that I could not!—this horseman appeared. I'm not sure if he intended to skewer de la Ville or not. Whatever, he seemed to care not in the least that the Prince was there, or that de la Ville was surrounded by others. He raced through, swept up the girl, and that was that."

Kat's tone was matter-of-fact and very calm as she told Robin what had happened. She had managed to still her own fears by reminding herself that Robin would refuse her help if she betrayed the least fear.

If they hadn't been children together—if they hadn't been in the forest together with her father that day—she knew that Robin wouldn't have tolerated her part in all of this.

But they had been together. They had both seen what had happened to the young Saxon lad. At first, they had only tried to warn the people when certain nobles were in the forest. But then Richard had become King and left England, and one by one, the neighboring barons had begun to grasp for power, nearly starving the people, taking everything from them.

Then Robin had had an encounter with a nobleman who had slain a man in the woods. And Robin had slain the noble in turn, and become a bandit in truth. Now only the King himself could pardon Robin. Now, as she explained all that had happened, Robin was watching her with a worried look. She had been careful not to tell him about Prince John's words to de la Ville about better prey to be had that night. Not yet, anyway. She had simply told him about Prince John's arrival with the others, and then about the way she had stumbled upon them in the forest with the girl.

And about the horseman who had so miraculously appeared.

She was seated on a tree stump and Robin was pacing, his fingers laced behind his back, his brow furrowed. Though a number of Robin's men were just beyond them in the large copse, the small clearing where she spoke with Robin was astonishingly quiet except for the natural sounds of the forest, the soft rustle of leaves, the twitter of a bird, the sudden, scratchy sound of a small animal moving on the forest floor.

The sky was beautiful that day, blue above them, just touched by the whitest clouds. The air smelled richly of the earth, of the green things that grew upon it, of the freshness of the sun. It did not seem so terrible a place to live, Kat thought. Castles and manors could be damp and dank and malodorous. Their roofs could leak.

And Robin had the canopy of the sky for his roof.

Well, that wasn't exactly true. They had built small houses in the forests in the nearby copse. Houses that blended with the trees, that were of mud and wood with thatched roofs. Quickly made, and containing little. Robin knew his base could be found and destroyed, and therefore they kept little that they could not move with them upon their backs.

Robin had been so silent as he paced, but suddenly he stopped and swung around, staring at her.

"Tell me about him again," he demanded.

She looked up at him, shaking her head. "Him? The Prince? De la Ville? Morti—"

"The horseman, Kat! The horseman!" Robin said, and sighed with exasperation.

Kat gritted her teeth. "Robin, if you would just be more precise with your questions—"

"Please?"

"There's nothing more I can tell you. The whole episode took place in a matter of minutes. And as for the horseman . . . he raced through, swept up the girl, and raced away. I have told you that."

"On a dark horse."

"Ebony-dark."

"In silver armor?"

"Mail, Robin. Silver, I suppose. Or gray. And he had the most intriguing helmet and visor. The helmet capped his head, then it seemed there was a very fine meshed mail visor designed to fall over his face, almost like a mask. A regular, thicker mail covered his shoulders and torso. It was so fast, Robin. He was difficult to see. He wore a tunic over the mail, I think. Aye. And a cloak. A fine black cloak. It looked like a cloud on the air."

"Did he say anything?"

"No, not a word. Oh, I forgot! Yes, I did hear something—before he came. A battle cry. Something ferocious and horrible."

Robin smiled suddenly, looking up at the sky. Then he looked at Kat and grabbed her hands, pulling her to her feet to swing her around before him.

"He's come back!"

"And you've gone daft!" she accused him, tripping, and trying to keep up with his sudden merriment. "Robin—"

She was suddenly sitting again, and he was by her side. "The Silver Sword. He's come back."

"The Silver Sword . . ." Kat repeated. So the man was more than legend!

The stories about him were all real, just as Robin was real—just as the Lady Greensleeves was real.

And there had been wonderful stories about him! A swordsman who stopped the wicked oppressors here and there throughout the land, demanding that knights and barons and noblemen alike meet his sword ere they thought to ladle out damage upon any other man.

The rumors had begun . . . and then faded away. Many thought that the Silver Sword had been slain, or that perhaps he had been an old knight, and perished because of his age. Whatever, if he had ever been real, he had disappeared.

But now Robin seemed convinced that he was back.

"So this legend is real!" she said.

"You saw him today."

"Perhaps I saw . . . some other man."

"And perhaps he has come back!" Robin insisted happily. He looked away from her. "A man in silver mail! I'll know soon enough. When I hear . . ."

"When you hear what?" Kat demanded.

He looked at her and blinked hard. "What?"

It was her turn to sigh with exasperation. "You'll know when you hear what?"

He shook his head lamely. "When I hear . . . well, I'll know when I hear more stories. Whatever!"

Kat sat there stubbornly, shaking her head. "I never really believed in the Silver Sword. You see, I believe in Robin Hood, because I know him. And of course I believe in the Lady Greensleeves, because I know her. But Robin, why don't we know this man?"

"Kat, he probably doesn't want to be known!"

"But is he really such a good man?"

"You said that he saved the girl."

Kat sighed. "I just wish I knew. I wonder—"

"Quit wondering," Robin said, suddenly crisp and in a hurry. "Maybe he hasn't come back. Maybe it was a different man. There are dozens of maybes!" he finished, rising once again and reaching down a hand to her. "I thank you for the information that you bring me, as always, cousin. I thank you with all my heart. You were careful?"

"Of course I was careful," she assured him.

"And what of the priest?" he demanded. "Certainly he was left behind to keep guard on you."

A twinge of unease swept through her. She didn't know whether to tell Robin about her fears or not. He could not risk coming to the castle.

But then she wasn't afraid of being in the castle.

"Kat?" Robin said worriedly.

"Oh, aye, I'm sure that the good father was left behind to guard me! But I'm equally sure that he couldn't possibly suspect that I left. I used the secret doorway and the tunnel. When I looked back once I reached the woods, I discovered that all was still quiet."

"What if the priest is demanding that he see his hostess, even now?"

"Then Marie—God bless her!—will ward him off. She is an ingenious woman."

"Indeed, then, God bless her!" Robin's good humor was swiftly gone then, a frown coming to his handsome face once again. "It worries me deeply, this picture I see here. John arriving with de la Ville, Father Donavan, and Gerald Mortimer."

"In truth, young Mortimer is not so bad—" Kat began.

"And not so good," Robin reminded her sharply. "After all, perhaps it was de la Ville attacking this young girl, but Mortimer was standing by, watching it all, if I am not mistaken?"

"He made no move to help her, that is certain," Kat agreed.

"Prince John—and two powerful young noblemen. And a priest," he murmured. He didn't need to hear anything from her to come to his own conclusion. "Kat, you're going to have to take extreme care!"

She nodded, trying not to appear uneasy. She waved a hand in the air. "Oh, I daresay that they are up to something."

"The Prince wants control of your castle, Kat. And your men."

"I haven't that many men left. Most of my knights followed Richard on the Crusade," she reminded him.

"But there is tremendous strength in your castle! Why, Kat, it is made so that it could hold off an army. That is what John wants. He plans to take this country from Richard in the King's absence. And if he holds a fortress such as yours, he will have one fine place to which to run, or from which to wage battle! Kat, he intends to force you into a marriage."

"Oh, aye, perhaps," Kat said, with far less concern than she was feeling.

"Perhaps you shouldn't go back."

"I have to go back. We both know that. If I don't, he'll tear this forest apart, and we'll both be found."

Robin was suddenly wearing that stubborn look of his, the male-protector look. "I cannot let you—"

"Robin! It would do no good for de la Ville to simply misuse or harm me. He must have a marriage to take over the castle and the lands. I will be all right. When the Prince demands that I marry, I will agree to a long betrothal, and that is all. Perhaps then we will even take de la Ville for more than he has ever imagined. Robin, I will be all right. You know as well as I that Prince John must take grave care. He dare not have the other barons rise too furiously against him."

There was wisdom in her words, and Robin knew it. He drew her to her feet, clutched her shoulders, and held her tight. His hands slid to hers and clasped them for a moment, too. Then he kissed her cheeks. "I'll take you back as far as I dare."

He called for his horse, and it was brought by his man, Roger Gray. She bade Roger hello and goodbye, then leaped atop the horse before Robin.

They traveled the forest in a strange silence, and Kat knew that she had deeply worried Robin. She touched his cheek when he drew in on the reins, intending to set her down.

"Robin, I will be all right. You must never, never come here, you know."

"Aye," he agreed quietly.

"Robin, once you made me promise not to use my sword against any man in the forest. Now you must promise me you'll not come to the castle. It would please them all no end to hang you!"

"Aye, that it would."

"Robin, promise me."

"Kat, I cannot."

"But you must! I demand it!"

"Kat—"

"Robin," she said stubbornly, "if you'll not give me your word, I will take back my own! I'll come plowing through your forest with my father's sword swinging before me. I swear it."

"All right, all right! I'll not come to the castle!" he said, and set her down, then quickly added, "Tonight! I'll not come to the castle tonight!"

"Robin!" She spun around, but he was already swinging his mount about. "Get on home, Kat!" he warned her. "I've got to hear from my men who went out in search of the Prince and his party after you reached me. I must discover what other mischief there has been. Go home! And tell me as soon as you can what takes place this evening!"

There was no room for further argument then. Robin spoke quickly—and then was gone, disappearing into the foliage.

Kat stared after him, sighed, swept her grass-green cloak around her, and started moving quickly through the foliage and brush, seeking the entry to the caves.

Before she reached the entry, she paused, as she always did. She waited, watched, and listened.

The wind picked up. Swirling cool and wild, it seized the leaves and grasses on the ground, sweeping them around her. She shivered, looking around. Night was coming. Darkness.

She was not afraid of the night, nor did she fear darkness.

Yet she shivered, for the wind that flowed around her seemed to whisper stark words of warning. She felt the power of the sky and of the trees. Branches now seemed to reach for her like gnarled and ancient fingers, ready to hold her back, to keep her there, part of the forest.

Whispers . . .

Omens . . .

Of tempest, of bad things to come. Shadows filled the forest; a new kind of darkness was descending.

Nay!

The cry was silent, but loud in her heart. She would not be afraid of men like de la Ville!

Ah, but she needed to fear them, to be wary of them! Take care!

The breeze in the forest seemed to echo the warning of her heart. She stood still, feeling the caress of the cool air on her cheeks.

These were dangerous times.

And there was nothing she could do but live through them to the best of her talents.

She stood still a moment longer, then, certain that she was alone in the forest, she lowered her head and sought the entry to the cave. Quickly, she moved from natural rock formation to the tunnel that had been so ingeniously dug.

The sun was indeed dying. She moved in shadow, but she knew the way. Even when she reached the stygian darkness of the stairway, she was not afraid or uneasy. She knew every single step.

She didn't feel the first hint of fear until she had traveled both the tunnel and the stairway and come into the light of her room.

Marie was there, pacing and wringing her hands.

"Oh, blessed Jesu! You are back. Katherine! The Prince has returned with those wretched men of his. He is demanding that you make an appearance, and quickly!" Even as she spoke, Marie bustled around Katherine, drawing off her green cloak. "Hurry, oh, hurry! You have just taken the longest bath in the history of the world, Kat! Donovan has already warned that you've doused yourself in evil spirits and that you must not delay so long in water. Come, come, hurry!"

Kat's heart was pounding furiously. "What is John's hurry?"

Marie's troubled eyes met hers. "He has business to discuss with you, and he is anxious to settle it. Katherine, I've seen you talk yourself out of a great deal, but this bodes ill, I swear it does. What will you wear? Something old and somber. Perhaps we can veil your face—"

Kat shook her head, slipping out of the rest of her green. "Nay, Marie. I'll be battling the Prince as well as de la Ville. I think that I'll do it in grandeur. Let's see. I think that I should like the pale blue linen underdress with the fine embroidered blue tunic. Aye, the one with the very elegant undersleeves. That will do nicely, I think."

Marie might disapprove, but she drew out the garments Kat requested, along with fresh hose and Kat's delicate soft blue leather shoes. Kat swiftly donned the garments, the drew her fingers through the tangle of her hair.

"Jesu! What a snarl we have here. A brush! Oh, dear! I need time to replait your hair—"

"Nay. I'll wear it down."

"But Kat—"

"Down, I think. I mustn't let him think that anything is amiss." She sat on the small chair at her dressing table. "I mustn't let de la Ville know how very deeply I despise him!" she said softly. Then she smiled at Marie, her show of bravado finding substance within her. "I am the Countess Katherine, chatelaine here in my own right. And I will walk down with dignity!" she swore. She picked up her brush just as she heard what seemed like thunder erupting in the room.

"Open this door! Now!" a voice demanded.

"Donovan!" Marie mouthed.

"Now!" came the demand again. "Else we shall break it down panel by panel. By God, woman, what is going on in there!"

Kat braced herself.

"Kat!" Marie cried.

"May he rot in hell!" Kat spat out.

"The Prince has sent Father Donovan or one of his men again and again," Marie murmured heatedly. "I am amazed he has waited this long. Oh, my lady—"

"Open the door," Kat said, with a smile. "Quickly, open it, just as we are commanded."

And Marie did as she was ordered.

Chapter 5

Donovan had been about to pound his fists against the door once again with a fury.

To Kat's great pleasure, he nearly fell in, unbalanced when the door was opened as he had commanded.

He gazed past Marie to Kat, who sat calmly brushing out her tresses.

"Father! Goodness! You are in a hurry! 'Tis intriguing how guests behave these days!"

She could almost hear the irate click of his teeth. And still he controlled his temper—and his suspicions—and bowed deeply. "Ah, what great pleasure this gives me! It seems that you are ready—at last—to come join us again!"

There was never a man quite so cruel or cunning as a man of the cloth gone bad, she determined, but maintained her sweet and serene smile.

"Indeed, Father, I am," Kat assured him. She set down her brush and rose. "I have been told, however, good Father, that ladies must be indulged, the better to hostess their guests." The length of her hair swept behind her as she walked to join him. "Father?" She offered him her arm. Bowing slightly once more, he took it.

He led her down the stairway to the hall below. The Prince was indeed returned along with the others. Mortimer was sprawled before the fire, torturing her hounds by pretending to throw them morsels of the leg of meat he ate.

De la Ville, uninterested in food for the time, was far across the room, looking outward as if he could see into the growing shadows of the coming night.

Prince John had been seated at the table. He rose as Donovan brought her into the room. "Katherine. Forgive us. Our hunger grew. We began without you, yet felt such an emptiness despite the quality of your food and hospitality! We knew that it could only be fulfilled by the presence of our hostess herself."

"How very kind of you," Kat murmured.

"The Prince was beginning to suspect that you had deserted us, Lady Katherine," Donovan said. "I told him that it could not be so."

"Why Father, you must know that! You were seated here, before my door, the whole time!" she said sweetly.

Prince John's wife should have dined by his side, but since the lady was not present—and was with her husband as little as possible—and as it was Kat's home, she assumed the "honor" herself. When she was seated, John took his chair once again. Raymond de la Ville, with moody, brooding eyes, sat opposite her.

Mortimer kept his chair by the fire, where he could continue to torture the hounds. Father Donovan sat beside de la Ville and smiled.

"Indeed, you were absent from us quite some time," John said, watching her carefully.

"Was I? Forgive me—I had not meant to be so rude."

"You would not think to escape us?"

The question, asked by the Prince, was light. There was an underlying tone to it, though. Kat decided that it was a dangerous one.

"Why would I wish to escape you?" she asked. She offered him a sweeping smile, trying not to feel the heat in de la Ville's gaze from across the table.

"Your are ever absent when I come," de la Ville told her.

Her eyes narrowed. "Ah, but be assured! Though I am absent, my lord, you are in my thoughts!" She turned back to the Prince, smiling. "Truly, Father Donovan sat in this very room, I do assure you, my guardian!" she said, and laughed.

"Ah, but I had begun to wonder myself!" Donovan said. He lifted his glass to her. "Perhaps your beauty is magical, as some men have said. And you are able to spirit yourself away."

"Father, you are a flatterer indeed."

"But you are a jewel in our crown, most certainly!" John said. As ever, he watched her. Slyly.

She turned to him with her most radiant smile intact. "A jewel in our good King Richard's crown then, sire, if you insist!" she proclaimed.

He didn't move or flinch, but she observed a mottled coloring come to his cheeks. He lifted his chalice. "Let's drink, men, shall we? To the astounding beauty of the Lady Katherine, indeed a jewel in my brother's crown!"

"Here, here!" de la Ville cried. She looked across at him. At the lust and fever in his eyes.

Marie might have been right. She should have bound up her hair and worn dingy gray!

But it was too late now. Raymond de la Ville's hand was stretching out across the table. His long hard fingers were twining around hers.

"A beauty with no peer!" he assured her.

She snatched her fingers back as gracefully as she could. "Messieurs, I think that you do me unjust homage. I thank you for it. Excuse me. As it seems that you have had your fill of meats and seek something else, let me see to the kitchens and some sweets to tempt your palates."

De la Ville caught her fingers again when she would have swept by him. She paused, staring down into eyes that danced dangerously. "There is only one sweet thing I desire, lady."

"Really?" she inquired coolly. "It was always my understanding that you desired several. A multitude even," she said, and spoke in so pleasant a tone that he had released her and she had left the room, before John broke into a gale of laughter.

"Truly, de la Ville! I do not know if you deserve her or not! The lass is worthy of some fine noble knight— one to understand and parry such a tongue!"

"I'll parry her tongue all right," de la Ville muttered darkly, evermore aggravated by John's amusement at his expense. "I shall parry it from here into eternity—until death do us part!"

John speared a small leg of a fowl on the end of his knife and brought it before him, apparently studying the morsel of food. He was still delightfully entertained. "It will be interesting to see just who parries who unto eternity, de la Ville. This is no meek, frightened maid you seek."

De la Ville leaned hard across the table. "Are we forgetting something, my Prince? We seek land, and we seek riches, and men-at-arms. Do we not?"

John delicately bit off a piece of the meat. He was not against tormenting his own followers.

"I feel, de la Ville, at times, that I have set an emerald before you when a piece of dusty rock would have done just as well. A rare emerald. One with brilliance and a shimmer that is strong and unique."

"Bah!" de la Ville said impatiently. "One woman is the same as another!"

"Blind!" Mortimer suddenly spoke up from his seat before the fire. He was half gone in his cups. " 'Tis true! You give him a fine filly, when what he craves is a team of oxen!" He broke into bellows of laughter.

De la Ville stood with abrupt fury, drawing his sword.

"Mortimer!" de la Ville growled. "I'll skewer you through like so much meat!"

John flicked away a piece of meat from his sleeve with distaste. "Sit down, de la Ville! You might be better off with a team of oxen. This emerald we speak of has a temper, and a will."

"That will can be bent to mine! Her temper will be broken!" He smashed one large fist against the other. "I will see to it!"

"And that may well be a pity," John said idly, his light eyes narrowing. "Perhaps we should look elsewhere, since—"

"Nay!" De la Ville was sitting again, his sword sheathed, but his fist slammed the table with a vehemence that sent the Prince's platter jittering.

John stared from the platter to the man. "What a shame that I am in need of your sword arm, de la Ville!"

"You promised her to me!"

"Alas, alas! Ah, but I want the maid myself!" John said, purposely stoking some of the fire within de la Ville. "She is worthy of a man who will be King, don't you think?"

"But—" de la Ville began.

"If ever a maid were worthy to be concubine to a King! Pity that she isn't a princess, eh? Pity that I have a wife!" he added, with a touch of true passion. "And still, at times, I do entertain thoughts . . ."

De la Ville was on his feet again. "You promised—"

"Sit down!" John spat out again. Then he laughed. "There, there, then. You shall have her." John suddenly folded his hands, set his elbows on the table, and leaned close to de la Ville. "Now listen, dear brute, for if you would snare this prey, you'll have to have some sense of delicacy. Mind your manners for the moment, and we will speak gently to the maid."

"She will refuse me," de la Ville muttered.

"Maybe—maybe not. She is not a fool. But whether she says aye or nay does not matter. We will see the situation solved. We will wrest a promise from her this very night—you will see."

De la Ville said something in return. What it was, Katherine did not hear.

She had not really left the men, but rather had lingered in the hall. Marie stood beside her now, listening, while Howard had been sent to fetch some pastries and cakes and sweetmeats.

"What in God's name are they saying!" she moaned softly to Marie. Now Mortimer had actually risen from his seat and stood at the end of the table, listening attentively. Father Donovan had his head bowed closer, and the four of them, hovering so close and furtively over the table, resembled nothing more than a set of cutthroats and thieves.

They *were* cutthroats and thieves, Kat reminded herself.

And very, very thick at the moment!

"Something foul, assuredly!" Marie murmured. "What will you do? Oh, Lady Katherine, what will you do? The Prince means to have you agree to marry that lout tonight!"

"But I am Richard's ward," Kat said bleakly.

"That argument will not sway him," Marie warned her.

She didn't need the warning. She had known. She had known this afternoon just what was afoot. Now she had to play the game.

"It's all right," she told Marie. "I can take care of myself. Truly I can." If only she were certain! Or if only she had managed to hear everything that they were saying! She would be better prepared.

"Wish me luck!" she urged Marie suddenly, squeezing her servant's hand warmly. Then, before Marie could stop her with any more words of wisdom or warning, she regally sailed back out to meet her guests.

"The sweets shall be along almost instantly, Father, my lords, Your Grace," she said, nodding to each man in turn, a calm and beautiful smile on her face. She took her seat at the head of the table, feeling as if vermin crawled on her as Raymond de la Ville's arm came close to her own.

She swallowed hard. How would she play this game? Was he senseless, mindless? His father had threatened hers!

And he had been there, learning his cruelty from that man!

She forced herself to speak. "And I've a surprise for you. A special coffee, from the Holy Lands. I'm sure you've had it many times before, Your Grace, but my traders have managed to procure an enchanting blend from some merchants just returned with a score of injured knights."

"Coffee! That heathen brew! Why, give me good French wine every time!" de la Ville said flatly.

The Prince picked up Kat's hand, rubbed his fingers over the pads of her own, and pressed a kiss against the back of them. "I shall be pleased to try your brew, Countess."

She nodded, bowing her head slightly. John leaned back and waved a hand in the air. "Have your servants bring us the last course now. We've business to discuss!"

Delicately, Kat arched a brow to him. "Of course, Your Grace," she said evenly. She rose and clapped a hand.

Instantly, Howard appeared with several young maids who worked in the kitchens. She clenched her teeth as she saw de la Ville size up every girl who entered, the younger the better, so it seemed. She was sure that he would have reached out to touch—had not the Prince frowned at him so fully.

"I shall serve the coffee myself," she informed Howard, inclining a head that he should gather the others and leave. She stood, serving the hot brewed Arab drink from the shining copper pot into delicate porcelain cups, passing one to each man—except for de la Ville to whom she offered more wine. Then she sat and smiled at John. "Your Grace, what is this business you would discuss with me?"

John didn't hesitate. Staring at her gravely, he replied, "Marriage, my dear."

"Marriage? But my Prince," she reminded him, as if she were troubled, "I am Richard's ward. Certainly I cannot marry without him here. Not in good conscience." She gazed innocently at Father Donovan. "Would such a marriage even be legal, Father?"

Donovan seemed to know that there was nothing innocent about her question at all. "Richard is not here, my lady—God bless the King, but he is absent. Therefore, in that absence, Prince John must act for your well-being."

"Ah, I see!" Kat murmured. She frowned. "And still, marriage must be legal. Else all that I possess could not pass to my husband. And what man would not want control of this castle? I believe I would do any man an injustice to wed him without Richard here, no matter how . . . noble . . . a prince his brother might be! In such a case as mine, it is most likely that the King would reward a noble knight from his field of battle with marriage—and this castle. What is done here could too easily be undone."

"Control is in the holding!" de la Ville announced. Then he grunted suddenly.

John must have kicked him beneath the table, Kat decided.

John lifted his hands. "Richard is very far away. His knights cannot help you from the Holy Lands, lady, while there sits in this very room a man so enamored of you that he cannot speak his own suit. He is a man who is . . . er, dear to my own heart. And one quite powerful enough to hold this castle. For you, of course."

"For me. Of course."

"He heartily desires your hand in marriage. And he has my blessing, and approval. In fact . . ." John moved closer to her, smiling a smile that was a warning. "I ask you, as your Prince and guardian—in lieu of my brother, of course—to accept this suit. I know that you will be well guarded and safe from the realm of banditry!"

They all waited—certain that she would refuse.

Dear God, she did long to do so! With every aching fiber in her body! She longed to leap up, to tell de la Ville that she would die a thousand times over before letting him touch her with his bloodstained hands.

She dug her nails fiercely into her palms beneath the table. She did not leap up. She maintained her air of innocence. "Well, Your Grace, I would not presume to become a Princess, even were you free, sire. And," she continued softly, with a slightly wicked smile, "it cannot be Father Donovan who seeks my hand. So, who, Your Grace, does me this honor? Gerald Mortimer or Raymond de la Ville?"

Mortimer almost spewed her sweet brewed coffee from his lips. De la Ville choked on his wine.

John, bemused, sat back, then indicated de la Ville with a wave of his hand.

"Raymond de la Ville seeks your hand in marriage, my lady. What say you?"

She allowed the flush of fury to stain her cheeks, and quickly lowered her eyes. "I say that it is a great honor, my Lord de la Ville. I say also that I am still troubled by Richard's absence, but that—with the grace of a few months' time—I might well be persuaded to accept a betrothal to such a . . . unique man."

John's eyes narrowed. "You will have a few days' time, my lady."

Her eyes were flashing with hatred, and she had to keep them lowered, lest the Prince see that anger. "As you wish it, Your Grace," she said sweetly. She rose, afraid that she would scream out loud and rant and rave if she were left with them a single second longer.

But she didn't need to fear. The Prince rose, too, and with him Donovan, de la Ville, and Mortimer.

John told her, "We will thank you, my lady, for your most gracious hospitality. And we will take our leave."

"So soon?" she breathed.

De la Ville took her hand. His lips brushed over her fingertips.

"The sooner to return!" he told her huskily. Again, she felt as if all manner of evil, slimy creatures crawled upon her. Odd. He was a handsome man— but so wretchedly cruel and odious. A touch of his perversion seemed to permeate even his voice, and the tips of his fingers.

"I am ever your servant," she murmured, and drew back quickly.

John bade her goodbye with kisses on both cheeks— thankfully, neither Donovan or Mortimer made any attempt to touch her.

And again, she had only to lift a hand to have her servants hurrying about. The hounds moved among the people as the castle villeins performed their duties, bowing low as they brought the Prince and the others their cloaks, and following behind Kat as she saw them from the hall to the courtyard, where other men quickly procured their horses. When they had at last ridden away, the frozen smile was wiped cleanly from Kat's face. "Close the drawbridge!" she ordered, choking on the words. And even as her command was obeyed, she ran back into the castle, and quickly up the stairs.

Marie followed her and found her in her bedroom, pacing the floor in a fury.

"Oh, what will you do, what will you do?"

"God's blood, I know not!"

"A few days' time! Richard will not return in a few days. There is nothing left for you to do! You cannot marry this horrid man. You must run. You must ask Robin for help, and flee this country."

"Oh! That's perfect!" Kat cried, relieved at last. "That is it! Oh, Marie, you are a dear!" She caught her servant's round cheeks between her hands and kissed her on the nose. "A few days . . . tomorrow I will get my things in order. I will see that the castle is emptied, and that my men are sent to other households. Then I will slip away myself. I will follow Richard to the Holy Lands!"

"Aye, aye!" Marie said. Then she frowned. "Nay! That is too dangerous. You must go on to Normandy, but then move no further."

Kat shook her head, her eyes wide and bright with excitement. "Nay. I shall go all the way to Jerusalem!"

"Lady Kat—"

"It is settled. And you'll come with me."

"Me! In that land of heathens! Oh, nay, nay, nay, my lady! Pray, think on it! Sleep on it!"

Kat smiled slowly, truly relieved for the first time at last.

The worst was happening. She had no choice but to escape it.

She could even sleep very well, she assured herself. "Help me off with my tunic and underdress and see that they are packed very carefully. I will take just one trunk, I think. I will travel light."

"But Katherine—"

"Eleanor of Aquitaine went on Crusade. There is a precedent for women other than camp followers to do so," Kat said, determined.

Marie groaned, collecting the clothing that Kat tossed about.

Slipping into a nightgown, Kat spun around to her. "Would you rather I wed de la Ville?" she demanded huskily. "Don't you see, Marie? I have to reach Richard. He is my only safety!"

"Mother of God!" Marie whispered, crossing herself. She remained there, holding Kat's clothing, looking up as if she could truly address the Blessed Mother. "Madame, assuredly my place in heaven is guaranteed for my years with this wayward girl!"

"For your years with this countess," Kat reminded her with a sigh for her dramatics.

Marie ignored her. "Holy Mother, please intercede! Don't let this foolish . . . countess . . . throw away both our lives in some distant desert, I pray you!" She crossed herself again, then smiled to Kat. "She will intercede!"

Kat felt a bubble of laughter rising within her despite her annoyance. "And I shall throw something at you quite shortly if you don't behave like a good lady's maid and pay heed to my words!" She caught her lower lip lightly between her teeth. "Marie, go now. I must get some sleep. I shall never sleep! Nay, I must sleep. I will need all my wits and all my strength!"

"Humph!" Marie responded. She hurried to the door and then waited. "Humph!" she repeated.

"Good night, Marie."

"Humph!" Marie said, making her disapproval as obvious as she could. But then she sighed deeply, and made her mutterings into more disapproving sounds. She went to the door, repeated a "Humph!" and then left Kat at last.

And Kat lay down on her bed, her mind in a whirl.

Dear God, it would be dangerous. She had to be so very, very careful! If she were caught . . .

If she were caught, what did she have to lose? No fate could be worse than marriage to a man like de la Ville!

Nay, she had nothing to lose.

Nothing at all. De la Ville was the epitome of everything she hated. Truly, death would be preferable. She had to escape. It was solved. It was easy. There was simply no other choice.

That thought, in the end, was the one that allowed her to begin to drift into the sleep she so desperately needed to function well in the morning. She did so with a half smile, curved with just a touch of bitterness, on her lips.

She was no different than the girl in the woods. A toy to de la Ville. Some poor maid to torment and ravish. The only difference would be that she happened to come with a castle.

Yet no knight would come to carry her away. She was on her own. A damsel in distress indeed, yet a damsel on her own.

She would prevail, she promised herself.

She would prevail, because she must.

She would indeed, but the path she was destined to take was not the path that she was recklessly determined to follow.

Not far from the castle, Robin felt the same cool swirl of the wind that had so touched Katherine before.

The wind had picked up, as if a great giant had suddenly leaned down to the earth and blown out a cold whistle of breath. It churned up the leaves at his feet, and the dust there, and it all swirled around them. He closed his eyes and listened to the rustle of the leaves.

This was a strange night, a dark night. Clouds played before the silver of a moon.

It was a night for the ancient gods, he thought. Christianity might be many centuries old here now, but there were still those who believed in the ancient gods, and the ancient superstitions. Why not, he thought with a smile. For they all still played around Maypoles on May day; and on Hallow's Eve, men crossed themselves and stayed far away from burial grounds. Tonight was a night for the old gods, indeed.

And for demons. The kind who came from hell below, and the kind who walked the earth in human form.

A night for . . .

There was a flash of silver in the trees. Robin smiled, and waited. He had been right. He had come to the cove here on purpose, and he had waited, certain that he was right.

The leaves rustled more loudly.

And a huge black horse stepped into the clearing, ridden by a tall man in silver mail and a black cloak.

"You are back!" Robin called delightedly.

The man dismounted from his horse and greeted Robin, warmly clasping the hand offered to him. The two men greeted each other with smiles: relations by birth; old friends, good friends, by choice.

By birth, they were different men. In their hearts, they were very much the same.

Just as Kat's father had inadvertently given birth to the Silver Sword, the Silver Sword had aided his younger relation in his own quest. He had been disturbed at the young man's determination to be the best bowsman in the world at first.

But as time had gone by, he had known that Robin, the young Saxon heir to Locksley, would be fighting all of his life.

He had best fight well.

And so he had taught Robin. And Robin had come to surpass him with a bow, even though the Silver Sword maintained his standing as the more accomplished of the two with a blade.

"Jesu! I believe in miracles!" Robin said. "How can this be?"

"A somewhat long story, I'm afraid," the man said.

"I heard about your adventure this afternoon."

"You did? How?"

"You forget. I have eyes all over the forest."

"Ah! Then I needn't have made my appearance. Your men would have intervened—"

"Nay, without you there, the lass would have been raped, tortured—perhaps even killed. De la Ville is a careless brute," Robin said dryly.

"Aye, a cruel one."

"But maybe he is a man who can now be kept in check."

"Indeed. Lord Montjoy has been sent home for that very purpose in mind."

"Is that true? The Lionheart has sent you home?" Robin demanded. And then he smiled, and looked to heaven. "Thank you, God above! Oh, thank you!"

"Well, I hope that you will still feel that way when I tell you the rest," Damian said, a frown furrowing his brow.

"Tell me!"

"As Lord Montjoy I carry papers and dispensations to immediately take the Lady Katherine de Montrain to wife, and assume control of the castle."

"Jesu!" Robin breathed. "Montjoy! To have Kat!" Then he started to laugh softly. "That's wonderful!"

"Well, I don't believe that the lady will think so."

Robin shrugged. "Well, admittedly, Montjoy is among her least favorite knights. But then she really doesn't know him very well. And she might not be pleased with Montjoy, but—she'll have to be pleased that someone has interceded. You see, John has other plans for her, it would seem."

"De la Ville," Damian said softly.

"Aye! And you cannot imagine how she hates de la Ville."

"Aye, but I can!"

There was a silence between them. They could both look back over the years.

And indeed, the three of them shared a hatred of de la Ville.

"I am glad," Robin said. "Deeply glad. I've spent endless nights worrying for her. She is so passionately involved with the people here. I had feared for her."

"Well, she may consider Montjoy one of her own deepest fears," Damian said.

"Aye. It may be rough going!" Robin warned.

"I'm sure that Lord Montjoy will manage," Damian murmured flatly.

"Ah, yes, he's dealt with the infidels. But he has yet to deal with a Kat!" Robin smiled, but then his smile faded. "Be gentle, for I love her dearly." He hesitated. "And you do not. Everyone is aware that Montjoy still mourns the fair Alyssa."

"I intend to be gentle, Robin. Yet in fairness I tell you—if given a wife, I shall have one."

"In fairness, I accept that."

"One that I would die to defend, as well."

Robin smiled. "If only you knew one another as I do!" he said. Then he added hurriedly, "I think that you've truly come in just the nick of time. And thank God, indeed! Now I am absolved from breaking a promise. And you, Silver Sword, are in a good position to protect the property granted by Richard to Lord Montjoy."

"How so?"

"I am afraid, dearly afraid. John and de la Ville were at the Lady Katherine's castle this very day, putting forth the Prince's proposal. Kat was certain that she would be safe, since Raymond de la Ville would need a true marriage to take hold of her property. And one would think that the Prince would not dare anything too open, but then again . . ." His voice trailed away. "I had meant to keep guard over the castle tonight myself, but Katherine made my plan very difficult for me."

"How so?"

"I gave my word that I would not come to the castle. I didn't mean to do so, but she forced me."

"Robin, my dear fellow, you do not know how to handle women."

"Nay? Do you think you will do so much better?"

"Indeed, my friend. My wishes will be law in my household."

Robin smiled. "Well, we shall see." His smile faded. "I am worried."

"Then so am I. But you needn't fear longer. You may keep your word and still know that the castle is well guarded." He stepped forward again and offered his hand once more in a sure clasp.

"I'm glad you're back!" Robin said. "It hasn't been the same without you."

"I had to go. You know that."

"I do. You are rightly Richard's man."

"Despite that, we may both still hang."

Robin grinned. "Aye, we may. But we'll have taken a lot of them with us down to our fiery hell!"

"Aye, that we will have done!"

Robin stepped back, watching. The Silver Sword mounted his ebony-black steed and rode into the darkness of the night, a ghostly shadow of silver and gray, glimmering, disappearing, beneath the pale glint of the moon.

Robin watched after him for a moment, musing.

Would Kat be any more pleased with this choice of Richard's for her hand?

Nay . . .

She would not! He smiled, thinking of the way Kat said Montjoy's name ever since he had accosted her in the forest—or ever since she had accosted him, whichever.

Damian, it seemed, was equally hard on Kat. He was careful when he spoke to Robin, but he found her reckless and headstrong and not at all the demure young chatelaine she should be. Damian would certainly be an honorable husband. He would never hurt Katherine, and in truth, he would protect her unto death. But he didn't really know her. He didn't understand her.

Kat didn't begin to know or understand him.

And Robin, well, Robin loved them both.

Perhaps Kat would learn . . .

Or perhaps Kat would teach Damian a thing or two.

They were both his friends, and both his kin, from opposite sides of his family.

He grinned broadly, then laughed into the night.

Indeed, fire would fly.

His laughter faded abruptly. Fire would fly—if the Silver Sword could keep her safe this night! It was becoming such a strange night. The wind was rising. Rustling through the trees. Swirling up the dirt and leaves at Robin's feet. Whispering . . . a warning.

Closer to the castle, the Silver Sword felt the same curious shift in the wind, the whisper on the air. Seated on his ebony-dark horse in the shadows before the castle, he, too, heard the rustling, felt the coolness of the night sweep around him.

Felt the swirl. Lifting, curling, causing a ripple in the leaves, forcing the boughs to bend. It was a breeze that whispered out warnings, that whispered of danger.

Clouds again covered the moon. The wind caused the water in the moat to ripple like quicksilver.

For a moment the clouds lifted from the surface of the moon. He could see the castle, tall and formidable and stark in the night. Stone upon stone, independent, defiant. Like a painting, it was cast there, still and silent.

His horse pawed the earth, anxious. The animal worked the bit.

"Not yet!" he said softly in the night. "Not yet!"

Then, even as he spoke, the stillness of the night was suddenly shattered.

A screech of metal sounded.

The drawbridge was being lowered, gears cranked against gears.

Then a raw cry rose high in the night. Riders surged out of the forest, and from the parapets high above the castle walls, a guard suddenly plummeted to his death, an arrow through his heart.

"Now!" he told his horse, and gave the animal free rein.

Chapter 6

They were coming for her.

Katherine had been sleeping at last, deeply sleeping, and she wasn't sure how or when she heard the first faint clink of metal against stone, or how she managed to wake up entirely aware that they had decided to throw caution to wind and solve their problems with a simple abduction.

Why had she been so sure that they would dare not do so? she wondered with dismay.

She tried to assure herself that the sounds did not mean that they were coming for her.

But they did.

In the soft expanse of her bed where she had lain sleeping so deeply at last, her eyes flew open instantly, and just as instantly, she was wide awake and aware.

She listened.

Again she heard it. A clink of metal. Far below.

How dare they? Outrage burned through her. This was her castle, these were her people. And though she was woefully low at men-at-arms due to the machinations of Prince John, someone, or perhaps several someones, had died trying to keep these wretched invaders from coming so close to her.

She leaped out of bed and raced to the tower window, ripping away the tapestry to stare down at the drawbridge and moat far below.

Then she heard the first cry. And even as she watched, one of her guards hurtled down before her to splash into the moat below.

Men had come to cause this!

Men in the darkness, men in the night! And they dared to claim that others were bandits and thieves!

Indeed, yes, men had come. Their horses' hooves were covered in cloth to keep them silent as they moved across wood and stone. Someone had let out a cry, and the clank of the drawbridge had been unmistakable, but they had come here in stealth. She was supposed to have slept through it all.

They carried no flares against the darkness. Even as she watched, the horses moved quickly over the drawbridge and into the great yard within the castle walls.

Prince John was gone and could not be blamed, or so he would determine. And the defenses of her castle, the impregnable defenses, had obviously been breached because someone had been left behind, a man from among de la Ville's ranks, someone to slit the throat of the man at the drawbridge, and lower it to the invaders.

For a moment she heard nothing. There was only silence. A half moon hung low in the sky, creating a night of shadow and illusion. A soft glow of amber light touched the deep dark waters of the moat below, and illuminated the near-octagonal shape of the castle with its various turrets and towers and parapets.

A cloud covered the moon. Katherine shivered fiercely. The horses were gone from the bridge. As if she had imagined them.

The moon appeared again. Far across from her tower window, upon a parapet, she thought she saw the figure of a man. Dark, foreboding, hands on his hips, his face in darkness, the only glitter about him being that of . . .

His sword. Flickering like a silver fire in the night. Held high against the darkness . . .

Her heart thundered. Was that he? The wretched traitorous rat, left behind to come stealthily upon the good men of her castle, take them unawares, stalk them from behind and with a quick swipe of that blade, steal their life's blood from them, letting it flow into rivers of crimson.

Vile bastard! Knave of knaves, she thought furiously.

Clouds, like black shadows, passed again. Quickly, oh so quickly, they came and went. And then, when the light appeared once again . . .

He was gone.

Had she imagined him? Were the curious moonlight and the depths of her fear creating flights of fancy within her mind? Her heart kept pounding, fiercely. So fiercely.

And what difference did it make if the enemy walked the parapets as well as the stair?

She knew who had come for her, and she knew why. De la Ville was very much aware that she wasn't a fool, that she would have agreed to anything.

And that she would still never willingly become his wife.

"I shall die first!" she whispered fiercely. But would she? Really? Looking down the heights to the moat below, she was quite certain that she didn't want to die.

She absolutely hated heights. She couldn't possibly throw herself out the window.

Perhaps that would be nearly the same as surrender, she told herself. No, she would not do it!

But death would be a sweeter fate than life with de la Ville. Her heart thundered, and she pressed her hands against her eyes.

No. She would never, never allow de la Ville to touch her. Never.

She would fight. To the bitter end.

Or perhaps . . .

She would run.

She hurried across the room to the secret doorway that led to the ink-dark, winding stairs and the dank tunnel that ran beneath the moat. She would escape into the forest. And if the doorway was discovered when they searched for her, well, that would surely be tragic, but certainly no more so than her capture by de la Ville. Once in his hands, she would be of no use to anyone.

But even as she touched the secret stone as she had done dozens of times before, she heard a curious grinding sound.

Nothing happened. The door didn't give.

"Jesu!" she cried in sudden desperation. She struck it again. She pounded it. Bleakly, almost numbly at first, she realized that something in the aging mechanism had failed her. The secret door would not give.

What she faced now was stone. Just that. Solid stone.

"Nay!" A cry of anguish and stark denial escaped her. The numbness fell away from her.

She might really be taken. To de la Ville.

Silence followed her cry.

And then . . .

Again, a sound. Closer now. The slight clink of metal against stone.

They had entered the keep. They were already coming up the spiral stone stairs that led to her room in the north tower.

She ran to the window again. She stared out to the night, and up to the sky. Then down again. The moat. It stretched out before her, yawning huge and black, like some beckoning pit of hell.

She couldn't do it. Even with escape cut off. She just couldn't do it, not until the very last moment . . .

There was a flash of silver again in the night. She looked to the parapets. Nothing. She was imagining things. And she was just standing there now, while her doom pressed closer and closer upon her.

But there was a tall figure there, upon the parapets. And the silver that flickered in the moonlight and disappeared with the shadows was from that figure's sword blade!

She stared at that figure, furious. Surely, he was one of de la Ville's men.

The one who had stayed behind within her castle like a thief in the night. The one who had murdered a guardsman to lower the drawbridge. She stared at him.

He stared in return—watching her.

It didn't occur to him that she thought him the traitor. His thoughts were on her.

This! This was what had brought him home, with Jerusalem so close!

There had been no great difficulty reaching the castle walls once he had been able to leave Lucifer in the woods and tread silently behind the attackers. But they had left a guard of their own at the gate, forcing him to scale the castle walls. He had done so, casting a noose around a parapet and precariously climbing the rope to reach this catwalk.

He was breathing very hard. This type of work was best done by men not weighed down by a coat and cape of meshed-mail armor!

All this . . . for her.

Had she been a well-behaved and demure damsel, Richard might well have had her safely wed long ago! He wouldn't be here, crawling around in heavy armor to save her.

Ah, but nay! Determined on her independence, the wench had all but financed Richard's Crusade by her own efforts.

And so she had been left free to roam the forest, to wreak havoc on the unwary, and to set herself into danger time and again. These were not the qualities a man sought in a wife.

Especially not when he had loved once before. When he had thought to wed before. When the lady had been the very essence of gentleness and kindness, with a smile to light the heavens, with a whisper to rouse the spirit and the deepest desires, with eyes to give promise—

Those eyes were closed now. Forever closed. This castle was his reward. This castle—and the girl.

And this castle was just about to be swept away from his waiting hands!

Yet even as he watched in the darkness, waiting, his heart took a curious turn. By the soft fluttering candlelight, he could see her through the slit in her tower wall, for his angle had been carefully chosen for just that design.

He lifted the mask of fine mesh mail that concealed his features, the better to see in the night. And even as he did so, she suddenly pushed away from the window and the wall, and upon her toes, she spun in a circle, somewhat like an animal realizing itself trapped.

And somewhat like an ethereal creature, a goddess of the ancient Greeks or Romans, or of the very Druids who had once trodden these lands.

As she circled about, her gown and the wondrous length of her hair moved with her. The gown was diaphanous and white, both virginal and . . . erotic, for the dim candlelight played upon it so completely.

Ah, she was wayward indeed. Temperamental, troublesome, willful—surely he could go on.

But beautiful, too. Strikingly so. For as she turned, her perfection could be clearly seen. Breasts full and firm, a winsomely slender waist, a flare of hips, and long ivory legs that were beautifully shaped and slender still. In that muted light, she was all ivory and gold. A goddess sculpted in alabaster, and cloaked in the endless gold of the waves of shimmering tendrils that flew so majestically around her as she swirled. Ah, and her face! Her features so very fine and delicate, lips so full and red, cheeks high, her eyes alive with fire and anguish, deep and dark from this distance!

Something burned within him. He wondered at the startling fever that suddenly filled him, at the ferocious strength of it. Ah, love could die perhaps, but desire was some rough creature that could live well and heartily within a man when love was gone.

She touched him, indeed.

And she was to be his wife . . .

Not if he didn't move well and quickly this night, he reminded himself.

He slid the mail helmet back over his face, and as he did so, a shudder tore through him.

Ari's words came back to haunt him. He was a thousand miles away, standing in the desert sands.

She will betray you . . .

Those words, before Richard had even spoken to him! He would wed her, but she would betray him in darkness . . .

Never, he swore abruptly and savagely to the night. None of it mattered, he told himself. Not tonight.

Tonight . . .

Tonight the Silver Sword had only to do battle . . .

And for both their sakes, they needed to win.

They would win, he vowed to himself. They would win. And then as to their own lives . . .

Well, they would see.

At the moment, Kat wasn't the least concerned with Montjoy or the Silver Sword.

Her mind was focused on another enemy.

Damn him, Kat thought furiously of de la Ville, and damn every one of his rotten henchmen! She would have none of it! Were they such fools that they thought they had only to break into the castle, slay her most noble defenders, and make demands—and she would accompany them?

Perhaps they imagined that they would take her asleep, quickly kidnap her, and perform whatever evil deed they had in mind. After all, these men were but the henchmen for a leader who might or might not be with them.

She would not let them take her. She would fight them. Perhaps they wouldn't really dare to harm her, and as long as she was able to hold them off . . .

What then?

A moment's despair tore through her. There was little that could help her now, no matter how long or industriously she fought. Only the King had the right to decide her fate.

She turned her anger toward Richard.

Richard! The King was far away, storming some Moslem stronghold in the Holy Lands, battling with Saladin, the great caliph of the people of Islam.

"Damn you, Richard!" she swore aloud.

Her father's slender dress sword hung on the wall of her chamber, and Katherine quickly leaped atop one of her trunks to lift it down. With the weapon in her hand, she felt somewhat better.

She shivered, determined again that she would fight to the bitter end. She thought again of the terrible height of her tower, and the great distance down to the dark swirling waters of the moat far below. The prospect of a lifetime committed to de la Ville made the dark waters seem almost welcoming.

There was no more time to waste. They were in the castle now, in her very tower, and it seemed that they were no longer terribly concerned with keeping their presence a secret. She could hear the footsteps on the stone stairs now. Their movements had been so stealthy.

Perhaps they were throwing caution to the winds as they felt that they closed in upon their prey.

Where could she go from here? There was only up, higher up, to the tallest parapets of the tower. Higher and higher . . .

She felt dizziness assail her, and she shook her head fiercely as if she could shake her fear away. She certainly couldn't stand here, just waiting, any longer.

She threw her heavy door open and was instantly alarmed to realize that they had nearly come upon her. A knight in half armor stood upon the stairs, his face covered by his helmet and visor, his chest protected by a cuirass of steel, but his thighs and calves were left barren of metal, and the fine worsted material of his short tunic and hose gave credence to the man's service not only to a nobleman, but to a rich one at that.

"My lady!" he said, startled.

Indeed, they *had* planned to come upon her in her sleep.

But she wasn't sleeping, and she was very aware of their mission; that much must have been obvious in her eyes. He cleared his throat and spoke quickly. "You must come with us, Countess. Now. At my lord's command."

"And who is your lord, good sir?"

"I am not at liberty to give you his name—"

"And I do not feel at liberty to give you my person, sir!" she snapped back furiously. "Get from my castle! You've no right here, none at all."

The man held a moment. His companions were quickly coming up behind him, and Katherine's heart sank as she counted their number. There were at least ten men in this party that had come for her. She couldn't possibly fight them all.

"Lady, I'm sorry," he said, and she thought that there really might be a certain sorrow in his voice. "You must come with me."

Katherine shook her head slowly and produced her sword.

"Lady Katherine, we seek your safety with a good and Christian knight, so do I swear it!"

"Good and Christian?" she repeated softly. "Oh, I think not! You come from a man spawned of the devil, and you have no authority over me. I am King Richard's ward, and no other has any right to order me from this property."

"It grows late," one of the men muttered behind the first. "Let's take her and have done with this!"

"What would you have me do?" the first hissed in return. "Skewer her through? My lord wishes a living bride, if not a willing one." His full attention returned to Katherine. "Please, lady, we will have you with us one way or another. If you'll only—"

"If you came in any good way, sir, you'd not have your face covered with that armor! When Richard hears tell of this outrage, there will be hell to pay, sir, I swear it!"

"Richard cares nothing for England, or anything English!" swore the man behind the first. "Come, lady, have done with this! We will take you willing or nay!"

"I think not!" she snapped back. Oh, her voice sounded good! She did not give away the fact that she was trembling, or that the cold of the stone beneath her bare feet now seemed to have entered into all of her being.

"Lady—"

The first of the men took a step toward her. She swirled out her sword with the expertise she had learned so long ago from her father, and she was pleased to see that the motion itself had given the men just a moment's pause.

"Dear sirs! I shall defend myself if you would take me!" she promised in a deadly tone.

"Why, she's little more than a girl!" someone wailed.

"Nay, friend, see the moonlight play upon her bounty, she is much more than a girl!" another bellowed.

"And chosen to be his lordship's bride!" the first man reminded them all fiercely.

Her sword drawn and ready, she backed away up the stone stairs, praying that she didn't trip on the sheer white linen hem of her nightdress.

"Lady!" cried the man in the lead. "Throw down your sword. We've no desire to hurt you!"

"You've invaded my property, murdered my people, and seek to seize me, and that is not to hurt me!" she retorted scornfully, a brow arched imperiously. "I think, sir, that you've caused me great pain already."

"Throw down your sword! You could be harmed!"

"I warn you—keep your sword raised, for if you seek to take me, you had best take great care for your nether parts, lest they be severed from your body!"

For the first time, the man in his helmet and half armor seemed to take pause. His eyes even fell to that nether part which must have been most important to him, as if he had heard, perhaps, of her reputation and was assuring himself that he was still whole at the moment.

"Go on there, Michael," teased a man behind him. "The lady is innocent, surely, and may not know quite where to strike."

"She knows, Michael," Katherine warned.

"Lady!" Poor Michael was growing desperate. "You must come with me."

She lifted her sword, the point wavering just a breath away from his body, at precisely that place upon his tunic he must surely want most protected.

"And they said we'd not need full body armor!" someone guffawed.

"Get her, Michael!"

Michael swirled around, defeated at last. "You get her, Clifford!"

And Clifford was suddenly thrust up before her. He meant to reach out and take her arm. She didn't want to use her sword against him, but she had to make them realize that she could not be intimidated.

And that she could not be taken.

She lifted her sword and brought it down expertly, just slicing through the muscle of the man's upper arm. He screamed out in pain, then stared at her, and she could feel, even at their sword's length distance apart, the growth of his indignity and fury.

"Lady, you will pay!" he cried, and lunged forward.

"Nay!" someone shrieked. "You cannot harm her!"

Ah! And that was in her favor. She held the steel high again, facing them all. She backed up another step. "Get away from me!" she warned.

"Charge her!" Clifford cried out angrily. "She cannot best us all!"

The assault was suddenly on. One by one they forced their way up the winding stairs, swords swinging to catch her blade. Katherine parried blow after blow.

Then she began to feel the weight in her arm. Aye, she was good. She'd had lessons with the best. The only child, pampered daughter, she'd been able to intrude upon her cousins' lessons and her father's patience, and she'd made good use of all that she had learned.

But no matter how talented she might be, she hadn't the arm strength of these muscled henchmen, and she knew that she had only moments left to spare before one of them was able to wrest her sword from her.

Thinking quickly, she slashed down on a sword, then stared above the throng of men and cried out loudly, "You've come! God above, you've come!"

As she had hoped, the men ceased in their ruthless attack, and turned hastily to look at the winding stairway the best they could.

It was all that she needed.

She turned and fled up the last of the steps to the door leading to the high parapet above. She shoved on it and gasped, horrified, finding that it had stuck. "No!" she shrieked, and threw her full weight against it, praying all the while.

It stuck!

Had all the castle stones themselves decided to conspire against her this night?

Once more!

She slammed against the door, and it flew open, carrying her along with it.

Gasping, floundering, tripping over the white linen hem of her gown, she came out into the chill night air, then turned to slam the door behind her. Yet even as the wood shuddered against the frame, she felt a scream growing in her throat.

She had stopped the men from coming momentarily. It did not matter. In seconds, she would not be alone on the parapet.

Her back to the door, she stared in horror and disbelief as a cloaked black shadow came flying through the night like a giant raven. Dimly she realized that he had sent a clamp and rope flying atop the buttress above her, and that he now rode the rope to the parapet to reach her.

How he came did not matter. That he had come to meet her here when she had bested so many did.

It was he. The enemy she had seen before. Perhaps he was the bastard who had remained behind when the others had quit her castle. The enemy who had seen that the draw bridge had been lowered, rendering a near-impregnable castle into an easy target!

"Lady—" came a husky voice.

She did not intend to listen.

"No!" she shrieked. With quickly fading strength she lifted her sword against the man, ready to skewer him through, then and there. He leaped free of the rope, a black shadow then reaching to his waist for the sword there.

"Drop the blade, lady!" he growled.

"Never!" she called, and slashing with both hands, approached him quickly.

"Damn you!" he swore. His blade crashed down on hers. Hard. So very, very hard that it seemed her bones chattered as well as her teeth with the repercussions. "Sweet Jesu, drop it!" he ordered again. She could not. Her fingers were clamped around it too tightly. She tried to back away. He followed her, a lethal shadow in the night, for his face, too, like the faces of those who had attacked from below, was covered. He was not in a helmet or hard plate armor at all, but his head and face and features were covered by an extremely fine meshed mail, silver and gray in the night. Likewise, his shoulders and chest were covered in the stuff. Not as protective as hard steel plates against a blow, the mail was still an effective device against swordplay, for the fine mesh gathered tightly together when struck and could ward off many lethal blows.

"Coward!" Katherine cried. "You cower behind the walls of darkness! You let no one see your face! You—"

"Drop your sword quickly and listen—"

"I will jump!" she promised suddenly and fiercely. She could hear the others. They were pounding at the door to the parapets. Any minute now, and the other thugs would join this fellow here upon the parapets, high above the moat.

"You may have to jump," he said flatly. And in a second, his sword fell on hers again. This was a strength she could not combat for long, and the sword clattered to the ground.

A gloved hand reached out, dragging her against a body that was hard and tight and hugely muscled.

And as hot as any flame . . .

She nearly started to shriek in pure terror, but he jerked upon her so hard that she fell silent. "I am trying to get you from this place!" he rasped out angrily. "Now cease to fight me! 'Tis not bad enough my heart nearly gave out scaling the wall. Now you must try to fight me as well?"

"You must be mad! You caused this!"

"I caused nothing!"

"You're with them—"

"I am not with them! Give me half a chance here, my lady. I seek to save you! Cease to fight me now!"

Cease to fight him! How could she fight! She was so close against him that she could feel his flesh beneath the mail and the cloth of his tunic and chausses. His very skin seemed to burn her; the warmth of his breath was a blaze against her senses and her being. He held her with such tightness that she could scarcely breathe, much less move or fight him . . .

And surely, he . . .

He knew she held no further weapon. She was so tightly pressed against him that he could surely feel every single delineation of her body. The linen of her nightdress was nothing between them, nothing at all. In all her life, she had never stood so intimately with any man, and when she needed the fullness of her wits so desperately, the overwhelming strength and masculinity of this man seemed to be robbing her of all sense.

"Listen to me, you foolish—" he began.

It was enough. This had to be some trick, so that she would let down her guard. He had surely entered the castle by the drawbridge, just as the others had done.

She kicked him with all her might.

She hurt her toes, but that was all right. He growled with pain, and she knew that she had struck well.

"Let me be! You must be one with them!" she cried.

And then, just then, the door to the parapets burst open.

"Damn!" the dark-cloaked figure swore and thrust her behind him. He lunged quickly at the first man to come through the doorway. Amazed, Katherine watched the man fall. A cry went up, a cry of warning, and more men began to press against the door.

He knew how to fight. He knew his swordplay well, striking where the armor did not cover his foes, a quick blow to unbalance a man, a second blow to the throat, or lower, to the belly. In wretched horror, Katherine backed away against the stone. Then, as more and more men began to file out, she dove for her own sword once again.

"I shall have her! Damn our Lord, but she's a prize we will take!" someone cried.

"Not in this lifetime, my reckless sir!" the cloaked stranger refuted. He had the right to do so, Katherine determined, watching his efforts with swordplay. Her own weapon now in her hands, she faced a duo who had come upon the parapets while the stranger smoothly felled a man with a clean slice to his throat, then swirled to catch the companion who would have slit him down the back.

Katherine heard bone crack. She saw the man fall. Then a cry of dismay escaped her, for it had become a true fight for survival with two swordsmen backing her swiftly into a corner.

He was fighting them. Could he truly be against them, or was this some ploy to dupe and trick her?

Could he so coldly kill these men as enemies if he truly were on their side?

Perhaps! De la Ville would sacrifice his own men, more coldly than any other could slay them.

Had he come to save her?

Could he be . . .

The same man that she had seen this day. The rider on the black steed. The man who swept up the girl, and carried her away.

To safety.

Could it be?

She would never be safe, if she could not find life and energy enough to fight on now!

Her feet were wretchedly cold beneath her on the stone. The hem of her nightdress had become torn and dirtied, and ragged ends of it were under her feet.

And far worse, the sword was becoming heavier and heavier in her hands. She could not wield it much longer.

Two of them approached her. Came closer and closer. She strove with every bit of will and energy left within her to raise her weapon once again. She brought it crashing down, but the weight brought her down, too, until she was on her knees. She could not parry the second sword.

Its point was suddenly at her throat. She looked up, into the metal-framed eyes of her opponent.

"Lady, you are had!" he stated triumphantly.

Then those same self-satisfied eyes suddenly glazed, and the knight who had towered over her crashed down before her. Her hand flew to her throat, and she swallowed back a scream.

He was there again. The dark-cloaked stranger, standing over the downed man. "I think not, young man!" he said softly.

Then he reached out a hand for her. She stared at that hand, knowing that it belonged to a man far more dangerous than any foe that she had battled this night.

"For the sweet love of Jesu, lady, take my hand! I am good—nay, lady, I am near great with my sword, but even I can only battle so many!"

"Great!" she repeated. Her teeth were chattering. Men lay dead or wounded all around her, and still more were streaming into the castle. Fear chilled her as thoroughly as the night, and she fought against it.

She took his hand at last. "Great, sir!" she challenged. "And humble, too, indeed."

She saw the flash of a smile against the delicate mail that fell against his face. "Alas, your tongue is sharp, demoiselle, but it seems, at least, that you have found your wits once more. And you will need them now."

Standing once again, Katherine tried to free her hand. "Let me go!" she demanded. "How can I fight—"

"We can fight no longer!" he said sharply.

"Then—"

"You must come with me!"

Where? she wondered. There was nowhere to go. They had climbed to the highest parapet. Above them was nothing more than the stone decoration, gargoyles and gremlins and beasts to protect the lords and ladies within the castle.

She jerked at her hand. "I don't know you!" she gasped in sudden panic. "You may be as wretched as those others who have gone, every bit as great a knave—"

"My lady, we cannot argue the point now!"

"There is nowhere to go with you—"

"But there is!"

A gasp escaped her. He was looking down the stone of the castle, far, far down to the moat beneath.

Oh, so far down . . .

"No, oh, no!" she protested. He still had her hand. She jerked at it again and again. His fingers were like steel.

"Come . . ."

Those steel fingers were drawing her back to him. Closer to the wall.

"You mean to jump! You're a lunatic."

"A conceited one, remember?" he taunted. She stared at him, incredulous.

They both heard the clank of steel. More men were slipping through the doorway to the tower parapet.

He came closer to her. So close. Again she felt the vibrant warmth of his body, the power of his being and his will.

"They come from de la Ville. Are you so anxious to be his bride, then?" he whispered.

"Nay!"

"Then . . . ?"

"I cannot jump!"

"Then you don't mind a fate worse than death? Or perhaps it wouldn't be a fate worse than death," he said scornfully.

"De la Ville is an odious swine!" she assured him.

"Then?"

She couldn't move.

"Coward!" he charged her.

"Never!"

"Then?"

"I . . ."

Again, beneath the fine silver mesh she thought she saw the twist of a mocking smile.

"What . . . ?" she whispered.

"I can!" he stated flatly.

Then she screamed, for she was suddenly swept up tightly into his arms. And with her so imprisoned to him, he leaped to the top of the wall, and paused, just staring down to the water beneath.

"No!" Katherine cried again, struggling against him. "No! Oh, I fear you, sir, far more than de la Ville! You are a madman, a rogue, a devil—"

"My lady, shut your mouth and hold your breath!" he warned.

She pressed upon his chest. They were so high! But more assailants were coming, running now against the stone flooring of the parapet.

"Fool . . . bastard . . ." Katherine continued, torn between the danger of the coming men, and her terror of the endless black that seemed to await them.

"Now! Hold tight!" he warned.

He meant it!

And then a shrill scream tore from her and echoed through the night once again, for he tensed, a powerful constriction of muscles, and leaped from the wall of the parapet.

And she was falling . . .

Falling forever, into the swirling blackness beneath her.

Chapter 7

She hit the water with astounding force, and then it seemed that she did die. Perhaps she blacked out. Perhaps the darkness of the water was simply so deep that for blissful seconds, she was able to think that she had lost consciousness.

Not long enough.

The awful, biting cold wrapped around her even as the force of their descent brought her pitching deeper and deeper into the icy black water along with the lunatic knight-errant. It encompassed her. Cold, so cold, a suffocating blanket that crushed her lungs until they were seared, that set chilling fingers of dark death upon her. Yet even as she thought that she would sink downward into the frigid black hell forever, he managed to stop their descent. Something other than the cold touched her, reaching out to feather along her legs. They had neared the bottom of the moat. The mud and the muck and the green slime were just beneath her, tendrils of plants, snakes perhaps . . .

A scream formed in her throat. She almost opened her mouth to let it tear from her, but some instinct warned her just soon enough that she might well die in the effort.

And they did not touch bottom. Despite the weight of the fine mesh mail he wore, he gave a mighty kick, and

Katherine became aware that they were heading back toward the surface once again.

Had they really come so far down? They broke the surface. She gasped, desperate now for air to fill her lungs. He still held her with one hand; with the other he was treading water, keeping them both afloat.

"There! There!" someone cried from above them. "I see them emerging! There!"

"Where the hell are the archers?" someone else shouted.

"Shoot! Shoot! There in the water."

"Nay! You'll strike the lady!"

"Shoot, and be damned!" came the last cry.

Her eyes widened. They would kill her in this blood lust and fury.

"Jesu, swim!" he commanded, and she was suddenly swirling in the awful cold, barely able to move her limbs, which were entangled in the tattered remnants of her nightdress. Her teeth were chattering and her limbs were refusing to obey any commands from her mind. "Are you daft, woman, they mean to kill you!"

"And so do you, it seems!" she lashed back at last.

"Mother of God!" he exclaimed. "Am I cursed this eve? You cannot swim!"

"What?" she countered swiftly, indignantly. She was freezing. The horrid, swirling black and frigid waters of the moat were all around her. And he was bemoaning her talents!

"Damnation!" He let out the sharp expletive. "So you cannot swim, is that it? I'll tow you."

He was trying to pull her more tightly against his body. She let out a sharp oath herself, wrenching free from him. "Oaf! I can swim! Take your hands off me, and I will manage very well!"

It was better to swim. Better to move. The cold was still with her; she could scarcely feel her fingers. But even as she strove with all her power to progress through the frigid water, she felt a spark of warmth and life returning to the center of her body, like a promise that her fingers would find sensation somewhere, sometime, again.

Anger, too, spurred her on. An anger not abated by the fact that her knight-errant kept an easy pace with her, watching for her to falter any second, even as the shouts continued all around them, fading now as they began to make good their escape.

She would not falter, she swore violently to herself. She would not give this madman a chance to touch her again.

But even as the vow came to her heart, a gasp left her lips, for she reached the shoreline of the moat and her toes floundered into the sticky mud and all the growth there. Men wanted to kidnap or kill her, she reminded herself fiercely. They wanted to hand her over to Raymond de la Ville, and this stranger could probably never realize just how dire a fate that might be.

And still . . .

She couldn't quite manage to make her feet find the bottom.

"Hurry!"

"I am hurrying!"

And she was, but not fast enough, apparently. He was standing, and despite her best resolves, he was reaching for her, sweeping her up like a wayward child, holding her first by the middle, then tossing her carelessly over his shoulder as he strode through the mud, taking them from the waters of the moat.

The cold night air seemed to hit her then like a blow. Tears stung her eyes as her sodden hair and clothing clung to her closely, adding to her chill. She wanted to escape the man, but she could barely balance against his shoulder as he strode swiftly through the night, carrying them from the open ground before the castle toward the trees of the forest.

"You can . . . let me . . . down!" she gasped desperately. The fine mail he wore was wet and frigid in the cold air, biting against her hands and the length of her body. She couldn't see. He was moving so swiftly. Her hair and the night breeze were blinding her, and she was aware only that they were covering a broad distance with startling speed and that she was being carried away from her home and toward a deep and chilling darkness.

And she was freezing. And half naked. Humiliated and near dead!

"Put me down!" she cried out again. Who was this man, and where was he taking her?

"As you wish it!"

She was suddenly, and none too gently, deposited upon the ground. He stood above her, panting, shrouded by the darkness of the night.

"How dare you—" she began. But she was quickly checked as his sodden-gloved hand appeared before her in a warning gesture.

"I am running in mail, lady, to begin with. And as delicate as you may appear, your added weight was no great boon to me."

"Well, indeed, sir, who ever asked you to carry me!"

"We hadn't the time to wait for you to decide to let your little toe touch the mud."

"Bravely and well spoken, for a man in leather boots!"

"Lady, you have just been rescued. Not that I was seeking laurels, but a simple thank-you—"

"Rescued! You near drowned me! And now you seek to freeze me—"

She broke off with no interruption from him, for suddenly they both heard a new voice shouting in the night.

"I bloody well know that they came into the forest! We must find her, else de la Ville will have our heads!

And that wretched intruder must be stopped! He brought down near a full score of our number!"

Her eyes widened.

Truth, at last. He was not one of their number.

Aye, she was easily and quickly furious with this knight, but at the very least, he did not intend to hand her over to de la Ville. She started to rise, but before she could do so on her own, he had swept her up once again, and tossed her over his shoulder.

"If you would just—" she began in a soft hiss, trying to rise upon his shoulder.

"My lady—" he began politely enough. But then he continued, "Shut the bloody hell up!" He spoke like a commander on a battlefield. Then one of his long strides sent his shoulder jutting into her belly and her breath was stolen and she really had no other choice.

Branches and twigs tore at her hair as he hurried swiftly along the forest trail. Once again, it was all that she could do to manage to find her balance and hold tight to him as he moved. Then it seemed that they burst out into a small cove, and a soft, low whistle sounded from his lips. Katherine heard a movement in the brush, and her heart seemed to cease to beat for a moment. She struggled up on his shoulder, turning just in time to see a horse nearly as dark as the night prance as delicately as a kitten into the center of the small clearing.

She slid down the length of the knight, the fabric of her nightdress catching against the mail on his chest. She snatched it free, her cheeks reddening in the darkness. He didn't seem to notice, indeed, his attention was now concentrated on the horse that stood before them.

"Good boy," he crooned to the animal, his voice suddenly soft and tender. Katherine felt a shiver sweep along her spine. What would a woman feel, she wondered, if this dark and dangerous man were to speak so gently to her.

"Come on, my lady, here! We've still miles to travel this night!" Again, his voice grated. Katherine gritted her teeth. Had she really been rescued? Or had she escaped one nightmare to enter another?

"Wait!" He was not one of their number, she was certain of that at last. But who was he? And just where did he intend to take her? "If you'll just—"

But he wouldn't. Impatiently he lifted her again, tossing her up on the black horse, then leaping up behind her with a small clank of metal and steel. His arms wrapped around her as he reached for the reins, and she had to admit that, at the very least, the arrogance of his hold sheltered her somewhat from the cold of the night.

She felt the movement as his heels struck lightly against the horse's flanks, and the huge animal seemed to burst into flight.

"Jesu!" Katherine called out. They would be killed. This reckless knight was commanding his more reckless mount into the trees at a daredevil gait that would kill them all. "You fool!" she cried.

"I can leave you for de la Ville," he reminded her, his voice touching her ear as they raced into the blackness of the forest and beyond.

"At least he'd not have my head loped off by a branch!" she retorted.

"You'll live, my lady. Even if you discover that there is more to life than rich tapestries and fine foods—and your own way with all things!"

"What!"

"I said—"

"I heard you well enough, sir! And I am very aware of life, and how many unfortunates share it with me!" she cried out indignantly, but she wasn't at all sure that he had heard her, for she was speaking into the wind and her words were being thrown back against her own lips. The pounding of the horse's hooves was very loud, the breeze seemed to whistle loudly, and above it all, she was nearly deafened by the slamming of her own heart against her chest. It was a merciless ride. She didn't think she could have held her seat if it was not for his strong arms encircling her. And after a moment, she closed her eyes. She was really an excellent horsewoman herself, simply because she had spent so much time on horseback.

But she had never taken a ride like this one, and the wild and manic zigs and zags they made through the brush and trees was making her dizzy and nearly ill. She would not be sick. Come what may—death itself—she would not be sick. Not before this man. And yet, as they rode, she closed her eyes against the black landscape that threatened to crash into them at any moment.

He had to ride like this, some sense of reason cautioned her. There were men after them that night. If he were truly to bring them to safety, only a bold drive into the very depths of the forest would do.

And still, their force and speed was like nothing she had ever experienced.

Then, so suddenly that she might have pitched over the horse's head if it were not for the man behind her, the great destrier came to a halt.

She dared to open her eyes, swallowing down hard against the bile that had risen in her throat.

"We're here," he said briefly, and dismounted behind her.

So they were here . . .

Where in God's name was *here*?

All around her there was nothing but darkness. They had come to a halt in a copse of trees, and the pale light of the moon lit on nothing more than an occasional branch or leaf.

She was chilled to the bone. Her hair was an awful tangle about her, damp and matted. Her nightdress was nearly dry, but torn and ragged and dirty. Her feet were bare, as frigid as icicles, and surely torn and muddied, too. Her sense of misery was great.

"What is it?" he demanded irritably, swinging back around, his hands on his hips. She still knew so little of him. The mail covered his face except for his mouth and eyes, almost like a glove. The cape that surrounded his shoulders, now dry, added to his vast size. It seemed that he was accustomed to being wet and cold, and didn't seem to understand why she was wretched.

"What is it?" she said sweetly. "Oh, nothing at all. It's really a lovely night for a soaking and a race!" Who was he, anyway?

He was the man she had seen in the forest that very day. He was the miracle that had occurred. He was the rescuer who had thundered from the trees in time to snatch the pretty peasant girl from de la Ville.

He was a legend. A living legend, just like Robin.

The Silver Sword.

And he had come for her tonight, too.

But who was he, really? What manner of man to treat her so carelessly and recklessly. And rudely. Why, she was quite certain that he had dealt far more gently with that poor girl in the woods today.

It was time, perhaps, to remind him that she was the Countess of Ure, King Richard's own ward, and a power in her own right.

"I am cold and wet, sir!" she said sharply.

"Do excuse me, my lady!" he said, sweeping her an exaggerated and courtly bow. "There is more at stake here than your simple comfort for the night."

"I am the Countess of—"

"You are a spoiled child," he said flatly. "Seeking to twist a king around your fingers. You should have been married to some decent baron years ago, and not tempting men like de la Ville. Nonetheless—"

"I am no child, sir," she warned him, her eyes narrowing dangerously. "And don't ever delude yourself upon that fact!" she added icily. But what now? All the warnings in the world couldn't do her much good at this moment. Perhaps he had rescued her, but she was, at this moment, very much his prisoner. And he might well be a lunatic, she decided.

He had saved the girl this afternoon, but that didn't necessarily make him a sound man!

Perhaps he was insane. But maybe that didn't matter now. He was on the ground, and she was on the horse. She could be free from him. If he was sane—and simply rude—she could discover who he was at some later time, and thank him then.

He was the Silver Sword. The man, the legend in the flesh, she reminded herself.

And he had definitely not been with de la Ville's men.

Yet it seemed that he had just traveled blindly into the woods. He had brought her here . . . to keep her here.

She could be no man's prisoner, she determined. She couldn't afford to be a prisoner. Perhaps he was the Silver Sword. Still, he did not quite know with whom he dealt!

"Lady—"

"Sir, you must be well aware of my importance, else you wouldn't have arrived at the castle tonight. But since I can really trust you no more than I can the creatures who battled their way to my tower, I will bid you adieu for the evening!" She slammed her heels against the horse's flanks.

The great black animal dutifully began to trot through the trees.

Katherine was just congratulating herself upon her escape when a soft whistle sounded in the night.

And the horse came to such a sudden and abrupt halt that she was not in the least prepared.

This time, there was no muscled arm to restrain her. She went flying neatly over the animal's neck and head to land flat on her back before it. Solicitously, it seemed, a black nose came sniffing down at her.

"Damn you!" she whispered to the horse, so winded that it took her a second to try to rise, and then, when she tried, she discovered that she could not.

He had reached her. And when she would have stood, a booted foot landed upon the white and muddied linen of her hem.

She clenched her teeth, fighting the wave of fear that washed over her. She hadn't really realized his size until he towered over her so. He was at least as tall as the King, with arms as heavily muscled, with a physique as taut and corded. He was perhaps half crazy, and now he was very angry as well.

He leaned down low, resting his elbow on his knee as he addressed her. "You'd repay your rescuer by stealing his horse? Why, my lady, how rude!"

He reached out, snatching her hand and pulling her to her feet even as he moved off her clothing. She faced him there in the darkness of the forest, cold and miserable, and very aware of the ferocious heat of his body.

"If I am so rude, and so terrible a spoiled child, why in God's name did you rescue me!"

He released her suddenly, walking away, toward the horse. He spoke to her over his shoulder. "You are not to wed de la Ville. You are to wed another, my lady. So says the King."

Katherine inhaled sharply. "The King?"

"Indeed, my lady. The King."

"Richard is in the Holy Lands—"

"Indeed he is. But he has chosen a husband for you, my lady."

Could it be true? she wondered with amazement. Perhaps it was. Perhaps Richard had decided that she had been humored long enough and he was determined that he would choose for her himself.

Nay. Most likely, Richard owed some knight who had done well for him on his Crusade. She would be the gift, the sacrifice!

"And who has the King decided I should marry?" she demanded, her chin high.

"Damian Montjoy, Count Clifford," he said flatly.

"What?" she whispered.

"Damian Montjoy, Count—"

Katherine hurried up behind him then, slamming a fist against his back. The mail hurt the side of her hand, but she had struck with some force, for he swung on her angrily.

"You're a liar!" she cried, amazed at the fear that had riddled through her body at the words. Montjoy! Suddenly, and all too fiercely, she could remember being within the man's hold. She could remember the feel of the flat of his hand against the curve of her backside, and worse, she could remember the feel of his body against hers.

He hadn't recognized her! Robin had assured her.

He was everything that she hated in the noblemen today; he was Norman; he was autocratic; he was awful!

No, she tried to tell herself. He might be awful, but he was not de la Ville!

Her teeth chattered, and she tried to clamp them tightly together. With a wife he would be like a field commander! Hard, intense. She could still feel the force of his hold upon her that day. Still see the taunting, sensual curve of his smile.

Feel the flat of his hand!

He would demand everything . . .

She didn't dare dwell on all the aspects of marriage, not now. What was important was the impact that it would have on her life. She would have no freedom. And the Lady Greensleeves had to be free.

Montjoy would never understand. He hadn't seen the lad in the forest. He hadn't heard the screams. He hadn't seen the blood.

She shook her head vehemently. Heedless of his mail, she slammed her fists against the arrogant knight's chest, this time with such a fury that he swore softly, catching her wrists, holding them tight. She ignored his grip, still accusing him.

"You! You are nothing more than a henchman for Montjoy, just as those animals tonight went about on the dirty business of Raymond de la Ville!"

"I honor the King, my lady, and myself, and no other man!" he declared angrily, thrusting her from him. He had undone the saddle girth and now lifted the heavy saddle from his obedient war-horse. He walked away with it, leaving her there to fume in the darkness. She didn't even know where he was going until she realized that there was some kind of thatched-roof structure there, hidden within the trees. By daylight it would be hard to see. By night it was almost impossible to discern.

But even as she stood outside shivering, he opened the door with his shoulder, and disappeared inside with his saddle. A moment later, there was a soft flare of light from within.

Still, stubbornly, Katherine remained outside, shivering.

Montjoy! This night was one nightmare after the other!

She should simply run into the forest. Not on the horse, but on her own feet!

She would not get far, an inner voice warned her.

He appeared again a moment later, striding toward his horse. He paid her scant heed, though, and Katherine realized that he had come back out with a leather bag of grain for his mount. He scratched the animal's ears, then poured grain on the ground. Then he turned and stared at her. As he did so, the clouds in the night sky parted somewhat. Pale moonlight flickered through.

The mail mask even hid much of his eyes, and yet she knew that he studied her keenly. She didn't so much see his gaze as she felt it, sweeping over the length of her. Perhaps it touched her mockingly. And perhaps it touched her . . .

. . . with some other emotion.

She was suddenly and keenly very much aware of her state of dress.

Or undress.

The linen of her nightdress had begun to dry, but it was sheer and near tatters now. The bodice was low, and the swell of her breasts rose above it. And as he watched her, she felt, to her great alarm, the hardening of her nipples beneath the fabric. She crossed her arms over her chest, but then realized that the golden triangle at the juncture of her thighs must be at least as apparent as the curves of her breasts. She might as well be naked.

But then he sniffed suddenly, and she felt a red flame rise to her cheeks.

She had assumed that she might be desirable.

He seemed to think that she looked about as desirable as a drowned and sodden rat.

This was ridiculous. She let her arms fall, raising her chin, standing defiantly before him. "Sir, just who in the King's name are you? Or better yet, sir, who is it that you think yourself to be?"

He bowed very deeply, and with a vast exaggeration. "Why, my lady, I thought you knew. I am he they call the Silver Sword."

"Who are you really?"

"No one, my lady. No one really. Just a knight to come in the darkness—and rescue a damsel in distress."

Chapter 8

The Silver Sword, indeed. Just a knight to rescue a damsel in distress.

"I daresay, sir, I am still in distress, so it seems! The Silver Sword, is it, sir? Boys will play at names, will they not? But I am not interested in games and play in the forest, sir. The Silver Sword! It is a silly name, no more. Who are you really? Or again, I dare wonder, just who is it that you think yourself to be?"

He laughed, a soft husky sound that seemed to touch her despite all her enmity—and dignity. He was not duly impressed. "Oh, my lady," he assured her, vastly amused, "I think myself exactly who I am."

"And that is—?"

"I've given you my answer. You don't need to know my given name."

"Or your face, so it seems," she commented dryly.

"Suffice it to say that I serve the King."

"Then beware, for I intend to report to the King exactly what happens this night."

"You can report so far that, despite the wretched problems you caused me—and the fact that I had to battle your sword as well as the blades of those men!—I rescued you this night."

"I believe that I became a damsel in deepest distress the moment you arrived!" she assured him. "I was doing quite well on my own."

"A child playing with steel," he said dismissively.

"Oh, you are impossible!" she cried out, truly affronted. "And what good were you? I could have plunged into the moat by myself, thank you very much!"

"Never," he replied lazily. "You hadn't the courage."

"I am well endowed with courage, knave!" she said indignantly. "I simply do not care for heights."

"Or mud," he added pleasantly.

"Well, it seems I shall grow fond of it then, for I am covered in it still. And I shall grow equally fond of icicles, for they will soon be forming over my nose and toes!"

She was startled when he at last seemed to be aware of her condition, his eyes seeming now much better than hers in the darkness as he focused on her. Then she was sorry that she had spoken, for he was striding across the short distance toward her, and sweeping her up in his arms. "Set me down!" she cried, struggling against the rock-hard muscle of his arm. "I can walk of my own accord—"

"Aye, you'll try to walk right out of the forest," he said wearily.

"And what will it matter?" she cried. "You'll have done your good deed! I am away from de la Ville's men—"

"But you are not yet turned over to the forces of your betrothed," he informed her.

She gasped, ceasing to struggle against him as he bent slightly to bring them both through the doorway of the thatched-roof structure in the forest.

"You mean to keep me a prisoner until we come across Damian Montjoy?"

"You aren't a prisoner, lady. You've been rescued."

"But I—" She broke off quickly. She still couldn't really see his eyes.

"You do serve Montjoy!" she accused him furiously.

He hesitated just a second. "I serve myself, my lady. But Montjoy is the King's baron, a count whose land neighbors your own, and a man to help hold this kingdom together while Richard fights on his bloody Crusades. Pray tell, my lady, what is your difficulty with a man who is the King's own choice?"

"Richard would not command this if I just had the chance to talk with him!" she said.

She suddenly found herself set down roughly on a small stool. He had lit a fire when he had entered the place the first time, and Katherine quickly discerned that they had come to the type of hunting lodge that was common among members of the nobility. She wasn't on her own land anymore, she was certain.

A chill swept through her.

This place probably belonged to Montjoy, Count Clifford.

"Stay here!" he suddenly commanded, then turned again, his black cloak sweeping behind him. The door slammed closed in his wake. Where had he gone now? she wondered.

She couldn't escape him on his horse.

But perhaps her idea about escaping on foot had not been such a bad one. She could eventually find her own way home. And de la Ville's men would be gone by now, and the neighboring barons would have heard of his attempt to kidnap her.

She needn't go home! She need only find Robin.

There might be all manner of places she might run, if she could only escape this knight who had rescued her.

She rose—just as he came back in through the doorway, carrying a leather bucket of water. She felt the sizzle of his gaze upon her as he approached her. A curious heat and a sudden discomfort assailed her. The breadth of his hand fell against her chest as he pressed her back to the stool. Flickers of lightning and unease coursed through her limbs.

"I told you to stay!"

She tossed back her hair. "And I have told you! I am a countess in my own right—oh!" she cried out, startled as he lifted her foot and gently bathed it with a cloth drenched in the clear cold water he had brought in.

The chill swept through her, and a startling pain as he washed the dirt from the myriad tiny cuts she had accrued on her soles. Without thinking, she braced herself against him, her hands upon his shoulders, her teeth biting into her lower lip. He finished with one foot and went on to the other in silence.

She was amazed at the competence and ability of his touch. His hand seemed nearly twice the size of her foot, that size perhaps enhanced by the tight-fitting leather gauntlets he continued to wear. Despite them, she felt a startling warmth to his touch, and a practiced gentleness that she had not expected.

She felt his gaze upon her when he was done, as he said sharply, "You haven't answered me. What is your difficulty with Count Clifford?"

She tossed back her hair, quickly letting her hands slide to her lap.

She hesitated a moment, wondering again just who she spoke with.

Though French was the language of the court—and certainly the language of the King—they had been speaking English, the common language of the Saxon people.

"He is a Norman," she said suddenly, coolly, knowing she owed this man no explanation.

"As is the King," he reminded her.

"But Montjoy is not the King," she told him succinctly. Then she added in a sudden rush, "I met him once," and she did not refer to the day in the forest. "I know the man, you see. I met him years ago. He is brash and arrogant. When he was betrothed to Lady Albright, there was to be a feast and dance at his manor outside London. But there was some argument going on even then between Henry and Richard, and there she was, poor Lady Albright, all alone, while Damian Montjoy ran in and out, determined to mediate between the two. He walked through the hall spouting orders, paused quite indifferently before the woman who was to be his wife, and away he went. Clanging! He was armed to the teeth, so it seemed, with a long sword hanging on one side and a short sword hanging from the other. I tell you, he may think himself a courtly fellow with his great Norman lineage and his friendship with the King, but he is nothing short of rude and barbaric!"

"And you gained this all from the one meeting with the man?" he asked seeming to be amused once again. Yet there was an edge to his voice. Almost as if he accused her of lying. "He loved his betrothed, my lady."

Katherine shrugged uneasily, wondering how this man could sense that there might be more. The "more" was something she did not want to think about herself. She ran her fingers through the tangle of her hair, as dignified as she could be seated upon the stool in the very tattered remnants of her nightdress.

She didn't answer the question. Instead she cried, "It's quite out of the question. I cannot marry him either."

"Because he is a Norman barbarian?"

She shrugged. "For that—and many other reasons."

"He's known to be a great hero. They say that he saved Richard's life on the Crusade."

"Trust me. He is little more than a beast who walks upright."

"Yet you wanted nothing to do with Raymond de la Ville. Had he captured and wed you, you'd not have had to worry about any other marriage plans being made for you."

She sighed. "There is no man quite so horrid as de la Ville. I suppose even Montjoy would be preferable to him."

"I am sure that Montjoy would be flattered to hear your words."

"It doesn't matter in the least to me. I cannot marry Montjoy."

"But it is the King's command!" he snapped suddenly.

She glanced down, frowning. The once-gentle hands upon her foot had suddenly constricted. "You are hurting me, sir."

He dropped her foot as if it were a hot coal. "Do excuse me, my lady." He rose suddenly. "I've wine in a skein in the saddlebags. Whatever the future might bring, some rich red wine, warmed by the fire, should do us both good."

Katherine hesitated. At least she was growing warm at long last. Her feet did not sting so badly. But she was still clad in the sodden linen nightdress and she was certain that if she touched her cheek, she'd find dried mud from the moat bed upon it.

And he intended to give her over to Montjoy! He had rescued her from one man to give her to another.

She needed so desperately to escape. To reach Robin's realm in the forest. If she could just hide there awhile. She needed to reach her friends. She had helped them time and time again. They would willingly help her. Robin was her cousin. She could be safe, hiding, waiting for Richard to come home.

Richard cared little if he came home or not, she knew that well enough. But still . . .

If she could only speak with him, beg her cause!

Before she could be handed over to Montjoy.

She stared at the man, at the towering stranger in his mail cowl and black cape. She gritted her teeth, wondering if there was any way to escape him. His presence filled the room. His every movement spoke of life and vitality and keenness of perception and being. She had felt the force of his muscled form.

He would be so difficult to escape . . .

"Let me go," she said suddenly, watching him as he set the wine skein high above the fire to warm.

He turned to her, and she felt the force of his gaze once again.

"Let you go?"

She stood, approaching him. She set her hands upon his arms and gazed pleadingly into his eyes. "You say that you honor Richard. I . . . I have friends who honor him, too. They would look after me. Actually, I can look after myself very well. I am able with a sword. You know that—"

"I know that you have a certain talent. I also know that I bested you quickly."

"I was weary then. I had already been fighting. I am truly competent with a sword and with—" She broke off, suddenly unwilling to give him too much information. He spoke to her in English, in the old Saxon tongue, but still, there were many among her mother's people who were more than willing to be lap dogs to the Norman aristocracy if it filled their own pockets with Norman gold coins.

"I can take care of myself."

"Ah. I should let you go, half-naked, running through the forest. Oh, aye, lady! That would be a noble gesture, indeed!"

"I'm telling you, I can take care of myself. And I would see that you were well rewarded."

"And would it matter how well I was rewarded if Montjoy decided to take my head?"

"He wouldn't."

"You say he is such a wicked monster."

She smiled, as beautifully, as beguilingly, as she could manage. "Perhaps he is not so bad. He is really only a monster to women. Please, sir, let me go."

"Hm," he murmured thoughtfully.

"Please?" she repeated softly, rising on her toes, her eyes brilliant, her whisper feminine and seductive. Robin had told her once that she was truly beautiful, and that she needed to take great care because of it.

He had also told her that she could probably seduce an angel into visiting hell on her behalf.

Was any of it true? Had she that kind of power?

"Please . . . ?" she repeated, just as softly, as seductively, as she could manage.

The man before her touched her chin with his thumb and forefinger. His leather-clad knuckle moved lightly over her cheek.

She lowered her lashes quickly over her eyes. Her heart was suddenly beating too swiftly. A flush of warmth was growing within her.

"Sir, I beg you, have pity on me!" she whispered softly. Yes, the voice was good. There was a quivering in it that she hadn't intended. The quivering came because he was too close. Because he was touching her.

I am seducing him! she reminded herself furiously. But the warmth remained with her, and the trembling sensation very deep within. "Be merciful. Let me go." She caught hold of his gloved hand. Her fingers moved over it gently. She kept her head lowered.

"I know that you have it within you to be merciful. I would give . . ." Her voice trailed away.

He freed his hand from her touch, lifting her chin so that he could stare into her eyes. She made them wide and luminous.

"What would you give?" he whispered. The husky sound of his voice seemed to dance along her spine.

"My undying gratitude!" she promised.

"What if I wanted more?"

She moistened her lips, trying to hold on to a sense of control and seduce him at the same time.

It was not an easy task.

"You are the Silver Sword. Valiant. Honorable."

"I am flesh and blood. A man. Tell me, my lady, what more would you give for your freedom. A kiss?"

Amazed at the bolts of heat racing through her body, she replied, "Perhaps, once I was upon the path of freedom . . ."

"A kiss? Really?"

She murmured an assent, her lashes and head lowering.

"I should betray a man and perhaps die for the honor of a kiss?" he queried softly.

Her head rose, her eyes flew open. There was a mocking curl to his lip now. "Just a kiss? You wouldn't even want to bed me when I might well die for your freedom?"

"Oh! You let me go—" she began.

But he was still laughing. His fingers tightened momentarily upon her chin, then she was free from his touch at last. "Release you, lady?" he queried very softly. "Not on your life!"

"Oaf!" She spat out. He would have turned away, but she was on him in a fury, slamming her fists against his mail-clad chest, in such a whirr of motion that she didn't even realize the power of the enemy she fought.

Not until he caught hold of her, his arms coming strongly around her. Suddenly, she could scarcely move. She gasped, trying to breathe, her eyes rising to his with a passionate vengeance. Slowly he eased his hold, then wound his fingers around her wrists and forced her back down to the stool.

"Lady, you do test me sorely! Now sit!" It was a command she was forced to obey.

"I hope you rot in hell," she said sweetly.

He laughed huskily, and again, the sound of it swept through her. "That I may, my lady. That I may," he assured her. He lifted the skein from above the fire then, drank deeply, and offered it to her.

"But if I do so tonight, Kat de Montrain, then we shall rot in hell together, and so be it."

She pushed the skein away and swirled on her stool, offering her back to him. He laughed again. "Dear Lord, but I pray this be the last time I'm called upon to rescue a damsel in distress!"

"Scarcely rescued!"

"As you like it," he said softly. "There's something of a bed in the corner there, my lady—the furs upon it are clean and warm." He came closer to her, and she felt his whisper as his lip lowered to her ear. "If this be your hell, my lady, we are consigned to it together here this night. Make the most of it."

She sat very still.

"Well, if you cannot find the bed in the darkness yourself, perhaps I can help you find it in my ever delicate and courteous way—"

She was up before he could finish the sentence, seething as she walked across the room to the pallet of furs on the floor.

"Pray, give me no more aid in your delicate and courteous way!" she cried, finding comfort in the warmth of a fur. "I fear I would not survive it!"

The soft, husky sound of his laughter followed her. "Ah, but you will survive, my lady. You will survive."

She turned her back on him, curled up in surprising comfort.

More surprisingly, in time, she slept.

And as the fire snapped and crackled and later burned low, he walked over to the pallet to stand above her, looking down upon her.

No mud could mar the beauty of her countenance. The furs could not hide the memories of her perfection in his mind's eye.

Nor could the sweetness of her sleep allow him to forget the sharpness of her tongue, and emotions churned deeply within him, emotions that warred.

"Indeed, lady, you will survive. And survive more of me. Oh, aye! You will survive much, much more of me!"

Yet as he stood there, a curious feeling swept through him. He longed to touch . . .

To possess . . .

Aye, and to protect her.

Chapter 9

She was a restless sleeper, this betrothed of his!

He should have slept much more himself. The journey to England had been long, and the journey here to the north had seemed even longer. Then Sir James Courtney, the knight he had named castellan for his home in his absence, had been quick to tell him that Prince John was in the neighborhood with his loutish sycophants and that Raymond de la Ville was assuredly up to no good. And just as James had glumly assumed, the Prince and de la Ville had been in the forest, seeking amusement with the peasantry. He'd been grateful to arrive in time to save the girl.

And even gladder to discover that he had returned home in time to save his own intended.

Even if she wasn't quite so grateful for the saving!

She tossed and turned in the night as if she still fought demons straight from hell. At first she cried out softly, flinging one of the furs from her. That left her nearly naked. Certainly her hair had dried with the muck of the moat still upon it. Splashes of that same drying muck marred her limbs and gown.

But they did nothing to mar the girl's beauty.

He felt his desire for her growing stronger as he watched her, fascinated, as the firelight played over her.

The white linen bedgown was tattered and torn, enhancing far more than it concealed. It had dried conforming to her every curve. As she flung upon her back, her breasts rose full and high, the dark, dusky nipples pressing against the fabric and the very sheerness of the white linen emphasizing the fullness and firmness of her flesh. Then, as his breath grew rapid and shallow, she struck out at some enemy in her sleep and twisted about, and the white linen cradled her derriere, hugged the rounded form of her hip, draped with a strange elegance over the wickedly long beauty of her legs.

He grated his teeth and swore an oath, realized that he did so in his Norman French, and remembered that the Silver Sword was a Saxon savior, and that as such he must remember to swear at the wretched wench in the proper language.

For a moment he played with the idea of honesty. Complete honesty.

No. She despised the Norman Lord Montjoy. He dare not let her know that he was one and the same as the husband she would soon have. He didn't dare let on about his connections to Robin, or to the forest. If she chose to betray him in any way . . .

He dared not think of the consequences. He might have a noble head, but noble heads too easily came upon the block. And he knew that he risked his head— or his throat—each time he rode, but he'd be damned if he'd die just because of the whims of his very wayward betrothed. Perhaps Richard knew just what he was up to. Perhaps Richard was very glad of his protecting the royal crown while Richard was away.

But John was here.

Give John the slightest knowledge that he was in any way an outlaw . . .

And he would die. Quite simply. Nay—he'd be stripped of his possessions.

Then he'd die.

He shook his head slightly. It didn't bear pondering any longer. He could not let the girl know his identity. And that meant sitting around in the wretchedly uncomfortable mail while he watched her sleep.

She was so careful herself. She knew that he was the Silver Sword, but she wasn't ready with any confessions about the fact that she was the Lady Greensleeves. She was so passionate in her cause!

That was to her credit, he had to admit. But she was far too headstrong, and reckless. He tried to understand her commitment—heaven knew, he had his own.

It had begun before the day when Raymond de la Ville's father had hunted down the Saxons in the wood. When Damian's own father had still lived. They had ridden across property belonging to de la Ville, and they had come across a man who had been hanged, and left there, swinging from the branch of a tree. He'd worn a collar about his throat. A brass collar. And French words had proclaimed him to be Cuthbert, thrall to some lesser nobleman.

Damian had seen many such collars before, though his father would not allow them on their people. "No man is an animal," his father had insisted. "And men do not wear collars. You can beat a man into submission, but you can never beat him into giving his love or his loyalty. Men will serve a fair master, and a fair master has no need to collar and chain his servants."

Whoever his master had been, it seemed apparent that Cuthbert had tried to escape him. And he had tried to find sustenance from the land.

He had died in the trying. A placard hung about his neck. "So shall die all who would poach in this forest!"

Cuthbert seemed so tragic there, swinging in the breeze. Birds lit down atop his head, to peck at the corpse. And as he watched the corpse, he had heard the laughter of the richer thanes who rode in the forest.

Those men had found it so amusing to hang this poor fellow here. There were laws in this land, aye, that there were.

But there were no laws to protect the weak when men of wealth and power were around.

He had never really intended to become any kind of outlaw. He'd been raised and trained to become a knight, to stand by the King, to do battle against other knights.

But then he had happened to be home, to be hunting, when Lord de Montrain had come through the forest with Kat and Robin. He had heard Lord de Montrain's shouts, and stumbled upon the scene there. And he had let fly those arrows against de la Ville because he had hated the man, and all that he did, with such a great passion.

Then he'd seen the treacherous bastard come back to kill de Montrain, and he'd been forced to show himself.

But he knew that de Montrain had never given him away. Rather, the man had suggested the disguise that had led to the nickname of the Silver Sword.

He had always admired de Montrain. And there was that peculiar relationship between them, for de Montrain had married Rob's father's sister, while Montjoy's mother had been cousin to Rob's mother. Robin had used the relationship, of course, demanding that Damian take him under his wing to teach him. He'd really had no choice. Robin would be called upon to fight again and again. Damian had determined he had best know how to do it well.

Beside him, Kat tossed and turned.

Oh, Jesu. The mud-spattered gown fell away completely from one lush breast. She was bared except for the wild tumble of hair that swirled and cascaded around her form, hair with a magnificence that no dunking in a moat could begin to dim. In the firelight each strand seemed to pick up highlights of shimmering red and gleaming gold as it curled against the pure ivory of her flesh.

The warmth in the room suddenly seemed explosive. He felt his cheeks growing hot beneath the helmet and a swift and painful constriction of muscle and body from his groin to his throat.

He swore softly, rose, and started to draw a large pelt back over the length of her body. Yet once above her, the fur in his hand, he froze.

She was going to be his wife. Soon. And all this would be his. For the taking. Their marriage was going to be a tempest.

But, oh . . . what a storm! he determined. None of it mattered. Wrapped in the golden glory of her hair, she seemed the most delectable, tempting flower. They needn't talk politics together. They needn't plan and dream. She need only await him in the darkness and the shadows, and he need only lose himself in the physical pleasures of their marriage. She was bringing him all that might be required. Land, wealth. And she was a stunning beauty as well.

If only Richard had seen fit to hand her over well-muzzled!

His muscles were tightening again. Arms growing rigid, a pulse at his cheek ticking, a sure drumbeat to go along with that forming within his loins again. He swore softly and dropped the fur abruptly upon the tantalizing display of body spread before him. He turned away, heading out into the night.

Before the stars, he stripped the helmet with its concealing mask of mail from his face. He breathed in deeply, then rubbed his cheeks.

He should ride away now. Then Lord Montjoy could ride by and pick up his betrothed in the morning. He could be rid of this wretched costume.

But underneath the stars he smiled slowly—and not without a certain wickedness.

Nay . . .

The Silver Sword would spend another day with the lady. It was so very intriguing to learn what he could when she assumed him to be a Saxon.

It could be a very entertaining day. Aye!

Either that, or . . . torture.

He gritted his teeth, feeling the awful strength of the longing that ripped and tore through him. And suddenly he was remembering Ari's words in the desert.

Ari, foretelling that she would betray him.

"No!" he swore furiously. Ari's prophecy would not come true. He would not let it. He glanced down. His fists were clenched. He raised them, looking at them. They had tightened just as they might around that fragile neck of hers.

Nay, he wished no violence!

He needed only to watch this wayward damsel, to learn more about the working of her mind. Knowing one's enemy was besting that enemy.

Enemy? She was to be his wife.

And what enemy could be more dangerous?

None, he assured himself.

He inhaled the night air deeply and turned and walked back to the hunter's lodge, pushing open the door. The fire had burned down. The room was nearly in darkness.

He closed the door. He couldn't even see the girl in the shadows. He might dare to take off the helmet and mask of chain mail.

He walked to the bed. She was sleeping peacefully for the moment.

Sprawled out, the furs thrown off. Long legs. Tempting full breasts.

Breasts. Damn.

He turned away and set the mask down, thanking God for the darkness. His mail beneath the tunic was heavy and cumbersome, and he was weary now, more weary than he had imagined possible. Impatiently he stripped away his cloak and tunic, and took down the heavy dress of mail. Muscles bulged tightly within his arms and shoulders as he lifted its eighty pounds of weight from his body. Then he stood only in his shirt and chausses, and wished he might shed them too for a greater feeling of the wonderful lightness and freedom that had come to him now.

Mail had not been fashioned for comfortable sleep, though he had, on occasion, been called upon to rest in various degrees of armor.

He started to stretch, but as he did so, he was startled and taken off guard by a sudden, high-pitched, anguished screech. He spun around, expecting some danger, only to see in the darkened shadows that she was sitting up in the bed. Even as he rushed to her side, he realized that she was not looking at him. He could barely discern her features in the darkness, but he knew that she was not looking at him at all, but rather staring straight ahead at some unknown demon. Some demon that plagued her dreams. She was shaking, trembling. The linen shimmered over her body. "No!" she screeched again, a hand flying out. "Nay, nay, never!"

"My lady—"

She heard his voice and turned to it, wildly flailing. Her small, elegant hands came flying hard against his chest. He caught her wrist, shaking her slightly. "Lady, cease! Wake up! You are dreaming. There is no danger."

She shook her head wildly. "He's coming. He's coming. It's he. And he's a monster. He's sent men. So many men. But he's behind them, I know that he is. You don't know him. You haven't seen his face when he—"

She was in his arms. Despite their dunking in the moat, her hair still smelled of rose petals, her flesh was like lavender. Soft to his touch. She was a burst of fire against him.

And at this particular moment, she was all vulnerability. Near naked in arms. Beautiful, hot, twisting. He could feel far too much of her body—and her nakedness. He felt a burst within himself. A startling explosion of raw and lusty desire. She was his. He could cease to make believe at this very moment, shake her from her fear of de la Ville—and rush the nuptials. She would be his when they were wed, for he would not allow himself to be wed and governed by her whims. She would understand. She would be his wife. In every sense of the word. He could just do the inevitable this evening.

Ah!

He gritted his teeth, trying to still the harsh and brazen fires that had seized hold of him. Take her . . . aye. When she shook so. When he would be no better than the man he had swept her away from. Ah, nay! She might have a tongue like a rapier and a will of the same steel. She might accuse him and accost him at every turn.

But when she shook so, trembled like this in his arms . . .

He sighed, pulling her closer, breathing in the sweet aroma of her hair. "It's over!" Within his hold and startlingly tender arms, he shook her slightly. "It's over. De la Ville will not have you. We are gone from them. You are safe. You are dreaming."

"Dreaming!" She went limp in his arms. Then he felt her stiffen. She tried to see his face in the darkness, but the candles had gone out. The night was all around them now. He felt her distress, and he had to soothe it.

"It's all right. I am not going to hurt you. Don't be afraid."

"I'm not afraid. Of you."

He was still holding her. And oddly enough, the stiffness was easing from her.

"Put your head down," he advised softly.

And she did so. Now his arms were around her, hands entangled in her hair. Her head rested on his chest. His chin rested on the top of her head. She trembled convulsively. He smoothed his hand over her hair. "Sleep. It's all right. You're safe."

She inhaled on a great shudder. Exhaled.

He continued to stroke her hair. It teased his nose. Her cheek moved against his chest. Her shuddering ceased.

A minute later, to his amazement, he realized that she was sleeping again.

He lifted his hand as she snuggled more closely against him. Oh, that hair! It was wound around him. Drifting softly over his torso, over his face.

He let his hand fall gently upon her shoulder. She breathed so easily.

And he . . .

He groaned in the night.

Indeed, this was going to be very interesting.

Intriguing . . .

Torture!

Even before she fully awoke, Kat could feel the discomfort of the mud she wore. There was a certain scent of moat slime about her, and she hated it.

Then there was more.

Her eyes hadn't begun to open, but she could suddenly feel a great discomfort. The night all came rushing back in on her and she knew—she knew without opening her eyes—that he was there. Before her. Watching her.

Memories of the previous night came rushing in on her, the truth blending with the nightmare, for there had been little difference at times. Perhaps the nightmares had been worse, for while the castle and she had been under attack, she had been moving too swiftly and too desperately to feel the complete onslaught of her fears.

And in truth, de la Ville had not come after her himself. He had been in the nightmares, taunting her as he had taunted the girl in the forest.

But then, the nightmares had ended. Because she had suddenly felt so safe and secure.

Because he had been there! A rock in the darkness. No longer a mystery clad in metal, but a man, a friend, warm flesh and blood, holding her.

And she'd let him do it. Let him put his arms around her. Hold her. Sleep beside her. She, with all her supposed courage. Nightmares had claimed her, and she had fallen into a stranger's arms for simple solace.

Aye, and he was watching her now. That same stranger. She could feel him watching her!

She opened her eyes. And indeed, he was there. If he had really shed his mail armor in the night, he was clad in it once again this morning. His mail helmet shadowed his face, his great black cape covered his shoulders. He was seated at a chair not five feet from her, one great booted foot resting upon his knee.

And his eyes, as she had expected, were hard and fierce upon her.

It was then that she realized that she had kicked away every fur. Her gown had dried hard to her flesh in certain places, and then had fallen completely away in others. The linen was bunched to her thighs. Her legs were bare. Half her breast was bare.

And he was watching her. Just watching. Beneath the mail she thought that she could see the amused curve of his lip, and she was suddenly furious. So she'd had a few dreams. And perhaps she had been a bit of a clinging vine in the night. That was his fault! He had brought her here, and forced her to stay here. But the fact that he had comforted her certainly gave him no right to watch her so now, with such vast knowledge and amusement! She let out a soft oath, springing upward to gather a brace of fur around her to her chest, and staring back at him with her own eyes snapping fire, her chin raised. "What do you think you are doing!" she cried out.

"Why, my lady! I am watching over you," he said, his tone injured, as if she had done him some grave injustice. "You did not mind it so in the night."

The words were smug. As if they'd shared something great.

"You did not stare at me like this in the night!"

"Nay, my lady. I touched you, a touch so infinitely sweet—"

"Oh, cease! You did not touch me in any such manner. If anything, sir, I touched you—"

"I cherished each and every caress," he exclaimed.

She realized the mistake of her words and swore in aggravation. "You know exactly what I mean!"

"Oh, aye. I do."

She was not going to win. The taunting amusement was there within his voice, and it was going to stay there. She let out a long sigh, and spoke then with the edge of command to her voice, a countess reminding him that the world, their world, was run by class distinction.

"My dear sir, you've no manners, no morals, no chivalry—"

"Lady! I've risked my life for you."

"You've risked your life for gain," she returned swiftly. "You intend to serve Montjoy."

He lifted his hands. "Truly, I am hurt. How many men would have scaled castle walls to combat de la Ville?"

"To rescue a lady—only to turn her over to another?" she said. "After amusing yourself vastly at her expense?"

"The dreams, lady, were yours. I sought only to comfort you."

There was some strange tone to his voice. Some deep note of warning. She was too upset to heed it well.

"All because you expect some return from Montjoy. I'm sure he'll pay you well."

"I'm sure it will depend upon what he determines as your worth, my lady."

"And what have you determined it to be? Surely, you've had time to assess it well!" she told him sharply.

She felt the very slow curl of his smile, and to her dismay, she knew that bloodred rush of color was flying to her cheeks. How he could madden her!

"Well, now, let me see . . ." he murmured. "Ah, of course, I did not touch you. But those pieces of you that did touch me, hm . . ."

"Oh!" she cried out, her temper flaring hotly. "Some fine knight you are, sir! I say one might call you the Silver Swine rather that the Silver Sword! Speak, as you seem so adept with words. Tell me! Shall your reward be great?"

To her dismay, he rose. He was an imposing figure, perhaps made even more so by the mystery of the mail. "Montjoy, my lady, is a warrior nobleman, as you are well aware."

"Hungry for power," she replied, disturbed that her words should be so breathless. She was not going to shrink away. Just because the vast bulk of his body towered over hers. Just because she could feel the dangerous vitality and energy of the man. Feel his eyes. Aye, even feel beneath the air in the room the very pounding of his heart, a pulse that went on and on.

Maybe she would shrink away.

She curled her feet beneath her, holding tight to her cover of fur, and shimmying into the corner of the pallet. She kept her head high, despite the fact that she must look absurd, her flesh muddied, her hair tangled, and her form decked in torn clothing—and using a wolf pelt as if it were a protective shield!

"Um," he murmured darkly, and still too close. "I think that the Lord Montjoy will find himself a prize. With such delectable . . ." He paused, his hand reaching out as if he would touch her cheek. Again, the mail nearly covered his mouth, yet she could sense the depths of his smile. "Very delectable lands," he finished.

She didn't know that she had been holding her breath until she released it in a rush. "You are horrible!"

"For admiring your lands?" he queried, as if hurt.

"You were not admiring my lands!"

"Then?" He lifted his hands. "Ah, lady! You are far too accustomed to adoration. The men in your life have too swiftly fallen to your bidding. You do flatter yourself indeed!"

"Do I? Well, I am sorry that it seems you were forced to stare at me all night when what you were required to witness was so displeasing."

"Displeasing! Why, I derived the greatest pleasure. I watched every twist and turn with deepest fascination! I felt every twist and turn—"

"You just said—"

"Oh, aye! Lord Montjoy is a nobleman who must always look to his back and guard what is his. While I, lady, Silver Swine that I may be, have no need to worry about material gain. And I, lady, found the night to be entirely engaging!"

She cried out in frustration, swearing softly. "Will you please get away! I swear, if you do not take care, I shall see to it that Montjoy hangs you!"

"But you don't even wish to wed the man!"

"I abhor the thought. And I will not marry him."

"But you won't mind asking the man to hang me?"

"Not in the least."

"If you don't marry him, how will you get him to honor such a gruesome request?"

Her anger won out. She cared not for her appearance, and really, what did it matter? They'd spent the long night together. With all her might, she threw the fur at him.

Despite the sayings, fur did not fly well at all. He lifted a hand, laughing, and the fur fell to the pallet before her, and she was left with nothing.

Suddenly, his laughter faded. She was near naked again. Slim yet delectably curved. Beautiful, bewitching. He stepped back. "Lady, take my cloak." He swept it from his shoulders and gave it to her. He walked back to the fire, using a piece of wood to stoke the dying embers. "If you wish to rise, do so. I'll show you where you can bathe."

"Bathe?" Delighted, she leaped to her feet, the heavy cloak about her exceptionally comforting. Silver Swine. He liked to tease and taunt. He was no great rich Norman baron, and perhaps, in his way, coveted those things that could not be his.

He had saved her from de la Ville. And he had given her comfort in the night. Despite her anger with him and the fact that he could so easily bring her temper rushing to the fore, she was suddenly a bit more grateful. His words were one thing. He was still a man of a certain honor. He was intriguing.

He had held her through the night, but he had done so honorably, despite his words.

Maybe he was expecting some great reward from Montjoy. He couldn't have expected much reward when he had saved the peasant girl in the forest, and he had risked death then, too.

None of his virtues—or lack of them—really mattered right now. Not when he was offering her what she wanted more than anything in the world at the moment. A bath.

"Lady, you are easily pleased," he said, studying her.

"I feel that I am wearing half a moat, sir."

"I shared your bed. And I am the Silver Swine, remember? Perhaps I might try to share your bath."

"I do not dream, sir, while I bathe. You'll have no need to comfort me."

"Ah, but you forget. I am wearing the other half of the moat."

"If you don't intend to allow me this simple and easy pleasure—" She broke off suddenly, then, with his heavy cloak wrapped around her, she took a step toward him. He was so covered by the mail and his tunic that she wasn't at all sure how she knew, but suddenly she was certain that she did. He was not wearing half of the moat any longer.

"You've been bathing!" she accused him. She didn't know why she was so outraged. Except that he was already free from the muck and the slime that still clung to her.

"I wished to ask you to join me, but by morning, you were sleeping like one dead," he told her. "Then I wondered if you might be one of those poor souls convinced that the devil would take your body if you were to immerse it all at once. I can't offer you a tub, my lady. Or scented soap from the provinces of France. But just beyond our doorway there does lie an exceptional brook. The water is cold, but the sun is peeking through—"

"I care not what the water is, or if you wish to torment me to tears," she informed him with her nose high but a slight curl to her lips. "Lead onward!"

"Aren't you afraid that I shall find you irresistible and seek to join you?"

She paused for a moment, her hands on her hips, and studied him as if with great care.

"I think not."

"And why is that?"

"Because Montjoy is known to be aggressive in the extreme. I wouldn't need to ask him to hang you."

"You seem to know him very well."

She shrugged uneasily. "We've met. And I assure you, sir, I was unimpressed with his manner. He is rough and ruthless, with no more finesse than those ancestors of his who first invaded this place. You would take your life in your own hands were you to come too close!"

"But I've already scaled great walls for you! Taken my sword against a multitude on your behalf! Why should I fear any other man?"

"But you saved me specifically for Montjoy, or so you told me," she pointed out.

"Perhaps I did it for Robin."

She inhaled sharply, watching him. What could one gain from studying the face of a man in a mask of mail?

"Did you?" she asked him softly.

His answer seemed long in coming, and when it did, it was curt. "Nay. I saved you for Montjoy."

He turned from her. "If you will follow me, my lady, I will show you to the brook. As you have ascertained, I have already bathed. I will be near—"

"To watch over me?" she suggested softly.

"To watch over you. But most certainly, you may enjoy your bath in peace." He swirled about again, offering her a deep and mocking bow. "That is, of course, unless Montjoy should arrive."

"What?"

Soft laughter curled around her. "After all, my lady, we are on Montjoy's lands even now. So you are quite safe from any unwanted attentions. Except, of course, for his attentions, that is. Should he be so rude as to appear."

Once again, he turned abruptly to lead the way out. With her heart racing, Kat followed.

She had suspected that they were on Montjoy's land. "Wait! Is he going to appear?"

The Silver Sword had no answer. He was walking onward.

"He had best not appear!" she muttered fiercely. But her fingers were trembling, and she clenched them together tightly, and she added a silent prayer. Please, dear God! Don't let him appear!

Please . . . !

Chapter 10

She hadn't realized in the night what a beautiful place they had come to.

The land was completely carpeted in deep, rich green, with strong trees that reached high to the sky where the branches formed great arbors. Sweet, rich grasses grew beneath the trees and led the way down a nearby embankment to a delightful winding curve of water. It was a large brook, dancing its way over a multitude of rocks and boulders, creating tiny falls here and there and enchanting little pools by the embankment. To her further delight, the embankment became gravelly rather than muddy, and the water was exceptionally clear and clean-looking.

With his great cape about her shoulders, she had left him on the pathway, running ahead, gasping with delight. Then, as she turned around, she saw that her escort had disappeared. He had, indeed, intended to leave her in peace.

She stared after him for long moments, thinking. He was not so bad a man. His words were outrageous, but despite them, his actions were chivalrous. She was safe with him. Safe from de la Ville, or anyone else Prince John determined might be made to pay for her.

She looked from the trail into the beautiful green of the forest. Still, he had been well and good the night before. He had arrived in the nick of time. But he was right about Montjoy. She didn't want to marry the man, and didn't intend to do so. Not until she managed to see Richard herself and throw herself—tearfully, of course—at his feet. So even if she would be just a little bit sorry, it seemed that she needed to escape the Silver Sword.

She was on Montjoy's land. She had to get off it.

If ever she meant to escape, now was the time. She couldn't even see him anymore.

Carefully, she paused a moment longer. Then she turned northward along the water, getting her bearings from the sun that filtered green and dropped down upon her from the canopy of the branches. If she just walked to the northwest, she could come through Robin's territory. Or her own, she thought with a chill. Montjoy's lands actually bordered hers in the southeast corner here.

Still, she wasn't sure about going home. She must find Robin first. Then she could try to use the tunnel and pray that the door might be unjammed! So that she could go home secretly, until she knew what had happened at the castle.

She looked up the pathway one more time, then sprinted directly into the woods, holding the cape tightly to her body lest it snag on the branches. Within minutes it seemed that she was completely within the sanctuary of the trees. She was certain that she could no longer be seen. If she just kept her eyes on the sun . . .

It worked for what seemed like hours, but was probably only minutes. The beautiful, gentle, shielding trees were filled with barbed branches. She stepped on tree limbs and on twigs. She swore. She paused, holding an injured foot and trying to blow on the pain where she had bruised it against a rock.

Weary, she sat. She'd come through enough forests. But usually she wore shoes!

She started off again, finding her way through one of the narrow trails to the road. She discovered that things went much better. Still, her feet were very sore.

She had been gone long enough for the Silver Sword to realize that she had left him, she knew. And once she had reached that point, every little noise behind her made her ready to jump out of her skin.

Certain that she heard a rustle of branches, she plunged back into the trees, running too wildly. She tripped over a fallen branch and went sprawling, landing right in a mud pool. And even as she came to her feet, sputtering, it seemed that the forest had become dead silent once again.

She couldn't go on the way she was. She had to make her way deeper through the trees to the brook at this end of the forest and clean her face enough so that she could see. Struggling, tripping, swearing, grabbing at branches that threatened to slap her in the face, she slowly made her way to the water. On the embankment she fell to her knees, cupped some water, and washed the mud from her face. Then, as her eyes cleared, she stared into the brook and let out a startled scream. There, reflected in the rippling mirror image, was the Silver Sword. He was mounted on his ebony horse and seemed comfortable, completely at ease—and monstrously powerful so high above her.

"My lady, I have never seen anyone take so circuitous a route before in all my life!" he told her. "First that difficult walk directly through the foliage. Then that canter down the trail only to plunge into a mudhole."

She leaped up, hands clenched to her sides. "You followed me? All that way?"

"Well, of course." She could sense his eyes narrowing. "I am watching over you, remember? I could hardly claim to do so were I to let you out of my sight."

"You followed me! All the way. You could have

stopped me at any minute?" Furious, she charged him suddenly, heedless of his size and his great horse. She slammed a fist against his thigh. "You let me wreck my feet! And plummet into that mud! When you had me all the while?" She slammed a fist against his side again, and then again, and then suddenly both of her fists were flailing wildly against the hard-muscled wall of his thigh.

"Whoa!" he called sharply. But she didn't listen. She vented her frustration against him recklessly until she could do so no longer because he had determined to reach for her.

Then suddenly she was rising. Her bruised feet no longer touched the ground. For a brief moment she was lifted high enough to see the sharpness of his eyes beneath the mail helmet, then she was being laid flat over the front of the saddle.

"Wait!" she cried breathlessly.

"Oh, I think not!"

He didn't intend to wait. She tried to struggle up, but the great ebony horse was in motion, splashing through the water and back up the brook. Kat pushed against the animal's taut shoulders and the man's thigh once again, just trying to see where they were going. It was difficult. She was encompassed in the cloak, draped over the horse's shoulder and the Silver Sword's thigh, and blinded by the tangle of her own hair.

"Let me down!" she demanded. He ignored her. "Let me down now!" Still, no word from him. "Oh, I hope you rust to pieces!" she cried out. "I hope that mail rusts right over your face. And over your chest. And every single little thing that protrudes from your body—"

"From what?" he said incredulously.

"From—nothing! Just let me down!" She pressed against him again, trying to see.

But even as she struggled up, she gasped suddenly.

She had tried so hard! She had cut and wounded her feet, plowed through foliage and branches!

And she had barely come a stone's throw from the hunter's cottage she had so recently left. Even now she could see the very path from which she had first taken flight.

"I am shocked," he told her, "simply shocked that such an exquisite, poised young noblewoman would be so very familiar with protrusions."

"I'm not! Really. I'm just very indignant. Let me down!"

"One would imagine that you might be contrite."

"I am contrite. Immensely contrite."

"You're sorry you've been caught, my lady, and nothing more."

"All right!" she flared. "I'm incredibly sorry that I've been caught!"

He was silent. And the longer he was silent, the more nervous she became.

"I am back! You can let me down now!" she cried out, trying to twist free.

The ebony horse came to a halt.

"If you'll just let me—"

"I thought you wanted a bath."

"I do. I'm dying for a bath."

"Then you shall have one."

She gasped again sharply as he gave her a little shove. It sent her flying from the back of the horse to land in the shockingly cold three feet of water directly before the horse's hooves. It closed over her head and she rose, sputtering, furious, and scarcely able to breathe.

And still she staggered to her feet. "Why you—" she began, seeking the energy to pummel his thigh once again. "Oaf! Bastard!" she cried. Then she went on with a number of more guttural and colorful oaths, slamming her palms against his thigh all the while. As she ranted, he stared at her. Then suddenly, he thundered out in reply. "Enough! Indeed, my lady, I have had quite enough!"

Quite suddenly, she found herself in retreat. Dragged down by the weight of the cape, she staggered backwards as he dismounted from the horse and came striding through the water, intent upon reaching her once again.

"Wait!" She cast out a hand as she walked away from him. "Get away from me. Don't you even think of coming any closer. I'm warning you, you had best get away! I mean every word that I'm saying, do you understand? I—" She broke off because he had reached her at last. Because his hands were on her shoulders and his hold was very fierce.

"Let go of me! Now!"

"I don't think so. Certainly not now."

"You can't hurt me—"

"I don't intend to hurt you."

"You can't have—"

"I can have whatever I've the power to take, lady!"

For the briefest of moments, she was mesmerized. Caught within his hold, staring into his eyes, fascinated by what might lie beneath the mesh and mail that masked his face from her.

Then he was pulling her inexorably to him. She felt the startling coolness of that fine mesh mail as it touched her face.

"No!"

"Yes!"

And against that coolness, she felt the sudden, shocking heat of his mouth as his lips touched hers.

Wild, but furious and frightened, she tried to twist from his grasp upon her. She struggled fiercely. His hands were hard upon her, and his body pressed closer to hers. She couldn't breathe. She tried to pummel him with her fists, amazed at the sense of heat that was pervading her, surely, swiftly. She was not giving in, she told herself. She was not.

But the heat was lulling. And along with the fury and the fear she was discovering that something new grew within her at his touch.

Excitement . . .

She didn't know when she ceased to struggle. She never meant to do so. She would have said that she would have fought him to the death, and she would have meant it.

But it was different when he touched her. Different when the sure heat seemed to build to an incredible fire. A blaze that coerced and seduced. A kiss that went on and on.

Instinctively she pressed against him. Her hands had no effect. His arms crushed her hard against his body. His fingers wound into the hair at her nape, holding her head still as his mouth covered hers. With amazement she felt the subtle play as his lips formed around hers. Felt the ruthless thrust as her lips were parted. Then all the warmth was inside her mouth, flooding her, as his tongue played a hungry havoc there, tasting, teasing, exploring, dueling intimately with her own.

She should have been fighting still. Fighting and struggling until the waters closed over her head, until death itself claimed her.

Nay, she could fight no longer . . .

For the searing warmth of his fire upon her lips seemed to spread. Despite the coolness of the brook, the ravaging movement of his lips and tongue brought flames and heat to leap throughout her body. Her breath was gone, her strength was stolen. She was locked within his hold, and captured, too, within a heady fascination. Again, his hands were moving. Caressing her nape. Stroking forward, sliding between their bodies. His fingers closing around her breast beneath the cape, over the thin film of linen there. She felt the roughness of his palm over the hardened peak of her nipple and a gasp formed in her throat, one that he silenced quickly with the intensity of his kiss. The fire then seemed to burst at an intimate point between her thighs, and then, more shocked at herself than at him, she let out a strangled sound, fighting him in earnest. Shaking, trembling, she tried to twist from his kiss, escape from his hold.

Yet she could not do so. Not unless he chose to let her go.

His head rose from hers, eyes blazing briefly into her own. He did not drop her this time but set her cleanly away from him, and she was almost certain that he trembled himself as he did so. The cape had fallen away and floated toward shore. She was shivering fiercely in the remnants of her linen nightgown as she stared at him across the few feet of water.

He pointed to her gown. She glanced down, coloring as she realized that in this dazzling green forest light the material had given completely, her breast was exposed, the mound full and ivory, her nipple a dusky dark hue, hardened by the cold, by his touch . . .

She cried out softly, reaching for the fallen material. She pulled it up, but it did no good, for she might as well have been naked, the way that the material clung to her body. Everything about her was visible. The rouge peaks of her breasts, the curve of her hip, the triangle at her thighs.

"Most enchanting, my lady!" The words were to mock her, she was certain. Yet he seemed in pain himself, anguished, tense.

He had caused it!

Blindly, both hurt and angry, she raised her hand, determined to strike him, and strike him hard. Her blow did not fall. He caught her wrist. She gritted her teeth against the pain.

"Take your bath!" he ordered.

"Go to hell!"

"Lady," he said softly, "Fear not—I am there!"

Then he turned from her and strode to the shore.

Kat felt her throat go dry, the rampant beating of her heart beginning to find a more normal pace. All her energy left her and she sank into the cold water, praying for its cleansing touch. But even as she rose to breathe, she found herself touching her lips, feeling the pressure of his there still. And she tried to tell herself that she was indignant and angry and that he'd had no right, certainly no right. She hated him, loathed him. Aye, she did!

Yet no matter what she claimed, what she felt was a startling sense of awe and wonder. Come cold! Come seep into me! she thought in silence, sinking into the water again. What was the matter with her? The rough stranger had swept into her life, a double-edged savior, entirely rude, and nearly barbaric. And still his touch had awakened sensations in her that she hadn't begun to dream might exist, all the while holding her here for another man. She should despise him.

She did. Surely she did.

How could she despise a man who had scaled castle walls to come for her? Who had entered into a den of danger, blood and death, on her behalf?

Ah, for mercenary reasons . . .

Nay, not that alone, for she had seen him in the forest. She had seen him race into another arena of danger to rescue the peasant girl, heedless of the fact that he thundered in against royalty. No matter what his manners, no matter how recklessly he liked to tease and taunt her, there were decent things about this man. There was a sense of justice about him. That very thing that their world seemed to be lacking since Henry had died and Richard had gone. *Honor.*

Still, the man was impossible! How dare he kiss her

and touch her and torment her so boldly?

She groaned softly, remembering the hot sensations his kisses had evoked in her, and slipped into the water once again. It surged over her head and she threaded her fingers through the flow of her hair, shaking her head to loosen the tresses. Then she rubbed her hands along her arms and legs, trying to sluice away any of the dried mud that might have remained on her.

She rose again, now shivering fiercely from the coolness of the water. She looked to the shore, but she didn't see him anywhere. Continuing to search the surrounding forest, she saw him come near the water again. He was carrying a coarse wool blanket for her and stood at the water's edge, watching her, waiting to wrap her in it.

She rose, walking out of the water, meeting his eyes and lifting her chin as she strode toward him. The wet torn fabric of her nightdress clung to her like a second skin. She didn't bother to wrap her arms around herself in any way because her arms couldn't cover all that the gown displayed. She walked toward him and did not turn until she was just before him, feeling the shadowed but potent fire of his gaze.

She spun around then, and he wrapped the blanket about her shoulders. He left her on the shore, wading out to retrieve his cape, now drifting in the water. He threw it over a pile of rocks to dry.

"There's a new fire blazing inside. Go dry yourself before it," he said, not glancing her way.

She watched him curiously. "And where will you dry yourself, sir?"

"In the sun."

"There is not much of it."

"Then, as you wished, my lady, I will rust."

"I am not afraid of you, you know," she informed him. "You can cast aside that mail and come in, too."

He swore, spinning to her. "Damn you! Go inside!"

"Why are you so angry with me! You caused this situation, not I!"

"Nay, lady, I did not! I merely went out of my way to scale walls to rescue you. I battled strangers, and I drew their blood. I dived into a moat."

"You sought to drown me, I believe!"

"Which seemed preferable, drowning or de la Ville?"

Her cheeks pinkened, but she stood her ground. "De la Ville, Montjoy—you. What difference does it make when a man intends to have what he will?"

He moved toward her quickly and grabbed her shoulders. "What difference, lady? Oh, I pray that you never discover it!"

She started trembling, instinctively aware that he was very right. She had been goading him. She had wanted him to strip away the mask and reveal himself to her.

And she should stay away. And she should be grateful.

Her lower lip began to tremble, and she caught it with her teeth, looking up to him. "De la Ville is a monster," she whispered. "I know it, I've heard it, I've even felt it—"

"What?" he demanded.

She shook her head. "I've felt the evil in him, when he's touched my hand. When he's looked my way. But what of Montjoy? He is probably not much better, don't you see?"

His hands fell from her shoulders. "He would never hurt you," he told her simply.

"He is a Norman, just—"

"Your father was a Norman lord, just the same, my fine damsel," he reminded her with a grate to his voice.

"My father was different!" she whispered.

"Different, aye, your father was different, but a Norman lord! There are other men like him. Men who admired him for his mercy and his strength."

Kat frowned suddenly. Maybe the Silver Sword had given away something at last. He had spoken of her father very familiarly.

"You knew him," she said suddenly. "You knew my father!"

"I didn't say—"

"You did! You knew him. I heard it in your voice. Why are you lying to me?"

"All right, I knew your father."

"And you're a Saxon, a Silver Sword. The great sword of Saxon justice!" It would have been unthinkable for an outlaw like the Silver Sword to have known her father unless he had been the outlaw in the forest that day who had saved her father's life. She gasped, her eyes growing wide. "My God!" she whispered. "You were in the forest. It was spring. My father had just returned from a campaign. De la Ville was there. He was very young. He was with his father. And his father had ordered that a young villain's hand be severed for poaching and that the Saxon lad's father be hanged for the offense. My father interfered, and the de la Villes would have killed him—would have killed us all perhaps! But there was a bowsman in the forest. And a rain of arrows sent them flying. And it—it was you!"

"I am the Silver Sword, my lady. Robin Hood is the great archer."

"But it was you! You have been around for years and years! The legend, that is, but the legend was real."

"My lady, I am not all that ancient!"

"But shortly after that terrible incident in the forest people began to talk of the Silver Sword. From then on the legend came alive."

He waved a hand impatiently. He was silent for a moment, admitting nothing. Then he continued.

"My lady, you have confused all Normans with the perversions and greed of John Plantagenet. Not all barons in the land are so licentious or cruel or grasping. Perhaps you should give Montjoy a chance."

"You are trying to make me forget something that will never leave my mind. Tell me the truth."

"There is nothing to tell you."

"I will not say another word about anything else unless you admit to being the mysterious archer that day."

He sighed. "What difference does it make now?"

"Admit it."

"Fine. I shall admit it, whether it is truth or not, so that we may get on with this. What is your difficulty with Montjoy? Why are you so against him?"

"You forget! I know him!"

"And he stands judged and damned?"

"Damned, truly."

Her sodden knight let out another irritated oath. "I tell you again—he would not hurt you."

She inhaled and exhaled on a soft sigh, disturbed to feel a rampant beating of her heart again, a breathlessness as she stared at him, feeling the warmth of his body emanating toward her, seeming to sweep around her with its vitality.

So they had been saved by the Silver Sword once before . . .

"Talk to me, my lady!"

"Perhaps he is not so vile a man as de la Ville. But Richard has offered me to him. He wants the castle. He wants the land. I come with them. And men—men do want heirs. Therefore, he will want a wife, and it will not matter if she is willing—or not. Deny that," she challenged him.

He threw up his hands. "Indeed, lady. He will want a wife. But not one to torture or abuse. Merely one to mold to a proper—"

"One to command and tame!" she retorted.

"I tell you, he is a just man. And where, my lady,

did you ever learn that you would have a choice about marriage? Thank God that Richard lives, and that John's rise to the throne is not an assured thing, for he could demand that you marry de la Ville, and no man on this earth could change that command! You will marry Montjoy, and that is the way it is!"

He turned away from her abruptly. He walked back to the large rock where he had laid his cape and turned around, taking a seat upon it. "Lady Katherine, go inside. I beg of you. You wear us both down."

"I'm not worn in the least—in fact, sir, if you were not so impossible, I would be somewhat in awe. You see, I will never forget that day. Or cease to thank the man who saved my father's life."

"If you are not worn, I am, my lady. And I swear, I will make it hard for you if you choose to tire me even more!"

She sighed with exasperation, then turned and headed for the cottage.

Inside, a fire blazed warmly once again.

Something was laid over one of the chairs. Curiously, she walked to it and found a lady's robe. The material was some of the softest linen she had ever touched, and rimming the neckline and the whole hem was a fur as fine and pure a white as the material of the robe.

He had left it for her, obviously. But where had he found it?

She spun around the cottage then and felt a shiver seize her. She pulled back the hand she had been about to place upon the gown.

This was Montjoy's property. The gown belonged to some woman Montjoy brought here. A woman he brought deep into the woods for secret trysts.

Lady or whore? Kat wondered, stepping back. She didn't want to be Montjoy's wife, and she didn't want to touch the cast-off clothing of one of his mistresses.

Yet neither did she want to parade around naked. Still, she didn't touch the fabric. She sat before the fire, pulling the rough wool blanket around her shoulders. She had been so cold. Slowly, the fire warmed her.

The door opened, and she didn't turn around. The Silver Sword had come back, she knew.

He was silent for a moment. Then he said curiously, "I left you something to wear other than that blanket."

"So I saw."

"It was not to your liking?"

"I don't care for the cast-off clothing of Montjoy's whores," she said coolly.

At first, she was not surprised by his lack of response. Then she was stunned to realize that he was so silent because he was striding toward her furiously. He wrenched her back to her feet. The blanket fell away, and she met him clad in her nearly dry but well-frayed nightgown.

He had cast off his sheath of body mail, and wore only his shirt and chausses—and the mask and helmet of mail. Somehow the lack of that body mail made him all the more formidable and powerful. She could feel the length of him. His legs were solid, his hips and belly lean and taut. She felt the ripple of muscle beneath his tunic and the sword-wielding power of his arms.

Hot with fury and emotion, he pulled her too close, his fingers biting into her. "Just who, my lady, do you think yourself to be? Some ungodly prize?"

"Let go of me!" she cried, truly alarmed, fingers pressing furiously against his chest. How could he have been the mysterious man in the woods? How could he be so very decent one moment, and so hard and arrogant the next? "Who do you think you are! Some luckless, landless knight—pretending to do good! Seeking what reward—"

"This isn't about me! You are not worthy to kiss the little toe of the lady that wore that robe before!"

"His wh—"

He almost struck her. His hand raised and she cried out quickly. "Nay!"

She could hear the grating of his teeth as he fought his temper. His hand fell. She was silent, watching him. Had he struck her with such violence, she would surely have been cast across the room.

She moistened her lips, amazed at his fury. How well did he know Montjoy?

Or this woman of Montjoy's who he so idolized?

"My lady, go naked then!" he said angrily. And once again she saw the movement of his hand. It fell against the tattered bodice of her nightgown and tore hard at the fabric. Already worn and ripped, the gown gave with a little flutter of sound, and lay at her feet.

She gasped and swallowed hard, this time allowing her arms to wind around her as she backed away.

But he wasn't even glancing at her body. His eyes held hers. Then he turned away again, walking back to the door.

She hated him at that moment. She wanted to throw something at him. No, she wanted to rush after him, to beat him furiously with her fists.

She didn't dare. She didn't dare come so close in her naked state.

She watched as he stood at the door, his shoulders squaring. Then he turned again, his gaze flickering over her as she reached down for the blanket to wrap around herself once again.

He bowed very deeply. "My apologies, my lady. My temper is very quick to peak with you, so it seems." He was silent for a moment, and to Kat's annoyance, she felt her own fury slipping away. Maybe it was the feel of his eyes now. The way they moved over her. He said things to her that . . .

That he didn't mean.

He cared for her in some way. Even if it was only desire.

And even if she wasn't worthy to kiss the toe of the woman who had owned the white robe before.

Perhaps he cared for her in his way because he had known and honored her father.

And perhaps she needed to bend just a little.

With the blanket hugged about her, she inclined her head slightly, a regal gesture. "My apologies, sir, if I offended you. I am being forced—by everyone, so it seems!—to marry this man. You will understand if I do not care for the belongings of his women."

"It did not belong to his 'women,' as you say, Katherine. It belonged to his first betrothed. The Lady Alyssa Albright."

Katherine gasped. "And he came here with Alyssa? And they—" she broke off, her cheeks flooding red again. They had been lovers? When Montjoy had always appeared to be cast of steel and stone, impatient to do battle, to ride with the King, as seemed their Norman way. What could Alyssa have seen in him?

"Cast aspersions upon the memory of Alyssa Albright, my lady, and you will truly risk my temper."

She was quiet for a moment, watching him. "You do serve Montjoy in some way," she said. It wasn't an accusation, it was a statement of certainty. "And it seems to me, sir, that you were in love with his betrothed yourself."

He shifted his stance, and she almost felt the rush of heat and violence that seemed to exude from him. She raised a hand. "Nay, don't take offense from me on this matter, sir! I admired Alyssa greatly myself. And if the robe was hers, sir, then gladly will I clad myself in it."

He bowed deeply to her. His temper seemed to have come under control after he heard her last softly spoken words.

She wished so desperately that she could see the shape and contours of his face, and read the emotions upon it. But the helmet and mask of mail had been well designed for the purpose of subterfuge. His eyes were always shadowed by the steel of the helmet. The intricate mail mesh fell just above his mouth, and hung so that not even the shape of his lips could be clearly discerned.

Yet she could remember so vividly the feel of them!

Had Alyssa known that this knight was in love with her? Had she returned those emotions? Poor, beautiful Alyssa! So stunning and sweet a woman, taken from life and beauty by the same fever that had taken Kat's parents. It was a frightening life, even without the likes of a de la Ville at one's heels.

But Alyssa had been loved. Really loved. By this man. The Silver Sword. Kat had seldom heard such passion in the words of a man.

"Well, I am glad that you are determined to cover up at last, my lady," he said softly. "For I do swear, lady, whatever your heart and mind, there are other things within a man, above and beyond his temper, that you do manage to bring to a peak!"

She didn't know whether to smile or to take offense.

Or to allow the strange feeling of heat to come through her again, as it threatened with just the touch of his eyes, and the intimate implication of his words.

It didn't matter. He was leaving her.

"I shall see to procuring something to eat," he said briefly. "I will be back."

The door closed behind him. She stood there, feeling the warmth of the blaze from the fire.

And that other strange warmth.

Then she suddenly ran across the room, dropping the blanket, sweeping up Lady Alyssa's robe and slipping it swiftly over her head.

He would be back.

A man far more dangerous than de la Ville, though he couldn't possibly know it.

De la Ville could threaten her person. Never her soul.

While this man . . .

She trembled slightly.

This man might well steal a section of her heart.

Chapter 11

To his amazement, she seemed rather subdued when he returned.

He had taken his time outside, feeding his horse, rummaging through his saddlebags for the loaves of bread and cheese that he had brought along. He hadn't thought about food for a while, but after following her through the forest and as the morning had passed away, he found he'd acquired a magnificent hunger.

It wasn't for food! an inner voice taunted.

He gritted his teeth. This was truly a fool's errand he had set himself today. One moment he wanted to slap her, then he would discover himself swept into the web of her beauty, taut with the blinding desire she could elicit. One moment she would make him furious and then she would be soft, and sweetly noble, and he would find his temper in check once again.

Well, Lord Montjoy had no cause for complaint, he told himself. Richard had granted him whatever he might desire for his return. Land. Men. Knights and villeins, good farm wives and good serving women.

And Lady Katherine. Marriage would be no torment, trying to get heirs upon a hairy-chinned old crone.

Nay, life would be this tempest! If she were so unwilling to bend to the Silver Sword she would surely never surrender a thing to Lord Montjoy!

We will, he assured himself, come to some agreement when the deed of marriage is done.

They would, aye . . .

For her, it would be a simple matter of acceptance. She hated him. Or, rather, she hated Montjoy.

While for him . . .

One moment he was tormented that she was not Alyssa. The next he was furious with her words or her cool assumption of absolute superiority. Then all that he could see was her beauty, and all that he could feel was the wrenching knot of desire.

He never should have held her. No matter what his temper, he never should have kissed her. Never should have tasted the sweetness of her lips, felt the fullness of her breasts, touched her flesh . . .

Never felt the fire in the woman. Passion lay deep within her. The passion to determine she must slip through the forest in green, the passion for right and for justice . . .

And a passion for love, one she had yet to taste.

And one she certainly wouldn't bestow too easily upon Lord Montjoy.

"Damn her!" he said aloud, patting his horse so hard that the faithful animal looked to him reproachfully. "Sorry, fellow. I might have been better off with a crone! Whatever, I suppose I must feed the maid, what say you? But you know what? I should have left her to the likes of de la Ville. He'd have stripped the spirit from her in a matter of hours."

Would de la Ville have been able to do so? No, and Damian felt an admiration for her that he had not expected. No, not even de la Ville's hideous cruelties or perversions would have killed what lived within her. For she wouldn't have let him touch it. And unless de la Ville had actually brought a knife to her throat and slain her, she would have gone on, finding new ways to fight him.

"Lady, you are lucky to have me!" he exclaimed. "Perhaps I will curtail your activities, but behave and learn your place, and I will leave you in peace!" Well, what peace he *could* leave her in. He was sorry, he would treat no wife like a nun. Perhaps love had been denied him. Heirs would not.

"I must go back in," he murmured. He'd been gone a long time. The morning had come and gone already, and they were well past noon. He had yet to offer her a single bite to eat.

"I can't starve her, eh?"

As if in answer, the great black stallion snorted and shook his huge head. Damian smiled grimly and turned back to their shelter.

When he strode back inside the lodge, she was subdued. She had slipped on the beautiful robe, and now sat before the fire, trying to dry and untangle her long golden hair.

He held still in the doorway for a moment, watching her, feeling the warmth steal over his own body. The length of her hair might have consisted of spun gold. It seemed to hang now in fine, rippling sheets of sunlight and fire. She was trying to undo the tangles with her fingers, a task that surely could not be an easy one.

For a moment, the strength of his longing kept him motionless in the doorway, fighting the painful surges that tore through his body. Then he walked on in, setting the food down on the rough wooden table and turning to search through the crate by the loft window. He found a skein of wine and two leather cups and placed them on the table with the food.

She knew that he was there, of course. Her eyes turned to him surreptitiously, then returned quickly to study the blaze.

"My lady, what meal we have is here."

Maybe she had been trying to keep her distance from

him. But her hunger had to be as great as his, and so
she rose.

He was sorry then in truth that he had given her the
robe. The fur was so soft and white against her flesh.
The fabric molded to her body, clinging to her legs even
as she walked. The deep V of the garment at the neck
displayed the rise of her breasts in an incredibly enticing
fashion.

He drew out a chair for her, and she sat, her hands
in her lap at first, her eyes downcast, as he positioned
himself across from her. Then she looked up. His breath
caught for a moment, he was so startled by the deep
aquamarine of her eyes. Damn this! He'd be tormented
his life through, wondering just what this damsel was
about!

She was not Alyssa!

Ah, but her beauty was greater than that of any maid
he had known. Perhaps he could not love her, nor she
love him, but he would be a harried husband, always
determined that no other man should lay claim to that
which was his!

"Eat," he told her, and the word sounded almost like
a growl.

She didn't seem to need another invitation but reached
for the loaf of bread and the cheese, breaking both into
several pieces. He was disturbed to see that she took only
small portions herself, careful to leave most of the food
for him.

It was a generous gesture. But he didn't care to admire
her too much.

Watching her, he shoved the cup of wine in her direction. She inclined her head in a thank-you. He started to
wolf down a piece of bread and found it difficult with
the mail nearly over his lips.

She lowered her eyes again, smiling. "Sir, I'm hardly
likely to tell anyone the identity of the Silver Sword.

You can cast aside that helmet and mail."

He shook his head. "You forget! You already plan to ask Montjoy to hang me. It will be far better for me if Montjoy does not know who he seeks to hang."

She waved a hand in the air. "How is this, sir? I shall not ask Montjoy to hang you—if you do not persist in handing me over to Montjoy."

He was still for a moment, clenching his teeth against the hope in her eyes. He shook his head. "I'm sorry." He picked up his cup of wine and swallowed it down as if it were water, shuddering fiercely then, but glad of the warmth that filled him. If she was startled by his behavior or dismayed by it, she gave no sign, but lifted her own cup to her lips. Her eyes met his for a moment, shimmering with their aquamarine beauty. There was the definite light of challenge in them.

She swallowed down the whole of her wine with one quick flick of the mug, just as he had himself. Then she smiled sweetly. "Have we more?"

"Indeed, we do."

He poured out another cup for them each. She lifted hers to his and, bemused, he allowed their cups to touch. "Salut!" she said, and swallowed down her wine again, waiting for him to drink his own.

"Salut!" he replied, and did so.

He poured another cup for each of them, somewhat amused.

She never quit. Never gave up. He realized she hoped to leave him passed out in his cups—while she darted away through the woods.

"I assume that this wine belongs to Montjoy," she said, making the words more a statement than a question.

"Indeed, it does." He poured them both more.

This time she swirled the wine in her cup. "A very fine vintage with rich, smooth flavor. And kept here by Montjoy. A clever man. As clever as John. Everything here for his bidding for an intimate tryst in this little—"

She broke off abruptly, guilt curiously touching her eyes as she glanced swiftly to him. What had she been about to say? Love nest? Den of iniquity?

He leaned forward. "In this what?" he demanded.

"In this lovely cottage," she said lightly, and hurried on. "Shall I pour you more wine?"

He lifted his hand in a gesture that assured her she must go right ahead and do so. "So this is Montjoy's wine. Perhaps we should not touch it."

"Why not? I hear that Montjoy is a generous man—when it comes to food and drink, that is—and I imagine that he would very much like his lovely betrothed to enjoy whatever creature comforts he might offer her in his absence."

"But what of you, Sir Silver Sword?" she inquired sweetly.

"I think that he would be willing to offer me far more than a mug of wine for seizing you from the very grasp of de la Ville!"

"Hm," she murmured, her fingers plucking a piece of bread. She managed to consume it very quickly—even as he knew she was busily hatching a scheme in her mind. She was both very hungry and very eager to escape him. Were he not the cause of her scheming, the entire situation might be amusing.

Her eyes touched his. She rose suddenly, coming around the table. Her knee touched his as she leaned against the table, reaching over to pour more wine into his mug. "So you are looking forward to a reward, eh?"

Just what was she getting at? He could feel her closeness, breathe her sweet feminine scent. Her eyes were shimmering in their aquamarine beauty. Her hair swept around her in tendrils that seemed to be crafted of pure gold, brushing the flesh of his arm. At this distance she was indeed a tempting morsel. She watched him so intently with those magical eyes, and her smile was surely the most seductive he had ever seen.

He picked up his mug and drained the wine from it. She refilled it quickly. He caught the skein from her and refilled her own. She swallowed it, still smiling, an invitation for him to do the same with his own.

"You drink far more like a tavern wench than a great lady," he said flatly. "Where did you acquire this . . . er, talent?"

Her lashes swept over her eyes for a moment, and a wistful, very poignant—and honest—smile curved her lips. "My father," she said softly. "It would be late and I was supposed to be in bed, but I would know that he was down in the hall, just watching the flames sometimes while my mother bathed or rested. Just biding his time before he would go to her. And he would say that we would share just a sip of wine, but then he would tell me the most glorious stories."

"About?"

Her smile deepened.

"About my mother. He loved her so. I'm sure that it was embellished, but he would tell me about their meeting, and somehow it all became very magical, a fairy tale." She gazed at him then and suddenly seemed to remember what she was about. "Well, you know, one sip led to another. Then sometimes he would be with his knights, and I would join them. And we all knew that I was my father's heir, and I had to take care that I never betrayed a weakness . . ." Again, she was telling him more than she meant to tell him. She leaned close, trying to make it appear that the wine was beginning to make the world just a bit hazy. "Ah, but you, sir, are a hardened knight! Yet a poor one, it would seem. Have more! If we are both here, guests of Montjoy, we should enjoy this, eh?" Again, she poured wine into his mug.

He poured wine into hers, offering it to her.

"Salut!" he said.

"Salut!" she replied.

Still smiling so seductively, she started to pour from the skein again, allowing the silk of her hair to fall over his arm as she reached for his mug.

He clamped his fingers suddenly and tightly around her wrist. Startled, her eyes flew to his. He held her there firmly.

"I don't think so," he informed her.

"You don't think what?" she tried.

"My lady, I am not going to pass out cold on the floor. And you are not going to go running off, a smug little smile on your face, while you think to escape me, Montjoy—and destiny. It will not work. For one, my lady, you could drink until you were ready to drop, and I would still feel less the fruit of the vine than would you! I have drunk and whored and gambled with some of the most loutish fellows you might ever imagine."

She tried to snatch her wrist free from his grasp. The sweet smile was gone. Her eyes were narrowed and snapping. Anger had etched hard, stubborn lines about her mouth.

"I have no difficulty in the least imagining you with horrid louts!" she assured him. "Indeed, I have no difficulty imagining you being the most horrid of the knaves! Let me go!"

He did so. She had been straining so hard against him that she went flying back, nearly striking the wall. She recovered her balance just in time and stared at him furiously, rubbing her wrist. "I swear, Sir Silver Sword— You will hang."

He pushed back his chair and rose, watching her. "Perhaps I shall. Will you really be so glad to see it?"

She hesitated a moment. Always thinking! Plotting,

planning, conniving! Honesty seemed the best choice to her at the moment. "Truly, I don't hate you! Despite your disgraceful behavior and terribly crude manners, I do not hate you. I saw you save that girl in the woods—"

"What?" he demanded, frowning.

"I saw you save the girl in the forest. And there could be no great reward for her. Some decency lurks in your breast, I know it!" She paused a moment. "Robin thinks highly of you. Therefore, I do not want to see you caught, a prey to others."

"How magnanimous, my lady."

She took a step back toward him and spoke very softly. "I cannot understand why you are so eager to see me made a prisoner when we are both so aware of the pricelessness of freedom."

He pushed away from the table with an explosive oath, standing and walking around the table to survey her. "My lady, you are tiresome in the extreme! Understand this. I will not let you leave here. You don't begin to realize your peril. Do you think that Richard is a fool? Why do you think he has sent Montjoy home to claim you?"

"He has done so because he is not here, because he doesn't realize that I can manage on my own—"

"As you did the other night."

"I was faring quite well—"

"Not well enough."

"I'm quite sure that I could have jumped into the moat by myself."

He shook his head. "I don't think so. And I do think that you underestimate de la Ville. He will not quit. He dared a raid on your castle. In fact, he left a man—or several men—within your walls to lower the bridge for his assault. De la Ville is not clever enough to have planned so himself. John was in on it—and John is determined. Your only safety is in marrying—and marrying as Richard has ordered."

Her hands were folded before her. She walked to the fire, her head slightly lowered. Had she accepted his wisdom at last? She stood there in silence.

Then she spun around before the fire to face him again. The highlights of red and gold flared against the beautiful crystal-pure white of the furred robe, and against the flowing cascade of her hair as she swirled.

"You have mentioned that you are interested in rewards, sir," she said very softly.

Just the tone of her voice made a curious, searing tension sweep through him.

"Perhaps."

"Perhaps I can offer you a greater reward for my freedom than Montjoy could offer for my person."

"Montjoy is a very wealthy man."

"I can offer more than wealth."

As he stared at her, he made a great effort to conceal the anger growing within him. "What?"

"I am willing to do almost anything to escape Montjoy!" she said swiftly.

He was dead silent for a long moment. "Almost anything?" he asked harshly.

She inhaled, and exhaled. He could see the rise and fall of her breasts beneath the softness of the fabric and the fur of her gown.

"All right," she whispered. Her eyes met his fully. "Not almost anything. Anything."

Stars seemed to explode within the sudden blackness that clouded his vision. His fingers wound into his palms, nails cutting into his flesh.

"Truly, my lady," he muttered furiously, "you jest!"

"I do not."

He fought raggedly to control his temper. He leaned back, crossing his arms over his chest. "Spin, my lady."

"What?"

"Spin around, please. Let me see what I am offered."

"You have already seen plenty!"

"You are offering your person as a reward. I am entitled to judge this reward."

She stamped a foot suddenly, forgetting for a moment what a seductress she intended to be. Her eyes were truly a blue-green fire, blazing and hot. Her chin went very high, and her hair rippled and glistened down her back.

"Sir, I am not a whore—"

"Oh, but exactly, my lady, for you would sell yourself for gain!"

"Not for gain, you bastard!" she hissed.

"Spin! And do it prettily and well, for I have had some beautiful women in my day. I need to see what would be worth risking my neck and revenue for!"

She spun around, her eyes flashing angrily. The gown swirled around her slim ankles and beautiful legs.

And she did it well. Very well. When she paused before him again, her breath came quickly. "You wretched clod! You'll never again be offered anything so fine in your miserable life!"

"Watch it, my lady. A maid refrains from calling a man a 'wretched clod' when she wishes to seduce him. Truly, my lady, you do not know what you are about!"

"Perhaps!" she shot back furiously. "But truly, sir, you do not understand how I value my freedom!"

"And loathe Montjoy?" he added.

"Oh, indeed! And loathe Montjoy," she agreed.

It seemed the final straw. He strode across the room to her and wrenched her into his arms. As he had held her before, he held her again. This time there was no mercy in his touch. He bent her back, fingers taut and cruel as they raked through the golden length of her hair. His lips descended upon hers, rough in their demand. His mouth ground against hers, his tongue demanded entrance. And with a thorough fury made ruthless by the depths of his desire, he ravaged her lips and mouth, demandingly, brutally. His fingers brushed over the ivory length of her throat, slipped within the folds of her gown, and curled around the fullness of her breast. She could not breathe, and he knew it. Could not protest in any way. And still he gave her no quarter, drinking of her lips, exploring her flesh with his bold caress.

And then his lips did slide from hers. Down her throat. And he thrust open the V of the robe, causing the front to fall open. And he slid his mouth swiftly from the pulse at her throat down to the deep tempting valley between her breasts, and down farther still to tarry at the naked flesh of her belly. His hands clamped over her hips. The mail of his mask made patterned images against the softness of her bare skin.

Then he felt her shaking. Shaking like the earth when a hundred horses rode. A roaring came to his ears. Her long delicate fingers were on his shoulders. She was fighting now, and he wondered if it was too late.

He thrust himself up against her and saw the anguish, the fury, the tempest in her eyes. Thunder touched his voice as he railed at her, "Anything, my lady! Anything at all! You want to betray Montjoy. And you would have me join you? Tell me—what will be my reward? Would you stand passive? Would you not fight back? Well, I tell you, lady! That is no reward! Have you spent so many years hearing about your beauty that you assume it will buy you anything? Alas, not with me!"

"Stop it!" she cried, drawing the cords of the robe and wrapping them around herself tightly once again. "Knave of knaves—"

"No!" he protested furiously, catching her shoulders. "Nay, nay, lady! You made the offer! You would do anything. Well, let me tell you what I would require! Let's see . . . you would cast off the robe. Slowly. Very slowly. Sensually. From a distance, I think. And you would walk the length of the room to me. Slowly. Very slowly. And with the certain walk that a woman knows. You would come to me, to a bed we would create on the pallet with the furs. And you'd kneel down before me, and wrap your hair around me. And I would see that fire within your eyes, and your lips would part to kiss me. And my lady, that you would do. Those lips would travel sword-scarred flesh and more. Until I swept you down and took your mouth again with my own. And more. Do you begin, even begin, to know what I demand?"

She struck him full across the face. She swung so fast that he didn't see her, nor did he expect to feel the pain when her palm caused the mail mask to bite so brutally against his flesh. He reached out and caught her arm, wrenching her forward, but she cried out.

"Stop! I am desperate! What right have you to humiliate me so?"

"What right have you to betray Montjoy?"

"Jesu!" she swore, wrenching free and backing away from him. "Montjoy surely had no inhibitions against betraying me! The man has had his mistresses and lovers, and well as his precious Alyssa. He seeks to acquire property and a brood mare, and no more!"

"What?"

"That is the truth of it, sir, and you know it as well as I!"

"He would not hurt you—"

"No more than he would beat a decent horse!" she cried out. "Oh, never mind! I think I hate you as much as I hate him!" She spun again, turning from him. And now her beautiful golden head was bowed as she watched the flames. Her proud shoulders were ever so slightly fallen. She seemed weary beyond belief, and he was ever more furious with himself that he was beginning to feel sorry for her.

She was willing to sell herself to a bandit to escape marriage to him! An honorable state, if nothing more!

He turned to walk to the door. He had to escape her, if only for a few moments.

But at the doorway, he stopped, slapping his fists against the wooden frame. And he turned back to her, amazingly touched by that small, exquisite figure with the bowed golden head.

"Jesu, lady! I am tempted!" he told her.

"And I am amazed," she murmured.

"Why is that?"

She turned to face him again, not beaten at all. "You are every bit as loathsome as Montjoy!"

"Am I?"

"Perhaps more so."

"But your offer still stands, does it?"

Her eyes narrowed, smoldering and dangerous. "I will not be mocked by you more, sir!"

Tension seized him. He walked back into the room, stopping just feet before her. "I do not mock you, Katherine. At the moment, I am trying to understand you!"

Her chin rose just a bit higher. The challenge, the fury, the independence shone in her eyes once again. "Montjoy seeks to own me. You would seek only to use me," she said very quietly, and with a startling dignity.

"My lady, you seek to use me!" he reminded her harshly.

She smiled. "Can you be used, sir?"

He threw up his hands. "I don't believe this!"

"Nor do I," she murmured, her lashes sweeping her cheeks once again. "And I am acquiring a splitting headache." She looked at him balefully. "I drank too much wine."

She turned away and took her seat before the fire, rubbing her temples now as she gazed into the flames. He watched her for a moment, and was startled by the tug upon his heartstrings once again.

The things he would do to her once they were wed! He'd thought once before that she'd needed a good oak stick.

Now he was determined that she needed the whole tree!

And still . . .

He strode across the room to the cupboard where he had kept the robe all these years and found a silver-handled brush. He came to stand behind her and picked up a length of her golden tresses.

She started at his touch, realized that all he held was a brush, and seemed to slump back into her lethargy.

"There's no need to be disturbed. The brush—"

"Belonged to the Lady Alyssa," she finished.

"Aye!" he said softly.

"You serve Montjoy, and you've served him many years, and you're foolishly loyal. Do you think that Montjoy knows about the things you do in the forest as the Silver Sword? Do you think that he knows about Robin and the others? Are you so foolish as to think that he wouldn't hang you instantly if he knew that you robbed from his kindred to give to the old Saxon aristocracy?"

"I do not rob from the rich to give to the poor," he said, hesitating to clamp down hard on his jaw as a length of that glorious hair of hers curled and wrapped around his hand. "That is Robin's domain. I merely do my best to see that some of the robber barons do not practice their crafts upon the poor people of this region." He let fall a length of her hair. It nearly brushed the floor.

She shifted on the chair, turning so that her hand rested on the back of it, and her chin rested on her hand. "There is goodness in you, sir—"

"Sir Swine?" he interrupted.

"Please!" she whispered softly. Hers was such a beautiful face. And the plea was uttered with such a sweet and feminine appeal. It was easy to see how she might have twisted her father, or Henry, or Richard easily around her little finger. "Please! Just think about letting me go?"

"Ah! About accepting your . . . er, bounty instead of Montjoy's reward."

"Mine would be the sweeter reward, I swear it," she promised solemnly.

He caught up a lock of her hair once again. "You said that I humiliated you, my lady. I assure you, I would ask no less than I have already described! And you have said that I am as loathsome as Montjoy."

She shook her head. There was something honest about the motion, and even about the way her lashes fell, sweeping her cheeks. She couldn't quite meet his eyes. "I am being given to one man. One who has known many women. Before being handed over to him, perhaps I would have a tryst of my own choosing."

"To avenge him?" he demanded hotly. "Lady, I tell you! Montjoy will be looking for purity in his bride."

"He will have no right—"

"He will have every right!"

She shook her head again. "You can be wretched, sir, and horrible. But . . ."

"But?"

"Your—your person is not so horrible. It might be better to . . ." She paused, needing another breath. "Better to know you before being handed over to Montjoy!"

"And why is that? I am the man you think Montjoy should order to be hanged. The knave who brought you swimming in the moat."

"And you are the man who saved my father's life in the forest that day," she said very softly. "You saved my life, you—"

"I never said that I was that man!"

"I know that you are. You gave yourself away when we spoke before. I would offer you anything."

"But you are asking for your freedom in return!" he reminded her harshly.

"Aye, that I am."

"For a reward well given."

She colored. But she didn't protest his words. "Think about it! Oh, please!" she whispered.

"I'll think about it!" He dropped the brush in her hands and turned about, determined that he really had to leave the cabin at last. He paused only a second at the doorway, speaking to her over his shoulder.

"Rest assured, my lady, I will be thinking about your words in all the days to come. In all the weeks to come. Maybe even in all the years to come!"

He slammed his way out of the cabin.

And Katherine, watching him go, couldn't help wonder at the depths of his fury.

After all, it wasn't he she intended to betray!

Chapter 12

It was later, much later, when he dared to return to the cottage.

By then, the fire had burned low within the hearth. The room was cast in almost complete darkness and shadow.

He strode over to the pallet. She was there, lying upon it. He could easily see the white of the robe, but in the darkness he had to come close to see her face. She lay within a tangle of her hair and the robe, as if she had tossed and turned a great deal already. The material had fallen away from her long legs, and the sculpted forms of her calves and her small slim feet were just visible. She seemed to sleep very deeply.

With a sigh he lifted the helmet with its attached mail visor and set it upon the table. He rubbed his hands through his thick dark hair, stripped off his tunic and shirt, then sat to remove his boots. It was very late. He prayed that he could get some sleep.

He lay down beside her. He was barely stretched out there more than two minutes before he knew he was a fool. He would have a better rest if he slept on a rock outside!

Comfort, bah! There was no comfort beside her!

He started to rise, but before he could do so, she suddenly bolted up beside him. An anguished scream tore from her lips. "Jesu!" he cried out, putting his arms around her, pulling her back down beside him.

"Katherine, you're dreaming again!"

Her eyes were open. They were wild. He was certain that she did not see him at first, not that she could have seen more than a shape in the dark anyway. "Kat, Kat! It was a dream!"

She shuddered and turned to him, burying her face against his shoulder. He smoothed back her hair. "It's the wine," she moaned. "I drank too much wine. Not enough to elude you, and too much to sleep at all well."

She pushed away from him suddenly. She tried to open her eyes, tried to focus on him. He realized then that she had imbibed a really good quantity of wine in her pursuit of escape, and that now—with the dream leaving her—it was having a mellowing effect on her.

He suddenly felt her hand on his cheek. "Who are you?" she whispered. She was trying to see him. Too late. Her eyelashes were fluttering.

But her fingers were warm. Their caress was seductive.

He caught them. "No one . . ."

She shuddered fiercely. "The dream is horrible. De la Ville is so real in it! Tonight the Prince was there, too. I keep trying to believe that he isn't evil. But there's something about him. And the stories I hear . . ." Once again, a shudder ripped through her.

"When you marry Montjoy—"

"Montjoy is one of them!" she said fiercely.

He sighed, catching her hand. "My lady—"

"It's so awful. I'm running and then I know that I'm caught. And then—" She broke off, groaning, and turned against his shoulder once again.

He touched her cheek, touched her hair and smoothed it back. His lips brushed her hair, and her forehead, and fell against her earlobe. "It's all right. It's nothing but a dream."

Her face twisted to his. He wanted to kiss her in the darkness. Taste her lips without the mail between them.

His mouth found hers. Lightly. So lightly. Touched on it and molded to it. Parted, and parted hers beneath it, savoring her, exploring her.

And all the while . . .

Explosive things found root within his body. In his limbs, and in his loins. His arms wrapped around her. He had to touch her. More and more of her. Her fingers were shaking as he began to stroke her throat, to thrust the material from her collarbone.

To plant his lips there.

She inhaled sharply, and twisted within his hold. The supple form of her body touched him and seduced him in a way she might never have planned.

At his bidding the ties fell free from the robe and it was parted completely, baring all of her to him. Thought was gone. The desire that had eaten at him, torn at him, tormented him throughout the long day—nay, since the moment he had taken her!—surged forth to rule supreme. He rose, trying to see her face. He saw the spark of the eyes in the darkness that joined them, saw just the contours of her face. Saw her lips, glistening in what dim light they had with the moisture left from his last kiss.

His mouth lowered to hers once again. He tasted the richness of the wine they had shared, tasted the sweetness of the honey that was hers. This touch was not so gentle. Now his was a forceful kiss, one that demanded she yield, that there was more than that, for he seduced, wanting what was good and sweet, and not what could just be taken. Even in the dark desire that knew no bounds, he would have her acquiescence. His mouth molded over hers. His tongue teased her lips, worked its way past her teeth, caressed her mouth, played with her tongue. Her heart lay beneath his hand. Beating. So hard. He kissed her and kissed her, allowing his hand to move. Stroking her flesh, touching her breast, his thumb rubbing over the peak of her nipple.

Soft, muted sounds rumbled from her throat, in protest or in agreement, he did not know. Nor by that point could he really care. Her hands were upon his shoulder and chest, her fingers rubbing the taut muscles of his flesh. It had been her game. Time and time again she had been willing to play it. And now the game had commenced.

His face rose above hers. He trembled with the force it took him to move away from her. He tried to read her eyes in the darkness, yet the night that protected him also shielded her from him.

He did not want this! She was to be his wife, and his temper would forever flame at what she had done.

Ah, but his temper flamed already at her willingness to do it!

And he did want this. Wanted it with every painful, throbbing sensation in his highly aroused body. Aye, he wanted this . . .

"It's tease and taunt no longer!" he warned her, his tone husky, shaking with both anger and desire.

He felt her trembling in turn. Was she afraid?

Of him? Of Montjoy?

"If you are afraid—"

"Never afraid!" she whispered back. Her words were so soft. Slightly slurred. Bravado? The sweetness of the wine talking?

"So you would give—anything?"

"So you would ask—everything?" she returned, and a curious smile curled her lips. "You're the Silver Sword, champion of justice. A kiss, sir, I freely give!"

"A kiss, lady! I've warned you, Katherine, you value yourself too highly!"

"Do I truly? Perhaps my kiss should be worthwhile, more reward than you might imagine!" Her arms were suddenly around him. Her fingers delicately played upon his naked chest.

Her lips touched his. The tiny wet point of her tongue suddenly moved around them, licking them deliciously.

Tantalized.

She practiced her power on him, he thought, and he drew from her, though every fiber of his being demanded that he not. A kiss. A kiss she meant to give. How much more? "So you think to play and tease!" he whispered, his mouth so close to hers. Oh, she did tremble! Her flesh seemed nearly as hot as his own. That web of golden hair was around them, soft as fur, entwining them. There had never been a more beautiful or more desirable woman, even though the darkness shielded most of her from sight. Perhaps she knew it. Perhaps she was certain of her power. Perhaps she did not know quite with what she played.

Or perhaps she did know.

"Be certain!" he warned. "You are not afraid of me— or Montjoy?"

Did she, in truth, tremble fiercely then in the darkness? There were too many tricks of shadow and ebony in this room!

"I am not afraid of Montjoy!" she cried out.

And that was it for him. His anger and the feel of her beneath him seemed to explode into something together. Hunger smashed through his body, hardening the whole of it into knots. His hand fell upon her cheek, and he held her face as he kissed her again. With all his strength he tried to lessen the brutal impact of his sudden hunger, though he knew not why. Somewhere inside him he wanted to hurt her. And somewhere else inside him, he did not. His passion barely tempered then, he kissed her.

And kissed her. And did so with such demand that she was drawn into the kiss. Lips parting to his again and again as his mouth touched hers, rose just slightly, found it again. Devouring. His kisses rained down over her forehead, her cheeks, touched her eyes. Moved to her throat. Found the pulse there, massaged, caressed, demanded. And then his onslaught eased, and he used just the tip of his tongue to follow a trail down the length of her body, teasing just the side of one breast and then the other. Then he held her taut, hands on her hips, and closed his mouth on the peak of her left breast. Nuzzled it hard, tormented it with his tongue, encircling it again and again, then sweeping it deeper and deeper into his mouth, sucking seductively, and with that same hell-bent hunger. And all beneath him he could feel the vibrance of her body. Feel its quivering, as taut and as expectant as a bowstring. Sounds escaped her once again, soft cries. A thunder entered into him. A sure pounding. A pulse that beat against the shaft of his desire, and throughout the length of him. The taste of her breast, the supple movement of her body beneath him, inflamed him.

A great, sweeping shudder streaked throughout her as he kissed and touched her, his hand roving over her hip, then coming curtly and boldly between her thighs. He touched the tightly ringed curls there and she gasped. He gave no quarter, thrusting, probing, rubbing intimately.

With a cry she rose against him. He pressed her back firmly into the furs, his legs straddled over her, his weight a force against her. He met her eyes. Caught her lips again with his kiss. Then he lifted his face from hers, and she was still, her eyes closed. He lowered his body against hers. Pressed his mouth hard against her belly, then caressed the soft flesh there with his tongue. He lowered himself still further against her, fingers touching the soft, intimate petals of sex, his kiss lowering blatantly, determinedly there, the wet heat of his tongue sweeping and bathing and seducing with raw and relentless desire.

She was suddenly a swirl of protest against him, trying to rise, trying to twist. He caught hold of her hands and held them tight. The twist and writhe of her body brought her more fully against his mouth, and he probed more deeply with the thrust of his tongue. She cried out, trying to deny him. It was far too late. The very subtle but completely feminine scent of her sex surrounded him. The taste of her body filled him. The tension within him was harder than any steel, and in this moment of intimacy between them, he had claimed her in a way that she would never understand. Perhaps he would never understand it himself. The darkness, the night, the wind, all seemed to wrap around him. He would have her. Now. With the taste of her on his lips, with the air hot with the sexual tension between them, with the blood running in a rage throughout him.

"This kiss I did not offer!" she cried out in a strangled voice.

He rose over her, adjusting his chausses. "My lady, you said anything! You are far too late to barter the fine points of your contract!" he warned her in a hoarse whisper. "You offered everything!"

"I said—"

"Oh, lady! Think of all that you have said!"

He could not see her eyes, or her face, for no light seemed to enter the room then. All that he could do was feel her in the darkness. She swore suddenly, and shied away. He reached out, capturing her knees, parting her thighs, and pulling her to him with the length of her limbs spread around him. She screamed, fighting his hold then, but she was pinned by his merciless hold. His hand brushed her mound, still damp from his lips. He lowered himself against her. He could then feel that silky wet and beckoning triangle with the tip of his shaft, and a blinding lightning seemed to tear through him, wretched, cascading fire in his blood and sinew and sex. "Oh!" With a furious cry she tried to rise against him. Her wetness seemed to capture him further, to tease ever more mercilessly. And movement at all would bring him closer, closer—

And into her.

She went still.

He caught either side of her head, fascinated even now by the soft, seductive beauty of her hair, tangling more tightly about them.

He found her lips once again.

His kiss then was oddly gentle as she stiffened beneath him. Coercive.

Near tender.

And he kissed her long and lullingly. Until the tight constriction began to ease from her beguiling form.

Until the fire within his own aching body seemed hotter than molten metal. And he whispered then softly against her lips. "Lady, take care when you play! For men are made in such a way that they will be determined to win any game!"

She was silent, eyes closed, lips slightly parted.

He moved. Thrust into her. Slowly, deeply.

Her eyes flew open. A shriek tore from her lips. Her fingers clawed at his naked flesh. He did not move, but held her more closely. Felt the beating of her heart. Felt her inhale, shivering, sobbing.

"This was your doing!" he told her. "Ah, lady! You were so determined. You would learn something about men tonight!"

She did not deny it, but neither did she accept it. "Stop now!" she commanded in a tense whisper.

He shook his head. He doubted that she could see the movement. "Ah, nay, lady, those words come far too late! You are the damsel who offered everything."

Even as he spoke, he felt the give of her body to the thrust of his own. A slow, tearing give, but one that was natural. He heard the grating of her teeth as she felt him enter her more and more deeply, become a part of her.

"So it is met then!" she cried out. "The bargain is made, and I am free. Have done with it!"

He held himself over her briefly. The muscles in his face tightened with anger. He brought his lips closer to hers. "Lady, lady! You've much to learn about the fine art of negotiation. I gave you no promises, made no bargains!"

She shrieked out in fury again, rising against him.

Perfect.

By her own movement, she forced him to tear through the last of her maiden's barrier. A startled sob escaped her.

And a surprising need for tenderness seized him once again, despite the rage of desire that now seemed to scream like a war cry throughout him.

"Gently, my lady, ever gently," he whispered, and folded his arms around her. He kissed her cheek and tasted the tears she would deny were there. He found her lips, her eyelids, the lobe of her ear.

And he began to move. Slowly. Subtly. Achingly. He would take the night, if need be.

Perhaps it would . . .

But then, as he kissed her, it seemed that she kissed back. A soft sound muffled from her throat. The tension of her fingers against him eased, then began anew. Her hands moved upon his shoulders, upon his chest.

He cupped her breast. Kissed it. Teased and caressed the mound and peak with his hand and with his lips. Aye, she was beginning to give . . .

Then he knew no longer just how much he had managed to seduce her. The fires of hell seemed to burst within him. A raw and ragged drumbeat sounded and the rhythm of his thrust and stroke became a savage one. Sweet wildfire seized hold of him, demons swept through him. He drove more and more deeply into the sheath of her body, creating a raw, wild friction between them. He whispered to her. Words about her beauty, about his need. She gave him no reply, but her limbs remained locked around his, her fingers burned into his shoulders. She tensed against him. Gasped, shrieked, and buried her face against his shoulder. To his amazement, he felt a new, nectar-sweet warmth between her thighs. She had learned more than something of men this night.

She had learned something of herself.

That sweet proof of her pleasure enhanced the wild need within him, causing it to echo and rise and plummet within him. Then the fires burst. A thundrous cry tore from his throat, and a savage shudder shook the great length of his entire frame. Then again, and again. And even as he fell to her side, little aftershivers shook him anew as he slowly came down from the frantic climax that had exploded so sweetly within him. It was worth it, Jesu, anything was worth it! He didn't remember feeling like this, certainly not with Affa, and not even with . . .

Alyssa.

He ground down hard on his teeth, trying to forget the woman he had loved.

Nay! It had to have been much, much better with his beloved. She had not sobbed softly, ever, when it was over, turning away from him to try to muffle the sounds of her tears.

He started to swear in his exasperation, and almost did so in Norman French, for the words *Mon Dieu!* were on the tip of his tongue. He caught himself in time, and still his words were explosive.

"Jesu, lady! What would you have of me! All day long you have teased me and tormented me. Could you have been so innocent of men that you had no idea of what you did?"

She didn't reply. Her silence added fuel to the—perhaps unreasoning!—anger that was already growing within him.

She had betrayed him. Well, she had betrayed Montjoy, with him. Maybe she really hadn't intended to, not when it came down to it. But she had offered. Damn her! She had bargained. A night with her for her freedom.

Another oath exploded from him. "I did my very best not to hurt you, my lady. And I did very well, so I believe. Few women feel pleasure with their first experience—"

He certainly wasn't prepared for the whirlwind of her small frame turning on him. Her fists were flying furiously. She caught him in the jaw. Then beneath his eye.

"Blessed Mother!" he cried out, imprisoning her wrists, holding them tight. He had her captured then above him, her legs straddled over his hips, her hair blanketing them both. She had no idea of her perilous condition though, for she was swearing wildly at him.

"Oh, you pompous jackal! How dare you, how dare you! Bastard, knave, bandit, fool! Your conceit is incredible beyond belief, you faceless wonder! Whatever makes you think—"

He rose slightly, his fingers tensing around her wrists. "I don't think, lady. I know. And if don't take the gravest care, you will find yourself initiating a second very intimate tryst between us once again!"

"Oh!" she gasped. Then she must have felt the pulsing rise of him beneath her for she gasped again and tried valiantly to free herself. He let her struggle until she realized that she could not combat his strength. Then, regretfully, he let her go.

She had curled up against the wall. He couldn't see her, but he could feel her there. He swore again. "I tried not to hurt you, lady," he said very softly.

After a moment he heard a ragged sigh, and then her reply. "You did not. Aye, you did, you did! But then . . ."

He smiled in the darkness. There was a wonder to her tone. She hadn't imagined that she could actually enjoy what she herself had offered.

"Oh, God!" she cried out suddenly, and he sensed that she was burying her face in her hands. Memories, intimate, detailed memories, were surging through her, he was certain. "Never, never!" she whispered. "I didn't think—oh, Jesu! I could hang you myself!"

"But think about it!" he advised her lightly, warring with his temper once again. "Better this with me—than with Montjoy."

"Oh, God! Never! I'll never, ever be so with Montjoy! Never so—intimately!" she stated passionately.

Oh, just wait, my lady! You cannot imagine just how intimately you will be with Montjoy! he swore in silence.

"I'm free now—" she began softly.

"I gave you no promise!"

"But you are the Silver Sword! You must behave decently. You must give me your word."

"I cannot do that."

"You will! You must!"

He leaped up from the bed, adjusting his chausses. He wrenched his shirt from the chair where it rested, then fumbled in the ebony darkness for the rest of his clothing and mail. At last he spun around to her. "One thing is certain, my lady, you've the hours till dawn in peace!"

He threw open the door and paused there, looking back with a raw fury. "Indeed, you've the hours till morn!"

He slammed the door behind him and stared blindly into the night.

"Oh, aye, my lady! You will be so intimately with Montjoy! Trust me! And soon, my lady! Very, very soon!"

He sat on the rock, as he should have done in the first place.

He waited for the hours to pass, alternately furious and bemused.

Vengeance, he promised, would be his.

In that tempest, he let the hours of the night pass, making certain that she was trusting in her certainty that the Silver Sword meant to let her go, and that she did not intend to escape.

As dawn neared, he whistled for his horse, and then swiftly rode the distance to Clifford Castle, his own home and inheritance.

He was barely there before he turned around.

Katherine had spent the rest of the night in a tumult of anger and wonder and fear. What had she done! She trembled, wondering what a husband would do when he discovered her to be . . . less than a maiden.

She replayed within her heart and mind each small thing that had happened.

Each little thing that he had done.

Each caress. Each touch.

She remembered the pain and the fury.

And she remembered the burst of wonder . . .

And her body colored, and she refused to let herself think anymore. But the truth would come back to haunt her again and again. She had let herself be taken by a total stranger in an ebony darkness.

A man whose face she would not recognize were she ever to see it!

"Oh, sweet Jesu!" she cried out, and hugged herself, and swallowed hard.

It was only the amount of wine she had drunk in her determination to be free that finally granted her an hour's solace at last. She could sleep. She had to sleep. And it was all right. He was gone. He did have his honor. He meant to honor the bargain, though he had said that he had made no bargain. He would not turn her over to Montjoy.

And indeed, both her life and her virtue had lain in peril. She didn't know what the future would hold. He had managed to give her . . . something. Something sweet. And she couldn't hate him or despise herself because . . .

No matter what he said, she knew that he had been the hidden archer in the forest the day that she had ridden in with her father. He had been the man to save them, when it had seemed that all was lost.

He had saved her father's life. For that alone, she would have given him anything.

She didn't know that she had finally slept until she was rudely awakened by the sound of a multitude of horses prancing within the copse beyond the cottage wall.

Her eyes flew open, and she wondered at the sound. Then panic seized her.

She was still alone. Alone in the bed she had shared intimately with the Silver Sword. Her head was still spinning. It had been the wine. It had blurred everything.

Nay, none of it had been really blurred in the least, not the pain, not the pleasure.

Oh, what had she done?

And who was coming now?

She clutched the white furred robe to her breast and leaped out of the bed, trying to wrap her garment more tightly about her. A million fears swept through her.

It was de la Ville. He had found her.

It was Prince John.

It was . . .

The door burst open. The sun blinded her for a moment. She stood there, wrapped in the white robe, her hair still a wild tangle from the night of intimacy that had so recently passed, trying to shield her eyes from the brightness of the day.

And then she saw him.

Montjoy.

Tall, hard, and ebony-haired, the man stood imposingly, his muscled shoulders filling the doorway, his silver eyes blazing as they seemed to pinion her there. He was fully, nobly clad in his family colors, his Norman lions emblazoned on his tunic. Handsome, arrogant—and Norman!—he stood there, assessing her.

"My lady. I had heard that I would find you here. Safe, and waiting."

The French tones fell over her courteously—with no affection. For a moment she felt her knees quivering.

Damn him. Damn the Silver Sword! He had betrayed her!

And damn Montjoy. She would have none of him!

"Come, Katherine. We do not know one another well, perhaps, but we are not strangers. You know that I am Lord Damian Montjoy. Count Clifford. And Richard has commanded that we shall be man and wife."

She found her courage. "I understand that the King has ordered a betrothal—" she began, but Montjoy chuckled softly.

"A betrothal, my lady! Ah, but these are dangerous times. We shall be married immediately."

"But we cannot! The Church—"

"Immediately, my lady. Why, a priest awaits us this very minute. And you are beautifully dressed for the occasion in pure, virginal white."

Color flushed her cheeks. "My lord, I tell you that I cannot—"

"Ah, but my lady!" Sharp, furious silver eyes narrowed upon her. "I assure you. You will!"

Chapter 13

Kat paced the confines of her bedchamber in a fury of thought and motion.

God in his heaven! What was she going to do now? She damned the Silver Sword to a dozen painful deaths, still unable to grasp the fact that the man had betrayed her.

He had never made her any promises, she reminded herself. He had been set on turning her over to Montjoy. But if he had been so set, and if he admired the man so very much, how could he have made love to her?

And how could she have enjoyed it?

No!

She couldn't think about it. She dared not think about it. Her cheeks grew too hot, and a wild sense of panic swept through her once again.

He had not just given her to Montjoy. He had betrayed her, and then given her to Montjoy. And after bursting into the cottage and so coldly informing her what was to be, Montjoy had ordered that she be given a cloak and taken home. One of his men had rushed in with a cloak, and that same man had courteously escorted her outside to a small mare that had evidently been brought along for her use.

Montjoy had had nothing else to say to her. He had been impatiently waiting at the head of his party of men, and as soon as she was mounted, he was ready to ride. She had been afraid that he planned to take her to his home, Clifford Castle, but thankfully, he had not.

But upon their arrival at the castle, he had lifted her down from the mare himself. He had tried to speak with her then—to push the idea of an immediate marriage, she was certain—but her wits had come about her at last and she had tossed back her hair, forced her voice to be both soft and caring, and pleaded exhaustion and a chance to bathe and rest before he should speak with her anymore.

And so she was now upstairs in her own chamber, awaiting bathwater, while Montjoy was downstairs, speaking with her household servants, introducing himself as their new lord and master.

A tap sounded on her door. She strode across to it and threw it open. Marie was there, red-cheeked and beaming. "Kat!" she cried, enfolding her mistress tightly in her arms. And Kat hugged her in return, suddenly riddled by guilt. She had forgotten just what good people she had, and how concerned they must have been for her safety. "Ah, love! We worried about you so! The whole of the castle knew that you had escaped those wretched henchmen of de la Ville's." She paused, clapping her hands. "Ah, that wonderful man! It was a miracle! He'd come to save you!" Marie sighed deeply, and with pleasure, looking heavenward as if the Silver Sword had arrived by some divine intervention. "The saints be praised, for they sent one of their own down among us!"

"The man is no saint, pray trust me on that!" Kat said, and drew Marie into her room. She was ready to shut the door, but Howard was right behind Marie, and a half dozen of the kitchen lads were behind him, all carrying heavy buckets of water. Howard bowed to her, looking as if he ached to give her a great hug, too, but knew that propriety would not allow it.

"Dear Howard!" she said, and gave him a quick kiss on the cheek that made him blush.

"'Tis grateful we are, lady, to have ye back!" he said. "All the lads and I—and the guard. Of course, 'tis bitter sorry the men are to have been so deceived by some traitor in our own midst! Why even now, my lady, Sir Gunther begs pardon to Lord Montjoy about the travesty of it."

"He begs pardon to Montjoy!" Kat gasped. "He owes Montjoy no pardon, nor does he even need beg it from me. I shall see to this situation myself. Why, men were injured, killed here in my defense—"

"My lady!" Marie warned softly. The lads dumping the steaming bathwater into her tub were watching her with a certain awe. Of course, that meant gossip would fly in the kitchens and stables and servants quarters this night. They all seemed amazed that even she would think to cross a man like Lord Montjoy.

She tossed back her hair. "I don't care! This is my property! Not his!"

"Very shortly his," Marie murmured uneasily.

Kat shook her head fervently. "Nay, I cannot marry him, Marie! I cannot."

Howard frowned. Marie shook her head likewise to him, and clutched Kat's arm. "It seems the water is delivered and that it might be a good time—"

Kat ignored her and turned, heading for the stairs. Her hair was still in a very wild tangle, but she was wearing the cloak that Montjoy had provided her, and she refused to feel like a child confined to her chamber while he went about her castle chastising her servants and her guard. She had descended the stairway more than halfway before she realized that she was afraid of Montjoy, and with good reason. But even as she reached the great hall, she knew it was too late to back down. He was seated at the banqueting table, and Sir Gunther, tall, slim, lean, hard, and gnarled as an old oak, stood before him with a drawing of the castle plan spread out on the table. Jenny, one of the young kitchen wenches, was busy pouring Montjoy a chalice of wine, while Meg, an older woman, second cook after Howard, was setting out a plate of cold smoked meats.

"My lady!" Sir Gunther cried, and took long broad steps to meet her, kneeling down and taking her hand. "Forgive me!"

"There is nothing to forgive," she said quickly. "Rise, Sir Gunther. We were tricked—"

"And should not have been tricked so easily," Montjoy said, rising, his voice already harsh with an authority to overrule hers. "Sir Gunther, as the Lady Katherine seems so determined to speak with me before resting from her ordeal, we will continue this later."

"Aye, my lord!"

"We, Sir Gunther, you and I, will continue this discussion later," Kat said firmly.

"Aye, my lady," Sir Gunther said, looking a bit unhappily from one of them to the other.

"I will send for you when Lady Katherine returns to her chamber for her bath," Montjoy said softly. Kat stared at him, dismayed at the shiver that seized her, and determined that she must find a way to have her temper and her wits keep her from the wretched hands of this new enemy. Ah, no! Montjoy was no de la Ville. Far to the contrary. As he stood he seemed the darkest, most dangerous knight. His hair was so deep a color that it seemed to be as black as a raven's wing. It was not cut so short as the usual Norman fashion, and curled somewhat at his neck. It framed a face that was handsome with its very high cheekbones and hard, squared jaw. There were minor scars upon his cheeks, attesting to the fact that he was a warrior lord, as the kings he had served were warrior kings. Those scars, however, were faded and pale, and took nothing away from the cleanly chiseled appearance of his countenance. She had heard that many women found him irresistible.

Those women, she was certain, had never looked into his eyes. They were silver-gray, menacing—ruthless!— hot as fire one moment, and cool as slate the next. This was all business to him. Acquisition. He was here assessing his gain, and she was no more than an annoying piece of that gain.

After Sir Gunther left Jenny and Meg looked at each other quickly, then scurried from the banqueting hall.

Kat realized they were left alone, she and Montjoy.

She was starting to shake as he stared at her. It seemed that he was looking right through her. As if he carried a deep-seated fury against her. And yet, he could not! Not unless he knew that she had been the girl in the forest that day. Nay, Robin had told her Montjoy had taken her for a peasant. He couldn't recognize her now when she was dressed so differently.

But what if he knew what had gone on in that cottage?

He could not. The Silver Sword would surely have risked his own neck to carry such a tale!

It was suddenly hard to breathe. She had to speak quickly. "I will thank you, sir, to leave the affairs of my castle to me," she said.

He leaned against the table, his arms crossing formidably over his chest. "I will thank you, my lady, to see to women's affairs. Like your bath and dressing, so that we may be wed."

"This castle, the people who abide within its walls and beyond them, are my concern. Falling stone is my concern, food and clothing are my concern, and our strength and our loyalty to King Richard are all my concern. I have done well here. It is my birthright. As to the other, I cannot marry you. I—"

"I beg to differ, my lady. I have all the proper documents and dispensations. We will be wed this very day, just as soon as you are prepared."

She quickly ascertained that she was not going to talk him out of a wedding. Perhaps arguing was a mistake.

She lowered her head, and her words were very soft. "You don't understand, my Lord Montjoy. I have just endured a most horrible experience—"

"Aye, two days in the wilderness," he murmured, and she thought his tone was sympathetic.

She raised her eyes to his. "After a dive into the moat! Freezing by night, starving, thirsting—"

"How amazing! From all the stories that I have heard of this Silver fellow, I was quite certain that he would have seen to it that you had food and drink. They say, in fact, that he must be some fellow who owes his loyalty to me, for he seems to know his way about my lands quite well. There was wine in the cottage."

"I know," Katherine said, trying to keep her voice light and sweet. "There was wine. I had wine. Too much wine—"

"What was that? I do beg your pardon, my lady."

"Nothing, my lord! Can't you understand? It was a trying experience—"

"Trying?" he repeated politely.

She nodded emphatically. "Wretched!"

"Wretched? The Silver Sword was wretched? Did he threaten you?"

She almost stepped back at the violence in his voice. And to her annoyance, she was afraid for the Silver Sword.

She did owe him something.

Even if he owed her much, much more!

"Nay!" she said quickly. "Only if I attempted to escape. You see—"

"Escape? Why would you want to escape a man who had rescued you from de la Ville and meant to hold you safe for me?"

"Safe for you—!" she began, her temper rising, but then she remembered herself quickly. "My lord, there is so much treachery these days, I dared not trust anyone. I knew nothing of Richard's plans until he told me, and how could I know, truly, what to believe?"

"Ah!" he murmured.

"So you do understand," Kat said. "You will give me time."

"Nay, my lady, I think not."

"What?"

"I said, I think not. We will be wed this afternoon."

"You don't understand—"

"You don't understand," he told her bluntly. "There is always rebellion afoot, so it seems, and I will not add fuel to the fire, engaging in a fratricidal war if you are left a tempting prize, dangling there even a second longer, for someone to think to snatch!"

"But—"

"Do you think that de la Ville will stop trying to seize you? Aye, lady, you are important. This castle is important. We cannot leave the strength of this place at risk, not for a moment longer. I missed the fall of Jerusalem for this, my lady! I will argue with you no longer!"

"Well, sir, I will not say the words! I have had no time to prepare my soul, to speak with my confessor—"

"To prepare your soul? My lady, you are marrying, not dying. And if you think you need a confessor, I will be happy to send you a priest immediately."

"Forget the priest! My sins are not so great!"

Weren't they? What of last night . . . ? she asked herself.

"I shall be happy to listen to any confessions you wish to make myself," he remarked, watching her with cool speculation.

"Hell shall burn with icicle flames ere that shall happen, my lord, I assure you!"

"Then you may confess to yourself while you bathe. My patience grows very short."

"As does mine! Your insistence is terribly unchivalrous. I am not ready to wed—"

"Who ever is, my lady?"

"I am not ready to share anything with you!"

"A pity. We will be wed."

She thought quickly. "All right. I shall agree to the wedding. If you will swear before God right now that you will not insist upon our—our sleeping in the same quarters. If you will not—"

"Demand my conjugal rights?" he suggested, amused as she sought the words.

"Aye," she said coldly. "If you will give me a year, perhaps—"

He was smiling.

"Six months," she amended quickly.

"Six hours, perhaps," he said very softly, "depending upon my mood. But fear not—I swear that I will see to it that you know me very, very well, and quickly so!"

Speechless for the moment, she stared at him furiously. She wished that she were a man. She longed to take a sword to him.

She had taken a sword to him once. And he had beaten her easily. Then he had taken a hand against her, and spanked her like a child.

He wouldn't dare behave so now! Now she was a lady. Back then he thought that he had captured a village wench.

Ah! She wished that she could tie his hands behind his back and then take a sword to him. That would do it.

But even as the thoughts of bravado came to her, she felt a shivering inside. He meant to wed tonight. And he would know then that he hadn't received the wife he had expected.

"Bastard!" she hissed, heedless of the fire that leaped to his eyes. "You will be very sorry, sir, if you marry me."

He threw up his arms in exasperation. "Pray, lady! I am sorry at this moment! But we will wed. And if you are capable of being demure and quiet and well-behaved, we will have an easy enough time of it. And if not . . ." He let the words trail away. "No matter," he warned darkly. "We will wed."

She fought the fear that swept over her. "I am not demure and I am not well-behaved! This is my castle, my inheritance, and I—"

She broke off because he had pushed away from the table and was striding toward her. She was not going to run from him! He wouldn't dare commit any violence here, in her own home!

He continued coming toward her purposefully, menacingly.

"My lord, I am warning you—"

"And I am warning you, my lady. You've two seconds to turn around and march up those stairs and bathe. Else I will take you there myself."

"Nay, my lord, you will not!"

"One second."

"Nay!"

"Aye!"

She gasped in astonishment as he ruthlessly swept her up into his arms. For a moment she clung to him lest she should fall, meeting the silver glitter of his eyes. Then she swallowed down fear and surprise, and cried out, slamming a fist against his chest, struggling fiercely in his hold. It meant nothing to him. Ruthless step by ruthless step, he made his way to the stairs, and then up the length of them. Marie and Howard, their hands folded nervously before them, still stood in the doorway in front of her bedchamber.

"Out!" he charged them in a thundrous voice.

"Marie—" Kat managed to gasp.

But Marie didn't want to hear her. She and Howard both dashed away down the stairs. Montjoy carried her inside and kicked the door closed behind him.

Kat twisted wildly, whispering. French curses, desperately trying to free herself.

"And you, my love, are risking great damage to your posterior section!" he promised.

She was suddenly on her feet, spinning around to meet his eyes. At least he had put her down.

"Jackal!" she cried.

He was not done with her. His hand reached out, snatching the cloak from her. In dismay she watched the heavy material give in his hands. His eyes were on her. Flickering over the robe.

The robe he had given the Lady Alyssa.

His gaze met hers again. He meant to have the robe back, and right then and there.

"No!" she cried, and turned to run. He caught her hair and spun her back. She shrieked in protest, near tears.

For his hands were on her. Blatantly on her naked flesh, slipping beneath the robe to untie it. The garment fell to her feet. Once again she turned to run.

And once again a furious and mortified cry tore from her lips, for he was, indeed, ruthless and relentless. She was swept up into his arms, made acutely aware of his rough knight's hands on her soft flesh. She squirmed, she writhed, she fought against him, then she gasped, astounded, near drowning, as he quickly dropped her into the tub of now-cooling water.

She emerged, furious, choking and coughing, and looking at him with all the malevolence in her soul. When she could breathe at last, she said simply, "You bastard!"

He nodded, arms crossing over his chest once again. "Know it well, my lady. I will be whatever it takes. I pray that you will come to understand. I, at the very least, pray for your continued good health and long life. De la Ville has never cared for anything but his own amusement. I wish to be gentle—"

"Gentle!" she gasped. "This is gentle?"

"I am what you make of me," he promised her softly. His hand was upon her nape. She felt the startlingly seductive movement of his fingers there. His voice sent a tremor along her spine as he spoke again. "Now, can I safely leave you to bathe on your own? Or shall I help you? Wash your hair, scrub your back?"

"No!"

He bowed courteously, with as much finesse as if they were at court.

And then he turned to leave her.

Stunned, Kat sat very still in the cooling water. Then she swore violently.

She heard the door open tentatively. She gripped the rim of the tub, shaking, trying to summon her forces to do battle once again.

But it wasn't Montjoy. Marie stood there, waiting. "My Lady Kat!" she exclaimed, and she slipped quickly into the room, closing the door behind her. "He—he wants the wedding to take place in an hour. I've come to help you."

Kat stared at her. Marie hurried across the room, delved around Kat's dressing table, and found sweetly scented soap and a sponge. She came to the bath with both, and began to wash Kat's hair.

But Kat swung around on her. "I cannot marry him!" she said, near panic.

"Well, he does seem very fierce, but if you were just a bit more agreeable yourself—"

"You don't understand! I cannot marry him!" Her panic was growing. "For so many reasons. He's probably had half of the women in Richard's retinue! Queen Eleanor once said that men could do what they pleased—that she was quite certain that Henry had even had affairs with Rosamund Clifford's sheep!—but that it was different for women."

"My lady, what are you talking about?"

Kat shook her head, her fingers gripping the rim of the tub. She couldn't tell Marie about what had happened last night. She longed to tell her, but she couldn't.

Not even Marie would understand. So she said simply, "I really, truly, can't marry him."

"Let's rinse your hair."

Kat didn't move. Marie ducked her head beneath the water, trying to smooth out the wet skeins of her hair.

Kat came back to the surface. Marie swept up the length of her hair and started to soap her back. "Kat, it will be all right. Truly. Think of it! King Richard sent this man back, one of his best warriors, on your behalf. He cannot be so bad a man. And I have heard that he was devoted to the Lady Alyssa—"

"I saw how he was devoted to Alyssa!" Kat murmured.

She had seen him that one day with Alyssa, yes. And she had assumed that he was harsh and cold and distant with her. But even then, Alyssa had smiled warmly; her eyes had been adoring.

Maybe he had loved Alyssa. The Silver Sword had been certain that Montjoy had loved her. But the Silver Sword had loved her himself. Alyssa had been worthy of such adoration. She had been so gentle, kind, and warm.

So perhaps he really had cared most tenderly for Alyssa. He did not love her, Kat!

She grabbed the soap from Marie and suddenly started to scrub her arms, and then her breasts, with a fury. De la Ville, Prince John, the Silver Sword—Montjoy! They were all alike! She hated them all. She wanted the touch of that traitorous Silver Sword off her!

Oh, aye . . .

Because Montjoy's touch was coming!

Nay, nay, nay, it couldn't be.

With soap and sponge, she still bathed as if she were covered with a soot that could be removed. Marie watched her worriedly, wondering if her usually level-headed mistress had lost her mind.

The fall into the moat might have done it.

"Kat!" Marie knelt down by the tub and loving-ly smoothed back her wet hair. "I had not imagined that marriage would frighten you so. But then you're always so very certain and strong. I wish your dear mother were here. She would say all the right things, and you would not be so afraid of what will happen. If you just knew a little more about men—"

"I know all that I wish to know about men," Kat replied dryly. "I'm not afraid, I'm just—" She broke off and then she stared at Marie. "I have it!"

Kat rose, water sluicing from her body. She reached quickly for the huge linen bath towel Marie offered her and wrapped it around herself as she stepped from the tub. "Find me something a bit rugged to wear—"

Marie gasped. "You don't mean the green—"

"Aye, that would be fine!" Kat said, then she paused. No. Not the colors of the Lady Greensleeves. If she was discovered escaping, she could not risk the other identity that was so important to her.

She could not be discovered! she told herself. But she said softly to Marie, "Nay, not the green. Something similar. A very simple undergown and tunic. Both a bit short. Wool hose, and my plain wool cloak."

"For your wedding?" Marie said in dismay.

Kat didn't reply. She was at the door to the secret tunnel. It had failed her when she had tried to escape de la Ville. She could not let it fail her now.

She pressed upon it, praying. It stuck. She wet her lips, and pressed again with force.

It gave, and gave so suddenly that she almost went flying right through it in her bath towel.

"Blessed Jesu, God you are above me!" she cried.

"Oh, nay!" Marie wailed. "Kat, you cannot run away from him!"

"Marie—but I can! I must!" she insisted. She hurried away from the tunnel doorway, quickly donning the clothing that Marie had brought her, then plucking up her brush to work on her hair.

Her hands froze for a moment. She remembered the feel when the Silver Sword's hands had worked on her hair.

Then she remembered the feel of his hands elsewhere and started to tremble. Ah, men! If the lot of them could just crumble into the earth!

"How can you even think of doing such a thing when you were in such horrible danger before! When you had to leap from the parapets—into the moat! There won't be a legendary savior at every twist and turn in the days to come, not so many miracles—"

"So he's a miracle now, is he?" she interrupted irritably, throwing her brush down on her bed. "Trust me, Marie, the legendary Silver Sword is neither saint nor miracle!"

"But you are still threatened by de la Ville! Montjoy will, at least, keep you from that monster. Kat, this is the King's command—"

"The King is not here," Kat said flatly. "How do I know his command?"

"Montjoy carries his orders, and his signet, and all the Church's dispensations so that the wedding can take place at any time," Marie argued.

"You are afraid of him," Kat accused her.

"Ha!" Marie chortled in return. "You are afraid of him, my lady—and there's the rub to you!"

"I haven't the time to carry on with this conversation," Kat said sternly. Then she gave Marie a fierce hug. "Get yourself downstairs and say that I insisted on being my own lady's maid. That way you will not be blamed when I cannot be found."

"Oh, Kat!" Marie eyes were worried. "Don't do this thing. Montjoy is not so bad."

"He is arrogant to the very teeth! Muscle-bound and reckless and—"

"Aye!" Marie agreed, her voice carrying a little breathlessness. Kat stared at her incredulously.

"You . . . like him! He's been wretched. He came in here spouting out orders, he humiliated me in my own hall—and you like him!" Her tone was hurt.

"Oh, I'm sure he never meant to humiliate you. He will just have his way, so it seems. You're very much alike."

"I beg your pardon!" Kat exclaimed.

Marie sighed, and smiled. "He seems bold and adventurous and exciting. Kat, please, think about this!"

But Kat would not be dissuaded. "I'm going! Get downstairs now. I'd not have you accused of complicity."

"Kat, please—"

"No!"

Kat felt Marie's eyes on her as she disappeared into the secret doorway.

Then she was alone. Blinking against the darkness in the narrow corridor, she carefully pushed the door closed, making sure that it was properly in place. She caught her breath for a moment, wondering if she wasn't really a fool.

But if she didn't run, she would soon be wed to Montjoy, sharing—everything!

She thought of meeting with the man in her hall below, and of how he had swept her up, heedless of anyone around them, to bring her back to her room. Of how he had taken her robe away.

Plunged her naked into the tub. And set his fingers on the flesh of her nape, warning her . . .

Blindly she turned around in the darkness.

And fled.

Chapter 14

Damian stood outside the castle walls, in the forest across the moat, and stared at the edifice, studying it. The castle was magnificent, he determined. It wasn't nearly so large a place as nearby Nottingham, nor was it so very different from his own stronghold of Clifford Castle. It was just that the planning of it was ingenious. The walls were high and stark. The encircling moat was a fantastic barrier, not a cesspool of complete filth, as so many moats were, because the builders had seen to it that a drainage system had been dug connecting the moat to Lake Ure, a beautiful body of fresh water with many free-flowing tributaries. If the bridge was up and the towers and the parapets were manned, the castle could probably withstand almost any army, any siege. Though the villeins' fields were, of necessity, beyond the walls and moats, the great courtyard of the castle housed many trades. The blacksmith, the cooper, carpenters, stone masons, merchants, and more kept their businesses against the inner walls of the castle. As he had just gleaned by the castle plans, there were vast storerooms of food and grain and hay beneath the living quarters. One tower housed armaments.

The place was, indeed, an incredible prize. He had been lucky to acquire it.

Aye, he had given up the fall of Jerusalem for this,

but perhaps it had not been so bad a trade. With his own property, he now had vast and extensive holdings that would surely place him as one of the most important barons in England, certainly in the north. Between the Clifford Castle and the castle at Ure, he would have the power he needed to carry out King Richard's order that he keep Prince John and his rapacious minions in check.

All he need do was keep *her* in check . . .

The thought rankled him anew. It was time. He had been admiring his new holdings long enough. Now he needed to go secure them.

Despite himself, despite his absolute determination to think of his loyalty to Richard and the strength he would gain from this marriage, he felt the hot fire of emotion licking into his heart—and loins—once again.

"I do not want to hurt you, wench!" he whispered aloud through clenched teeth.

But maybe that was a lie. She'd been willing to use anything to escape him, even her virtue, her honor. What should have been a great prize to her husband, she had cast aside.

What if he himself were not the Silver Sword!

She would have betrayed him already. Not for the sake of love, but out of hatred. The only gentleness he had ever seen about her had been when she spoke about her father, and his love for her mother.

Nay, maybe there had been more. She loved Robin. That was obvious. And she was so very passionate about her people. She was dedicated to them, determined, and had great strength of spirit. The lady was no coward.

She was seeping her way into his soul! he warned himself. Aye, she was courageous, she was lovely, she could fight like a little tigress. She was far more than he had expected, even knowing that she had prowled the forest as the Lady Greensleeves.

Well, her father had spoiled her. And now there were things that she would just have to learn, and he would have to continue to treat her firmly and coldly.

Coldly! When he burned inside and out, thinking of her? He might long to wind his fingers around her neck and shake the very defiance from her eyes, but even as he did so it seemed that the blood and fire within him created their own resolve. He wanted her. Again. Like some sweet potent wine he had tasted, he craved the taste again.

His wedding was about to commence. And just how, he wondered, was he going to deal with this traitorous little bride of his?

More intriguing still . . .

How did she intend to deal with him? So far, she had not rushed forward with any confessions!

Well, he would discover her intentions very soon, he thought. He mounted Lucien, the black stallion who was half-brother to Lucifer whom the Silver Sword rode, and started for the castle. Even as he rode toward it, he narrowed his eyes, for a horseman was racing across the drawbridge. It was his castellan and very loyal retainer, Sir James Courtney.

Knowing that something was very wrong, he nudged his thighs against Lucien's flanks, and the stallion burst forth in tight gallop to meet Sir James at the end of the drawbridge.

His redheaded, freckle-faced young servant was fraught with tension as he drew his horse to a halt before Damian.

"What in God's name has happened?" Damian began.

"Damian—she's gone!"

"She—who?"

"The Lady Katherine. The announcements had been carried into all the villages as you ordered. The kitchen villeins have all received their orders for a wedding feast.

Father Jacob had arrived. All was in preparation. But when the serving woman went to the Lady Katherine's room to escort the lady down, she found nothing but an empty bedchamber."

Damian's eyes narrowed fiercely. The fire shot through him. Damn her to a thousand hells! She did not learn!

Damn her, indeed, he thought furiously. So she was out there somewhere. She didn't begin to realize that de la Ville might be out there, too. And if de la Ville found her before she was legally wed . . .

He would kill de la Ville with his bare hands before ever allowing the man to touch what was his.

"You're quite certain that she is gone?" he thundered.

"Aye, Damian! For when her lady's maid gave us the word, we searched first her chambers, then the castle, high and low."

"Perhaps she is hiding. Maybe her people would hide her, thinking they did her a great service."

Sir James shook his head. "I don't believe it can be so. Her maid is white with worry. We can put pressure on these villeins, of course, but . . ."

"Aye, pressure! Torture! And be no better than the men we must combat!" Damian said angrily. "How in all of hell might she have escaped?"

"We watched the hall, I swear it, Damian!" James told him passionately.

And he had watched the drawbridge himself, Damian thought. Who had come and gone? Men to the fields. A few lads with a flock of geese. Had she costumed herself?

"Damian," James said in confusion, "I watched even the faces of those who came and went. Is she a witch?"

"She is a witch all right, thought I do not believe in witchcraft," Damian muttered darkly.

Yet, was there such a thing? He suddenly remembered

Ari on a dark desert night, feeling the wind, watching the stars up above.

She will betray you . . .

And she had done so. The exact beauty he had described. The woman with her golden hair and aquamarine eyes, eyes to rival the rippling waters of the seas . . .

"Is a horse missing? Did you speak with the grooms and stableboys?"

"Aye, Damian, I did. She rides a gray mare, Elisha. She has not taken her mount, or any other."

"Then she has escaped on foot, and I will find her," Damian said flatly.

"I will ride with you. Let me call out the others—"

"Nay. I will find her myself. Go back, pray. See that the wedding preparations continue."

"But, if you cannot find her—"

"Do as I say," Damian commanded. He felt his temper soaring like a dark fever within him. "I'll find her. So I swear it, I will find her!"

Could he really do so? he wondered briefly. The forest was immense, and she could be anywhere.

Nay. She would head straight for Robin. "Aye, I will find her!" he repeated. He tugged a command upon his reins. Lucien rose with a wild, excited snort, pranced upon his hind legs, then stormed into a gallop that carried him away from the castle.

And into the woods.

Afternoon shadows were already coming to the forest when Kat left the tunnel behind her.

The late afternoon was clear, cool, and beautiful. She felt as if she were surrounded by a comforting blanket of green. This was part of the forest she knew very well. The grasses here were exceptionally soft. The lush embankments led to beautiful brooks. Trees formed exquisite canopies over her head.

For several long minutes, she ran. She wanted to go as far from the castle as quickly as she could. But though she was swift and surefooted, she quickly tired. Gasping, panting, she looked back to the castle.

Had they discovered her missing yet? Maybe not, maybe she still had time. All that she had to do was come deep into the forest and find the first of Robin's lookouts. Then she could reach her cousin, and God help her, she would be safe from all men, once she had thrown herself on his mercy. Perhaps he would disapprove. It didn't matter. He would help her. And she wouldn't risk his all-important function within the forest. She would see to it that she left him just as quickly as she came. Some help outside the forest—even a touch of monetary help!—and she could make her way secretly to London, and then onward to find the King. It would be difficult, but it could be done.

Ah, especially if she went straight from Robin to Eleanor of Aquitaine. The Dowager Queen, in her old age now, was still a formidable matriarch. John had been a favorite of Henry's, but not so with Eleanor. She loved her youngest son, but knew every one of his weaknesses and perversities.

She blamed them all on his father, of course.

When Henry had been king, Eleanor had been imprisoned. One of Richard's first orders at the news of his father's death was that his mother be released.

And so it had been. And now Eleanor was free, and very powerful, and as wildly independent as she had ever been. She had been married to two kings, Louis of France and Henry of England. She and Louis had very willingly divorced, and her two daughters were half-sisters to King Phillip.

Eleanor had outlived both kings. Her outlook on life was very pragmatic. She was not, however, without a vivid sense of romance and adventure, and she might very well understand that Katherine wasn't defying Richard, that she merely wanted to see the King herself and present her case to him.

It occurred to her as she saw the tall towers of the castle rising above the trees behind her that she was giving up a great deal because of Damian Montjoy.

She was leaving her own home behind her. Leaving a people who had learned her ways, who depended her.

And it was surely true that it was a woman's lot in this world to be wed. Perhaps marriage was a sacrifice, but maybe, just maybe, it was one she should have made.

If she left England, she could no longer be of any assistance to Robin. If she had wed Montjoy, she might have been privy to even more information that might have stood Robin very well.

A little shudder streaked through her, bringing with it a chill of dismay. Maybe she had acted like a fool. She was left out here now with nothing.

Montjoy had everything.

Damn! It was all his fault. He had been so heartless! He hadn't begun to understand.

But it would have been so much worse once they were wed . . .

It didn't matter now. She had run. There was nothing to do but keep on running.

She had caught her breath, but she didn't feel quite so afraid now. The afternoon was growing darker and darker. She would be close to Robin soon.

Her stomach suddenly growled. How long had it been since she had really eaten? There had been those bites of bread and cheese and nothing more.

Oh, no, there had been that wine! That wine that had dulled her wits, that had made her thoughts and her words so very reckless. The wine that made something magical of a stranger's caress in the dark . . .

"No!" she whispered out loud. And she looked to

heaven. "Damn them all!" she swore. "Dear God, forgive me, but they are knaves, every one of them!"

God did not answer her. Her stomach did, growling once again. There was nothing to be done for it, not until she could find Robin. But she turned her feet toward the brook, hoping that a long swallow of cool water would help to fend off her hunger.

She found the brook in the growing green darkness and bent down on her knees before it. She drank a long cool swallow of the water, then bathed her face. She closed her eyes, shivering as trickles of water trailed down her throat and beneath her tunic and underdress. She bent down to the water once again, cupping her hands for a last drink.

But then she froze. For in the darkened pool of rippling water before her she could see the weaving mirrored image of a man on horseback. She stared at the water as the ripples began to fade, her hands cupped above it without moving.

Then she swung around, incredulous. He was there. Behind her.

He wore no cape or cloak against the encroaching coolness of the night. He did not seem to feel cold or dampness—any more than he might feel the least sensitivity to her position. He was as deaf to the whispers of the wind as he was to her pleas. He had come after her in his undershirt of plain fawn linen, his dark chausses, his crested tunic, his high leather boots—and his low-slung scabbard and sword.

"Get up!" he commanded sharply. She stared at him, dazed for a moment, unable to believe that she had risked so much for freedom—and lost it all so swiftly.

She gasped as he slipped his sword from his scabbard, urging his horse forward, and setting the tip of the blade to her throat.

"Get up," he repeated angrily.

She jumped to her feet, eyeing him as she backed away from the blade, trying to skirt around him. His eyes were like silver daggers, no less sharp than the honed edge of his blade, piercing through her.

He could not have come upon her! He could not have caught her so easily here! She knew this part of the forest! He did not!

But apparently he did, for he had found her, and quickly.

"What kind of coward are you, Montjoy, to come after a woman with a sword?" she demanded quickly.

"What kind of coward are you, my lady, to run so quickly from one who would protect you!" he roared in return.

There was some distance now between them. He had never meant to use a sword against her, she realized. He just wanted her on her feet. He expected those around him to jump when he commanded them to do so.

There was a clearing before her. And then a dense group of trees. Perhaps too dense for him to travel through with his huge black war-horse.

She gazed into his eyes—and then made a break, sprinting ahead of him with a wild burst of energy. Yet even as she ran, she heard the pounding of the horse's hooves and she drew up short as the great animal swung around before her, directly in her path. She turned again to run.

And once again, the horse cut her off.

One more time . . .

And again the animal was too quickly there.

With Montjoy.

Exhausted, winded, she held still, staring at the ground, unable to bear the awful feeling of being trapped so. "Lady, give it up!" Montjoy warned softly. "You weary us both."

"But not enough, so it seems!" she murmured.

The sword touched her chin again, forcing it to rise. She didn't fight him any longer, didn't protest, but looked into his speculative and pensive eyes. "Nay, lady," he said very softly. "Nor will I grow too weary for you! Merely more impatient. Give it up. It is over." He drew the sword away, replacing it in his scabbard. He reached a hand down to her.

"You can't just take over my home!" she cried, and despite herself, there was a desperation to her words.

The wind rose and seemed to whisper, too. The trees rustled. The wind fell. He watched her all the while.

"I do not mean to take over your home. Only to give it strength. Take my hand."

She swallowed hard, and accepted it. She gasped as he easily swept her up before him on the horse. She straightened her back, dismayed by the feeling of his muscular arms and thighs around her. But the ride did not last long. She had not come so far. Within minutes they had reached the drawbridge, and there he slowed his horse so that they clattered over it.

"We've guests," he muttered suddenly, his voice husky and warm against her ear.

She stiffened instantly, amazed at how very afraid she was that Prince John had come again with de la Ville, and that he would somehow overrule this knight and pass her over to de la Ville.

He must have felt her fear, for he chuckled softly. "Nay, lady, 'tis not the Prince. See the pennants flying. They're the colors of Aquitaine! 'Tis the Queen Mother who has come to visit here!"

"Eleanor!" she gasped with relief and pleasure. The Dowager Queen! She hadn't reached Eleanor, but Eleanor had come to her!

They entered the courtyard where a dozen servants were dismounting from horses and pack trains and scurrying about with trunks and satchels and barrels.

Katherine started to squirm, anxious to get away from him.

"Let me down! Eleanor is here! There's much to be done! I have to—"

"You have to stand by my side and wed me, my lady, now!"

"But the Queen Mother—"

"Will understand."

He held tightly to her, refusing to let her slip down from the horse before him. He dismounted first, holding on to her arm.

Then he lifted her down. His eyes met hers, and held them still as he set her upon the ground.

"I cannot be wed like this—"

"Dear God, do you think to delay the ceremony further! Lady, if you were naked at this point, you would be wed so!"

"Really, it sounds divine to me!" a soft, musical voice said. They both turned around and saw that Eleanor was indeed there with them.

Katherine didn't know just how old Eleanor was, but surely she was in her sixties at the very least.

Yet she was beautiful. She walked with a springing step and her dark eyes flashed continuously. Her smile belied the wrinkles on her face—a knowing, sage smile, yet one that still laughed at the world, and at herself. Her dignity was unsurpassed, and yet life still offered her incredible pleasure and enjoyment and enormous vitality. She displayed that now, opening her arms to both of them. "Katherine, my sweet! And Damian, you handsome devil. How glad I am to see you both!"

And how glad I am to see you! Katherine thought in silence, hugging the Queen fiercely. You will truly be sorry now, Damian! she thought.

But he did not intend to be sorry. Nor was he awed by Eleanor's presence among them.

"You've come just in time for a wedding, Your Grace!" he informed her.

"Ah, so I have come in time!" she said, smiling at Katherine. "How glad I am! I do love a good wedding! And I will make a very remarkable witness for the marriage documents, what say you?"

Katherine's mouth went dry. "Whatever is the matter, child? You've gone quite white. And surely this is a sudden affair, but you're not dressed at all properly for the occasion!"

"I—"

"Katherine wanted a drink of water," Damian said blithely. "The water here would not do."

"Oh?" Eleanor looked at Kat, her interest piqued, a smile playing on her lips again. "I see. I think I see. Well, Damian, if you'll give me but a moment with your bride—"

"She's had many moments, Your Grace."

"But a proper gown is required."

"She went for a proper gown. And the next thing I knew, she was determined on drinking from a stream in the forest!"

"Ah." Eleanor seemed perplexed. Then she set an arm around Kat. "Kat would not leave me sitting alone in any room in her castle. It would not be courteous, would it?"

Kat still couldn't seem to speak. Eleanor nudged her. "Katherine! Upon your honor, you would not do so!"

Kat sighed, giving in. "Nay, Your Grace, I would not," she admitted, her eyes upon the dust-covered ground.

"Then it's settled. I shall produce her for the wedding in a matter of minutes," Eleanor promised. And with her arm still around Kat's shoulder, she led the way into the castle which she knew well, having come there often since Richard had ascended to the throne.

There was a clamor within the hall. Kat saw that the

table was being set with a great feast. Her own people were hurrying about with a purpose.

They had never been advised that there might not be a wedding, Kat realized.

It was all a den of confusion. Even Marie was there, directing Howard to do something at the table. Her eyes rose to Kat's, and she flushed with dismay.

Eleanor's retainers were all still hurrying about, bringing in the Queen's belongings for her stay.

She did not travel lightly.

"There's Marie!" Eleanor said lightly. "Marie, come soon, we'll do up your lady's hair together, eh?"

"Ah, Your Grace!" Marie said, dropping into a low bow for Eleanor.

The Queen quickly steered Kat up the stairway and to her own room. Just as quickly, she closed the door behind her. Then she stared at Kat.

"Just what is going on here?"

It was her very last chance. Kat was determined to play it to the hilt.

She flew across the room and knelt before Eleanor, taking her hand. "Oh, my lady! I am ever so grateful to see you! I beg you! Stop this! Don't let this wedding take place!"

"Whyever not?" Eleanor demanded incredulously.

Kat lifted her head, meeting the Queen's eyes. "Because I cannot marry this man! He is harsh and hard and merciless—"

"And my dear son John intends to give you to de la Ville for his loyalty—and for a great sum of money, which John always seems to need," she said dryly.

"Aye, I know that. But if I could just speak with Richard—"

"Why?"

"Well, to tell him that it must be some other knight. Not this one!"

Eleanor disengaged her hand from Kat's grasp. "Up, young lady. It was Richard's command that you marry Montjoy."

Kat felt as if her heart sank to her feet. She had heard the finality in Eleanor's voice.

Of course. Richard had always been Eleanor's favorite child. She refused to see ill in him at all, ever. In her eyes, he did not make mistakes.

"But—"

"Montjoy is the perfect match for you, Katherine. His lands adjoin yours. Together you will form a formidable force here. Powerful enough to offset John's constantly grasping fingers."

Katherine sank down on her knees, watching as the Queen walked purposefully to Kat's trunks, opening them up to throw out masses of her underdresses, hose, tunics, and veils. She sprang to her feet, rushing to Eleanor one last time. "Eleanor, you do not understand. I could be in serious trouble with this man."

"What do you mean?"

Katherine inhaled and exhaled wildly. She wanted to tell Eleanor the truth.

The truth failed her.

"He's . . . he's been betrothed before. He's—"

"At the least, Katherine, he's had dozens of mistresses, concubines, and simple whores before you," Eleanor said flatly. "Such is the way of men." She paused, holding a beautiful blue headpiece before her. "However, I don't believe I've ever heard any word of his having any affection whatsoever for animals." She touched Kat lightly on the cheek with a cheerful smile. "Be grateful. I am quite certain now that dear Henry did have quite a penchant for sheep!"

Sheep! Because Rosamund Clifford had been the child of a shepherd and of all Henry's women, Eleanor had been jealous of Rosamund. So jealous that many had accused her of Rosamund's murder. Eleanor had been locked up at the time, but even Henry had seemed to think that she might have had her fine hand in it.

This was not getting her anywhere.

"Eleanor, what of me?"

"What of you, my dear?"

Confess! Kat thought. After all, it was not all her doing. The Silver Sword had been the knave to go forward when she had demanded that he stop.

But she could not say those words. She didn't dare admit what had happened. Eleanor just might tell Montjoy.

And Montjoy just might . . .

Seek out and slay the Silver Sword.

The traitor deserved it! Kat thought.

Nay, she couldn't let it happen. Not that she wouldn't like to inflict some injury upon the vile rat herself!

But he did keep the forest clean of vermin such as de la Ville. Robin needed him.

And she . . .

She felt her breath coming more quickly.

If only she were being wed to the Silver Sword. She could close her eyes. Accept the magic.

"What is it?" Eleanor insisted.

Kat shook her head. She didn't dare speak.

"I think, Kat, that he may come to love you very much."

"I don't think that he will."

"And you, my dear, may come to a point where you defy both heaven and earth for him."

"Never!"

"Sooner than you think! Ah, the blue gown it shall be," Eleanor told her. "Come. Let's get those things off, and these things on."

The door opened. Marie, her eyes wide, came through. She carried a huge chalice. She bowed quickly to Eleanor, then focused her gaze on Kat. "I thought that a bit of wine might help."

"Oh, aye!" Eleanor said gaily. "A bit of wine always helps!" She took the chalice from Marie and sipped, then offered it to Kat, smiling. "Actually, a lot of wine helps!"

Kat swallowed down nearly the whole chalice full. Then she shuddered.

Wine!

It was what had gotten her into half of this trouble to begin with!

But it did help. Before she knew it, she was dressed in the soft blue underdress with the rich royal-blue tunic set over it, and both Eleanor and Marie were working on her hair. "Ah, I do remember when I married Henry. There was never a question between us. I had the Aquitaine, you see, and Henry coveted it. But he was a man to behold, I tell you. Those were wild and tempestuous days, when all our lives and ambitions were before us. How I envy you!"

"Envy me!" Kat cried.

"Aye, indeed, Kat! For you've gotten yourself a knight truly wondrous to behold. Dark and dangerous, with all those years of delicious tempest before you. I daresay, you'll come to adore him."

Adore him? A curious trembling swept through her. For a moment she remembered his words by the tub. *I am what you make of me* . . .

She felt the stroke of his fingers at her nape. And she remembered the gentleness of his words in the forest. He did not mean to take her castle. He meant to give it strength.

Could their battles end?

They would just begin tonight. When Montjoy discovered that he would receive no maiden.

Kat caught her breath, watching Eleanor, then daring

to remind her, "You came to detest King Henry!"

Eleanor paused, catching her lower lip lightly with her teeth. She didn't look at Kat; she was seeing some far distant path.

"Nay, I never hated him. I battled him. Year after year. I had to pray for his death for my own freedom. Yet in the end, I wept. I never ceased to love him. Neither of us knew how to love. Maybe you will have a chance to do much better. If so, seize it. There is no greater glory in life. Not lands, not riches, not crowns. We were blinded by the glitter. We forgot people," she said softly. "We forgot love. But, well—I'm sure that you will fare very well. Oh, he is a wondrous-looking man, isn't he, Marie?"

"Oh, aye!" Marie agreed.

"A fine lover! And you will love him one day."

Kat shivered. "Never!" she whispered.

Eleanor laughed softly. "You'll see, he will make you love him."

"Never."

Eleanor's and Marie's eyes met over her head.

Aye, she'll learn to love him, Eleanor thought, and sorrowfully so. For then she would learn the pain of jealousy, and so many other agonies.

But perhaps not.

For few men had been given so beautiful a gift as Katherine de Montrain.

No knight had been more loyal than Montjoy had been to his Alyssa. No knight had been more loyal to Henry, and then to Richard. No knight, she decided, was more striking, sensual, or intriguing.

She smiled. She hoped they would do very well.

And if not . . .

Well, then, there would be a very desirable blending of property, and a good firm check on that naughty boy John!

She stepped back. "I think we're done. Katherine, are you ready for your vows?"

"No!"

Eleanor issued a soft peal of laughter, clapping her hands together.

"Alas, we've left an impatient bridegroom below. Marie, give us the chalice for another sip of wine there. Trust me, love, it will make the proper words slip more easily from your tongue!"

Perhaps it would be so. It did not seem quite so painful as Eleanor and Marie led her from her chamber.

It didn't even seem quite so horrible when she saw Montjoy at the foot of the stairs, awaiting her.

It didn't seem quite so terrible at all until he took her hand.

Then she felt the fire and steel in his fingers. And when he looked at her, she saw the silver triumph in his eyes.

It was all that she saw. She knew that the priest was there. She heard him saying the words.

Then she felt Montjoy's iron grip upon her tighten so that she cried out.

She must have cried the proper words, for the ceremony continued. Montjoy clearly stated his own vows. She gritted her teeth, despite the feel of his grip upon her.

Bastard! So he would marry her! He would not find any triumph over her; she would not allow it.

She would not fear him . . .

But then the priest proclaimed them man and wife before God and all assembled there.

And Montjoy looked at her again.

Silver eyes sizzling, his mouth sensually curved into a wicked, wicked smile.

And then he kissed her . . .

Chapter 15

This was no fine, gentle kiss bestowed upon a new and tender bride! Kat determined, reeling beneath the passion of the man's touch, of his hold. It wasn't as if he sought to hurt her, for he did not. But neither was there any give whatsoever in his grasp, for his arms were firmly around her.

"Bravo!"

Kat was dimly aware that the Queen cried out, laughing softly. But then, as the kiss continued, as she felt the fire of his touch engulf her from head to toe, she was aware that the priest was clearing his throat. "Lord Montjoy—"

But the priest needn't have worried. At that moment, one of the guards rushed down the inner steps from his position atop the high tower.

"Riders coming, my liege, my lady."

Then it seemed that Montjoy was quickly distracted. He let go of her and looked to the man who had brought the message.

"At what distance?"

"They're still quite far. But, my lord, you ordered that I warn you the moment I saw anything at all—"

"And quite right. I thank you," Montjoy told him quickly. "Can you tell what colors they wear?"

"I believe it is the Prince who comes, my lord, though

even from the tower, we cannot see the pennants and colors clear as yet."

Then Montjoy was quickly issuing orders. "Marie, help your mistress in her chambers. Sir James, I'll speak with you now. Eleanor! Thank God that you arrived when you did!"

"How very lovely to be so appreciated!" Eleanor said delightedly.

"And one and all!" Montjoy's voice rose to include all who were present in the hall—mainly his own men, a few of Eleanor's ladies, and some of Kat's own people. "Enjoy the food and festivities!" He turned to walk away.

This was her home! Kat thought irritably. "If you don't mind, my lord—" she began.

But he swung on her then, his brow arched in surprise. "I said that you must go to your chambers!"

"But this is my home!"

He lowered his voice. "And you are still determined not to see the danger!"

"Danger stands before me."

"Go to your room with Marie like a good little bride, else I will see that you are taken there."

"Take care, Lord Montjoy," she warned, "lest you should awaken minus that arrogant tongue of yours!"

He arched a brow to the challenge. A smile curled at his lip, and he moved a step closer to her. "You take care. This is a rowdy enough crowd we have on hand here. One word from me, and I'm quite sure they could be convinced that a traditional bedding might take place here. They could sweep you up those stairs for me, strip us both, and stand about like drunken gawkers while—"

The blood had drained from her face. That last thing she wanted at this moment was a pack of witnesses!

Without another word, she spun away from him. Then

she swirled back to him. "I swear, Montjoy, I will make you very, very sorry for this marriage!"

To her surprise, she had touched upon some sore spot. An anguish seemed to leap swiftly through his silver eyes. "I am sorry for it, madam, and for us both! Now go!"

Kat did so, seething. She took the stairs two at a time and burst into her room well ahead of Marie. Her dear friend and servant followed her, silent at first, wringing her hands while Kat paced the room like a caged tiger. "Ah, look, my lady! Flowers. Beautiful flowers on the trunk by the bed. Bless the Queen that she thinks of such things! See the exquisite red roses, bright yellow daffodils!"

Kat vaguely saw the flowers, strewn attractively over the trunk. Under other circumstances she would have been delighted with their beauty and wonderfully pleased with the touch of scent they gave the air. She would have plucked one up to feel the softness of the bloom's delicate petals.

But now she barely glanced their way.

Marie kept trying. She pointed awkwardly to the bed. "Katherine, you must see this gown! Eleanor had it sent during the service. She told me about it. She acquired it in the Middle East some years ago. The fabric is the softest you can imagine. It is cool against the skin. Let me help you—"

"I want no gown in which to meet this man."

"Kat! You are a bride tonight—"

"With no love for her husband!" Kat said. Husband. It had happened; they were wed. Nothing that she could do would change that now. And even the thought made tremors run hotly along her spine.

"Lord! What will I do?"

But even as she spoke, her heart leaped and then catapulted back to her feet. Someone stood in their now-opened doorway. But it wasn't Montjoy. Not yet. Eleanor was there, smiling, her eyes shimmering with amusement—and sympathy, and understanding.

"What will you do?" she inquired lightly. "Ah, youth and beauty are their own reward. I believe a great deal will be done for you!" She laughed softly. "Come now, Katherine! Chin up. Let me help you again."

Kat swallowed down her tension and the feeling of being so desperately trapped. "Nay, Your Grace! It is not right for a queen to aid a countess—"

"Dowager Queen," Eleanor said. "And a very, very rich young lady!"

She made a motion to Marie, urging her away. She knew that Kat would not fight her, and she quickly helped her discard her wedding finery and don the ivory gown that she had given as an impromptu wedding present.

The material barely clung to Kat's shoulders and fell against her like cool hands. The feel would have been exquisite, had she been able to feel anything at all. "Sit now, and let me unwind this blanket of hair," Eleanor told her.

She sat. The gown slipped from her shoulders. "It's wonderful, thank you, Your Grace," she said very properly. "But it won't stay on!"

"I do believe that is part of the very idea of the gown. It came across long trade routes from Persia, so I was told. And the fabric is wonderful. Ah, if I were just a few years younger!" She laughed softly. "Maybe not. I think I'd need to be a few decades younger!" She bent and kissed Kat's cheek. "He'll adore you. You'll wrap him around your finger in no time at all."

Montjoy? Never!

After tonight, he would probably want to kill her!

"If the Prince is coming, we must be ready. No matter what, he must be entertained. I—" Kat began.

Eleanor rose. "Don't worry about a thing, my dear.

I do believe that it's that young monster of mine arriving quickly here. And I shall entertain him, I assure you. Enjoy yourself. John remains my son, though had I been the father rather than the mother, I might have questioned the relationship!"

Kat leaped up. Eleanor was heading toward the door. "Wait!" Kat cried out. "This is all wrong. Montjoy and I should greet guests together—"

"Not this evening, my girl! You may greet my son in the morning, Lady Montjoy. That will certainly do well enough." Eleanor smiled suddenly. "Oh, I can't wait to see his face when he arrives!"

Eleanor disappeared despite the wild plea in Kat's eyes.

It was only then that Kat realized that Marie had already escaped her room.

She had been deserted by everyone!

"All those years of loyalty and concern, and he steps in, and even Marie runs like a mouse!" Kat said aloud. She started to pace the room again. There had been no way to fight this. He was coming here, and coming very soon. She didn't dare try to run again. She might give away the secret of the tunnel. And John was coming, he would be there any minute, and—

She heard a quiet sound. She spun around, her breath catching.

Montjoy was there. In her room. Standing against the doorway. So very tall, and so casually, arrogantly assured. Arms crossed over his broad chest, his stance easy. Silver-gray eyes glittering as he watched her. And waited. With the lazy regard of a great animal that toyed easily with its prey, knowing full well that the prey was trapped, and had nowhere else to go.

Was he amused, or filled with that deep-seated anger that so often seemed to fill him when he spoke with her? She couldn't tell. Not from the way he watched her. Not from the curious, mocking smile that curled so slightly into the curve of his lip. Not from the cast of his hard, handsome face, or that cool speculation in his eyes.

She stopped dead still, one hand fluttering to her throat. As she stared at him she could feel the very fierce pounding of her heart. Perhaps he could see it himself against the form-hugging softness of Eleanor's beautiful garment.

"Well, this is it!" he said, his voice surprisingly low and soft. "The moment of truth!"

Truth! Oh, he couldn't imagine the half of it.

He hadn't been there when she had come to know the Silver Sword. Oh, the Silver Sword had been equally arrogant and determined, but there had been something between them . . .

Maybe because she had known that he had saved the girl in the woods. Or more probably, because she was so certain that he had been the archer to save them all that long-ago day. Maybe she had just come to know his touch. Maybe it had been that first kiss in the water, the one that had made her feel warm from head to toe . . .

Yet even now she could still feel Montjoy's wedding kiss upon her lips. Feel the force, and the power, and even the persuasion. The startling heat of that kiss, too. Eleanor was right. He was not a horrible man. Not in the physical sense. He was every bit as tall as the Silver Sword, as broad, as tightly muscled.

As powerful.

And his face was striking, despite the small scars that nicked it above one eyebrow and across one cheek. His ebony-dark hair and silver eyes enhanced that rugged, masculine appeal. If all she had to do was look upon him . . .

But that was not all that she had to do. One look at his very speculative features and she knew well that her waiting game was near over.

The moment of truth . . .

She shook her head fervently. If she could just buy a little time! Time to know him better. To learn to control her own temper, and therefore manage his!

She quickly decided that dignity and reason were her best weapons now. "Sir, you have what you wish. We are wed before God and man. The castle is yours—"

"As are you, my lady."

Trying to keep her temper under control, she quickly lowered her lashes. He was watching her, waiting. She didn't speak quickly enough, for suddenly he was walking toward her. She sensed his movement and looked up, walking away from him. "Love, sir, cannot be forced!"

"My lady, the number of men and women who are man and wife and most certainly not in love would reckon into very high numbers indeed!"

She backed away further. "Truly, you are the most magnificent of Richard's loyal knights. With strength and power tempered with justice and mercy. The Prince is coming. We should both be downstairs, hands entwined, strong together against any trickery he might devise!"

Montjoy paused, a sparkle to his silver eyes as he rubbed his chin. "How passionately, how beautifully spoken!"

"Then, if you will just listen—"

"You do flatter me well, my lady. Had I time, I would be tempted to let you go on."

"We haven't time, so you must listen to me!" she insisted. "We must go downstairs together now—"

"No!" The smile left his face. She suddenly found herself pinned against the cold stone of the castle wall. He leaned against it casually, a hand on either side of her head. "The Prince is coming. I will not risk an annulment of this marriage I am sorry to alarm you—for you do seem to be very alarmed. You were eager for a confessor before. Have you something to tell me now?"

She swallowed hard and shook her head fiercely. Just what did men know about women? It didn't matter. She couldn't confess a thing to him.

Dignity was not working, she saw. His eyes were as sharp as blades. He had no intention of letting her be.

"Confess? To you? I owe you nothing!" she hissed. Perhaps she surprised him. She pushed against his chest with an energy born of fury. "This place will be filled with guests and you intend to idle away the night—"

"I will not be idle."

"Everyone will know—"

He sighed, watching her walk by. "That, my lady, is exactly my intent. Aye, everyone will know. With any luck whatsoever, the Prince will burst in upon us. Therefore, we will make haste."

She spun to face him. "Nay! I will not do it—"

"Lady, off with that gown, and onto the bed! Else you want it ripped from your person."

She gasped, her eyes narrowing. "The gown belongs to the Queen! You wouldn't dare—"

"Oh, I would dare with astonishing pleasure," he assured her cordially. He stood five feet away. He said he wanted to hurry, but he seemed in a leisurely enough mood himself. Of course. She was trapped. He knew it well. He did nothing but toy with her now.

She stared at him in an absolute fury.

And it was then that her stomach growled again, giving her a whole new argument.

"I can't possibly do—what you want me to do. I am starving to death. What chivalrous man would want a maid who hungers as I do?"

He laughed out loud, sweeping her a deep bow. "My lady, I swear that I will most chivalrously teach you a new hunger."

"You've an amazing conceit, sir, but I will not remain here to foster it!" she announced coolly. "I intend to have something to eat!" With those words she turned from him and started for the door.

She had not gone two steps before she felt him at her back. He was amused no longer. Catching her arm, he swung her around. With a determined grasp he caught hold of her gown and ripped.

The elegant, beautiful fabric gave way and drifted like clouds to her feet. Naked, alternately searing hot and icy cold, she stared at him. Jesu, was there no way to best him, no way to shame him?

Nay, for he stepped back then, in his eyes as he looked her over from head to toe. "The castle was what you wanted most!" she snapped furiously. "Did you pay too great a price in a bride to achieve it?"

He met her eyes squarely. "I know, my lady," he said flatly, "that you are very aware of your own beauty, and your own assets. You are painfully wild, willful, and determined, but even I grant you this, madam, you are a very beautiful woman. And you are my wife. Mine!"

Something in that last word seemed to send the most awful fear of retribution racing through her. Stark naked but heedless of it, she turned to bolt.

She barely even moved. His arms were around her naked form, and before she had even caught her breath, she was losing it again, swept up into his arms to be cast wildly upon her bedding.

Her heart thudded fiercely. She stared at the ceiling, stunned for a moment, then realized that he was stripping himself.

Boots fell hard against the cold stone. The dark-matted and muscled breadth of his chest was bared as the tunic in the Montjoy colors was cast heedlessly atop them.

Her face flamed.

It had been dark when she had been with the Silver Sword. She hadn't even seen her lover's face, much less . . . anything else.

Now she was seeing. Chausses were gone and the man approaching her was clearly visible in the candlelight. Naked bronze shoulders glistened. She could see the flex and pull of every muscle. He was hardened from head to toe; taut, sleek, fine.

And ready. Ready and determined. Her eyes flew unerringly to his large, fierce shaft standing so boldly.

She leaped from the bed, to the side opposite him, and stood there shivering.

"Jesu, lady, do you ever quit?" he demanded in a soft roar.

Her eyes narrowed fiercely. "No!" she exclaimed. "See how very sorry you will be? An annulment would be the kindest grace to befall you, sir!" She started to move, but even as she did so, he pounced across the covers, and his fingers wound into her hair. She cried out softly, wrenching her golden tresses from his gasp. Tears stung her eyes. "All right! Be so wretched and vile and horrible." She threw herself down flat upon her back, and stared up at the ceiling. "Go ahead. Act like de la Ville. Rape me."

She closed her eyes and crossed her arms over her breasts, just as if she were dead and ready for burial.

And still she did not dissuade Montjoy. She felt him lie down beside her.

Then he laughed. Loudly, bluntly, and with true amusement.

She felt his fingers winding a strand of her hair.

"Poor little maiden!" he whispered very softly. She felt the heat of his words at her earlobe. "Am I truly so very wretched—threatening your . . . innocence?"

Her eyes flew open. What could he know? Why that so very subtle shade of mockery to his tone?

Confess now, she thought. But she could not. And she could never tell him about the Silver Sword.

He might decide to slay the man . . .

She moistened her lips, wishing that he were not so

very close, and wishing even more fervently that he did not seem to take her nudity—or his own—so very casually.

Silver eyes touched hers. A smile curled his lips so slightly and wickedly once again. He ran a finger over her lower lip. "I told you," he said quietly. "I do not wish to hurt you."

"Well then, don't! Let's not do this!" she whispered in reply. He was very silent, which unnerved her, and she turned to see his face fully. "You could be chivalrous, sir, truly! I would swear to anything below. You could be the great knight in truth, so strong that you dared be gentle and tender—"

He was smiling again. Touching her cheek. "I do intend to be gentle."

"You could be so very heroic—"

"My lady, your head is just filled with romantic notions," he said softly.

"Then you won't—"

"Nay, lady. I will."

She flung around, giving her back to him. But it was a bare back. And in just seconds, she felt . . . something along her naked flesh.

Just a touch. A gentle, near-elusive touch. So very soft against her skin. And a sweet smell was suddenly on the air.

The smell of a rose.

She closed her eyes. He held one of the flowers, she realized. And the bloodred soft petals of the rose were just brushing over her. Along the length of her spine. Down lower. Trailing over the rise of her buttocks, sweetly over her thighs.

"Perhaps you're right," he mused. "Love cannot be forced. Perhaps it is even like the bud of a rose. Petals closed so very tightly, yet suddenly bursting into a most magnificent bloom!"

Kat swallowed hard, amazed by the sensations caused by that stroke of the rose. So soft! She did not want to feel it. It was so very light that she had no choice. Where it touched her her flesh seemed to become acutely alive! Alive, and vibrant. And then so warm.

She rolled again to avoid that stroke of the rose against her, forgetting then that she gave her front, rather than her back, to his touch.

Her eyes fell first upon his form.

He was stretched out lengthwise by her side, raised upon an elbow. The muscles of his chest and shoulders, though not constricted, remained taut and hard. Sleek. To her amazement, she was tempted to touch him. To feel the flesh and body that was so very honed and corded.

She swallowed hard and quickly looked to his eyes. Startlingly silver eyes. The emotion within them was neither amusement nor anger now.

Nay . . .

It was rather a shimmer of passion. So intense that it caused her breath to catch within her throat. She delicately wet her very dry lips to speak, finding it difficult to breathe.

"I will not—burst into magnificent bloom!" she told him.

He smiled. The rose he held suddenly fell between the valley of her breasts. He lifted the soft petal to encircle one breast, rubbing the petals over her nipple. She gasped softly, yet discovered herself too bewitched to pull away.

At his command, the rose continued a slow descent. His eyes followed the trail the petals took then, falling down to her belly. Teasing, just barely brushing the golden triangle below.

"Roses need time!" she gasped out suddenly, trying to catch the flower and stem. "A bloom will not open today if it is not meant to do so until tomorrow!"

She caught the stem, and he released it to her. She cried out softly as a thorn caught her fingers.

Then she would have cried out again, had she sufficient breath, for he had suddenly crawled over her. He took the rose from her and cast it aside, sweeping up the thumb that had been barbed by the thorn. "A good gardener can coax a flower to bloom," he assured her, and his lips closed over the small injury to her finger. His tongue was hot and wet. Slowly, seductively, he sucked the wound.

And she watched him. Just watched him. Wide-eyed, amazed at what the feel of the hot tug upon her thumb seemed to be doing to the rest of her body. Her eyes seemed captured by his, prisoner to his silver gaze.

And then she became more and more aware of his body. The hard-muscled thighs around her hips. The heat of the burnished shoulders above her. The soft teasing of his dark hair against her flesh.

The great pulsing protrusion of his sex lying so hotly against her belly . . .

"Nay! You are not a gardener at all, but a knight!" she whispered, trying to twist from his touch. "Certainly not a good gardener—"

"Ah, my lady, I do protest!" He leaned toward her. "I am the very best!" he whispered, his lips just over hers.

And then they fell upon her lips.

Her fingers pressed against his rock-hard chest; she was determined to elude his kiss.

But his hands were upon her head, and she could not twist from his questing tongue.

And neither did the force of her hands seem to mean anything at all against his muscular body. A whimper of protest sounded softly in her throat. She could not speak. She could only feel the determined sweep of his tongue within her mouth. Tasting. Ravishing. Coaxing.

She could scarcely breathe. The room, she was certain, was spinning.

She didn't know where or when she ceased to fight, but she must have done so. His hands were upon her body. Stroking the rise of her breasts, his fingers curling around the fullness there, then seeking the detail of her nipple, playing there, making the peak harden, making streaks of silver heat through her. His hand moved. Curving over her midriff, finding her hip. Slipping beneath her to cradle her behind. Exploring, demanding. Seducing.

And all the while, she felt the potent hardness and length of his shaft against her. So warm. Rubbing against her belly. Insinuative, sensual.

His stroke moved again. Falling too against her belly. Below.

Aye, somewhere she had ceased to fight.

Because this was inevitable, she told herself.

No . . .

His hands no longer secured her head to his kiss. She could have twisted from his kiss. She had not. His lips touched hers again and again. They teased at her eyes, at her earlobes, at her throat. His whispers touched her ears. She heard no words, but knew the tenderness of their cadence. Alarm filled her. Not that he hurt her, for he did not.

Nay . . .

Slowly, surely, his touch was evoking . . .

Fire.

She wanted to think, she wanted to fight . . . not so much Montjoy anymore, but the tremoring he awoke. It seemed almost good that he touched her so. Almost natural. Aye . . .

He was an exceptional gardener.

For it seemed that she knew him. That she had come this way before.

Were all men so similar? Did the kiss of one so equal in intensity the kiss of another?

Her thoughts fled. A gasp escaped her as she felt the sudden parting of her thighs. Felt the bold touch of his fingers, intimately. Inside her. Stroking. His hands forced apart her thighs, and she cried out in protest.

Then he was there, above her, the whipcord length of his body between her thighs. His eyes met hers and he smiled. "A very good gardener is most nurturing of those soft red petals of that rose. Caring for them with the utmost tenderness."

She started to speak, but gasped instead for he was suddenly on his knees, his hands around her legs. She could not imagine being spread so far, nor could have ever imagined the searing jolt of sensation that ripped violently through her as he . . .

Tended to the petals of his rose.

A scream tore from her throat, her fingers plowed into the rich darkness of his hair. Her touch meant nothing to him. She couldn't move for his knight's length.

And dear God! He was determined to tend those petals!

Gently parting them with thumb and forefinger, lathing there with his tongue, more and more intimately. She shrieked and struggled against him, a fierce panic seizing her that she could feel his touch with such . . .

Such sweet abandon.

For as he mercilessly held her to his whim, she felt desire growing within her. That which she had so briefly touched once before now seemed to come cascading down upon her. She didn't want to fight him. She wanted to feel him. She wanted to reach and reach for the crystal glory before her. She was keenly, achingly aware of every sensation about her. She knew the feel of her back against the linen bedding, knew the softness into which she sank.

She knew the scent of the flowers, the roses on the air. The coarse, masculine feel of his hair beneath her fingers. And she was so aware of that blinding, building fire within her.

Centering . . .

Then he was over her again. She briefly caught sight of his eyes, burning with such a shattering intensity.

But then she closed her eyes, crying out again, for the fierce pulse of him was suddenly inside her, deep, deep inside her. She braced herself, tensing for the pain that would come to wipe away the magic. She shuddered, her fingers winding into the bedding and then into his shoulders as he thrust himself into her. For the briefest moment, it seemed that she would shatter in two.

But there was no pain. There was the intrusion, swift, demanding, incredibly intimate. She could not take all of him.

But she could. And for a moment he was there, poised above her.

Her eyes had been closed. She opened them. Met his.

Panic seized her. The time had come. The moment of truth indeed. He knew. He knew women, he knew her.

He knew that she had had a lover.

Sharp silver eyes impaled her just as his shaft did.

Then a great shuddering seized hold of him. He closed his eyes.

And he began to move.

Once again, with all her heart, she wanted to cry out. She wanted to protest. But she could not.

There was no more subtlety about him. No tender stroking of the rose.

The desire that swept him was like a storm. It was like the high shriek of the wind, like the tumult of the rain. He moved so fast. Demanding that she come with him. Bronze muscles flexed with strain, and a fine sheen of perspiration began to break out on them. She did cry out, stunned at the force of him, entering deeper and deeper inside her, again and again . . .

But his tempest had swept inside her. She wanted so badly to fight him. But it was there, so close. That crystal glory that had beckoned her before. That she had so nearly touched.

She closed her eyes tightly against him. She felt the fury of the storm.

And she was part of it. Hips writhing to his command. His mouth seized hers as he moved. Lowered. Captured the rouged peak of her breast even as he thrust with greater demand. And each touch brought new streaks of fire and light cascading down upon her. Before she had known something.

But not like this!

Not this rising, soaring wonder. Twisting, undulating, wondering, seeking more. More and more of him. Reaching . . .

The climax exploded throughout her. Wild, violent. There was a scream, and she dimly realized it to be her own. A rush of heat flooded her as magic touched the length of her. She didn't know if the liquid heat came from her or from him.

Tremors shook and seized her. Bit by bit she became aware again of the things around her.

The feel of the bedding against her back. The scent of the rose, now musky and sweet. The coolness of the air.

The hair-roughened thigh of the man who stared at her.

He'd eased his weight from her. His thigh remained cast casually over her lower limbs. His hand lay just below her breast.

She bit into her lower lip, longing to cast that hand away.

Yet at this moment, she didn't dare. And so she lay there with her eyes downcast, waiting. Feeling the silver edge of those eyes trying to pierce into her heart.

"Poor, sweet damsel, eh? Dreading this encounter with all the purity of her heart?"

Her eyes lifted to his, issuing a challenge. He wasn't going to frighten her, she swore it.

"Dreading you with all my heart!" she said softly.

"Ah! So not this other lover, eh?" he demanded.

Her heart seemed to slam against her chest.

"His name, madam."

"You must be insane—"

"His name."

She shook her head violently. "It is ended. It never began."

"I would know—"

"He is dead!" she claimed wildly.

"Who?" His voice hardened.

She waved a hand airily before her. "Perhaps there were a score of others. Would you slay them all?"

To her amazement, he laughed softly. His face lowered over hers. "I didn't intend to slay any man, my lady."

But with those words he suddenly pushed away from her and walked the distance to his discarded clothing and rummaged there. Kat watched him warily and started to rise, trying to draw the linen sheets around her. Then she stopped, a scream forming on her lips, and freezing there.

He had taken a sharp dagger from the ankle sheath that lay with his chausses.

He didn't mean to slay any man. He meant to slay her!

She managed to gasp, backing away from him as he pounced upon the bed again, kneeling before her with the dagger drawn. "Jesu!" she breathed, closing her eyes.

No blade touched her. She opened her eyes, and a sharp breath caught in her throat again. He stared at her as if she had gone insane.

He had used the dagger against himself, slicing a small nick into his wrist. A few drops of brilliant red blood fell upon the sheet.

Kat looked from the blood to his eyes. "What—?"

He arched a black brow dangerously. "Don't you hear the clamor beneath us, my lady?"

She hadn't heard it. She had been too busy watching him, worrying about his actions. But now she was aware of the sounds beneath them. Music—her wedding music—played on. But voices rose above it. There was a certain clattering. Hard footsteps, the clang of metal. The sounds of men; their boots, their swords.

She stared at him with a certain alarm. The footfalls were coming up the stairway.

"The Prince!" She tried to leap up from the bed. He caught hold of her wrist, and she fell. His arms wrapped around her.

"Let me up!" she commanded. "You've had what you wanted. And people are coming. Let me dress, let me get a robe—"

"Nay, lady!" he said, smiling with grave amusement. "There's far more at stake here than dignity. The best you'll have now is a sheet and the bulk of my body. Get beneath the bedding, if you wish."

"But—!"

"Do it!"

The sounds of the footsteps were at the door. He rolled with her, his bulk atop her. He caught hold of the bedding, sweeping the linen sheet up high around them, that and his body covering hers as the door suddenly burst open.

Montjoy lifted up, keeping her covered and a bit behind him, just as John burst into the room. "Jesu!" Montjoy swore irritably, as if he hadn't realized that he was being disrupted until the form of a man actually entered the chamber. Then he sighed softly. "Why, 'tis the Prince! John, how come you here?"

"Montjoy!" John seethed as he stared at him. Kat dared to look around the huge bronzed shoulders of her new husband. John was furious—and perplexed.

"I came for the Lady Katherine. I had decided she should wed Raymond de la Ville. And I come here to find—you! By what right is this? The girl is my brother's ward—"

"You came for her?" Montjoy feigned surprise. "I am well aware that she is your brother's ward. I have his papers, the license, and the bishop's dispensation, all upon me! Surely, Eleanor informed you—"

"Eleanor informed me that you were upstairs with the Lady de Montrain—"

"Lady Montjoy," Damian interjected softly.

"I will see to the validity of this marriage!" John thundered.

"It is valid in word and deed," Montjoy said, and an edge of steel that could not be missed rang clearly in his voice. Even Kat could read so many things in the words that passed between them! Damian did not forget that John was a Prince of England. But that would not sway him while he still honored the King. And if John persisted, he would find himself a very formidable enemy.

"It would seem that the papers are valid," Father Donovan said lightly. "And that the marriage has been consummated," he added, pointing to the drops of blood upon the sheets.

Kat felt herself redden to a hot crimson. "My lords!" she cried out, "Could we all not discuss this in my bed-chamber?"

"The lady is mine," Damian said firmly, watching John, as if she had never spoken. She wanted to strike them all, yet just as she was about to speak again, reminding them that she was a person, an heiress herself, the door suddenly burst further open and Father Donovan was shoved out of the way.

Raymond de la Ville strode furiously into the chamber, staring at Montjoy and Katherine. His eyes seemed to bulge, an erratic pulse beat furiously at his throat. "Montjoy!" he spit out, flecks of foam flying from his mouth with his fury. "You! I swear, I'll kill you!"

He drew his sword. Naked still, Damian leaped from the bed, agile as a deer despite his hard-muscled size. He caught up his own sword from the floor and circled around, heedless that he held no protection whatsoever save that sword.

"De la Ville, you may well try! For if you ever come so near my bride again, I will slice every extremity from your body!"

De la Ville swore, and swung. Damian returned the parry, his sword meeting de la Ville's midair. There was an ear-splitting clash of steel.

Then de la Ville's sword flew and fell to the ground.

Prince John stepped between the men. "My lords, I command that you end this—"

"Whatever is going on here?" a new voice interrupted. A feminine voice. Intrigued. With an edge of cunning.

Eleanor's voice.

"Pray, John! Father Donovan, my lords! What does go on here?" Suddenly she, too, was in the room, her eyes upon them all. "Did you doubt the marriage to be real? Why, John, I told you that it was so!"

"Mother, cease your meddling in my affairs—"

"Your affairs?" Eleanor said sharply. "Why, last I heard, your brother was still alive, and quite hale and hearty. Matters of the crown are his affair!"

"There is no matter here," John said. He bowed deeply, some of the rich Plantagenet sense of politics and dramatics showing through. "I have told these lords. I believe these lords wished to pierce one another through. I have told them that the matter is ended."

"And it is ended," Damian said, his tone sharp. He stared at de la Ville. "For the moment." Then he bowed toward Eleanor. "Your Grace, I am not dressed—"

"Truly, Mother! Show some shame!" John reprimanded her.

"Ah, that coming from you!" Eleanor replied lightly, her eyes narrowed. "At my age, my son, my pleasures are not many. Don't begrudge me a sight of such finely honed male perfection. I don't see a one of you having the least difficulty ogling Lord Montjoy's bride! But now, shall the lot of us voyeurs leave them both in peace?"

De la Ville looked as if he would rather die.

"Out!" Eleanor commanded him.

He gritted his teeth. His eyes still looked as if they would bulge out of their sockets.

Kat couldn't help but feel a certain pleasure. She remembered the look of that poor, terrified girl in the forest.

"De la Ville!" John thundered. Then he whispered to the man, but the whisper carried. "You fool! Had I not stopped him, Montjoy would have skewered you."

De la Ville didn't say another word. He turned and exited the room, his feet stomping hard on the floor. "So it is legal, Montjoy," John said. "But don't forget—I am the Prince!"

He followed de la Ville. Donovan turned and followed him.

Eleanor blew them both a kiss, smiling. "Good night, children!" she said sweetly.

Kat stared at the door as it closed. She smiled, remembering de la Ville's look.

"Oh, you could have skewered him through!" she said,

then realized that her new husband was staring at her, his sword still in his hands.

She tossed back a length of hair, in a show of bravado. "If you wish to skewer me with that sword, then pray do so! I am weary of being threatened by your kind!"

"My kind?"

"Men!"

"What other men threaten you?"

Her eyes met his. He came closer to the bed. She prayed that she wouldn't choke on her words. "Why, de la Ville. The Prince. Of course."

He smiled and gazed at his sword. "Ah, lady! This is not the weapon I would take to you! But skewer you, madame? What an invitation. I shall accept it readily, I think."

She flushed, despite all that had been. She edged away on the bed. "Why did you do that?" she whispered suddenly, heatedly, casting her eyes on the droplets of blood. "What if there were another? What if I—" She needed all of her courage to continue. "What if I were to bear a child? All the world would claim it to be yours!"

He hesitated just a moment. Then he shrugged. "Lady, I promise, if you conceive a child, I will know the father!"

"But—"

"Lady, come here. The night has just begun."

Her eyes widened. "But we've already—"

He laughed, catching her, sweeping her hard into his arms. She struggled against him. He kissed her, hands delving into the mass of her hair. His husky whisper touched her lips.

"As I've said, lady, the night has just begun. And the rose has just started to bloom!"

Chapter 16

The green shadows of the forest were just beginning to fall. Damian, dressed as the Silver Sword, sat atop Lucifer, waiting impatiently for Robin to make an appearance. Time was of the essence at this moment.

News had come to them here in the north country in a frightening manner.

First, the news had been good. Richard's Crusade was finished.

Although Richard had not really bested Saladin—and Jerusalem had not really fallen—the English King and the Moslem ruler had come to an agreement. Travel was now made safe for Christian pilgrims to the Holy Lands.

Despite his tireless energy and resolve, circumstances had tied Richard's hands as surely as a cord of rope. King Phillip of France had given up the quest and gone home. Other European leaders had done the same.

Richard alone had gained this one piece of victory.

Hearing all that had occurred from the messenger sent specifically his way, Damian had felt a surge of bitterness. He should have been with Richard. He should have tasted the victory, and the sense of discouragement, with Richard. He should have been with him.

He had forgotten that he had wanted to come home just before Richard had summoned him to his tent. Forgotten the longing for the green coolness of the forest.

He would have liked to have forgotten his new bride, but that luxury was not allowed him.

He was angry half of the time, it seemed, and obsessed the rest. No matter what victories he gained over her, no matter how he sought through sheer strength to control her, she managed to fight him still.

She had been the most perfect hostess to Eleanor and Prince John and his retinue. There had been no reason to be diplomatic with de la Ville, for he had been so furious with the turn of events that he had turned around then and there to ride home—after denying, of course, that he'd had anything whatsoever to do with an attempted abduction of the Lady de Montrain.

Lady Montjoy now. And forever. Damian had stressed that last. For he was certain, now that de la Ville had seen her possessed by another, he wanted her more than ever.

Katherine! His wife. She was a complexity.

No woman could have been more tactful, more gracious, or more beautiful as she entertained their royal visitors. She was still seething at him, he knew. No matter what he had touched within her. No matter how he had held her. No matter how he wanted her, again and again, just watching as she moved about the hall.

She saw to meals, she offered interesting tidbits of information about the castle and the forest, telling tales about the day-to-day lives of both peasants and knights, making everyone laugh.

Not that he was so very amused himself. For though surely no man could have come to know a wife more intimately, she held herself carefully away from him. And she told him so with her every glance.

No matter, lady! he thought. You will learn to obey me, and that will be that! It was all he needed do, he told himself. Mold her. Teach her, tame her. And that he would do.

Yet every once in a while he would catch her smile. And first he would feel the steel and fever seep into his body, causing his muscles to tense and her jaw to lock. And he'd want to sweep her up and cast the chalices and plate from the broad table in the great hall and have her then and there. All of her. All that she held away from him.

He would remind himself that he did not love her. Perhaps he was acquiring a certain tenderness toward her. Perhaps he admired her, perhaps he even enjoyed the challenge of her, for when those cool, sea-colored eyes touched his, so often he felt a smile curl his lip, and a sizzle of fire touch his heart. But he could not love her, so he assured himself. He had done well enough. He had managed to take the castle and the girl, and make both his. He could expect no more. His heart he had given before, and it was not something he would ever think to risk in her furious fingers. And still . . .

Ah, indeed, she was becoming an obsession. And they played at a game of give and take. The first night following their wedding, she tried very hard to keep Eleanor and John and their retinues of nobles and ladies up just as late as she could.

Conversation and wine flowed—and very easily, at first, for the topic had been the assault on the castle. Prince John had pretended to listen to every detail with great concern—he had, of course, been completely ignorant of such an attack, and he clucked with sympathy over it. "It was wonderful for dear Katherine that this Silver person—" Eleanor began.

"Silver Sword?" John interjected, an edge to his voice.

"Yes, that's it! It's wonderful that he could come so swiftly to Katherine's defense!"

"The man is a bandit, Eleanor," John informed his mother. "A plague of these parts—just like that wretched Robin Hood."

"Yet, for Katherine's sake, we all must be grateful," Eleanor said. "Isn't it true, my dear?"

"Aye, isn't it true?" Damian pressed Katherine.

Her lashes fell as innocently as an angel's, but he detected a strangling tone to her voice, too, and he quickly hid his own smile. "I am most certainly—grateful!" she murmured.

"Kat rescued, honor saved!" Eleanor said delightedly. "It's a wonderful story, isn't it, Damian?"

"Oh, aye. And of course, I am grateful, too, beyond belief," Damian said, lifting his chalice to his wife in a salute. He smiled. Her cheeks colored just slightly. Her eyes clashed with his.

"If I find the man, I will be fully aware that he is a bandit still!" John announced harshly. "And he will be treated as such. Hanged, just like wretched Robin Hood and his companions, that huge Saxon Little John, the one they call Will, the Lady Greensleeves, and all the others!"

Damian watched his wife carefully as John spoke, and was startled by the strength of the emotions that swept through him as he studied her face. For there was some light of innocence in her eyes, and then a touch of fear as a small shudder seized her. But her chin went up, almost imperceptibly. She would not be frightened or swayed by anything that John said. She hated what she had seen in the forest that day so long ago.

And she meant to fight it, whether she was afraid or not, for herself or equally for Robin.

Or the Silver Sword.

John's eyes suddenly touched Damian's. "You, my Lord Montjoy, must take care now that you are here."

"Oh, how is that?" Damian asked, sipping his wine nonchalantly and leaning against the stone mantel at the hearth.

"Some say that the bandit Robin Hood is kin to your

wife. That he is the son of the old Saxon Earl of Locksley. That would make him your wife's first cousin on the maternal side."

Damian didn't allow himself to tense. His eyes narrowed as he watched Kat's golden head. Give nothing away! he longed to warn her, and he spoke quickly. "They say that no one knows the true identity of Robin Hood. In fact, the peasants say that there is not one identity for the man, that the name speaks of a spirit of freedom within the forest."

"It sounds as if you're near to speaking treason, Montjoy!"

Damian bowed low. "Never, Your Grace! I would honor our good King Richard to the grave and far beyond!"

Kat turned, watching him, a curious light in eyes, a picture of beauty as the wealth of her hair streamed behind her.

"Katherine?" John said acidly. "Tell me, do you agree with this?"

"Of course. I honor my husband in all things," she said softly.

Just as hell could freeze! Damian thought. He smiled wryly, watching her. Her eyes quickly turned from him.

This marriage was still war.

And later that night, she fought her battles with the beauty of her smile and the flash of her eyes. Wine flowed, wonderful food was served. She played the lute. She sang with a melodious voice, one to rival the angels. Even with a house filled with royalty and nobles, she was the one to hold court. A queen, a prince, knights and ladies, villeins and hounds, all seemed to circle around her. She charmed. She seduced. She brought easy laughter to the lips of so many.

She irritated Damian beyond belief, never stepping over the boundaries of perfect propriety, and yet . . .

Pushing. Ever pushing. She had the Prince just about at her feet, eating out of her hand figuratively and near literally, as she offered him olives brought back from the Holy Lands.

A dangerous play! he wanted to shout to her. John didn't really care one way or another if de la Ville wanted something.

But if John wanted something himself . . .

Yet she had the Prince talking. Bragging. Telling her all his thoughts and desires.

There, so charming, so sweet, moved the cunning mind of the Lady Greensleeves, Damian thought. But those days are over, my lady! You'll not run into the forest with your tales and weapons any longer. It is too dangerous a game, and if Robin could not stop you, I will.

But watching her, Damian realized that she seduced men to speak. To tell her anything they knew. She elicited the same response from the knight's ladies, sympathizing with them, advising them, laughing with them.

Beyond seducing all their secrets from them, Damian realized dryly, she was managing to keep them all up, and awake, and busy throughout the night.

She was quite determined to escape the hours alone with him.

She innocently protested Damian's command that they go to bed, telling him that they must be courteous. And she turned her back on him, drawing adoration from the eyes of even Damian's good servant, Sir James. She laughed with him, and flirted outrageously. And when Damian would have approached her again, she turned to Father Donovan, and what she said to that false priest, Damian did not know.

Anything, he thought, to avoid her husband!

He let her go so far, fuming inwardly, yet smiling to both the Prince and Eleanor with all the humor and tolerance he could muster.

He had no intention of allowing John to see that theirs was a house divided. Such knowledge could be very dangerous in those Plantagenet hands.

Then when a number of the knights, in their various colors, were snoring upon the floor and the rushes, their arms and their cups draped over the huge bodies of the castle hounds, he determined that he'd had enough.

Perhaps she saw the look in his eyes. Her own narrowed, and she bid her good-nights quickly to those who remained awake, and flew up the stairs, well ahead of him.

As he had expected, she was curled up, feigning sleep. He was weary himself, but very determined, so he lay down beside her and waited, half closing his eyes.

And when he saw the smug smile begin to creep into her lips, he rolled quickly, taking her into his arms. "Ah, you cannot sleep, my lady? Neither can I. I know a very brisk exercise that is wonderful for such restlessness."

"I can sleep very well!" she protested. "Truly, I am exhausted—"

"You will be more so. And so prone to smirk and smile, acts which must cause an awful wakefulness!"

Those beautiful aquamarine eyes of hers shimmered in the darkness. "Last night you would starve me! And now you would deprive me of sleep!"

"Aye, lady! That I will do. Until you have come to honor your vows to love, honor, and obey."

"I shall never love you! I detest you!"

"Lady, that is your misfortune. And something that means nothing to me. You will honor and obey me!" he promised. "If it means that you must starve, stay awake for eons, or even reside within the walls of the castle dungeons."

She gasped, eyes growing wide, amazed that he would say such a thing. He was startled to see that a soft glaze had come to shield her eyes. As if there just might be a trace of tears upon the length of those golden, wickedly long lashes.

"What of you, Montjoy? I am not your Alyssa, so you have no love for me. You vowed to cherish, my lord, but all that you seek is to command. May I also threaten to cast you into the dungeons, or into some awful hell on earth?"

He moved his fingers over the radiance of her hair. And he spoke the truth as he did so. "Lady, you spent half this evening sending me to every imaginable hell. Flirting, smiling, teasing, taunting, seducing—seducing my own men, at that! Poor Sir James. He's young, my lady. You did well setting your web about his heart. I might begin to wonder at how easily you seem to acquire men. So I warn you. Let's talk no more this night. Not unless you feel that you should bare your soul, and tell me of your past life, the lover—or lovers!—you have known."

She gasped. "Nay!"

"Then . . . ?"

To his amazement, her hands curled round his neck. And her lips touched down upon his. Softly. Tentatively. Yet with such a feminine and captivating appeal that he was inflamed, and more than willing to forget any questions—had he really had them. By nature, she was beautiful. By instinct, she could use that beauty to be an incredible love.

And when the night was over and he lay awake while she slept, he knew that in one way they had formed an intimate bond—they had become husband and wife, and perhaps more. It was almost as if he were drugged. He craved her. Wanted more and more of her. There was something magical about her beauty. About the golden tendrils of hair that would around and seduced him, soft, enchanting. Perhaps it was even in her eyes. Eyes with that fascinating aqua shiver, all fury and challenge one moment, and all fascination the next. How could they be such fantastic lovers—and such bitter enemies?

And though he knew that she would eventually come into his arms, each night it was something new. She must brush her hair, for several hours at the very least. There was a problem with their bed—the ropes were not right, the bedding was awry, and not one of the hundreds of villeins who lived within the place had managed to fix it to her satisfaction. She could always think of some reason to elude him.

One night when he had been entirely certain that she had gone to bed ahead of him, he was amazed to discover that she was not within the chamber. He had paced the confines of the room, then begun a silent search of the keep. Down the to hall below, and upstairs again.

She had awaited him then. And she had seemed extremely nervous.

"Where were you?"

"Why, just down the hall, seeking to see to—"

"To what?"

Those rich lashes fell over her eyes. Her hands folded demurely before her. "Seeking to see to my household duties, my lord."

He gripped her shoulders. "You were nowhere! I searched for you!"

She was, indeed, very, very nervous. Her tongue lightly touched her lips. Perhaps he had spent too much time taunting her, being fully aware that he himself was the Silver Sword, the lover she had first known.

This was not so amusing. This was something that he could not touch, and it was alarming.

"Where were you?"

And she had pulled away. "Nowhere, my lord, as you can see. I am here in the castle. With you."

He found himself worrying still. Although de la Ville

was gone, John remained. He was not hunting, or amusing himself in any of his usual pursuits. There was no one here with whom he could plot and plan. His mother ever sided with Richard. Why was he staying?

"Jesu!" He seethed suddenly. "If it is John—"

"John!" she exploded. And a smile curved her lips. "I do assure you, my lord, I have not been with John. He is truly a Norman rat!"

"But so am I, my lady. So you've informed me."

She lifted her nose regally. "Aye, that's true enough." Maybe something in his expression gave her cause for alarm, for she stepped back quickly. "You are not as . . . repulsive . . . a rat!"

"The Prince is a surprising man of our time, my lady. He seeks to bathe daily. At least he is not a dirty Norman rat."

She shuddered softly. "He could bathe forever, and he would remain filthy."

"So you wouldn't be with him—by choice."

"Never."

"But it seems that you did bed another before our marriage. Out of love, or out of spite? Was it something done to flaunt me?"

"It was not done on purpose," she said swiftly.

"Rape? I will have his throat!"

"Why bother? Is life so different now?"

"Aye, it is. For we are wed. And I have very carefully done my best to charm and seduce—as you do yourself!—rather than use any force. So tell me a name—"

"There is no name! No one name. Perhaps there were twenty names—"

"John among them?"

"No!" she protested. Then she swore in aggravation. "Leave it be! As I have said, you are not so repulsive."

"But I believe that you did go to another to spite me. So even if the Prince is repulsive, perhaps—"

He caught her wrist quickly as she tried to strike him. "My lady—"

"Don't you dare accuse me so! I owed you no allegiance before we were wed!"

He pulled her close. "You damned well owe it to me now!"

"And I truly despise John. Far more—"

"Far more?"

"Than I have ever hated you!" she whispered softly.

He laughed. "I believe I'm even entertaining to you upon occasion." He murmured. He wanted to stay away. Damn. She was hiding something from him, and he was determined to know what.

But he found himself holding her still. Looking down into the coolness of her eyes. Longing to shake her.

And slipping his fingers into the soft flowing cloak of her hair instead. "I think, my lady, that I am not nearly so horrid as you claim. You forget that I am the second skin that lies with you. You forget that I hear your cries, and your whispers, and feel the movement of your limbs beneath me."

She blinked and tried to escape his hold. "Montjoy—"

"Come, my lady, whisper it. 'My lord, you are really not repulsive at all.' That would hardly be a declaration of undying love and passion, yet it would be a start!"

Her head fell back. Her eyes challenged his. "You would have this? From me? When you come to bed each night and make your demands, then close your eyes and wish that I were another woman?"

"What?" He released her instantly, eyes narrowing.

She turned her back on him. "I am not Alyssa Albright, my lord."

"Nay, lady, you are not!"

Neither was she right, and he felt an odd sense of shame at the words. He had loved Alyssa. He had thought himself loyal to her memory.

Yet he had never wanted Kat to be she, never dreamed of Alyssa in the night. He was obsessed with Kat. His desire for her never seemed satiated . . .

"So what do you care, my lord," she murmured softly, "where I have been? Or with whom?"

He swung her back around to face him. "What I care, madam, is that you are mine. And if I discover you with any man, he is a dead one. What you are, Kat, is my wife."

She was trembling. Not fighting him with her usual fury.

Just where had she been?

The anger, the fear might have seized hold of him.

But her arms suddenly wound around his neck. "I have not betrayed you!" she whispered. Her lips were against his throat. His arms wrapped around her.

Hours later, he lay awake in the night, haunted by the memory of Ari's words in the desert.

She will betray you . . .

Had she done so? Was it yet to come?

Was Ari a fool? Was there such a thing as destiny, and could he change it?

She lay sleeping at his side, comfortable there now. The nights had made her his, as such things went. Her inhibitions with him were fading. She seemed as natural as a kitten, indeed his wife, naked within the shelter of his arm, sleeping so peacefully.

Ah, peace!

Aye, he wanted a touch of peace, he thought. Some gentleness in this world.

But now, as he sat upon Lucifer, waiting, he knew that there could be no peace. Not domestically, and not within their world at large.

He sighed, growing more impatient as the sun set in a burst of red beauty behind the high tops of the tall trees to the west.

Only days after word reached him that Richard had found a certain triumph in the Holy Lands, a second messenger had found his way to Damian. And this man brought news of disaster, not triumph.

England could well be at the brink of civil war.

Richard the Lionheart, Richard the great warrior, Richard the King was suddenly the prisoner of another monarch in another place.

Richard had left the Holy Lands to return to England, but his journey had been cut short. He had been captured by the Duke of Austria, who had immediately turned him over to Henry VI, Emperor of Germany.

And the Emperor wanted a hundred thousand marks from England as a ransom for King Richard's release.

John had departed the castle the moment the word had come, and Damian had been sorely worried by the look he had seen on John's face. Eleanor, too, had departed. The Queen was headed to London to start what efforts she could to raise the ransom.

While John . . .

John had already ordered that a nearby monastery be stripped of all precious relics of silver and gold.

They would not be sold for the money to ransom his brother. They would rather be sold to the highest bidder for the money to raise his own army.

If Damian knew John, and he was afraid that he did, the Prince intended to claim the throne in Richard's absence and see that his brother resided in a German castle until he grew old and rotted there.

However, to transport his stolen riches, John's men were going to have to travel through the forest roads. And there he might well be stopped. If only Robin would arrive so that the men might be gathered in time!

Damian heard a rustling in the trees and backed Lucifer more deeply into the foliage, determined to see before he was seen. But as he had expected, Robin came riding to him on a white mare.

"My friend!" He rode close, offering Damian his hand. Damian clasped it quickly. "Jesu, I am grateful to you. I hear that you rescued my fair cousin from the tower rather spectacularly."

Beneath the mail helmet and visor of the Silver Sword, Damian grimaced. "Spectacular—and wet," he admitted.

Robin grinned. "Oh, indeed, it seems my Kat was seriously outraged, and is as angry with the Silver Sword as she is with her new husband, Lord Montjoy."

Damian shrugged. "Robin, I did my best."

"Um. I tell you, Damian, there's much I'd have given to have seen the faces on our dear Prince John and the noble de la Ville when they broke in on the two of you on your wedding bed."

"Word travels quickly," Damian said.

"Very quickly. And now, we've little time. Did you come to assist my men and me this afternoon? Within the hour, we must be on the road, ready to attack the pack train with the religious relics."

"How in God's name do you know about that? I came here this afternoon to warn you that your men must be gathered, and that something must be done. And that Richard is captive—"

"Richard is captured, and a ransom must be raised before John can seize the crown. Aye, Damian, I know it all."

"And how? By God, I can see how you might know about the King, but I heard about John's plans in my own house—"

He broke off, feeling a swift simmering of anger within him. "Let me guess. Katherine. Ah, no! She's the Lady Greensleeves when she slips through the forest, right? Damn you, Robin! I thought that we were agreed! This is too dangerous a game now for her to be involved!

And damn her! She's my wife now! I swear I—"

"Damian, I know that it is dangerous. And we did agree. But we did not get Kat to agree, and therein lies our problem."

"She comes to you—"

"And I send her home. With warnings and threats and all. Damian, she does not heed me."

"Well, Robin, she will heed me. I will see to it."

There was a hard set to Damian's jaw that sent a chill of unease along Robin's spine. He started to speak, then reminded himself that Damian and Kat were now wed. It was certainly not a match made in heaven—not from Kat's point of view and, from Damian's look, not from his, either. But Robin loved them both dearly, and respected Damian as he did few other men. Few other men would risk so much in loyalty not just to a king, but to justice.

No harm would come to Kat in his care. Even if Kat's eyes did flash with fury every time she mentioned his name.

"Deal gently with her, Damian!" Robin said.

"Gently!" Damian snorted.

"She's a tender little thing—"

"As tender as a hedgehog, Robin."

Robin lowered his head, hiding a smile. "She claims you're the most arrogant jailer she's ever met. And she likes the Silver Sword no more. What were you, charming in the extreme as both men?" Robin inquired.

"You sent me to save her at the castle. I sent hooks flying to scale walls to rescue her, and the next thing I knew, she had taken her sword against me. Then I told her that I was holding her safe for the husband chosen for her by the King, and she tried every available means of escape. That was the Silver Sword. Now as Montjoy, I merely married her, and I promise you, hell can be no greater a tempest!" His eyes narrowed sharply. "How the hell is she getting to you? I've ordered my men to keep a strict eye on her. Ah, and before the wedding could take place, she managed the miraculous escape from the castle. I knew she would be heading for you, and so I found her in time. De la Ville was on his way at the very moment."

Robin laughed. "Ah! So the damsel is escaping the Silver Sword at every turn?"

Montjoy's eyes sizzled like the silver of the mail that lay against his face. "Robin, I tell you, this is not amusing. Perhaps she finds her lot a bitter one now. If de la Ville seizes her, or if the Prince finds a higher bidder for her now, we will be hard put to sweep her from their hands again! With Richard free, John knew some fear. While now . . ."

"Aye, I know!" Robin said quickly. Then he shook his head, somewhat at a loss. "I never told you about the tunnel?"

Montjoy leaned low over his horse's neck. "What tunnel?" he asked sharply.

"There's a tunnel that runs from the castle. There's an entrance from Kat's room. One pushes a false front, and there is a door there. Then a small hall, a circular stone stair, and at its bottom, the tunnel. It lets out in the caves just beyond the stream."

"There is a tunnel into the castle?" Montjoy repeated, his voice hardening.

"Aye!"

Montjoy shook his head. "I sent that wretched hook and rope up the parapets, scaled the castle walls—and there was a tunnel entry?"

"Jesu, Damian, I am sorry. I was deeply worried when I spoke with you that night. And I was right to be so concerned, as you saw."

Damian sat back. "Well, at the least, I am glad that you have let me in on this secret now." He paused a moment. "Why, that little witch! She nearly escaped me before the wedding, and she did sneak out the other night! That was why I couldn't find her!"

"She came to tell me what she knew about Richard and the Crusades," Robin said.

"I will wring her lovely little neck!"

Robin shook his head. "You can't do that. Not unless you intend to tell her that you are the Silver Sword."

Montjoy's eyes narrowed. "Nay, not yet!" He didn't tell Robin that he didn't intend Kat to be let off any too easily for her encounter with the Silver Sword. It worried her still, and he was glad of it.

She deserved it!

"Well, then—"

"I will find a way to stop her using the tunnel," Damian said quietly. "Perhaps I will block it somehow."

"Well, don't do so yet."

"Why not?"

Robin looked unhappy. "I'm not sure that she's returned home as yet."

"She came running out again this morning!" Damian exploded.

"She felt she had to tell me about John and the relics stolen from the monastery."

"Wretched little—" Damian began.

But there was suddenly a movement in the forest, and a small gray mare could just be seen through the trees. A soft feminine voice sounded.

"Robin! Robin!" The horse broke through the trees. Kat was riding it. Kat, caped and capped in a costume of green that matched the trees. Her eyes were on Robin. "The men are seeking you! The Prince's men have already entered the forest with their wagons—"

She broke off abruptly, for she had turned.

And she had seen him.

"You!" she gasped. A strangled fury entered her voice. "You—traitor!"

"Traitor?" Robin said, looking from one to the other of them with confusion. "Kat, this is . . . er, this is the man who rescued you."

"You!" Damian exploded in return. "The Lady Katherine—the Lady Montjoy! Madam, you are now wed, a wife and chatelaine. You shouldn't be here!"

"You have no say over me here!" she informed him coolly. "I'm not your prisoner any longer. Here I am the Lady Greensleeves, and a dozen men in this forest would die to protect me!"

"And you would probably have them do so!"

"Both of you, please—" Robin tried to interrupt.

But Kat was working into a rage. "You! You scurviest of rats and traitors—"

"Aye, my lady, me!" Damian replied, "Traitor, whatever you would have me be! The Silver Sword—ever at your service once again!"

Chapter 17

"Your pardon, both of you," Robin said. "This train of riches will pass us right by if we do not make haste to join with the fellows."

"Indeed, yes!" the Silver Sword said, bowing low to Kat. "My Lady Montjoy. Go home."

"Sir, don't you ever think to command me," she retorted in a low voice of warning.

"Kat, please, I am grateful, as always, for the news you bring me," Robin said. "Now go home, out of harm's way."

But she wasn't listening to Robin. She was still staring angrily at the Silver Sword. The aquamarine color of her eyes had taken on the forest hues, and they seemed to burn a green fire as they touched upon the Silver Sword. "I shall be out of harm's way," she assured Robin.

She was defying them both, determined to stay until she knew the results of the intended assault upon the Prince's men.

Damian leaned low over his horse's neck. "Lady, what would your husband say, to know that you were here? Think of my command as his!"

Did she hesitate, for perhaps just a second? Her chin lifted. "My husband, sir, was not of my choosing, as you well know. No man commands me!"

"I imagine that he thinks he does."

"Then he should think again."

"If we could just discuss this all later—?" Robin suggested.

Indeed, it would have to be discussed later. One of Robin's followers—the giant bandit farmer, a man as big as an old bear, with grizzled whiskers and flashing quick dark eyes, who was curiously known as Little John— came upon them on foot. Despite his size and bulk, he could run like a deer, Damian knew. He'd seen the man in action. He could fight well with a sword and aim an arrow with precision. His greatest prowess, however, was with a staff. He could take on half a dozen men with that weapon, and best them while they still assumed that he was scarcely armed.

"They're coming down the north road!" he informed them quickly. "And wary they are! A guard of near fifty, and armed to the teeth. If we don't take them at the angle in the road, we might well be in difficulty."

"Aye!" Robin said. He looked hard to Damian. "Come, sir, let's ride!"

Damian watched in amazement as Kat spun her horse about, still determined to join in the action. Little John was already leading the way on foot like an ancient Grecian runner. Robin's horse cantered behind him, and Kat would have followed, too.

Damian rode his horse alongside hers, reaching over for her reins. She gazed at him in astonishment, trying to back her mount away from him. "If you don't let go—" she warned him.

"If I don't let go, what?" he demanded heatedly.

She leaned close to him. "I will give my husband your name! I'll let him skewer you right through, hang you by the neck—"

"And he'll hang me, knowing that you're the Lady Greensleeves?"

"Aye!"

"What if I were to slay him?"

Her eyes widened somewhat, and he was maddened to realize that he couldn't read the emotion within them. Would she care if Lord Damian Montjoy were to be slain?

"Let go! I swear, I'll see you hanged myself!"

"And if you don't stop here this instant, I'll tie you to yonder oak!"

"You wouldn't dare!"

"I would indeed!"

"Robin would have your throat!"

"I think not."

She quickly changed her tactics. "I have no intention of joining in the fray. I am good with a sword, as you know, yet I swear I will risk no swordplay. I just wish to climb high above in the trees with Robin's archers—"

"My lady, the Prince's men will have archers with them as well. And in a tree, you will sit as pretty as a bird to be plucked!"

"Then I will stay behind the rock—"

"You'll stay here."

He saw the sudden stubborn streak in her eyes. She brought a small riding crop down hard on his hand where he held her reins. Surprise caused him to release his hold, and she nearly bolted from him.

She would have made good her escape, had it not been for Lucifer. The well-trained mount stopped her mare from racing forward, blocking the animal's path. And in seconds Damian had dismounted from Lucifer and was dragging Kat down from the mare. She cursed him, trying to flay him anew with the whip, but he was quick and determined. In a matter of seconds, he had her seated before one of the oaks in the copse, and though she hissed and threatened and tried her best to kick and struggle, he bound to the oak with a strip of green cloth ripped from her cloak. He stood then, surveying his handiwork, trying to assure himself that she was securely tied, but not bound so tightly as to cause her pain.

"So this is it!" she hissed, staring at him in fury. Her cloak had fallen back. The heavy abundance of her hair had been braided and knotted at her nape, but dancing tendrils had escaped that severe confinement and now trailed about the delicate beauty of her face.

Delicate! Her eyes were definitely filled with all the fury of Satan. There was nothing delicate about this maid's temper!

"So you would tie me! It is your way, eh? When your commands are not obeyed, when people do not fall down to serve you, you simply use blunt force to tie them up! Fine! I'm here! Is this your only way? Is there anything else you want while I am left so helpless?"

"Lady, a tigress should be so helpless!" he retorted, then felt the impact of her words and didn't know if he wanted to laugh—or to strike her. He started to walk away, but swung back. "Madam, I do not recall propositioning you, while you did your damnedest to sway me from the course of honor that was mine!"

"Course of honor! Why you despicable—thief!" He could have sworn that a glaze of tears touched her eyes. "You took what what was offered—and betrayed me!"

"I made no promises!" he assured her roughly. He didn't have time for this. Robin needed him against Prince John's fifty men.

He spent enough of his time as Lord Montjoy dealing with her!

But suddenly he was down upon one knee before her, staring into her eyes. "Was what I did so horrible to you, Katherine? Have you found yourself tormented, tortured, abused? Does he beat you? Abandon you? Is he truly so horrid a person? Are the nights hell on earth? Isn't there the least touch of heaven within any of it?"

Her eyes met his, flaming. Then her lashes fell in a honey-gold sweep over her cheeks. "You still do not understand."

"Does he have warts? Foul breath? What?"

"If anything, sir," she retorted, her eyes meeting his, "he is far too much like you! A Norman version of a Saxon knave!"

He rose then, angry with her, and with himself. What had he expected from her? He needed to take care. Perhaps she would begin to realize just how much they were alike, the Silver Sword and her husband, even if the languages they used were different.

"What do you want out of the man when he has a wife determined on a life of banditry?"

"He knows nothing of my life," she assured him airily.

"Perhaps he should."

Her eyes flew open wide upon him. "You jest! Perhaps he is Richard's man, but if he knew that I brought aid to the infamous Robin Hood . . ." Her voice trailed away. "If—if he knew who I was, he, too, might become determined that the forest must be cleared of the outlaws."

He felt his jaw tightening like steel. She still thought her husband to be an autocrat, with no sense!

And she was still willing to risk her life and limb out here in the forest! Well, this was her last excursion. He would see to that later.

He bowed to her. "I've no more time. I shall return shortly to free you."

He turned to leave her. She called after him in a fine temper. "And what if you are slain? What if that silver sword is sent flying, and that knave's throat is slashed? What then? Shall I rot here, sir! Damn you! Come back! Let me free!"

He felt a certain satisfaction, leaving her there. A smile curled his lip. He leaped upon Lucifer and nudged his flanks, racing after Robin and John.

He would have to take extra care not to be killed!

Kat listened as the sound of his horse's hooves faded into the sweet-scented air, unable to believe that she found herself in such a predicament. She hadn't meant to join in any fight, but she would have been there, just in case she could have saved some situation. She'd been very good since the day she had run into her husband in the woods. She'd never tried to attack any group of men, but she had stayed with Little John or Will upon occasion, and once she had managed to throw a rock at one of the Prince's men, distracting him long enough for Little John to find his staff, which he had lost.

But things were different now, so it seemed. The Silver Sword had returned.

She looked heavenward, struggling to free her wrists. "I am plagued! That Norman for a husband, this Saxon to wreck what private life remained to me!" There was no answer, and she gritted her teeth. The more she fought the tie he had created, the tighter it became. She felt her temper soar, and she studiously fought her anger. When she calmed it somewhat, she realized that she could fray the fabric by running it along the bark of the tree. Patiently, she began to do so.

Her patience ebbed. She began to curse the Silver Sword to no end. She rested, feeling a trickle of sweat slide along her face despite the chill of the day.

The air seemed very still here. Silent. The trees surrounded her like a green shroud. She could hear birds chirping. The earth beneath her was redolent, damp, soft. No leaves rustled in the stillness. There was a sense of waiting here.

It was a fine situation! What if a wild boar came along? Or a snake. Or worse . . .

What if her husband were to come riding in the forest with some men? She didn't know where he had gone. He had been quiet and moody and set on his course since he had heard that Richard had been taken prisoner. He had left this morning . . .

Would he come near here?

She began once again to work her wrists along the bark of the tree, her effort aided by her anger against herself. The fear of a snake or a boar hadn't done it. Thinking that Damian might find her here had sent her into very quick action. It had made her breathless, made her heart pound too quickly.

She was not afraid of him, she assured herself. What more could he do to her? He had taken over her life. He lived in her castle, in her room . . .

In her bed.

She trembled, and tried not to think of the man. If she was so sworn to despise him, why couldn't she do so with more purpose? Because he was so determined that hating him completely would be futile?

Or because . . . ?

She was finding a greater and greater fascination with the man. He dealt very well with people. Her guard admired him. He had made it a point to meet with and know every man, know his weaknesses and his strengths. He had also gone out among the villeins, and he had seen their work, and even seen to his own satisfaction that the people worked their own small holdings as well as giving their allotted days to their work for the lord and lady of the castle. To Kat's irritation, she had seen a number of the women look to Damian with wonder—and more!— in their eyes. Perhaps he did look like a great lord, tall on his black stallion, regal in his cape, indomitable with his silver eyes and ebony hair. Perhaps . . .

Perhaps there were even things that were truly admirable about him. His was a good shoulder to rest upon.

Strong. Even when he had been stark naked, she had felt safe from both John and de la Ville behind his back. And then there was the way his lips could touch hers . . . and touch her flesh. And there was the hot, tensed feel of his muscled flesh beneath her fingertips, and there was the fusion of their bodies . . .

And there was his temper, and his raw determination, and the way that he saw fit to order her about. So he was a careful enough lover. Tender, nurturing. All to his own end, for he wanted her. Aye, wanted her enough . . .

Even if she was certain that he sought to make love to a ghost. Alyssa Albright had been the woman he had wanted. Perfect, beautiful, quiet—obedient!—Alyssa.

She bit her lip, sorry, for Alyssa had been a beautiful lady. Always kind. Always caring. And some women might well say that it was better to have a husband in love with a ghost than a husband who carried on numerous affairs.

She didn't know anything about her husband, she reminded herself. She just knew him. The bronze of his shoulders, the dark mat of hair on his chest, the whorl of it that led in a narrowing line to his waist and flared out again at his groin. The tension and ripple of his muscles when he made love to her.

She could care about the man, she thought. Perhaps she did care about him, whether she wished to do so or not. She might never have realized it, had not the Silver Sword warned that he might slay Montjoy. And then she had pictured him. Damian. That warrior's bronzed body, broken and bleeding. The silver eyes closed forever. The proud, handsome face still in death, the sensual lips silenced forever . . .

A ripple of heat cascaded through her, and her breath caught. In truth, he was not so terrible. In truth, she even looked forward to the nights, to the tempest that lay between them, to the hours held tight and secure while she slept.

Aye, she could easily come to care for him . . .

Fool! she chastised herself, then grit her teeth. He was the selfsame bastard who had brought his hand down upon her in the forest! But he hadn't known her, hadn't recognized her then. And he never would, never, if only—

If only he never caught her red-handed, tied here to a tree!

Ever more strenuously, she ripped her ties along the bark. Then, to her pleasure and amazement, the fabric ripped through at last. She leaped to her feet, dusting the dirt from her green tunic, cloak, and hose, and rubbing her wrists. She had chafed them in her efforts to free herself, but it had been a pain well worth it!

She hurried to her mare, mounted the animal quickly, and rode through the narrow trail as rapidly as she could. As she neared the main road, she slowed down, her heart quickening as she heard the sounds of a battle engaged. There was no chirping of birds here. The air was alive with the ringing of steel, with the cries of horses, with the shouts of men.

She dismounted from her mare and carefully made her way through the foliage to the side of the road, peering through the bushes and around a clump of rock there.

Robin had set archers in the trees, and those archers had done fair damage. Men-at-arms lay strewn across the road, arrow shafts protruding from their bodies. Some arrows had pierced armor, and some had found the weaknesses of it, catching men through their throats, finding a mark through an eye, or one here and one there at a man's nape.

No one had needed to die, Kat knew. Robin never assaulted a party without first offering men the choice of laying down their arms and departing the forest. He was fair, and yet . . .

This carnage today seemed awful, for there were so many men!

And so many still engaged in battle!

The wagonloads of goods stripped from the monastery remained in the center of the road, and it was from there that the remaining men formed something of a circle to fight the bandits. And there, hard within the fighting, she saw the Silver Sword, Robin, John, and many of the others.

Beneath golden rays of the sun, with the green of the forest and the beautiful cool cloak of the day, men fought and died. Kat caught her breath with horror as she saw one of Robin's men, little Nat of Huntingdon, fall down as he was struck from behind by one of Prince John's men. He fell forward, eyes opened and glazed, and died there.

That same fierce guard hurried onward, wielding his sword. Even as she watched, he neared Robin's back.

Her cousin did not see him. He was engaged with the two swordsmen who harried him from the front. "Robin!" she shouted, leaping to her feet. She raced forward, entirely forgetting herself and her own safely.

She drew the sword she had carried at her side—for defensive purposes only—and thrust her way between the mounted man and Robin. The Prince's guard raised his sword against her. She met it coolly with her own. The clash of the steel reverberated all the way down her arm. The man was mounted, which added weight and pressure to his strikes against her.

"Kat!" Robin dispatched one man battling him and tried to come to her aid, but the other rushed him. Kat's hood fell back from her face and the guard whistled, and laughed. "Have at it, friends! A woman! A woman fights for the bandits! What have we here? Come, help me!"

She was suddenly encircled. No one dared come too close at first, for she was amazingly talented with her father's light sword, and sliced many an arm that came too near. But the men were all mounted. They were pressing her down the road, away from Robin. Away from help.

And finally, a deft blow from a fresh opponent sent her weapon falling to the ground. She cried out as the first guard drove his horse closer against her, sweeping her up. "It's Lady Montjoy!" someone called out. "Take her, take her alive! What a reward from Montjoy there will be!"

"Ho, to find his lady, here in the forest? More like he'll be ready to slay the messenger of this bad news!" cried another.

Kat fought the gauntleted hands that held her. She leaned forward, biting hard at the fingers that laced around her. The man cried out, but shifted his hold.

"We'll not get her out of the forest for a reward or any other prize at all," a visored guard told her tormentor, "unless we can escape this forest!"

"She will be our passage from here," the one who held her claimed. He caused his horse to rear and spin back to the action. "Robin! Robin Hood! We have a woman here. One who cried your name. Let us pass through here freely, else I'll slit her throat this minute, I swear it!"

All the clanging of steel stopped.

There was a silence in the forest, like nothing that Kat had heard before. The air itself seemed still.

"Drop your sword, bandit!" the guard commanded again. He quickly drew a dagger from a sheath at his calf, and pressed the razor-sharp blade to Kat's throat. She scarcely dared to breathe.

Robin stepped from the midst of the melee, standing before them. He paused, looking at her, and looking at the man.

"Don't!" she gasped. "Don't throw your sword down, Robin! He won't do it! He dares not kill me. Montjoy will have his throat—"

"Montjoy will never know when I have slain you, my beauty!" the man claimed. "If I don't escape this forest to live, it will make little difference to me! Lay down your sword. I leave here—with her!"

Silence reigned again. Silence in which the cool air seemed to shiver.

Then suddenly, a voice rang out. "Halt!" It was the Silver Sword.

Mounted upon his black horse, he walked the beast up behind Robin. He had strung an arrow in a bow. With deadly intent, he aimed it at the guard.

"Like bloody hell, sir!" he called. "Free her this second, or you are a dead man!"

"My blade is at her throat—"

"And my arrow is aimed at your eye!"

"I'll kill her!"

"Last chance!"

And it was the man's last chance. Kat felt his fingers tremble, felt the blade move against her flesh. Felt a trickle of blood . . .

Then she heard a whizzing sound against the stillness of the air. Then a horrible impact.

And she screamed. The knife fell away from her throat. The fingers that had fastened upon her loosened.

The man fell from the horse, dragging her along with him. She fell upon his chest, and stared with mounting horror at the arrow that protruded from his eye. She started to scream again, to scream and scream, totally unaware that swords were clanging in the forest again.

She tried to free herself from the body of the dead guard. Her cloak was caught beneath him.

Strong arms suddenly plucked her up, wrenching her garment free. Her teeth chattering, she gazed at the mail-masked face of the Silver Sword.

"Jesu!" she whispered.

"Death is seldom pretty," he told her sternly, and whistled for his horse. The obedient black stallion trotted up, and the Silver Sword mounted the horse, then reached for her, lifting her up behind him.

The fighting was near finished, Kat saw. Two-thirds of the guard were dead. The few remaining men were throwing down their swords and pleading for mercy.

Robin would grant it, Kat knew. Yet a shivering was stealing over her. When they fled the forest, they would bring tales with them. Tales about her having been here. Prince John would know.

Her husband would know.

Yet no one but she seemed aware of her predicament at the moment. The survivors of the guard were being tied, their wrists together behind their backs, and then the lot of them bound in a row together. And Robin and his men were opening the goods in the wagons, dragging them out, and commenting on the treasures they discovered. "Ah, now look at this cross! Have you ever seen such shimmering gold? There'll be no King John while good Richard lives, even if he does abide in captivity!" Robin cried. "This cross will help pay that fee to bring him back, eh, my lads?"

There was suddenly a startled scream from deep within one of the wagons.

"What new prize is this?" Robin demanded.

Little John pulled on a slender, blue-linen-clad arm. A woman fell from the wagon, and into his arms.

She was dark-haired and very beautiful, with deep, haunting dark eyes.

And she spit at Little John, and then at Robin, who stood atop the second wagon, looking down at her.

Kat was startled to see that her cousin had gone very white.

"How dare she spit at Robin!" Kat exclaimed. But Robin didn't hear her, nor did the woman.

"Aye!" the Silver Sword commented. "How amazing for a woman to abuse the very man who would rescue her!"

She slammed her elbow back against him, then listened hard, for Robin was speaking to the dark-haired beauty.

"Well, mistress, how nice to see you again," Robin said.

"So you are the bandit," she replied.

"That I am," Robin said, and bowed stiffly.

"And these mongrels are your men."

"I do take exception!" Little John exclaimed.

"They are my men, and you, Marian, are their prisoner, just as you are mine," Robin said.

"You make war upon your own people!" Marian exclaimed.

"These 'mongrels' are our people," Robin said flatly.

"We've work to do," another man reminded him softly.

"Oh, aye! Please pardon my distraction, my gentle friends!" Robin said. "Meet the Lady Marian, daughter of Sir Matthew Wheeler of Wiltshire—and, until she discovered that I was not popular among the court of Prince John, my betrothed!"

Kat gasped softly, having been unaware that Robin had ever been betrothed. But it had seemed years now that he had held this curious position as prince of the forest thieves. Surely it had been some time since this alliance had been broken.

But neither Marian nor Robin seemed to have forgotten anything that had passed between them. They watched each other now in a way that seemed to cause sparks to rise from the forest floor.

Suddenly the Silver Sword was twisting in his saddle to set Kat down upon the ground. She stared at him in astonishment and he explained quickly, "I think I had best step in here."

And he left her there, in the roadway, and urged his black stallion forward. "Robin!" he called, breaking something that had seemed to hold them all prisoner. "I will take Lady Marian to camp, and you may finish with this business here. Lady Marian, if you will come with me, you will be a guest here, never a prisoner."

And to Kat's wonder, the woman accepted the hand that the Silver Sword offered her. He lifted her up easily and sat her behind him. He raised a hand in salute to Robin, turned his mount, and began to ride.

He paused before Kat, staring down at her. The dark-haired girl, Marian, did likewise, watching her curiously.

"You, I will deal with later!" the Silver Sword warned her.

She gritted her teeth, watching the man go. A flurry of emotion was invoked within her. Anger, irritation . . .

Jealousy.

Nay . . .

She breathed deeply. Once again, the man had come to her rescue.

But then he had deposited her on the ground to sweep up another woman.

One whom Robin seemed to love, Kat speculated, studying her cousin. For Robin was watching the Silver Sword ride away with the dark-haired beauty, and it seemed that he wore his heart upon his sleeve. "See to these!" Robin said to Little John, and jumped down from the wagon. He called to a lean handsome man named Will to look after the prisoners, and started to walk down the road.

Kat hurried after him. She followed him for several minutes before he even realized that she was there. Then he turned to her in surprise. "Kat! My good Lord, Kat! You've got to get home." He hugged her suddenly. "Do you know how close you came to death today? What manner of man am I that I cannot control my own kinfolk? I've begged you—"

"Robin! That bastard would have slain you had I not been there!"

Robin inhaled sharply and paused. Then he exhaled slowly. "Aye, 'tis true. But I'd not have my life over yours, Katherine."

"Robin, in truth," she said ruefully, "your life is the more valuable of the two."

"Never. And you're married now, Kat. This has got to end. Can you imagine what might have happened if— if you had been killed?" He reached out and touched her throat, showing her the thin trickle of blood that touched his fingers.

Kat trembled. "Things worked out."

"But what of these men, Kat? Would you have me slay them all? When I release Prince John's men, they will carry back tales. And they recognized you."

"Perhaps I can speak with them. Perhaps—perhaps they can be persuaded to join you! Prince John will hardly be pleased if they return without his treasure!"

"Perhaps," Robin said. He was worried. He was trying to be attentive.

His mind was elsewhere.

"Why didn't you ever tell me about her?" Kat asked him softly.

He shook his head. "There was nothing to tell. Richard had just become King. We were in love. But then Richard rode to the Crusades, I was here when one of John's favorite noblemen nearly beheaded a peasant for taking a deer. I killed him, and the legend was born. And it was suspected that I was the bandit. Then John had more and more power . . ." He sighed. "Perhaps I'm not being fair. Marian's father died. He was a small land owner, a remnant of our own Saxon nobility. It probably had seemed a wise move to leave her under the protection of John Plantagenet." His voice hardened. "Or maybe she wanted his power herself, I don't know. She broke the betrothal when it was scarcely made. There was never anything to tell you."

"She spit at you," Kat said indignantly.

"I am outside the law, Kat." He paused, watching her. "As are you. Why didn't you go home, as I told you!"

She didn't reply. They both heard the sounds of horse's hooves coming along the dirt and stone road. They turned.

He was coming upon them. The Silver Sword.

The beautiful Marian no longer rode behind him.

"Robin!" the man called to him. "I have left Marian with your friend, the good friar. I believe she is somewhat reconciled to a lengthy stay in the forest. I will return, but I had thought perhaps I should take the Lady Greensleeves home."

"Home!" Kat exploded. "I cannot go home, Robin. Not now. What if these men talk—"

"They will not talk," the Silver Sword said softly.

"But—?"

"They are not leaving the forest. Twelve men lived— and twelve men wished to continue doing so," he said. "They have joined forces with you, Robin, and they are well aware that any betrayal of Katherine would be a betrayal of you. You will go home," he said firmly.

She turned to her cousin. "Robin, I—"

"You must do as he says, Kat."

She gritted her teeth and walked to stand by the flanks of the Silver Sword's ebony-dark horse. "A betrayal of me is a betrayal of Robin? My, I wonder if he is aware that his best friend, the noble Silver Sword, was more than willing to betray me!"

He reached down without a word, wrenching her up before him.

Surely Robin would protest!

But Robin's mind was not with them. He was staring in the direction of his base camp. He didn't say goodbye to her.

He didn't even realize that she was leaving as the Silver Sword nudged the huge black and moved them into one of the narrower forest trails.

"I have my own horse, you know," she said stiffly.

"I know. She's wandered off somewhere. We'll find her."

"I can make my own way home."

"I think that I will just see to that."

"Ah. Your mind is occupied now, too, I see," she said softly. He didn't respond. She added, "With the wondrous Lady Marian!"

The black stallion was abruptly reined in. "Why, my lady! It seems that you are jealous."

"It seems that seduction is part of your style."

He chuckled softly, and dismounted from the black, pulling her down and into his arms. Kat gasped, suddenly frightened. She *had* been jealous, she realized.

And how horrid. Just hours before she had been feeling curious twinges of jealousy where her husband was concerned . . .

She was legally wed to the man. And she slept nightly in his arms. She awakened to his touch.

She felt her flesh burning.

"My lady!" the Silver Sword said, "what would you think if you knew that I had been obsessed with you, day and night, night and day, ever since our meeting?"

She tried to draw back from him. "I would say that

you were a liar. You are ever eager to see me made a prisoner—"

"Nay, lady. I wished only to see that you were safe."

"And to receive a reward from Montjoy? Tell me, did my husband ever reward you? After all, it was work well done!" There was sarcasm to her tone. She didn't wish to be this close to him. He and Damian were of a size. Both were reckless, demanding. She even imagined that they touched the air with the same subtle masculine scent.

"I had my reward that night," he said hoarsely.

"Let me go!" she whispered.

But he was suddenly very intense. "So, is there a glimmer of happiness in that wretched home of yours? Yet you are so willing to run away from it!"

"These are my people—"

"Your father was a Norman lord!"

"And a very special, unique man!"

"So you've no desire to go home—not to a Norman lord. But what of the man, my lady?"

"I don't—I don't know what you mean!" Perhaps she did. Perhaps she understood his persistence exactly. But there was nothing that she was willing to say to him. She couldn't begin to explain that she hated her husband less and less as the days went by. She couldn't explain that she even looked forward to the nights. That she felt safe in his arms. She couldn't explain that he was clever and fascinating, and that she just might be falling . . .

In love.

No. She could never explain that. She would never love a Norman baron, not really. And especially not the Norman baron who had caught and spanked her in the forest! The same one who had taken over her life.

The one who came to her at night with such passion, while loving the ghost of Alyssa Albright.

"He is my—"

"Your what?" To her amazement, the Silver Sword shook her shoulders. Hard. And she swallowed, alarmed at what she felt for him, too.

"He is my enemy."

"He is Richard's man, I swear it."

"He is—Norman."

Was there some curious disappointment in him? His next question was sharp. "Then what of me, my lady. I am not your enemy. And I swear to you, I have thought of nothing but you!"

What was this curious persuasion of his? She felt so tempted to touch him. The passion in his voice was real. Did he truly taunt her?

Or did he truly want her?

She shook her head. Her lashes fell.

"I thought that you hated him."

"I—I do," she said. But it was a weak whisper. There was no truth to the words.

"Then?"

She lifted her hands. "He—he is my husband," she said softly.

The Silver Sword was silent. Then he turned her around by her shoulders and she saw that her mare was grazing just feet away, beneath a large shade tree.

"Go home," he said softly. Then his voice hardened. "And stay there, my lady! For I promise you, the next time I tie you to a tree, it will be with rope, and you will be there—away from trouble!—when I return for you. And lady, trust me, it will not be with gentle words again!"

Chapter 18

Marie had been sitting by the entrance to the cave, ready to take Kat's mare, when Kat rode hurriedly through the forest to reach her. Marie leaped up nervously the second she heard the hoofbeats, then crossed herself with a brief glance to heaven. "Blessed Mother, you're back!" she exclaimed.

"I have not been gone so very long," Kat said defensively, but of course, she had been gone a long time, far longer than she had planned.

Marie caught the mare's bridle and warned Kat, "Get down, and quickly now, my lady. Oh, what will happen if Lord Montjoy decides to come to your chamber when you are not within it?"

Kat shrugged, "He has already done so," she murmured uneasily. Aye, he had done so, and he had been suspicious, too. But actually, she was amazed at the leniency he was showing her, knowing how ruthless he could be when he was determined on something. She shivered suddenly, thinking that she might well be in serious trouble if she were caught betraying him.

But would he consider her activities in the forest a betrayal?

Not unless he knew about her and the Silver Sword.

She couldn't dwell on it any longer. She had been gone a long time. And though the lords of castles seemed to think themselves free to come and go with no word, they demanded explanations from their ladies.

"Kat, please hurry!"

Kat leaped down quickly. She patted her mare's nose. "Sweet Elisha," she crooned softly to the horse, "you serve me well!"

"Let me take her. Get back, please!" Marie insisted.

Kat gave up the reins and backed away. She'd be sorry for worrying Marie so—if she weren't still so irritated with Marie for bowing and scraping so quickly before Montjoy. The man had been here only weeks, and already it appeared as if the servants thought he had been here forever.

Marie leaped up on the little mare, a good mount, but a horse that might be ridden by a lady's maid as well as a lady. She really was worried. Kat smiled and waved, heading for the cave. "I will hurry, I promise! Meet me upstairs at the castle."

"Aye, my lady!"

As she had promised, Kat hurried. She nearly ran the dark distance through the dankness of the tunnel, and groped around in the few filtering rays of sunlight once she had reached the underbelly of the castle to find the stairway. With her hand on the stone, she quickly and carefully made her way up it, and then pressed against the stone to reach her room.

For a moment, a sense of unease stirred within her, as if she were not alone. Then panic swept through her. What if he were here? What if he caught her red-handed, coming through the door?

But a quick look around the chamber assured her that Montjoy was not in the room.

This was where they slept. He had managed to make it his room as well as hers. Now the lord's trunks were aligned with the lady's, and strewn about were various accoutrements belonging to a knight—one of his cloaks, a calf-sheath for a knife, and even his boar-bristle brush.

But he had chosen another room in the tower for his business, and he was often there, composing letters to be sent to be London and the justiciar and other barons, men who would help with the ransom to see that Richard was returned to them, safe and sound.

It was irritating. He went there for peace and solace. No one disturbed him there. Not that anyone disturbed him when he was with her—not now, not since Prince John had burst in that night.

But she had no place of utmost privacy, for he entered this chamber—her chamber—without ever thinking to knock.

That thought propelled her into action. She stripped off her green cloak and tunic and underdress and quickly stuffed the garments into the bottom of her largest trunk, then laid the false panel over them. Even her hose seemed to threaten to give her away, and so she kicked off her shoes and stripped them off.

For a moment, she paused, discovering herself to be very dizzy. She sat at the end of the bed, and waited for the sensation to pass.

This life, she determined, was wearing on her. Besides the dizziness, she almost felt as if she were going to be sick.

She closed her eyes tightly. She had no time! she reminded herself. She willed the feeling to go away, but when she stood, the queasiness was still with her. She ignored it the best she could. She had no time to be ill.

Marie had seen to it that a bath had been brought in her absence. Just in case the water had become too cool, a large kettle of it boiled over the flames in the hearth to be added to the tub when Kat was ready.

Kat was certain that the bath had grown very cold, and so she quickly took the heated water. Even as she poured from the steaming kettle, there was a tentative knock at the door. She reached hastily for the large linen bath sheet that had been cast over one of the high-backed chairs by the fireplace.

"My lady!"

It was Marie. Kat strode quickly across the room to let her in.

"He's not here?" Marie said, her palm against her heart. "Oh, thank the Lord!"

"Indeed!"

A smile swept across Marie's face, and she followed Kat into the room, catching the towel when Kat discarded it to slip into the water. "So, tell me, were you in time? Did you find Robin? You told him earlier about Richard's capture, so surely he must have been prepared for John's treachery. Tell me all about it!"

"It went very well," Kat assured her. "Robin was very glad of the chance to get his hands on the stolen gain. And also—" She broke off, for there was suddenly the sound of someone trying to open the bolted door, and then such a loud knock on the door that Marie leaped back, startled and afraid.

"It's he!" she cried, her hand flying to her mouth.

"Tell him to go away!" Kat said swiftly.

"I have to answer it. He'll break it down!" Marie said.

"Tell him that I am bathing, that I am not decent!" Kat pleaded.

She was shivering. She wasn't ready to meet him herself.

Marie hurried to the door and opened it. "My Lord Montjoy!" she bobbed a curtsy. "Ah, the Lady Kat—Katherine—is bathing. She's not dressed, my lord—" Marie broke off because Damian had pushed the door open, and stepped past her, setting her aside. He was grinning. "Marie, your lady is my wife, and I have managed to see her both dressed and undressed upon any number of occasions. You're excused, Marie. I'll send for you if the lady needs any assistance other than my own."

"Marie, wait—" Kat began.

But Marie had already bobbed another curtsy to him, and even as Kat spoke, she was fleeing out the door.

Damian grinned like a wolf seeing her in the tub, but then closed the door carefully and thoughtfully behind him.

"Bathing before supper, my love?" he inquired politely.

Something about his tone made the water seem very chilly. Despite the chill, Kat sank more deeply into it, rubbing her arms with the soap and the sponge, and trying not to betray either fear or secrets as she watched him in return.

"So it would appear, my Lord Montjoy."

His hands clasped behind his back, he walked around the tub. He was dressed simply in a white linen shirt, short golden tunic, and beige hose. It appeared that he had just emerged from a bath himself, for his ebony-dark hair seemed damp, as if it had just been washed.

"Is there something you want?" she asked growing more and more agitated as she watched him walk slowly around her.

He dipped down to his knees by the side of the tub, meeting her eyes. "There is always something that I want when I find myself near you, especially when you are in such a wondrous state of undress!" he told her softly. He dipped his hand into the water, then loosened his fingers and allowed a slender rivulet of it to run slowly over her shoulder. "You should bear in mind just how fascinated I become with the deliciously domestic sight of my wife in her natural state before deciding to change your dress and bathe in the afternoon!"

She stared into his eyes, wondering what he was insinuating with the comment. His eyes remained wide on hers, as silver-gray as burnished armor. Once again he lifted a handful of water and watched as it sluiced over her shoulder and breast.

She wondered how her cheeks could still redden so quickly and so hotly, after all that they had shared. She found her lashes quickly sweeping her cheeks. And her breath growing short, and a fascinating warmth from within her seeming to make her water all the colder.

"Why do you taunt me so?" she murmured. "I think that what I do matters very little. You will always have what you want, one way or another."

"Maybe. Maybe not," he told her. His gaze was on hers once again.

"You know that you will have your way!"

"Maybe what I want is not my way."

"I don't understand—"

"Maybe, once, I'd like it to be what you wish. I'd like to see you rise out of the water, intent upon the seduction of my body and my mind."

Kat was dismayed to realize that she was blushing fiercely again. "I no longer seek to fight you, or to avoid you in any way."

"Nay, lady, that you don't," he whispered huskily. "But neither have I ever seen you rise like an Eve from your water, the wondrous, wicked glint of sin in your eye, and that eye to fall upon me. Nor heard such a whisper as, 'My lord husband, we have been separated longer than I can bear, hold me within your arms, let me touch you, kiss you, make love to you . . .' "

The words in themselves were seductive, bewitching. The huskiness of his whisper, the nearness of him, all seemed to captivate and to charm, as did the curve of his smile. But she held her breath, refusing to respond. And as she watched him, he suddenly came even closer, lifted more water, and watched the droplets fall back into the tub.

"Your bath, my love, is very, very cold. Where were you when it was first intended for your leisure?" he demanded suddenly and sharply.

"I—" she began.

Damn him. He had managed to take her entirely off guard.

She dropped the sponge she had been holding so that the water sprayed up into his face. "I haven't been with Prince John, if that's what you're up to, my love!" she promised him in a cool snap, gripping the edge of the tub to rise. "And the moon will rest in the palm of your hand long before I ever come running to your bed with any wondrous, wicked glint of sin in my eye!"

She stood, reaching for her towel, but he snatched it away to mop the water from his face. He was laughing, she realized, and she swung, trying to hit him. Before she knew it, she was swept up into his arms, and he didn't care in the least that she was dripping wet.

"Let me down, wretch! All you ever intend to do is tease and torment me—"

"Nay, I intend much more!" he assured her. And he landed with her on the bed, the linen towel between them. She saw his eyes for just a moment, then felt the wonderful heat of his kiss explode on his lips, then take flight throughout her.

His mouth delved within and played upon hers, and she fought against the urge to hold him that so swiftly grew within her. But he was too fervent a lover. His arms encompassed her, stripping the linen from her. His kiss strayed, his tongue licked against her earlobe and stroked a long trail between the valley of her breasts. A soft touch fell against her collarbone and . . .

And then there was nothing. Her eyes had been closed. She opened them and shivered at the sudden fury she saw in his gaze.

"What . . . ?" she whispered.

And he touched her neck. "Let's see, lady, will you tell me? What is this thin line upon your throat? I interrupted your bath too quickly, so it seems. There's blood on your throat. Explain it, please!"

Her hand flew to her throat, and for once in her life, she was left entirely speechless. She floundered, her lashes flickering, her lips bone-dry. She touched them with the tip of her tongue. "It was a necklace. I tried a necklace that I have not worn in some time, and the band of it was so tight and so sharp—"

She broke off speaking because he had risen. Frightened of what he might discover, she rose quickly, grasping the towel to her breasts. Her heart beat hard as she tried to decipher his purpose, then she saw that he had taken the sponge from her bath and now carried it to her. He paused, his knee on the bed, and shoved her down to her back, pressing up her chin as he bathed her neck.

"It's not so very bad!" she cried.

"And done by a necklace! How very amazing! It appears to be cut—as if by a knife."

"It's not so very bad, really!" she insisted. He sat back now, watching her with interest, the sponge discarded.

"Where is the offending necklace? I shall get rid of it immediately."

"I—I don't know where I put it," she murmured nervously, rising from her back to sit at the foot of the bed. Why couldn't she have been dressed when they had this discussion? She felt ridiculously vulnerable, sitting there in her towel.

"Ah, well, perhaps then what I have to say will be very good, indeed. In this castle, my lady, you seem to disappear so easily. And now jewelry disappears likewise, after slicing through flesh."

She looked away from him, still holding her towel to her like a suit of armor. "I don't know what you're talking about."

"I think that things are running very smoothly here. It is time to take you home. To my home."

She swung around to stare at him with open dismay, too surprised to try to hide her emotions. "To your home! But—but that's completely impossible!" she told him.

"I beg to differ. It's not impossible. It's what we are going to do. I need to go home. I sent the majority of my knights there when I returned to England, and I must ready them all for war again."

"War?"

"John will rise against Richard. You know that. He is trying to raise the money to hire soldiers now, Englishmen, mercenaries, all that he can find."

"You will fight for Richard," she murmured.

"Did you ever doubt that?" he asked her.

She lifted a hand airily. "I knew that you were the King's man."

"So is Robin Hood, so they tell me."

She swallowed hard. "He is, of course."

"And how would you know?"

Her cheeks reddened. "I don't know, of course, but from everything that I hear . . ." Her voice trailed away. She turned to him. "You should go home, of course. Raise all the knights and soldiers that you can. I will stay here, because we will need all the able-bodied fighting men from this estate as well."

He was shaking his head. Slowly. A smile curved his sensual lips. "Nay, lady. I do not think so. You are my life. Where I go, you will follow."

"Please!" she whispered. "Don't make me go!"

"My home is very beautiful," he assured her. "Warm. Warmer than this castle, as a matter of fact, my love."

"I can't go with you."

He lifted his hands. "Convince me."

"What?"

"Convince me."

She gritted her teeth, wondering at his good humor— and at the very wicked gleam in his eyes. Then she caught her breath, and wondered if she could convince him. She glanced down at her trembling fingers for a moment, then smoothed back a rich fall of golden hair from her shoulders. Her eyes touched his, and she moistened very dry lips.

She rose, letting the towel drop from her. "What if . . ." she whispered softly. "What if I were to give you what you said you desired." She wasn't at all certain about what she did, but instinct guided her.

As did her fascination with him.

She curled her feet beneath her and brushed his cheek with her fingertips. She feathered a kiss against his lips, brushed his chin with her kiss, and touched the open V of his white linen undershirt with her lips and tongue. Her eyes met his again and she trembled as she rose against him, pressing her length against his, her breasts against the thin fabric of his clothing. She straddled his hips as he sat there, her arms curling around him.

He watched her for a moment. "Jesu!" he breathed, and his arms wound around her. A second later she was flat on her back, and he was stripping away his clothing. He was down beside her, glimmering eyes devilish, his whisper even more so. "Go on," he urged her.

She wet her lips again with the tip of her tongue. "What if I were to say . . ."

"Say and do," he reminded her.

It was not so difficult. She pressed her lips to his naked chest, and the heat of her breath bathed that bare flesh as she then whispered against it, "My lord husband, we have been separated longer than I can bear . . ."

She barely heard his groan, for suddenly it seemed that the words were true. It was tantalizing to touch that hard, rippling bronze flesh with her tongue. It was exciting to feel the pulse and power of the muscle beneath her, to stroke the length of his arm, to burrow against his chest. Her hair fell around them both, a soft cloak to tease and torment awakened and aroused flesh. She rose above him, then stared down into his eyes. A smile curved her lips, and a wicked green fire of seduction sizzled in her eyes. "Indeed, my lord, we have been separated so very long!" Then once again her lips touched his. "Let me hold you. Touch you!" she murmured against them. Then she used the whole of her body, rubbing against him, as she lowered herself upon his length. Her hair draped them, her kisses rained over him. Her hands and fingers caressed. Lower and lower.

She heard the sharp intake of his breath as she touched him. Then the expulsion of a low, startled groan of deep pleasure as she tentatively stroked him with her tongue, and whispered once again.

"Touch you . . . hold you . . ."

He seized her hard; his body shuddered as if he had been gripped by great seizures, and she felt a dizzying sensation, a sweet sense of power, and of wonder—and of desire. She grew bolder. Her touch was delicate, then more rugged, intoxicating . . .

Then she was lifted and flipped to her back so suddenly that her breath was stolen away. She met his eyes, and the searing heat of the passion within them caused a tremor in her heart. "Jesu, lady, Jesu!" he breathed.

She smiled, somewhat in wonder at her own power, and in wonder, too, at the sweet desire that lived within her. She reached out her arms to him. "What if . . . !" she whispered.

"Jesu!" he repeated, and swept her hard into his arms. She gasped at the searing blade of him as he swiftly entered into her; hard, vital, fully aroused. Then she closed her eyes, for she was suddenly swept into the whirlwind of the very desire she had elicited, and she was riding the wind, and riding a storm. She felt herself buffeted to excruciating new heights. She saw the pinnacle before her and knew that she had left behind her thought and reason to seduce, and entered into her own storm of desire. Soft cries were escaping from her, and she buried her lips against his shoulder to silence them. He brought her higher still. Then it seemed that the world exploded in stardust. Brilliant rays cascaded down upon her as she fought to regain her breath. She felt the immense power of the man as he found his own release within her, felt the hot sweet cascade of his seed pouring into her, and cried out once again, turning into his arms to be held as they drifted slowly back together.

They lay there in silence, and he stroked her hair. It seemed amazing to be so sated, so easy there with him. She had sworn to hate him. Too easily, far too easily, she was finding too many other emotions.

"If only . . ." she whispered softly, and she smiled as she curled upon his chest and met his eyes.

His eyes closed. He cast his elbow over them, still holding her with the one arm, but absently, or so it seemed. She laid her head down on his chest.

"If only . . ." he repeated quietly.

"So I will not have to go?" she murmured.

Then he shook his head. "If only . . . then you would please me greatly, as you did, my love. But that is all. I do not bargain, and I do not change my mind. I want to bring you to my castle, my home. Tonight."

Kat froze. She couldn't have heard him right!

"I will not go!" she stated. "I cannot go! I—"

His deep, weary sigh interrupted her. "Katherine, you will go, and you know that you will do so. If you fight me, I will bring you bound and screaming. One way or the other, you will do as I have said. It is necessary."

"It is necessary!" she repeated in a furious hiss. She crawled up atop him again, her fingers clenched into fists. "It is necessary!" She suddenly began to pummel and thunder against the chest she had so foolishly found so irresistible just moments before. "Damn you!" she choked out furiously. "You let me—you just lay there and let me—"

He caught her wrists, tensing as he raised himself up, his teeth grating with a warning sound. "You're my wife. I 'let' you honor the vows we gave to one another, and nothing more."

"Oaf!" she shouted, trying to wrench free. She was in such a frenzy that she nearly managed to do so. "I swear, you're all alike, there's not a drop of honor within a single one of you. You can't begin to honor a bargain. I—"

"You what?" he demanded, giving her a firm shake. His eyes blazed. "And if you'll excuse me, madam, but who are all alike? What bargains do you speak about? Did you make a bargain with another man, pray tell?"

Kat felt the fury ease from her as fear came swiftly slinking into her heart in its place. "Just you!" she managed to hiss. "You said something that you didn't begin to intend to honor—"

"I never made you any promises, Katherine."

"Just like—"

"Like who?"

She closed her mouth, her lips sealed. Her eyes fell. He never pressed her. She couldn't tell him the truth. She couldn't even explain.

"You play a dangerous, dangerous game!" he warned her.

She had nothing to say to him. He set her aside, and to his credit, did so gently. Kat remained kneeling on the bed, her back to him. "Whoreson!" she muttered suddenly. Then she stiffened, wondering if she had pushed his temper as far as she dared.

But she heard only a sigh of impatience. He was dressing, already clad in his white, full-sleeved undershirt and tunic, and pulling on his heavy wool hose. "One day, my lady, you will take back such words!"

"I think not."

He pulled his boots on and rose, then stood behind her naked back and leaned low to speak confidently against her nape. "I think so, madam. But it doesn't matter now. Be ready to ride in an hour."

"An hour? But are we not having supper? The cooks have worked all day. And we've entertainment—"

"There will be plenty left here to eat the food. And the entertainment will wait. You will be ready."

"You are seeking to do me harm in one way or another," she insisted. "Starvation is one of the ways!"

"You are not in the least starving. We have ample food in my kitchens, I assure you. You will be ready to ride."

"And if I choose not to be?"

"I will carry you all of the way, over good Lucien's hind quarters."

She spun on him, not doubting his words. "You, my lord, are among the most vile of all knaves! And you had best take great heed. One of these days, I might well slip into the forest and disappear so completely that not even you could find me."

He smiled grimly. "That, my lady, is another reason why we are leaving."

He strode across the room. Stunned, Kat leaped up, trying to drag the sheet along with her. She raced after him, catching his arm. "I won't. I won't disappear. I swear it. If we could just stay here. I'll—"

"You'll what?" he queried, intrigued.

"Apparently, what I promise means nothing to you anyway," she accused him, suddenly wanting to run again.

"You might want to confess all your sins," he suggested, and waited.

"My sins!" she exclaimed. "I do assure you, my lord, I have nothing to confess to you!"

"Then be ready to ride," he suggested. And before she could speak again, he had gone out of the room, heavily closing the door behind him.

Kat watched him go, then picked up one of her small shoes to hurtle it after him. "I hate you!" she cried. But the words were meaningless. She wanted to hate him so badly, he deserved to be hated . . .

But more and more . . .

"I will not love you! Ever!" she vowed out loud.

She swept the covers from her bed around her. His subtle, masculine scent seemed to linger, and she wondered how she had come to need the feel of his arms around her.

How she had come to reach such sweet glory from his touch. They were man and wife . . .

She froze suddenly, shivering violently, and pulled the covers more tightly about her. She was hungry one minute, sick the next, and dizzy when she exerted herself.

She leaped up, the covers about her, and began to pace the room, trying to count the days. They had all seemed such a blur since her marriage!

But it was true. She was late. Very late with her woman's time and . . .

A groan escaped her. She sank down to the foot of the bed. She couldn't be—she just couldn't be! They were scarce married, it just wouldn't be fair, and the Lady

Greensleeves just couldn't be—*enceinte!*—with child,
it would make creeping through the forest like a wraith
nearly impossible.

A babe. An infant. His, hers. He would have a handsome son, she thought. A little boy with those wonderful
gray eyes, eyes that were alight with curiosity, and never
so hard a silver with so much of the ways of the world
behind them! Or a daughter, perhaps, with that ink-dark
hair to flow down her back. His child.

His child, or . . . !

An awful shudder ripped down her back.

Her husband's child?

Or the Silver Sword's?

Kat was ready as he had commanded, mainly because
she knew that he wouldn't hesitate to carry out any
threat, no matter how much trouble she gave him.

And she felt the need to steer far clear of him this
evening.

She didn't toy with the idea of running away for more
than a few seconds. If she escaped, he would come after
her. If he didn't find her, the Silver Sword would, and
if he didn't, Robin would. One way or the other, she
would be returned here—and then she would be taken
to Montjoy's stronghold anyway.

When the time to leave came, she did so with energy
and grace and a beautiful smile. If she pretended to go
willingly, his men might well believe that there was
nothing wrong with her returning to her own castle—
the moment the first chance presented itself. And it had
to be quickly. She needed to be here! Her tunnel was her
one escape into the different world, the forest world.

As anguished and worried as she was, she even intended to be pleasant to Montjoy while they rode. She didn't
want any of their retainers to realize what a great deal of
trouble still lay between them now.

But as it happened, Montjoy did not ride with them. At the last moment there was some difficulty with the mechanism of the drawbridge and he meant to stay until it was fixed.

Kat received word of this when she was already mounted on her gray mare, with Marie riding behind her. She wouldn't have been alone, for Damian's right-hand man, the very courteous young Sir James Courtney, was at her side when Howard came out with the message. "My Lord Montjoy says that he will be detained no more than the night at most, and that you must journey on without him."

"But, Howard, if there is a difficulty here, then I must stay!" Kat insisted.

"Oh, no, my lady. Lord Montjoy was very adamant on the matter. You are to ride on."

She lowered her lashes, trying to hide her emotions. Damn him! She could jump off her mare and go in pursuit of him, she thought. But he might well drag her back out here and tie her to the horse so Sir James could take her onward.

And if she rode on cheerily without him, she might well be able to ride back without his realizing it if something important happened that she needed to tell Robin. She might only have one or two more chances to reach the forest. She had to make those chances pay.

And there was also the small matter that she wasn't really ready to deal with him tonight, not when she was so plagued with this new worry.

"Then, Howard, you must tell Lord Montjoy goodnight for me. And wish him a most pleasant evening."

"He says that he will miss you, my lady. That the long separation will be more than he can bear."

She felt her cheeks pinkening, and she wished she could bid her husband goodbye herself—so that she could throw something at him.

"Tell him—" she began. "Tell him goodbye!"

With those words, she turned her horse's head toward the road. Marie's mount trotted along behind hers, and Sir James followed quickly, and after them came the ten armed guards chosen to serve as her escort.

Kat kept up a steady pace, leading the party herself. But darkness was falling quickly. She had packed a number of belongings, as had Marie, and with the pack animals following behind them, it seemed to be slow going. On a fast horse, the two strongholds were probably not much more than an hour or so apart. Tonight, the ride seemed to take forever.

"Perhaps tonight's journey was not so very wise," Sir James murmured. He held a burning taper high against the darkness. "In these woods."

"Oh," Kat said lightly. "We are safe in these woods."

"Aye, I imagine that we are," Sir James agreed.

Kat frowned. She wasn't afraid of the bandits—she knew all the bandits! But Sir James Courtney was her husband's man, and Richard's knight or no, Lord Montjoy was among the Norman aristocracy. Shouldn't he have been afraid?

Perhaps not. She had been rescued for Montjoy by the Silver Sword. And he and Robin Hood worked in unison.

Not even Robin had been in the least dismayed to discover that she had been married to Montjoy. He rather seemed to have enjoyed the information.

It didn't matter. Not tonight. She was weary and aggravated, and very tired.

And to make matters worse, the ride was making her feel queasy all over again.

She needed this night's respite from Lord Montjoy. She wanted to be angry with him, she wanted to always remember that day in the forest when he had behaved so discourteously in his Norman fashion.

But even being upset, she knew that something was changing. Something that she could not control. Even when they fought. Even when he used his power over her. Even when she knew that she must best him in the end.

She cared about him. She might even be falling in love with him. There had been no hardship, other than the loss of dignity, in casting aside restraint to whisper the words he had longed to hear. *We have been separated longer than I can bear . . .*

She smiled suddenly. Maybe, someday, there would be a chance for them. If Richard was rescued and returned. If there was no longer a need in the world for the Lady Greensleeves.

If she could . . .

If she could forget her one night in the forest with the Silver Sword.

Well, she couldn't forget it. Not now. Not if she was right about her condition!

Perhaps she was wrong! Oh, she had to be.

Even as she fought both men, she felt drawn to them both, and respected them both . . .

Cared for them both.

"My lady, Clifford Castle lies ahead," Sir James informed her.

She reined in. Montjoy's castle stood tall and monstrous in the moonlight. It was larger than her Castle de Montrain, but there was no protective moat around the high stone walls. There were four main towers, but the castle was not built as a square or rectangle, but seemed to meander there, large and forbidding in the moonlight. Repelling invaders, yet welcoming those who were meant to come. She had seen it many times before.

She had never imagined she would dwell within it.

"Then let's reach the castle, shall we?" she said, and nudged her horse into a canter.

The party behind her followed her lead. Sir James called out to the guard as they reached the gates, and guards in the colors of Montjoy quickly appeared at the portcullis, calling out a welcome.

The few people out and about at night hurried close to watch her curiously as she entered the courtyard. Women held bushels of straw or buckets of fresh cool water, coming to and fro from their domiciles within the castle walls. All stood still at their distance, then bowed and offered shy smiles as she made her way among them. She smiled in return, surprised to feel the warmth of her welcome here.

It was not so bad a place, it seemed.

There was simply no escape tunnel here!

Sir James led them to a broad entryway in the north tower. "Here, my lady!" he said. Dismounting, he hurried to her side and helped her down. Huge wooden doors at the tower opened even as a young, toothless little groom came to take her horse. She thanked him and allowed Sir James to lead her into Montjoy's main hall.

It was mammoth, taking up all of the lower floor of the tower. The walls were lined with the armaments of the Montjoys. Full suits of armor were cast upon iron figures against the back of the dais, armor for the joust, dress armor, and the rugged, useful knight's armor that Montjoy surely wore into battle.

The arrow slits at the back wall, the exposed wall, were covered over with elegant tapestries. A Persian rug lay before the giant hearth, and a dozen hounds stood wagging their tails just beyond it, woofing, waiting to greet both her and Sir James, whom they knew so well.

Lined up in the hallway were a number of the house servants. The cooks, Elizabeth, Hubert, and Humphrey; the maids, Lisa, Arlaina, Tess, and Nan. Then there was the tall and lean Tom of Quincy, Sir James's own squire, and castellan when both Sir James and Lord Montjoy were absent.

The servants all seemed pleased to greet her, and sorry to hear that their lord was not with her. Tom of Quincy was anxious to see to all her needs, and she assured him that she was weary more than anything else. Elizabeth promised to have a warm and welcoming meal sent to her room, and Tess vowed to have her things in her room for her in a matter of minutes, with Marie given a chamber close by.

Kat thanked them all, then followed Tess to the master's chamber on the second floor, high above the great hall, much as her own chamber at home was located.

And like her own it was very large. She felt Montjoy the moment she entered into it.

There were more of the iron, skeletal figures here, all clad in different sets or pieces of armor.

A wealth of swords adorned the walls. Again, the tapestries were rich and varied, but mostly Norman work, she could tell. The pictures chronicled the victories won by William the Conqueror.

"Your maid will be yonder, lady, for there is a servants' wing just past in the hallway," Tess told her, remaining quietly behind her.

Kat didn't turn. She wanted to be alone in his room. "Thank you, Tess. Marie, please, go on to your room. Get some sleep. It has been a long day."

"And a rough ride," Marie said softly, but with feeling.

Kat smiled, lowering her head. Perhaps she had set rather a rough pace for poor Marie. She had not intended to do so.

But now she wanted to be alone. She had to be alone! She wanted to think.

And to feel . . .

"My lady, I shall see to your trunks and unpack—"

"Nay, not now, I beg you. I am fine. Just weary. Leave me for the time," she said.

Tess bobbed her a little curtsy in agreement and left her. Kat stood alone in the large room and tried to imagine Montjoy here. There was a table near one of the tapestry-covered arrow slits. In the day he must have the tapestry taken away so that he could work there. The table was piled high with various parchments, maps, and documents. His great seal lay upon it as well.

Far across the room were a bowl and pitcher of fresh water, and across from the very large strung-rope bed, there was an embroidered linen dressing screen. Various trunks lay around the screen.

There were mementoes from the Crusades. A silver coffee server sat on a trunk to one side. A jeweled dagger in a silk embroidered sheath lay on another. Curiously Kat moved to one of the trunks, paused, then determined to look through it. She went down to her knees, then opened the trunk, and gasped at the array of clothing she found there.

The trunk was filled with silks. Women's silks. Gowns in pastel and bright colors, soft, see-through, entirely flimsy pieces. She tried to imagine them on the female body, and she wondered if they had been purchased with a specific female in mind. Her? He had known that he would have a wife . . .

But these things bore a scent. A musky scent, an attar of some exotic flower. It was a scent not to her liking. A scent that had surely been worn by the woman who had been clad in the silky garments.

Suddenly, the dressing screen began to teeter precariously.

Kat backed away as it fell over.

And revealed the woman who had been hiding behind it. A small, dark-haired woman with olive skin and almond eyes and long, free, jet-dark hair. A woman encompassed in the same gauzy silks and veils as filled the trunk.

"Who in God's name are you!" Kat exploded.

"I am Affa," the woman said proudly. "I serve the great Lord Montjoy. And I serve him very, very well!"

This was too much! Oh, dear Lord! This was truly the wrong side of way too much!

A black fury seemed to simmer before Kat's eyes, sizzling to red. She nearly plucked her shoe from her foot to throw across the room at the woman.

Just in time, she restrained herself. No matter how she longed to scream and shout—and pummel Montjoy's too-handsome face—she would restrain herself. It might well work to her advantage.

"Affa! How very curious," she murmured.

Chapter 19

Damian stood in the fields outside the castle and watched as the drawbridge was slowly lowered over the moat. He lifted a hand and ordered it drawn, and watched as the newly repaired and oiled mechanism brought the bridge upward once again. The action was smooth—and swift. Well pleased, Damian let his hand fall again, and the bridge was lowered to allow him entry, and to allow the people to come and go from the fields beyond the gates. It was later than he had planned. The evening had come and gone, and now the morning had come and gone, and he still hadn't been able to leave. As the hours passed, he was growing more and more anxious to reach Clifford Castle. He was hoping that Katherine was well moved into his homestead by this time. There was no knight more loyal or chivalrous than Sir James, so he was certain that her welcome into his home went smoothly. His servants, to the best of his knowledge, were happy people. His fields were rich, his people ate well, and he was certainly a nobleman of a decent enough reputation. Katherine should have been greeted warmly and with pleasure, and made to feel quite comfortable.

Last night he had been determined to get her away from the tunnel and keep her from the chance of any more dangerous escapades. But now, as the hours passed, he had begun to wonder at his own wisdom.

James Courtney knew the truth about the Lady Green-sleeves, just as he knew the truth about the Silver Sword, and both were secrets he would keep to himself. He knew that Kat needed a careful eye on her. Nothing could happen.

But Damian had lain awake the long night anyway, worrying.

Worrying . . .

And missing her.

His hands clasped behind his head, he had stared up at the ceiling for long hours. He had grown so accustomed to sleeping with his arms around her. Sleeping entangled in golden hair. As he lay there, his heartbeat quickened. When he closed his eyes, he saw hers. Aquamarine, like the waters of the sea. Ever-changing eyes. Beautiful eyes. If anything were to happen to her . . .

He didn't intend to love her. She was willful, she was stubborn to an extreme. And as she had told him, she was not Alyssa Albright.

Nay, she was Kat. Lady Katherine, Lady Greensleeves. His wife. And since he had first met her upon the roof, trying to fight him even while he had tried to rescue her, she had somehow been winding her golden hair around his soul. He still loved Alyssa. He always would. But the love he had borne her had always been a gentle emotion. Soft. Tender. Perhaps he could even begin to lay it to rest now.

He had never felt . . . this. This tempest that governed him when he thought of Kat.

This need to touch her, when she had scarce been gone a few hours. This desire to hear her speak, to hear her laugh. To see her move, mercurial, beautiful, graceful.

This volatile desire to hold her, have her close to his heart. Lie beside her, sleep beside her . . .

They would be parted only one night. And he had been determined that they must be parted, so it was all his own doing. Yet he lay there still, not sleeping, just thinking.

Of her. Her scent remained in the room. Her clothing lay in the trunks. This had been her castle, her home, long before he had come to it. She was everywhere. She seemed to be there still, a whisper of memory, sweeping about the room. Defying him, aye, tempting him . . .

Coming to him.

And so the night had been long.

Then the morning had been even longer.

But now the bridge was fixed, and he could gather what he would take, and ride for his own home. He would not be encumbered, he decided, but ride with only a man or two at his side. Then he could spend no more than an hour or so on traveling.

But even as he left the field behind and started on foot across the bridge, he became aware of the pounding of horse's hooves behind him. There had been no warnings of an approaching enemy from the guards atop the parapets, so he knew that one of his own men was coming.

He spun around to see that the rider was Sir James, and his breath caught. There had to be something wrong. Something very wrong.

James's horse drew up beside him, and James was quickly off the mount, and down upon a knee before him. "My Lord Damian, God forgive me, I failed you!"

"Jesu! What the hell happened?" he exploded, shaking. "Is she all right—"

"Aye, she's all right! At least I believe that she is—"

"You believe?"

Sir James looked up, his eyes anguished. "She's gone."

"Gone!" Damian felt an inward trembling. He'd been a fool. A damned bloody fool. He never should have sent her there alone! "Since when? What in the bloody hell happened?" he roared.

"My lord—" James began, his voice shaking.

"Get on your feet man, and tell me simply what has happened!"

"She escaped us—"

"Jesu!" Damian raged. "I've men in my service who have battled whole armies of infidels! I left you in charge of a castle and lands where over a thousand men and women abide. And between you, you could not keep your eye on one small lady?"

Sir James was not accustomed to seeing Damian in such a temper. He was known for his ferocity, but never his blind rages. His mind was cool and quick, calculating at times. Though he could fight with a rare energy and vengeance, his mind was as great an asset as his muscle.

"Perhaps that is deserved, Damian," James said quickly. "But it does not seem to me that you have managed to do much better."

"Damn you!" Damian thundered, but then, even as he stepped forward with menace, he sighed, controlling his temper with the sheer truth of James's words.

"I do not blame you, I blame myself! I should have known better."

James shook his head. "Damian, you could not have been prepared for what happened."

"Which was? Come, tell me quickly!"

"More of our Clifford men had returned from the Crusade, Damian. And they brought with them more of the property you acquired."

Damian stared at him blankly. "Go on!"

"Property, Damian. Among that property, a number of fine Arabian horses, and a curious old man named Ari, and a truly curious young woman named Affa."

"Oh, Jesu!" Damian groaned aloud. "But the girl was never mine! She was a gift to Richard!"

"I hadn't even known that she was there," James continued. "By the time I discovered it, she had already introduced herself to Kat—in your room. And the man

Ari had tried to give Katherine some kind of an explanation—"

"But Kat ran out. My God! That must have been last night—"

James shook his head strenuously. "Nay, my lord, not last night. In fact, she was quite incredibly controlled last night. She talked with Affa for some time, then assured her that she was quite welcome to Clifford Castle—since Katherine wanted none of it. Katherine insisted on vacating your room herself, but went of her own accord about the castle to choose a room for herself. I talked with her last night. I told her that I was certain that you didn't know a thing about the girl. I said that I'd have her thrown out bodily, taken away . . . but she insisted that I not do so. She was charming, saying that she'd discuss the situation with you. She couldn't have been more gracious. She ate what the cooks prepared for her, complimenting them all. She was charming. Until this morning. And then—"

"And then?"

"Then Lord Morgan from south of the forest came riding hard into the courtyard to find you. I hurried down to tell him that you were held up here, and he told me that I must warn you quickly that Prince John was in an absolute fury about Marian—"

"Marian?"

James gratefully inhaled to speak again as Damian interrupted him. "The Lady Marian of Wiltshire, Damian. The girl Robin had once been betrothed to. She was kidnapped there in the woods—"

"Yes, yes," Damian said impatiently. So Robin was still holding Marian. He had expected as much. Robin was still very deeply in love with her. And if he was not mistaken, Marian was in love with Robin. She had heard of his exploits through John, so it was easy to see why she had turned against him. When Damian had ridden with her to Robin's base camp, and listened to both her anger and her explanations, he had been certain that confusion, and nothing more, had parted her from Robin.

Damian couldn't worry about Marian or Robin at the moment. Not while his wife was missing.

"Well, the Prince is taking up arms against the entire forest. He is raising an army to thrash its way through the forest, bit by bit, so said Lord Morgan. The Prince is convinced that if he can find Robin, he can retrieve all manner of treasure that Robin has taken."

"So Kat heard these words—and then disappeared?" Damian demanded.

"Jesu, Damian, I should have known, I should have been prepared! But I told you, despite everything that had happened, she was so very calm. She seemed even to be amused by the girl Affa."

Amused. She had not been in the least amused! She had been furious, and plotting her revenge, Damian thought. But that didn't even matter now.

He had to find her.

Well, she would be heading for Robin once again.

And for once, Damian prayed that she might reach him.

At least before any of John's men reached her.

"So when did you discover her gone?"

"Just minutes before I rode to find you here. I had the whole of the castle searched, and even now, your men are looking for her. Her mare is gone—"

"They will not find her," Damian said. "But I will!" he vowed.

He spun around, calling to the men at the end of the bridge. "My horse! Bring me Lucien, quickly!"

"I'll ride with you," Sir James said.

"No, I will move more quickly myself," Damian told him. He wanted to yell, and he wanted to rage. But he knew that James was sick with worry himself. "Stay here. Watch for her returning here. It's quite likely that she may do so."

A page had brought up Lucien. Damian leaped atop the seasoned war-horse, saluted Sir James, and left the castle behind him at a gallop.

His heart and mind were in a tempest. It seemed more imperative than ever that he reach her.

And quickly.

Kat had taken no time with any manner of subterfuge to ride deeply into the forest, and seek out the first of Robin's men that she could find. It was Hamlin, once a woodcutter from Willow's Creek, a man whose talent lay in his ability to throw an axe. But like all of Robin's men, he had quickly become adept with a bow and arrow, and as soon as he saw her, he sent sailing forth a message that she was on her way toward the base, and she rode even deeper in, toward the camp, past more of the men who were ever holding guard, silently, blending in with the trees in the forest.

Kat had paused just once to assure herself that she wasn't being followed. But as she had suspected, her break had been a clean one.

She had played the night and the day amazingly well.

Truly! Amazingly well, for she had maintained a calm and serene facade when she had been alive with fury and tempest within. How dared he? How dared he send her to his home when he had a woman within it! Her first instinct had been to set her hands on the little olive-skinned harlot and tear every silky dark strand of hair from her head. And when she was finished with that, she would have liked to have started on Montjoy, and truly, her anger was so strong that she felt she might have been capable of the feat.

But before she'd even managed to take a step across the room, a curious man had appeared in the doorway.

He was dressed in desert robes, and his face had seemed both ancient and ageless. The eyes set in the slim face had been sad and wise, and he had spoken very quickly to the girl Affa in their foreign tongue. Affa had seemed furious, but the man hadn't cared. He had come into the room, his wise eyes on Kat very curiously, and he had bowed low before her. "Affa apologizes from the bottom of her heart. She doesn't understand your ways. She had been informed that Lord Montjoy has a wife, a great lady in her own right, but I think that she believed . . ." He paused uncomfortably. Kat watched him curiously, and then her eyes flicked to the girl.

"She thought that she could sow the seeds of discord!" Kat murmured.

"Exactly, my lady."

Affa screamed something to him furiously and threw a beautiful clay pot at him, which crashed to the floor. Kat lifted a brow to him.

Flashing an angry look at Affa, he explained to Kat, "She said: 'You should go home, you old goat.' To me, my lady. I am the old goat, not you."

"Oh," Kat murmured. Now she was both amused and seething. And disturbed. When she glanced at the small, olive-skinned beauty with her sizzling almond eyes, she felt a curious boiling in her blood. So this was how Lord Montjoy had spent his nights in the desert. The great warrior! The King's right-hand man! The fury seemed hot enough to scald her.

And hurt her.

She had spent hours in agony for what she truly considered a sad indiscretion with the Silver Sword. She had alternately convinced herself that she was wrong, that there was no child, and then felt a cold sweat break out across her flesh because she knew that was a lie. It had taken her a while to comprehend the situation, but she was positive. There would be a child.

And now . . .

Now this woman!

By this time, all manner of people were rushing up the stairs to see what had disturbed her. Sir James came first, gasping with surprise at the scene, then bursting through the doorway to set himself down upon one knee before her, taking her hand. "My lady, forgive me! None of us knew, none of us expected that anyone would dare to assume this chamber! I swear, my Lord Montjoy knows nothing of this—"

"Please, Sir James! Rise." And she smiled with all the regal poise she could muster. "Do you mean to tell me that my husband does not know this woman?"

Poor, young, freckle-faced James! No lie could have saved him, for his face seemed to turn a thousand shades of crimson. "Know her? I . . . er . . ."

Kat looked to the doorway. The cooks had arrived, and the maids had arrived, and everyone was looking in. "My goodness!" she murmured. "You all must not be so distressed! You've done nothing wrong. James, see to it that my things are taken elsewhere. In fact, if you'll allow me, I'd truly like to decide upon my own domicile."

"Affa will not remain here," James stated.

"Oh, she had truly best not," Kat said softly. "But be that as it may," Kat said firmly, "neither shall I." She smiled at him. "Please, good sir! It is not your concern. I will take it up with Lord Montjoy when I see him again."

And so, with half the household behind her, she had toured the hallway and found herself a pleasant enough room. She hadn't been sure herself what she would do. She had assured herself only that she could use what had happened here against Montjoy, and she meant to do so. Yet it seemed imperative that she convince them all, all of his people, that she was extraordinarily composed and serene, every inch the lady.

She prayed that she managed to do so!

The night, however, had been a misery. She was humiliated that one of her husband's whores was so familiar with his house, and at the same time, she was ridiculously jealous that the almond-eyed girl knew the man she knew so intimately as well as she did herself. Perhaps more so.

Perhaps her husband had enjoyed the girl with all of her experience and teachings more. That thought was the one that irked her most, and the fact that it irked her most, when her dignity was at stake, made things all the worse.

She made herself summon Affa. She listened to her story about being given to Richard, and finding that she enjoyed the great Lord Montjoy so much more. They hadn't gotten very far when the man, Ari, came in once again, insisting that Affa be taken away. Affa tossed back her long mane of dark hair and informed Ari that only Lord Montjoy could order her away.

Kat smiled grimly.

That order would be coming. It was one thing that she would demand.

But for the moment . . .

"See that Affa is given somewhere in the castle to sleep."

"I will sleep—"

"Where I say," Kat finished for her.

Affa jumped up. "I can't go home! I must stay in England."

"Then I will see what we can find for you," Kat promised.

Affa had meant to stay. To talk down Kat. Actually, what Affa wanted to do was get rid of Kat, but it didn't seem that that would happen. Sir James insisted on taking the girl away.

Kat seethed. She boiled within.

She worried.

And she felt dizzy and ill all over again.

But she remained poised. She was entranced by Ari, who told her that he had seen her long ago, in a vision. "I told Lord Montjoy that he was destined to marry you. I saw your hair. I saw—" He broke off, shaking his head. "I knew that you would wed," he finished lamely.

Intrigued, Kat questioned him anew. "What else do your know?"

"I know that even now, storm clouds hover. There is great danger brewing in the night. My lady, you, and my Lord Montjoy, will have to take the greatest care."

"That is all that you see?"

He shook his head. "I see men. Men in armor. I see swords and pikes and a hail of arrows."

"It sounds like war," she murmured.

"A great battle, at the very least," Ari said. He was still looking at her. "Forgive me! For there was something that I saw in a vision that I do not see now. Nay, perhaps it's still there. But so darkly clouded! I cannot read the truth of it."

"But what is it that you do see?"

Ari shook his head again. He bowed down low before her. "You are a very great lady," he told her.

Then he was gone, and she was left to wonder at his words. But she could not dwell on them long, for despite herself, despite what epithets she slammed down upon her husband's head in his absence, she was fuming with jealousy. It was her pride, she told herself. Her dignity, her status.

It was her heart. Her soul, her longing.

In the morning, however, once Lord Morgan had arrived, excitedly looking for Damian to tell him that John was preparing to scourge the forest, she knew that her restraint had served her well. It was imperative that this news reach Robin.

And she would lose nothing for bringing it to him, for in all truth, she could tell Damian that she hadn't been able to stand his home with his whore in it one single minute longer. And she had been so very calm and tolerant of manner that she had managed to assure Lord Morgan that word would go to her husband immediately—and then had turned toward the stables herself, retrieved her mare, and ridden away, completely unchecked.

She rode now straight into Robin's base camp with its wooden, thatched-roof houses that blended right in with the trees. A number of the men were about, notching their arrows, dining on pieces of wild fowl, laughing, jesting with one another. Someone played a lute, and someone else sang a bawdy song.

All paused and saluted her the moment they saw her. Little John, the big bear of a man, hurried forward to greet her. "Lady Kat! You've come through the forest with no disguise! 'Tis dangerous enough when you come clad to blend with the forest-green, but this is foolhardy, my lady!"

"I had to come here, and come straight. Robin has to know as quickly as possible that the Prince is in a rage. It is over Marian, so they say, but I know him well, and it is probably over the dowry he meant to get from some baron for her hand. Or perhaps it is over the religious treasures taken the other day. He intends to bring a whole army into the forest. Robin has to be ready for him. Actually, he has to let the Lady Marian go. And quickly. He was insane to keep her a prisoner. Where is he?"

"Gone hunting," Little John said. "I should explain about Marian—nay, lady. Robin should explain. I will find him, and quickly. Come down from your horse. Rest, drink some ale. I'll bring him quickly."

Kat nodded, and John's massive, outstretched arms lifted her to the ground. "I'll just wait in Robin's place," she said, striding toward the tiny wooden domicile that was her cousin's.

"My lady—" Little John called after her.

But it was too late. She had pushed open the door to the hut. The shadows were deep and dark here, and it took a few minutes for her eyes to adjust.

She knew the room.

It was a very small homestead, with a bed of straw and furs across from the door, a fireplace dug in the center of the earthen floor, and a pair of chests far to the left, on top of which were set the simple things for living: cup, bowl, spoon, fork, knife, water pitcher, long-handled brush. Alongside them lay bows, arrows, quivers, swords, and knives.

But from the bed of straw and furs on the floor, a figure emerged somewhat in the shadows. Kat, surprised, gasped out loud as her eyes became adjusted to the darkness.

There was a woman in her cousin's bed. A naked woman. The Lady Marian. The one who had spit at him. And the one the Silver Sword had so swiftly— and so courteously—taken away.

"Oh!" Kat gasped again. Marian sat up quickly, dragging furs about her. "Your pardon, please!" Kat murmured. "I didn't know. I . . . er, I—"

She broke off at sight of the soft smile that curved Marian's lips, making her more beautiful than ever. "It's quite all right, Lady Katherine. Please, come in. Perhaps you'd be good enough to toss me yonder shift. And sit. We've ale in here. I'm glad enough to have some time with you."

Kat came through the doorway, then closed it behind her curiously. She tossed Marian the shift as the woman had requested, and sat at the end of the pallet of straw and fur. Dressed, Marian became the perfect hostess— despite the strands of straw in her mane of dark hair.

Marian hurried to the one trunk, opened it, produced leather mugs and a large canister, and poured them both some ale. She handed one mug to Kat and lifted her own. "To the outlaws in the forest!" she said, and winked.

Kat took a sip of ale and arched a brow to the woman. "I assume this means that you and Robin are reconciled. Is there a wedding planned once again?"

Marian blushed and sat down beside her. "I must have sounded horrible to you. But I loved him so much. I had never imagined loving anyone so much. And everything was set, and then Prince John came in one day and told me he was quite certain that my Rob was the one who had become a murderer and a thief in the forest. I didn't know the rest of it, Lady Katherine, I swear it. The Prince neglected to tell me that Robin Hood killed men who tried to slay the defenseless poor, peasants and villeins without a stick to take up in their own defense."

"So you are a prisoner here no longer?"

She smiled broadly. "Hardly, my lady. Unless I am a prisoner of my own heart. I love your cousin. Dearly. And I pray that you believe me, for I know that he believes the sun rises and sets in you, and I wish nothing more than to be your friend."

Kat smiled. "Well, that is simple enough. But now he can hardly let you go. John will instantly see you wed to some other man, determined to thwart Robin. I came to tell him that John intends to raise an army to bring against him here in the forest."

Marian tensed. "Jesu! Because of me?"

"Aye . . ."

"Then I must go back!"

"No, you must not! Prince John will raise this army one way or the other. This goes far beyond you or even Robin himself. John wants the throne. Richard is a prisoner, and John wants to seize the crown. This is only part of his maneuvering. Marian, of all things, you must not go back! Robin would be distracted then, and no good would come of it." A great sigh shook her. "Robin must fight him!" she whispered, terrified. Could Robin win against an army of men, fully armored and armed, under the command of the Prince?

Marian hugged her suddenly and fiercely. "He will not be alone. He will have the Silver Sword, and other such friends."

There was a reverence to Marian's voice when she spoke of the Silver Sword. Kat pulled back, bristling. "The Silver Sword cannot best John's army."

"Oh, but he can take down a baker's dozen men alone!" she said, her eyes bright.

"But he is one man! An army must ride against an army." She leaped up suddenly. "I really have to go. I have to . . ." She paused again. It hurt. She was going to have to put her differences behind her. Swallow her pride. She was going to have to go home and convince Montjoy that he must actually ride against the Prince. With his men. He was a seasoned warrior. So were many of his men. They were the army that could combat an army. No matter what the pain, the tempest, the jealousy in her heart, she had to convince him to come to an outlaw's aid.

"What?" Marian said.

Kat shook her head. "I must persuade my husband to fight the Prince," she murmured, sinking down again. Aye, Damian might have cause to be grateful to the Silver Sword.

If he were not grateful for her, at the very least he had to be grateful for the Castle de Montrain, a stronghold he seemed to covet.

"Well, I can't see how that should be so very difficult," Marian murmured.

"Oh, it might be awful! Some time ago, Robin and Montjoy met in the forest. Well, rather I met Lord

Montjoy, and Robin had to come to my aid. They fought each other!"

Marian was smiling. "I believe, my lady, that they were merely careful to fool you. Lord Montjoy would never take up arms against Robin."

"What are you saying?" Kat demanded incredulously.

"You don't know?"

"Know what?"

Marian hesitated. Then her eyes lowered. "I don't know what I am at liberty to say, but I will tell you this much, for it is common knowledge, and it's truly startling that you don't know. Robin and Lord Montjoy are kin."

"But they can't be! My mother and—"

"And Robin's father," Marian said, stressing the word *father*. "Robin's mother was first cousin to Lord Montjoy's mother. Lord Montjoy's mother died so very young—perhaps that is why you never knew. Lord Montjoy was raised in a Norman household, and Robin, of course, was strictly a Saxon's child."

"Cousins?" Kat repeated. "They staged that fight for me! The rogues!"

Marian laughed. "Indeed. But aye, Kat, go home! Convince him that he must take up arms against the Prince!"

"Oh, I do believe that he'll need to take up arms!" Kat stated softly. Impulsively, she gave Marian a fierce hug again. "Friends—and relations!" she said. "For I believe, soon enough, we'll be cousins-in-law! Goodbye for now."

She hurried from Robin's small hut and ran for her mare. Robin's man, Will, hurried toward her. "Katherine! Robin will return shortly—"

"And so must I. He'll have my message. I must see what other help I can bring," she announced.

Before any man could stop her, she was mounted on her gray mare. But even as she prepared to ride hard toward home, one of Robin's men burst into the small copse.

"Damian, Lord Montjoy, is dangerously near the clearing!" he announced tensely.

Damian. Her heart thundered. He was looking for her.

She closed her eyes and remembered that day when she had accosted him here, in the forest. She was a good swordswoman. He had cost her her weapon in a matter of minutes. He had refused to kill her . . .

He was Robin's cousin, she reminded herself.

But now he was in the forest, looking for her, determined to find her. And Robin's men might well feel that he was getting too close, that they might have to accost him.

And men could die.

Damian could die . . .

She was startled by the pain that cut through her. She wanted to kill him herself. Rage against him, pummel her fists against him. Because . . .

Because she loved him. More than she had ever imagined that she could.

Even as she sat atop her gray mare pondering the situation, Marian hurtled out of Robin's crude hut. "Katherine!" she cried, having heard the news, it seemed. "You've got to do something! You've got to go stop what may happen. They don't know! Robin's men don't know! A few do, but not most of them. It has been a carefully kept secret because of his position."

"It's such a secret that Damian is Robin's cousin? We can just tell them. We can explain—"

"Jesu, Katherine! It's far more than that!"

"What, Marian? Tell me!" Eyes beseeching, Katherine looked down at the girl with the large flashing dark eyes and wild mane of hair.

"You really don't know?"

"I really don't know!"

Marian inhaled sharply, then quickly made up her mind. "Damian is far more than just Robin's cousin. He's—"

"He's what!" Katherine cried desperately.

Marian exhaled softly, watching Katherine. "Your husband, Lady Katherine, Lord Damian Montjoy, is none other than—"

"Than? Please! Tell me!" Katherine exploded.

Marian lowered her eyes.

"He is the Silver Sword."

Chapter 20

Damian went near mad, searching the forest trails for Kat. When he rode deeply into the woods and still had yet to find her, he began to curse himself as a fool for having come here as himself.

Only James Courtney and Robin's closest fellows knew that Lord Montjoy was the Silver Sword. If he risked going much farther, he would have to pray that he was discovered by Robin, and none other, else he'd find himself engaged in combat with a man he had no desire to injure or kill.

"Damn her!" he swore aloud. Then he was angry with himself for having been so foolish as to have come after her this way. If his emotions hadn't become involved, he would have gone about this far more sensibly.

But his emotions had become involved. Damn him.

He slowed Lucien, patting the horse's neck as he looked quickly about, a sixth sense warning him that he was not alone in the forest, that a number of eyes were upon him.

"I'm looking for Robin Hood!" he called out. Robin's men would, of course, be scattered rather densely here. He was near Robin's camp. Damian dismounted from Lucien and walked closer to the trees. Would someone he knew be about? Some man who was a confidant of Robin, and did know his secret identity as the Silver Sword?

He needed to be careful, he warned himself. He could identify himself, and not be believed. But it would be very dangerous to give out the secret of the Silver Sword, and he did not want to have to do so.

But he didn't want to hurt any man.

There would be no need to do so, he told himself. If Robin's men came for him, he would surrender quickly, and be held for Robin's return, if his cousin was not about.

He took another step toward a copse beneath the dense branches of a number of oaks. Men were within those trees, he knew. Their rustling was heavy; the canopy of green and shadow was dark. The earth was damp and springy beneath his feet.

"I'm looking for Robin—" he began again, calling out. But before he could finish the sentence, he heard a curious whirring sound, looked up, and ducked instinctively.

Too late. A massive rope netting was being thrown over his head. Cursing, he felt the weight of it bear him down to the ground. Winded, he struggled to his feet, fighting the rope. The more he moved, the more it seemed to twine about him. He could still reach the knife at his calf, but he didn't want to engage in any deadly battle with these men. "I have told you that I am looking for Robin Hood!" he shouted furiously.

Leaves and branches began to rustle. Bodies suddenly began to fall lightly to the ground from the limbs of the trees. Feet thunked into the soft black earth beneath the trees. He recognized a number of the men, and did so with irritation.

None of these were Robin's closest associates. None were men with whom he had shared his most important secrets from the very beginning. They were good men, all, but not men Robin knew well . . .

Nay, not men Robin knew well!

"If this is the way you greet all noblemen of good cause who would visit your leader, my fine gents, you do a rather rude job of it!" he roared.

Then one of their number stepped forward.

One among them that Robin knew very well!

Kat—or rather, so it seemed, the Lady Greensleeves.

She wasn't wearing the costume he had seen her in before when she was so involved in her forest activity. Borrowed plummage? he wondered. For a crude wool knit mask in an earth-brown was pulled over her face, leaving open just a slit for her mouth and two holes for eyes. She wore a rough brown tunic and a heavy cape in a like color. She was very well concealed.

And yet . . .

He knew it was Kat. From the moment she leaped with such agility from the branches to stand before him, he knew it to be his wife. Instinct. He knew that she had come here.

And she might well feel that he had much for which to pay. And he might well pay for it before anyone thought to warn Robin that they had a prisoner in the forest.

"So, my Lord Montjoy!" she murmured huskily, facing him in his tangle or ropes. "You have come to the forest. Seeking Robin. Well, we shall see that you are able to find him . . . just as soon as he has time. But for now . . ."

She stepped back. "Do you come willingly with us, Lord Montjoy?"

Damian grated down hard on his teeth. He was torn between a searing gratitude that she was here and alive and well—and the utmost desire to drag her over his knee.

At the moment, the latter seemed impossible. For once, she had him.

Just what was the little witch up to? he wondered. She didn't know he was the Silver Sword . . .

And she didn't know that he was well aware that he was facing his own wife. She couldn't know that. He had never given it away in any word or deed.

"Aye, lady, of course I come willingly. I just told you, I seek to speak with Robin Hood."

"Then hand over your sword and the knife at your ankle."

"I can scarce move, my lady."

"I know you can reach that dagger," she replied in a deadly tone. "Toss it to me."

He did so. She barely motioned his way, and the half dozen men who had netted him moved carefully forward, both to free him from their trap and to accept his sword.

"Your hands, Montjoy. Put them behind your back."

He clenched down hard on his jaw, fighting the swift rise of his temper. This was not the time or the place to have it out with her.

He stared her way as one of the fellows quickly slipped behind him, binding his wrists together, and doing it very well. "His ankles, too, I think!" she suggested softly, and a rope was tied about his ankles, giving him room to walk, but not to run.

"My lady, I've come here seeking Robin. Why would I run?"

"You, my lord, are a dangerous man, best kept in check," she replied sweetly. "Let's bring my Lord Montjoy to a place where we might hold him for Robin."

He watched, his temper soaring once again, while one man came forward, leading the group of the bandits' horses.

She was being careful now, not riding her own horse, but a small bay. "Have Lord Montjoy's horse brought along," she ordered.

Then, mounted, she brought the bay near him and

cast a roped loop around his neck. His eyes narrowed at her, and he thought that perhaps she shivered. For just a moment, but . . .

Then the noose tightened around his neck. "Come on, Lord Montjoy. We've a bit of a distance to go."

She couldn't intend to make him stumble along in his hobbled state! he thought incredulously.

She did. She kneed her mount, and they went forward through a forest trail. She started off slowly enough. He trotted behind her, as well as the rope between his ankles would allow, over the soft dark earth, over tufts of grass, over beds of pine.

She sped up.

He followed, determined that he would master her game. A fine sheen of perspiration broke out on his forehead.

"My lady!" one of the bandits called out, riding beside her. In his Saxon tongue he whispered softly to her, "Should we be so cruel here? Robin wishes an alliance with this man—"

"Trust me," she said softly. "Robin will be able to talk him into doing anything he wants."

"But—"

He stumbled then, over a tree stump. He went down hard, pulling the noose taut about his throat.

"Have mercy, my lady—" a bandit murmured.

But she wasn't in a merciful mood. "Up, Lord Montjoy! Come now. We haven't all day!"

He rose, the muscles of his thighs and calves bulging as he managed to do so without the use of his hands. He bowed to her when he stood. "At your command, my lady."

She turned quickly. She did not urge her mount on to such a speed as she had before.

Damian assumed she would be bringing him to the base camp, but that was not what she had in mind. He was startled to discover that they were coming to his own hunting lodge.

That same place where the Silver Sword had brought her that night of her rescue.

She dismounted from her horse and drew her sword, placing it to his throat as soon as she had slipped the noose from around his neck. "You are familiar with this place, my lord?"

"Indeed. It is on my own property."

"Then you shall feel quite at home while we wait," she told him. "Go forward," she warned him, her blade at his vein.

He complied. The door to the cottage was opened for him, and he walked in and stood before the fireplace. He heard her give a command to someone, saying that they might go for Robin and that she needed no further assistance, and then she followed him in.

They were alone.

Now she pointed her sword at his gut, forcing him to back across the room to the bed of straw and furs. "Sit!"

He did so.

When he was seated, she set her sword upon the table and sought out the skeins of wine and the leather mugs, and poured herself a long draught.

"Lord Montjoy knows his wines very well," she said.

He inclined his head. "Thank you."

"Are you thirsty?"

"Indeed. I am near strangled, and therefore very thirsty."

She walked to him with one of the mugs and came down on her knees. She brought the mug to his lips, but when he would have drunk, she jerked suddenly.

The wine spilled over his chin and down his tunic.

"Your pardon, Lord Montjoy!" she said with feigned horror. "But then, you do have much to ask pardon for yourself, have you not?" She backed away. "Never mind. There's quite a supply of wine here."

With an effort he rose, the anger suffusing him giving an added boost to the efforts of his muscles. He backed himself toward the fireplace and the crude mantel, finding a ragged edge there among the wood.

Once she had escaped his bounds. Now he determined he would do the same. He had to.

Oh, she would receive her just rewards!

She sipped wine herself, watching him, then set down the leather mug and skein and swept up her sword again. She stared at him. "You do have much to beg pardon for, do you not?"

"Would you have me beg pardon for being Norman?" he queried her.

She picked up her blade again. "For being Norman? That, my lord, is an accident of birth. But let's see here, all the bandits in the forest take offense against a man for the sins he commits against his fellows. Perhaps, my lord, I am here to take offense against those sins you have committed against your wife!"

"Ah, my wife!" he echoed softly.

"Well?"

"Well? You tell me," he insisted. Once again, a fine sheen of perspiration was breaking out on his face as he worked his wrists against the stone, trying to do so without being seen. "I have committed no sins!" he insisted.

"No?" Her sword was suddenly up in her hands again, and she neared him with the weapon. The wicked blade suddenly swung, severing his brooch from his tunic. It clattered to the far corners of the room. His tunic fell to the floor.

He arched a brow to her and smiled grimly. "What have I done to the girl but wed her!"

"You have sought to command—"

"A wife is a husband's to command!"

"Nay! She is not property to be used and set upon a shelf and told to stay!"

"Perhaps she is kept safe upon that shelf."

She ignored him. "Then—then!—sent from her home, to live with a husband's whore!"

"Her husband has no whores!"

The claim seemed to enrage her.

Her sword moved again with a frightening dexterity, slicing through the fabric of his tunic and undershirt, and just missing his flesh. Just barely missing his flesh.

He forced himself not to move. To stand dead still while she taunted him. His body seemed to heat like a blaze, his muscles to tense like molten steel.

Her blade moved lower, hovering against intimate zones of his body. "How curious that you claim so! Perhaps I should give your flesh a nick or two, and give you time to recant those words while you heal! But, alas, I should have to take great care. I wouldn't want to mistakenly remove anything completely!"

Damn her! He felt the blade. Razor-sharp, just piercing through the fabric.

He forced himself to remain completely still.

"Lady," he promised softly. "You had best cease this game. You will pay."

"You are in no position to threaten me now, my Lord Montjoy," she said. He sensed her smile. Damn her. She was truly enjoying herself.

"I tell you again, I have done nothing evil to my wife. I have—"

"You have taunted her time and time again!"

"How so?"

"How so?" she repeated, her voice rising sharply with anger. "Oh, how so—how not! Let's see, my lord, there was the time when you met her on the parapets and near drowned her by dragging her into the moat!"

"I? That was the Silver Sword—"

"Oh, aye! And it was the Silver Sword who kidnapped her here in the forest to await Montjoy! The lying, licentious, evil demon known as the Silver Sword! He teased her, imprisoned her, taunted her—dear God! The Silver Sword? You Lord Montjoy! Master of lies and deceit!"

He stiffened. She smiled with vengeful satisfaction.

"Perhaps I am not the Silver Sword."

"Oh, but you are. Don't deny it."

"I tell you—" he began angrily.

"Tell me carefully, whatever it is," she warned, pressing the blade hard against his thigh and dangerously close to sensitive flesh, "Tell me very carefully, lest the great Lord Montjoy, the wondrous Silver Sword, the man who is one and all, shall soon be no one but a choir boy!"

"What of my wife?" he asked, his voice a very low roar. "She, who knew she was betrothed, bartered her favors to a stranger to escape!"

"But you were that stranger, playing her along."

"Oh, and shall I play her along now!" he roared.

"What?" she said quickly.

"Lady, when I am free, I promise, you will pay the price!"

"What price more than the things that you have done to her?"

"To my wife, eh?"

"Aye, indeed!"

"The things that I have done to her! Damn you! I have loved her!" he returned sharply.

"You've what!" She backed away, just momentarily. But as she did so, there came a pounding on the door. Startled, she spun around.

Damian took that opportunity to run the ropes of his bounds furiously over the stone.

At last, they gave.

Watching her back as she hurried to the door, he reached down and freed his feet in silence, casting the rope aside, following behind her as silently as he could manage.

She had thrown open the door. Over her shoulder, Damian could see that the Lady Marian stood there, speaking quickly and in a harsh whisper.

"Katherine! You mustn't keep going with this thing. I have just found Robin, and he is hurrying back to base camp, thinking that Lord Montjoy has been brought there."

"Fine, I'll bring him—"

"Katherine, wait! He knows."

Damian smiled like a wolf, sensing her frown. "He knows what, Marian?"

"He knows that the Lady Katherine is the Lady Greensleeves. He has known all along."

"He can't—"

"But he does!" Damian exclaimed sharply at her back. Marian gasped, seeing him then. Kat spun around, her eyes very wide.

Instinct was with her. She immediately tried to step out of the cottage, but he was too swift for her. His fingers curled hard around her arm. "If you'll pardon us, Marian? I think we need to continue this discussion alone."

"Nay, let go of me!" Kat protested wildly. "Robin will be waiting. Marian, isn't that true? There are important things to be clarified right now—"

"Indeed, there are!" He smiled at Marian. "Go on, now, my Lady Marian. Tell Robin we shall be along shortly."

Then he slammed the door.

In a frenzy, Kat tried to pull free from him. He held her hard, wrenching the knit hood from her face. Her hair tumbled around her, a beautiful frame for the shimmer of her eyes.

"The game has changed, eh, my love? You no longer wish to play?"

"Let go of me, Damian Montjoy—"

"Well, I do. Because it is my turn. So far you have roped me and snared me and dragged me along behind your horse. You have dunked wine all down my face and clothing, and threatened to lop off portions of my body that I deem incredibly important."

"Let me go!"

"Oh, I don't think so! Let's see, where is that sword? Perhaps I should take some slicing practice upon your clothing!"

She did manage to wrench free, because he let her do so. It was his turn. He found the sword and hefted it testingly in his hands.

"Oh, where shall we start? Where shall we start?" he murmured.

She lunged for the door. He stopped her, pushing her back. He set the point of the blade against the tie on her rough wool cloak. He barely moved his wrist, severing the tie, and the garment fell to the floor. There were ties all along the front of the tunic she wore.

One by one, he slit them. "Shall I go on, my lady? I can strip you bare in a number of seconds. Then I could dump wine on you. Um. It does have its appeal. The entire afternoon could truly be very entertaining."

She set her hands upon her hips and tossed back the golden abundance of her hair.

"You wish to be entertained? Oh, I think not, my Lord Montjoy! Where shall we begin?" she hissed in turn. "Oh, there are so many places one could start! There is Affa—that charming little olive-skinned creature who has taken up residence at your castle. In your bedroom. Where you sent me!"

"I didn't know she was there—"

"Oh, you lie! She knows you well, my Lord Montjoy. Very well. Then! There is this little matter of your being the Silver Sword! You bastard! You damned bastard! Snake! Letting me go on and on, seducing me—"

"I never seduced you! You seduced me!"

"You lie!"

"Lie! You witch!" he accused. "You were duly and honorably betrothed, and you were willing to sleep with anyone to escape your husband!"

"Not anyone! The Silver Sword. The man who saved my father's life all those years ago! But you! You rodent—" She lifted a hand, pushing the blade of the sword away from her. Heedlessly she came at him, her fists thundering against his chest. "And you knew that it was I! Lady Greensleeves, coming and going, and still—"

"I didn't know a damned thing about the tunnel until Robin told me, and you had me worried sick time and time again!" He let the sword fall. She was flushed and furious and ready to pound against him again. "Stop it!" he commanded her. "I swear, lady, you are going to be very sorry—"

"Sorry! Oh, my Lord Montjoy! You don't begin to know the meaning of the word!" Her eyes were brilliant. Deep pools of exotic color. He had never seen her more angry, or more passionate.

Or more beautiful.

"I will slice and dice you!" she promised. "I will rip you to ribbons—"

"Whoa!"

Her fury was forcing them both backward. He caught hold of her wrists just as her impetus sent them both sprawling on the bed of straw and fur. She was wild, a tigress, a whirlwind of fury. But at length he caught her wrists, pressed her back, and straddled over her.

"You! You are the most wayward, disobedient, and stubborn of all wives! Jesu, you should be whipped and locked in a tower. You—"

"You have already tried both!" she accused him.

"You haven't begun to see the half of it yet, my lady!"

"How could you! How could you!" she demanded. "Letting me stalk my chamber in torment, in fear—"

"You've never had the sense to be afraid of anything!"

"I was in agony—"

"And you deserved it! You betrayed me! You bedded the Silver Sword, a complete stranger!"

"I didn't even know you! And you were busy playing with that little black-haired harlot—"

"What do you mean I was busy! As you have reminded me, I was the Silver Sword!"

"Yes! Which you knew! And I didn't! Of course, the great Lord Montjoy could be magnanimous to his poor quaking bride. You knew! You were fully aware that there had been no man before you, and still . . ." Her eyes narrowed furiously. "Oh! You with your drops of blood! You wouldn't dream of letting any man question the paternity if I were to quickly bear a child! Because you had the benefit of knowing all along that any child would have to be yours, while you left me to wonder—"

"Why would you wonder?" he demanded.

"By nature, one would wonder!" she cried in return. "Oh, you! Get off me! Whoever you are! Silver Sword, Montjoy—whoever! You are both entirely wretched to me!"

He shook his head. "What are you wondering about?" he demanded.

Her eyes narrowed, and she stared at him. He had ten times her power, and his thighs were hard around hers while her wrists were imprisoned in his hands. She couldn't fight him any longer.

But she had no intention of surrendering.

"Whatever we have to discuss, my lord, we can discuss later! Robin needs both of us now!"

He shook his head slowly. "Nay, Kat. Robin needs me now. You are finished in the forest. Finished in truth, I tell you."

"No!" she cried out, trying to rise against him. The ties he had rent from her tunic left some of her beautiful flesh bare. Her hair streamed all around her, and he was near painfully reminded of their first time here. Then she had been clad in the flimsy gown. Though it was muddied and torn, she had still worn it beautifully. As now. Pleading with him, trying to rise against him, her eyes azure, her fair skin ivory, her hair a cloud of sunlight.

All women could be tamed, he had told himself once.

It did not seem that Kat could be so.

Yet maybe she could be loved.

"Damian!" she protested, and her voice was earnest, her lower lip trembled slightly, and her eyes brimmed with liquid color as she entreated him. "Marian told me you are the Silver Sword. She wouldn't lie, she'd have no reason to do so. And so I know—you were there! You were there that day, so long ago, when we came into the woods. Damian, you saw what they did to that poor fellow's hand, and they meant to hang his father, Damian, and—"

"Kat! Aye, they meant to do many things. And men try to right the wrongs. But this battle is no place for you anymore!"

"If you think that I'm not useful—"

"I know that you've been useful, Kat," Damian admitted softly. It was a difficult thing for him to say. Aye, she had been useful. She had been necessary. With her will, her determination, and her courage, she had surely saved many a life, and helped stem some of the flow of cruelty. "Katherine, it's coming down to something very close to war now. I'm going to meet with Robin. You're going to go home."

The softness left her tone. Anger returned to it, and he was sorry. We're on the same side! he wanted to cry out to her. But it was clear she already thought him her enemy again, and no words were going to change that now. "You are sadly mistaken, my lord, if you think that I will return to your home—and live with that black-haired witch! You can have me bound, gagged, and tied to every tree on the property, and I swear that I shall escape you! You can beat me—"

"When did I ever beat you, Kat?" he demanded furiously, "As either man?"

Her chin inched up. "In the forest, my Lord Montjoy. There was no oak stick about, so you found your hand to be a readily available switch!"

He started to laugh. He couldn't help it. It was a mistake. She was suddenly twisting with a frenzy beneath him.

"Montjoy—"

"I'm sorry! Truly, I'm sorry. In fact, I'm quite sorry, but you did have it coming. And it didn't seem to do a thing for you. You attacked me again anyway."

Her eyes sizzled with azure fury. "I shall attack you again when you least expect it, my lord, if you dare to command me—"

"Let's get this straight!" he said, sitting back on his haunches to ease his weight from her. "I am the lord and master here, my lady. And I will command you," he said very, very softly. But as he spoke, he leaned closer to her. Her eyes remained on his, widening with wonder as he spoke. "But I'd never command you to live where another woman abided, for no woman could hold a candle to your grace and beauty. So the woman knows me, Kat, aye, that she does. It was a long war in the Holy Lands. Long, and I had grown hard from the loss of a gentle lady."

"One far more gentle than I!" Kat murmured, and he smiled.

"Different, my lady. Far different. But in truth, from the moment I heard I was to wed, I was with no other woman. Perhaps not because I knew in my heart that I should become so fascinated with the one who would be mine, but rather because there were other matters at hand. Still, it is true. I had no notion that Affa would think that she was to be mine. Ari, I knew, would follow me. He longed to come to England. He is a seer of the future, and he announced that he would accompany me." He paused. Aye, and he had said that Kat would betray him. But she would not do so, could not do so, he swore silently to himself. Ari could be wrong.

That didn't matter now. "Affa will be sent back. Or sent somewhere, I swear it. Yet, if you obey me, there is no reason to send you to my home. I ordered you to go because I could not keep my eye on your tunnel constantly!"

Her lashes lowered. She nearly smiled.

"What will you do?" she asked him.

"Meet with Robin. Gather my forces, and yours. There will be a battle here. John will order de la Ville to come against Robin and the bandits—and Lord Montjoy. And we will fight in return. Kat, please, go home now. See that the guard is kept well. That no man can breach our defenses again and seize the castle, for that is one thing that de la Ville covets. There is only one thing he wants more.

"And that is—?" she asked him.

"You," Damian told her softly. "He would sacrifice anything for you. You must remember that, Kat, and see to it that you are never in danger from him."

She had ceased to fight. Maybe she was even listening to him, and paying him some heed.

He rose and pulled her to her feet before him, pulling her tunic closed where he had slit the ties. "Will you go home?" he asked her. "Will you obey me? If in nothing else, Katherine, I beg of you, obey me in this!"

She hesitated, lowered her head, and nodded slowly.

He caught her shoulders and brought her hard against his chest. His lips touched her hair. The golden-blond strands teased his chin and his nose. The scent seemed to fill him.

"Roses . . ." he murmured. "You always carry the scent of roses, my love. And I am ever reminded of that rose on our wedding night. The sweet scent of roses, and the beauty of their petals as they lay against your flesh, all as soft as silk!"

There was a sudden pounding on the door. Kat pulled away from him in alarm.

But there was no need to fear. It was only Little John who had come. "My lady . . . er, Kat! Lord Montjoy! You must hurry. The armies are forming. Robin is waiting. They say that de la Ville's men have gathered east of here, and your own men-at-arms are riding in from the copse before the castle. You must come, now!"

"Aye!" Damian called. His eyes remained on Kat's. For once, they wore no masks.

He pulled her into his arms and kissed her.

By necessity, the kiss was quick. Yet it carried with it a hungry passion. A simmering heat. Force and coercion . . . and a promise.

He drew away. To his amazement, there seemed to be the slightest shimmer of tears in her eyes. "Take care, my lord."

"I am a very good knight," he told her gravely.

She smiled and lowered her head. "Aye, so I've heard. But a mortal one."

"It sound as if, perhaps, I am growing less horrid as a husband?"

"You saved my father's life once," she told him.

He couldn't quite let her go. He pulled her close again. "Say it, Kat. Just because I am the Silver Sword, and you are the Lady Greensleeves. Say it because we are legends, and because it would be a pretty tale. Say it . . . say, 'I love you, Damian, Lord Montjoy, my husband. Stay safe from danger, because I love you.' "

His lips touched hers once again. Parted from them. "Because it is the stuff of legends," she explained softly, and then her words were a whisper he barely heard. "I love you, Damian, Lord Montjoy, my husband. Stay safe from danger, because . . . I love you."

"Kat . . ." His lips just touched hers, then rose regretfully from them. "Please, now! Ride home. Give me the strength of knowing that you are safe."

He released her, and she turned quickly from him, almost running to the door.

But when she had reached it, she paused. She didn't quite turn fully to him, and her words remained soft, but they were crystal-clear and promising.

"You must stay safe in battle, my lord. I'm not at all sure which, but I do believe that either the Silver Sword or Lord Montjoy will soon be a father. And in the troubled times ahead, a boy—or a maid, at that!—will surely need a father."

"Kat!" he murmured, and started for her.

But she had already escaped, with the door closing quickly behind her.

And he thought that maybe—just maybe!—she had left the softest sound of a sob to linger there upon the air.

Chapter 21

Ari watched as the Montjoy's men prepared for battle, mounting their horses to ride from Clifford Castle. From his distance, the sounds of preparation were muted and muffled, the clang of steel, the hurried shuffle of booted footsteps, the neighs and whinnies of scores of excited horses. They had survived the endless jaunt to the Holy Lands, the endless months of warfare, and the long road home. They could make ready at a moment's notice to go to war.

Now they needed only their lord's hand to lead them.

Ari paused upon the parapets of Clifford Castle. He felt the breeze, and an uneasy sensation swept through him. This was such a different war from those in the Holy Lands. A Christian prince struggling to seize a crown from his Christian brother. Greed was the driving factor here, and such an emotion promised catastrophe from the start.

He had seen the battle coming. He had known that it would take place. He couldn't see a clear ending to it, because it was all . . .

Gray. There was so much darkness about it. The darkness he had envisioned when he had first seen the vision of Katherine, Countess of Ure.

Darkness. No matter how hard he tried to see, it swirled around him. He had barely met his master's new lady, but he was convinced that she loved Montjoy. And he was convinced that she was a woman of passions that ran as deep as her beauty. Not evil passions, but those that would demand the rights of men, those that would cry out for justice. Would such a woman never betray Montjoy?

He had seen it . . .

He had been wrong.

The darkness had distorted all that he had seen.

He clenched his arms across his body and looked to the sky. Clouds moved in gray now up above them. There was a fierce rumbling of thunder, though he'd seen no lightning yet.

Perhaps the thunder was a warning.

He closed his eyes tightly. Aye, he had seen her betraying Montjoy. He had seen it because he had envisioned her in the cottage in the darkness. And the man with her had been faceless.

Because he had been the Silver Sword. But she had not really betrayed him because the Silver Sword was Montjoy, and Montjoy was the Silver Sword.

That had to be it.

But the sense of unease remained with him.

Then, as he stood there, feeling the air turn cooler with the portent of rain, he looked down on the men-at-arms again, those men with their bustling preparations for war, one shouting an order, another gathering up a shield and calling to a squire for a certain saddle.

Someone moved among the men. Someone who was not one of them.

It was Affa.

No one paid her the least heed.

Ari had never been quite sure how the girl had managed to gain a place in the party of Montjoy's men and possessions that had left the Holy Lands in his wake.

He had not been asked about her, and there had been no word left regarding her. Ari had been certain from the start that Montjoy would not have ordered the girl brought along. She had not belonged to him. Yet she had entertained Montjoy, and so none of the English would have thought to refuse her wish to join them when they had made ready to leave.

Had Ari known what she was about, he would have refused her. There was simply something evil about Affa. There was a selfishness in her that did not suit with the followings of Allah. The girl would try anything to have her own way.

Well, it seemed now that she was leaving. Good riddance! Perhaps she had dreamed that Montjoy's wife would be a haggard old crone.

Had that been her thought, she must have seen the truth by now. Lady Montjoy was golden. Her hair was golden, her face had the radiance of sunrays, and even her spirit seemed to shine golden. Ari had seen her ride away, and he had kept his silence. She had gone with warnings to the others, and that he knew well. He wouldn't have stopped her.

But she would have rid Clifford Castle of Affa; that was quite obvious—had not the Lord Montjoy done it more quickly himself. The Lady Montjoy, however, was not one to hide in corners while others faced her adversaries for her. Nay, she was a lady prone to action.

Just as Affa was . . .

Slipping among the men who hurried about below, Affa had disappeared for a moment. Then Ari saw her again. She had taken one of the small, beautiful Arabian ponies from the stables and, unnoticed or unheeded, she had ridden straight from the courtyard to the gate and the wall.

Ari couldn't see the man, but he imagined that the sentry watched her with a puzzled frown, then shrugged, and let her go on by unmolested.

Was she leaving them for good? It would be for the best. Perhaps Allah would be kind, perhaps she would find what she sought with some other baron.

Ari continued to watch the preparations for some time.

Then the wind picked up, and a chill seemed to seize him.

He was a stupid, stupid old man.

No seer had ever been so blind.

The betrayal he had seen wasn't over. It hadn't even begun.

And it wasn't the Lady Montjoy who would betray her lord.

Rather, it was someone who would seem to be the Lady Montjoy, and therefore, the darkness.

Even with the battle poised before them, so inescapably that the air seemed tinged with the tension of it, Kat knew she didn't dare return to her home as she had come to the cottage, in the peasant garb. She rode quickly ahead of Little John and Damian to reach Robin's camp, and there retrieved her own clothing, then found time for one last goodbye before realizing that Damian meant it—he needed her at the castle.

Sir James Courtney had come to the copse, and he was given the task of seeing her safely home. She felt a moment's guilt, seeing his distress at being given so simple a task, and she was sorry that she had caused the poor man so much trouble. "I am coming with you, sir, with no difficulty, I assure you," she told him. Montjoy was looking up at her. There was no time for any further farewells.

"See to her!" he commanded James softly. Then he turned away to join Robin, and Kat paused only briefly, praying with a sudden and desperate passion that they would meet again, and soon. Then she dug her knees into her horse's flanks, and her mare leaped forward, and she was racing like the wind, Sir James following as quickly as he could behind her.

She raced for what seemed like a good twenty minutes before a streak of lightning flashed across the sky, followed by a bold crack of thunder. Her horse reared up wildly, and Kat fought to control her. She reined in after patting the mare's neck, waiting for Sir James to catch up with her.

"It's going to be a rough night!" she called.

"Aye! Rough weather coming! We should hurry. Come along ahead. Maybe we can reach the castle before the storm breaks!"

Kat wasn't concerned about herself. She could only think about Robin and Damian, and the men in the forest. Were Damian's men really on the move already? And what of de la Ville's troops? He had to be ordering them onward with promises of great reward—once Prince John became King John. Would they fight in this kind of weather?

Already the wind was whipping around. Leaves and grasses were lifted from the earth and tossed about in reckless motion. The air smelled damp.

"Ride, my lady!" Sir James reminded her.

She nudged the mare again, and the small horse leaped forward. After the lightning, it seemed that darkness, night, had descended, just as if a giant black hand had blocked out all that might remain of the sun's rays. Kat slowed the mare, moving more carefully over the trail, heading for the copse before the castle.

"My lady! Let me lead!" Sir James called to her.

"I know the way better, as does my mare!" she turned to call back to him. She was nearing the copse. Just as she turned from Sir James to look forward again, another jagged shard of lightning lit up the sky.

And illuminated the copse before her.

A scream rose in her throat, but it was ripped away by the wind.

There were men before her. At least twenty mounted and armed men.

And leading them, sitting there in silence in helmet and visor and armor, was Raymond de la Ville. His helmet was formed like the wings of a raven. His visor was beaklike.

"She comes!" he cried out, the tone muffled by his helm. "Seize her!"

Kat shrieked and tried to turn and spur her mare onward to escape.

But Sir James was there, unaware of what had happened, blocking her way. The mare reared in confusion. She rose so high that Kat lost her seating and plummeted to the ground. Just in time. The mare, too, lost her balance and careened over backward. Then the animal screamed and rolled wildly. Kat, stunned from the fall but otherwise unharmed, jumped up, crying out, worrying for her loyal little horse.

But the animal had not broken a leg. The mare leaped up, shook herself, and cantered off to the side.

Kat felt a presence near her and looked up.

De la Ville.

"Come, my lady, ride with me."

"When ice forms in hell, my lord."

"Perhaps not, Katherine. Look yonder!"

And she did so. Sir James had been quickly seized, taken by surprise. And now there was a noose about his neck, the end of which was held by a mounted man clothed in a tunic bearing the yellow and blue colors of the house of de la Ville with the three ravens etched across it.

"If she isn't mounted before me in three seconds, Gwillen, slit his throat," de la Ville commanded coldly. "My lady?" He bent down, offering her his hand.

She didn't dare hesitate, for Gwillen had already pulled his sword and set it to the vein pulsing at Sir James's throat.

"Well, my lady, I've got you where I want you at last. Or almost where I want you!" he said triumphantly. "But that will come later. Tonight. When the castle is mine!"

"You will not get into the castle," she told him. "The guard has been tripled at the drawbridge. Your treachery was our only weakness."

His arms tightened around her. "My lady, you will bring us directly into the castle."

"Never."

"Would you have this poor fellow slain?"

"I'll hang myself before I'll let you betray yourself and the castle, my lady!" Sir James called, his voice ringing out like steel.

"Um, well, my fair young fellow, you just might want to wait on that extraordinary deed of valor," de la Ville told him. "I've a far greater threat to use against my lady than your puny death!"

"My own?" Kat queried, hating the feel of his arms around her as she sat before him atop his dark horse. "I've contemplated death and you before, my lord, and found the first a far preferable attainment!"

De la Ville started to laugh. There was something just a little maniacal about the sound, and it frightened Kat greatly. "Where is your sense, my lord!" she cried out. "I am wed to Montjoy! No prize can be achieved through me. Damian will meet you in battle. Damian with all of his forces. Damian, and the outlaws, they will band as one—"

"I don't think so, my lady!" de la Ville said smugly. His arms were like bars. She could see nothing but his eyes because of his helmet. They seemed to burn.

"De la Ville—" she began, then stopped.

She heard a rustling in the brush. Riders were coming.

The wind whipped up with a sudden fury. Once more, lightning burst and flared across the sky. The thunder that followed was immediate. Another flash followed in just a matter of seconds.

And then the brush parted. The lightning allowed her to see those who were coming.

She paused, blinking furiously. For the party was led by a woman who might have been she. She was cloaked in one of Katherine's finest green capes. Her head was hooded by the cowl, but it appeared that a wealth of blond hair lay beneath that cowl.

Katherine's heart shuddered violently. The sky lightened. The woman riding the lead horse glanced up, a look of pure satisfaction and smug victory on her face.

Affa.

Affa. . . . The woman was in league with de la Ville!

Pulling away the blond wig that she wore even as she entered into the clearing.

"What in God's name—" Kat began.

"In God's name, lady, aye! You will order the drawbridge lowered. We will all ride across it—you will order the guards to lay down their arms." His voice came very close to her ear. "Or else, my lady, I will order your husband murdered!"

"But you cannot—"

"Oh, but I can."

"He will kill you first—"

"Lady, we will wait. And you will see for yourself!"

He should never, never have fallen for de la Ville's trickery! Damian chastised himself as he paced the forest.

Or Kat's proclamations of love.

The latter was by far the more bitter, for he thought himself the greater idiot for having ever believed. He had been warned. Again and again. Ari had seen it, Ari had told him.

But he had never imagined that she would deceive him. Not with de la Ville. With his whole heart he had believed that she hated de la Ville.

Even if she had never cared for him. Even if the way she made love was a lie, if the sob in her voice was a lie, the whisper of passion, the brilliance in her eyes!

The worse fool he!

Damian knew that even as he walked along the darkened forest path. But, ah, love! The brutal things that it did to a man!

Kat had scarce been gone before one of Robin's men had burst upon him and Robin Hood there in the deep clearing.

"Robin, Lord Montjoy! Something amiss has happened. I saw the lady, streaking through the trees, running like the wind, and screaming for help. I tried to follow—"

"Where the hell was James Courtney?" Damian exploded.

"I know not, my lord, all I know is that he called her name—"

"Damian, wait!" Robin urged him. "I will gather the men—"

"Nay, for we cannot reach my knights in time, and if this is treachery, then we all are lost. If Kat calls, then I must come!"

"Damian!" Robin called, but Damian had no time now for logic or thought of safety.

The storm was coming. Closer and closer. Lightning streaked raggedly across the sky. "Follow as best you can!" he told Robin, once mounted. Lucien could feel the tempest of the weather, of the sky. He pawed the ground in a frenzy, and Damian at last gave him free rein.

Robin's man came racing behind him, directing him along the trail. He could see her then, ahead. Color in the trees. Then he heard his name. Cried out softly. Carrying on the wind, whispering through the trees.

"Kat!"

The lightning crowded the sky again. He could see her clearly. She had donned her cloak against the wind and coming rain. He knew the cloak well. It was one of her favorites, and she had packed it when he had ordered her onward to his castle.

"Katherine, wait! Hold still, let me reach you!"

He couldn't see any danger about, but he knew that it was there. Instinct warned him. *Withdraw! It is a trap!*

"Damian!"

The wind ripped and tore at her voice. Distorted it.

"Katherine! Come to me!"

Then he heard the scream.

It came from the deep thicket. He could ride Lucien no further, and he dismounted and started to walk. "My lord!" cried Robin's man from behind him.

He turned, but the man was no longer there.

And then he knew. It was a trap. Kat had led him directly into a trap. And he had been warned.

"Damian!"

He walked, ever wary, listening to the whisper and echo of her sob, desperate to reach her, to understand.

He drew his sword, ready for the onslaught that would bring him down.

"Now! We'll take him as the outlaws have taken us!" came a triumphant cry.

And twenty men sprang from around the trees, all with swords drawn or bows strung or ropes looped and knotted and at the ready.

He sprang forward, lashing out with the brutal intensity of his steel. One man fell, another, and another. "We can't kill him yet!" someone warned.

"Aye, but he's killing us!"

His steel rang, hard, fast. He fought forward.

But the ropes were falling around him, too. He dodged and twisted and slashed his way through the men. Five were fallen, six. Seven. But he couldn't fight the swordsmen and the rope. There were countless bound around him now, distorting his aim, wearing down his strength.

He could no longer twist or turn.

Then, even as he roared out his anger and vengeance, struggling fiercely to free himself, to raise his sword one last time, something hard came crashing down upon his head. Once, twice, three times . . .

Then the darkness of the night had been nothing compared to the deep black void that had risen to claim him. Bitterly, bitterly, he had fallen to it. He had not been taken by the best of Saladin's archers or assassins. He had survived endless battles of hand-to-hand combat. He had triumphed as a knight in battle; he had fared equally as well as the Silver Sword.

But now, at last, the treacherous, golden beauty who had become his wife had brought him down, and hard. She had warned him that he would be sorry.

Aye, she had warned him!

But he couldn't fight the darkness, no matter how bitter it might be. As so he went catapulting into the black void. Falling, falling, falling . . .

"Ah!" de la Ville cried out with pleasure. "See, there, my lady, he comes! The great Lord Montjoy, brought low at last."

A party of men on foot came through to the copse where they waited. There were perhaps ten of them. And within their group was Damian. He was being carried on a litter that was dragged by the two of the somewhat bloodied fellows.

"You've got him!" de la Ville said triumphantly.

"He brought down Ivan and Leif, and eight others," one told de la Ville wearily.

"I don't care how many he brought down, as long as we have him!" de la Ville said.

Montjoy . . .

Did he breathe? They had folded his hands upon his chest. His handsome face was in complete repose, pale against the ebony of his hair. A small trickle of blood trailed along his forehead. He was bound by numerous ropes.

Kat tried desperately to elude de la Ville's hold, but his armored arms kept her prisoner before him on his horse.

"Let me go to him!" she shrieked. "Jesu, is he—"

"Dead? Not yet, my lady. His life lies there, within your gentle hands."

He could not be lying there. Injured. At de la Ville's mercy. Kat could not accept it. "You have not taken him down, you have not!"

"Indeed not, my lady. You have taken him down."

"I never—"

Kat broke off, hearing Affa's very soft laughter. Then Kat realized that the lithe Arabian beauty had ridden into the copse behind the men. She was wearing Kat's cloak, the green one with the low hood. "You claimed to love him!" Kat cried out.

"He will be mine," Affa said, her chin high, her eyes deep and dark, but touched by fire. "I have made a pact with Lord de la Ville. He will use Montjoy to obtain the castle. Then Montjoy is mine."

"Affa! How can you be so foolish! He cannot plan to give you Montjoy in any way, if he is threatening me with Montjoy's death, should I refuse him what he wants!"

Affa looked uncomfortable for a moment.

"Fool, heathen woman!" de la Ville shouted. "My Lady Montjoy is not going to let him die? Hush, and you will have what you're after! We've got to take the castle first, and Lady Montjoy must give the order that the drawbridge be lowered for us to seize it! Let's move now—"

"Wait!" Affa commanded. "Lord de la Ville. You said—"

"Affa, you can't listen to what this man says! He cannot give you Montjoy! What would you do with him? Where would you have him—"

"She will take him to Clifford Castle!" de la Ville announced furiously.

"Affa, think about it! He cannot afford to let Montjoy live!" Katherine said quickly. "You know Montjoy, so you've told me! So does de la Ville. If de la Ville holds me and the castle, Montjoy will tear down heaven and earth to get to him. De la Ville cannot afford for Damian to live, can't you see that?"

Affa's eyes widened in the darkness. "We made a bargain!" she told de la Ville.

"And Montjoy is alive!" de la Ville insisted.

"If he were dead now, de la Ville knows that there is no way on God's earth that I would command that the drawbridge be opened!" Kat insisted.

De la Ville's arm squeezed her so tightly then that she cried out.

"Maybe there are other bargains we can make to keep the man alive a bit longer, eh?" de la Ville said.

"You are a traitor!" Affa cried suddenly. "I will help you no longer!"

"I need your help no longer, bitch!" de la Ville announced.

Affa jerked on her horse's reins, trying to spin the animal about. "You will not betray me!" she shouted. "Allah's curse will be upon you!"

A brilliant flash of lightning lit up the sky. For a moment, Kat could see the woman, clad in her own beautiful green cloak. The blond wig was gone, and Affa's own glorious long dark hair was streaming behind her. She was a picture of wild, exotic beauty.

Then, in that same bright streak of lightning, everything changed. Kat heard the whizzing sound of an arrow streaking through the air.

Affa was struck in the back. She arched upon her mount, looking to the sky.

Looking to her Allah.

Then she catapulted forward, dead on the ground, while her mount raced away into the darkness.

A chill, a savage penetrating chill, streaked along Kat's spine. "My God! You murdered her! In cold blood. Her back was to you, a defenseless woman, and you murdered her!"

"And so will I murder Montjoy," he assured her flatly. "She was about as defenseless as poison, my beauty," he added. "As are you! I do not deceive myself about you, Katherine. I know, too, that you can be a formidable foe. So let's have at this, shall we? Let's finish with our business this night. Then we can get on to our . . . pleasure, eh, my lady?"

"Bastard!"

"You will have that drawbridge down, and quickly, madam. And you will order your troops to lay down their weapons, and obey my commands. Else he dies!"

She twisted to see his eyes beneath his raven's helmet and faceplate. "And I am a formidable foe, too! So you have told me. Like de la Ville, don't you suppose that I will come after you time and time again until the castle is mine again?"

"Lady, if you cause me too much trouble, an arrow can dispose of you, too. I do intend to keep you alive for quite some time, though. If you behave."

Her gaze fell over him thoughtfully. "I decided long ago that my death would be far preferable to my life with you."

"Your death, my lady. But what about his?" De la Ville inclined his head toward Damian, sleeping like one dead on his litter. It seemed that Kat's heart swelled within her chest and rose to her throat to near choke her, bringing blinding tears to her eyes.

Damian had always thought that she had meant to betray him. Would he ever believe the truth now? Would she ever hear him speak with tenderness again?

She tensed, desperate to escape de la Ville, to touch Damian, to kiss his silent lips, and with that kiss, swear her innocence. Yet de la Ville sensed her need, and jerked his arms hard around her.

"You may see him more closely. Soon! Once we are in the castle."

Kat exhaled slowly, blinking away her tears. "Then ride for the castle, de la Ville," she whispered, fighting to keep the tones of desolation and defeat from her voice.

But de la Ville heard them. He heard them, and his laughter rang out loudly, and with pleasure.

The snap and crackle and warmth of fire began to awaken him.

At first he did not open his eyes, because he could not do so.

Eons seemed to pass. Eons in which he drifted into and out of consciousness. He heard her as she whispered his name.

Then there was a time when he thought that his eyes did open, just a shade. And she was there. She was there with her exquisite aquamarine eyes flooding with the liquid brilliance of tears. She was there, whispering his name. He could almost reach out and touch the gold of her hair.

Then she was gone. He was back in the forest. Battling man after after man, feeling the chafe of the rope as it came around him and pulled him down. Dragging him, down, down, into darkness . . .

Dreams.

They faded.

He couldn't open his eyes, because he hadn't the strength to do so.

Then he was careful not to open them because he realized that his hands were bound behind his back, and that he was a prisoner somewhere, and that he must decide just where he was and how guarded before he dared to open his eyes.

It was amazing that he was able to worry about opening his eyes, he thought, fighting the pain that ripped through his temple from the blows there. Amazing that de la Ville had not killed him outright.

Why was he still alive?

He opened his eyes just a slit and tried to focus. He was surrounded by silence. It was cold here, but though he heard the sound of the wind and the rain, that sound was distant. The chill that pervaded him let him realize that he was in a castle, deep in the bowels of a castle, beneath the earth.

The Castle de Montrain?

Aye, it must be. And he had been taken here because Katherine had tricked and trapped him. Because she had given him and the castle to de la Ville.

Nay, it couldn't be!

Did his heart deny it, or his mind? Katherine . . . when he had come to love her, to need her with all of his heart. When he had let go of the past, and come to know that the beauty granted him had been of the soul and the heart, and that miraculously, he had been given love!

He had come to this . . .

Nay, it was not possible!

But bitterly he realized that it was. He lay here, a prisoner.

Where? The cellar. The deep cellar of the castle. The hall would be above him, and above that, Kat's chamber, his chamber. Where even now, de la Ville might be celebrating his victory.

His victory—or his alliance?

But then, even as he lay there fighting to regain his strength and assess his situation, he heard the sound of footsteps on the hard earthen flooring, and then he heard the rough sound of de la Ville's voice.

"You will see, my lady, for now I keep my side of this bargain. He lives!"

With his eyes closed, Damian was acutely aware of sound. He heard the soft flutter of fabric. Someone was trying to reach him.

And he breathed in the scent of roses . . .

"Let go of me!" Kat demanded. "Let me get to him! You said that I might come closer—"

De la Ville's laughter was harsh, and very pleased. "Lady, if I were to let you go to him, he would cast you from him with a vengeance! You betrayed him, lady."

"Never—"

"He followed you to his doom, Katherine."

She cried out, and it was all that Damian could do to remain still. But he had to do so. The bloom of hope had taken root within his soul, and he must hear this to the end.

There was more, of course.

If he hated her or loved her, he would have Kat back. Until the breath of life was completely torn from his body, he would fight for her.

But at the moment, he was laid out on a cold stone slab, and his hands were tied behind his back. To save her, he must wrest free.

"It's time, Katherine. Time to take me up yonder stairs, and convince me that he should continue to live!"

"You're an idiot!" Kat cried out. De la Ville was hurting her. Damian could hear it in her voice. By God, bastard, you will pay! he thought. Yet he could do nothing but listen while she continued. "A fool, and an idiot. I despise you! I have always hated and loathed and despised you!"

"They say you hated your husband, my lady. Perhaps you will get over it with me."

"Never! There is a difference, de la Ville! Damian would never take his amusement from harming the defenseless. Damian would never have had Affa brought down in cold blood."

"Don't fool yourself. She betrayed him to me. He would be glad to have her dead."

"Nay, de la Ville. You are so covered in filth that you would not know what it was to be clean! Damian would have pitied her. He would have seen that she was misled. He is far stronger than you, de la Ville. But his strength is tempered by mercy, something of which you know nothing!"

"Then teach me!" de la Ville ordered. "I will make you love me. You will do so!"

"Nay, I tell you, never! All that I will do, my lord bastard, is slay you the first chance I get!" Kat hissed in return.

Then she screamed again as de la Ville jerked her around. "Bitch! You are right. You will get no mercy from me when the time comes, and the time comes now!"

Kat screamed again.

And the scream echoed and echoed in Damian's heart.

"Wait!" she cried out suddenly, wrenching from him. "A moment! Give me a moment, and I will walk with you."

"And cease to fight me?"

She wanted to die before giving the promise, Damian knew.

"And cease to fight!" she breathed. "Let me just touch him."

"Try to free him and you are both dead."

"I do not seek to free him, just to touch him!"

De la Ville must have let her go. Damian heard the flutter of fabric again, the soft fall of her feet.

And then he felt the warmth of her arms around him. Felt the silken carpet of her hair, blanketing him. Her cheek was against his. Wet with her tears. And she was whispering urgently.

"There is a door, third stone beneath the stairs. It's part of the tunnel. Escape, my love, escape to the forest. Jesu, God, please let him hear me! Somewhere in his mind, please let him hear me! I did not betray you, love!"

Her tears caressed his flesh. Warm and liquid. Then her lips touched his cold ones.

"Katherine! Now!" de la Ville warned.

A touch, a breath.

And she was gone.

And the awful cold settled in all around him.

Chapter 22

Damian didn't know how he managed to split the ropes that bound his wrists so cruelly tight together. Perhaps it had been the feel of her lips against his.

Perhaps it was the knowledge that de la Ville was now taking her upstairs. To her room.

Nay, to their room! Their chambers, where they slept together, where he held her.

Rage, love, desire—one, or all three, had given him a miraculous strength. Rubbing his fists with a vengeance against the stone slab beneath him, he had at last managed to break through the rope. With his wrists free, he had been able to go on and tear off the ropes about his body, and those that bound his feet.

There was little to see here, for de la Ville had left his prisoner no light. He could still hear the storm. It had come in earnest now. Rain slashing down. Thunder abounding. And still, upon occasion, the lightning would come. And even here, in the bowels of the castle, the stone would brighten for a moment.

He could see the stairway.

And the stone. The third stone beneath it . . .

Freed, he was about to leap up when he heard the groan of a door opening. He lay back, pretending to remain unconscious. With his eyes barely open, every muscle taut and tense, he waited.

"Lord Montjoy! Oh, Jesu, have they killed him?"

The soft whisper came from Kat's serving woman, he was certain. Marie. But she was not alone. There was someone else with her.

"Nay, he lives. But we must rouse him fast. The guard will know quickly that I am not administering to his head wound. We must rouse him and take him from the castle!"

It was Ari, the old scoundrel. What was he doing here?

Easy enough. He had come somehow with poor Affa to England, and now ...

"Jesu, we cannot carry him! He is solid muscle and weighs like steel—"

"Shhh! The guard passes by!" Ari warned.

Damian allowed his eyes to spring open. Marie almost cried out with surprise, and he jackknifed up, clamping his hand over her lips. "You need carry me nowhere, Marie."

"Thank the Lord!" she said.

"Shhh!" Ari warned again.

"You must leave the castle. Kat bade me come here and see that you find the tunnel. She tried to tell you, but you could not hear—"

"I heard!" he said with soft vehemence.

"Anyway, our only chance now is for you to escape. Find your men, and Robin, and return here to wage the battle so ready to begin. Kat's men remain loyal to her, and to you, my lord, but they are afraid that de la Ville will kill you if they disobey him. Once you are gone, that threat is over."

"We haven't time to talk! You must escape!" Ari said urgently.

Damian gripped his hand suddenly. "What do you see, old man? What do you see this night?"

Ari shook his head dolefully, his dark eyes anxious.

"I see the rain, my lord, I see the rain and the darkness. I didn't see clearly before, either, to my greatest sorrow. I knew that she was with another man, but that man was you. And I knew that you would be betrayed, but I could not see that it was another in her stead."

"I can see that you must get out of here!" Marie said urgently.

Damian leaped to his feet. "Nay!" he said softly. "You must get out of here."

"What?" Marie said.

"If it is discovered that I am gone, de la Ville will not hesitate to murder you both. You will go and find Robin. Marie, I know that you will know how. You have helped Katherine come and go from this castle as the Lady Greensleeves for years now. You will know what you are doing."

Marie flushed. "My lord—"

"Go!" Damian insisted. "Come, let's reach the tunnel."

"But what are you doing?" Marie asked with dismay.

"This is the same tunnel by which she has escaped all these years, am I right?"

"Aye, my lord, but—"

"Then it leads to my bedchamber above, where de la Ville thinks to take my wife, right?"

Marie nodded. She moistened her lips. "But she said that whatever befell her, you must live!"

"I will live," Damian promised her. "I will live, I swear it! De la Ville is the one who will die!"

She had promised not to fight. Promised—for that one near-impossible prayer that she might whisper some words to Damian.

Words of freedom.

Yet she had touched his lips, and his lips had been cold. If he were to awaken, if he were to live, he would despise her! Could he ever believe in her again?

Did it matter? she wondered with desolation. De la Ville held the castle. De la Ville held her. And it seemed that there was nothing that she could do, for she would not let him kill Damian. Nay, she could not let that happen ever.

Even if she did not love him the way that she did, he had been the man with the arrows in the forest that day. And he had been the man to defend so many for so long . . .

Nay. She would not let him die.

And though she had sworn not to fight de la Ville any longer, she found ways to do so. When he wrenched her from the cellar, she warned him in a hiss that he must loosen his hold upon her, or all within the castle would know that she was no willing hostage.

So he let go of her, and she walked into the great hall on her own, and she ordered Howard to bring up more wine for their . . . guests. And de la Ville sat before the fire, his evil, handsome face brooding while he watched her, his fingers drumming impatiently upon his chair.

And while she tasted wine, she managed to speak to a very frightened Marie, who trembled while she poured out goblets of wine, but she nodded, understanding.

Then, from far across the room, Kat saw that Ari was there. Ari! He watched her gravely, then nodded imperceptibly Hope sprang into her heart. What could one little wizened old Arabic seer do? She wasn't sure, but she was glad that he was there, and glad that he could see.

But then both he and Marie managed to disappear. And when Kat walked across the hall again, de la Ville caught her hand.

"Where is your maid?"

"Gone only to see to my lord's wound. Your guard will wait beyond the door, I am quite certain."

"I don't like it!"

"He is bound and trussed like a deer." She couldn't help it. She leaned close, taunting him. "Do you fear him still?"

De la Ville was up then, wrenching her around. He lifted an arm to those of his men he had brought with him into the hall. "Good night. Guard this keep well!" he commanded. He nodded one man. "Rothwell! You will keep guard at my door. And you likewise, Gunther."

His eyes fixed on Kat's. "Now. Now, lady, you will pay for your lord's life!"

He shoved her ahead of him. Kat dared not look back to the hall. Her people within it would be instantly slain if they saw her distress and fought.

And so she walked slowly ahead of him up the stairs. She tripped, trying for any ploy whatsoever to buy time.

Time . . .

For what?

Robin hadn't the strength to attack the castle. His men hadn't the arms and the armor to do that kind of battle.

Damian's forces were out there. Awaiting Damian. Awaiting his orders to fight . . .

But were they there? Did they even know that he had been taken?

De la Ville jerked her up and around. She balanced precariously on the stair, meeting his furious gaze. "Lady, I have known you for years! And I have never known you to be less than nimble on your feet. Now move!"

And she did so. She walked ahead of him. He followed. She paused before her door, her head downcast, her eyes on her hands. He strode behind her, thundering the door open with his fists. "Keep guard well!" he warned his men, then shoved her forward, and slammed the door behind them.

He pushed her closer to the bed. He had shed his armor below in the hall. Now he stripped off his riding gloves, watching her with that same brooding intensity with which he had watched her in the hall.

His gloves landed on a chair. She felt his eyes. Felt them stripping her inch by inch.

"Jesu!" he screamed at her suddenly. "What is wrong with me? Is my person so repugnant? Is my face so horrid?"

"There is nothing wrong with your face or person," she said coolly. She realized then that de la Ville had not won. He thought that he had won when he dragged her here. But now they both knew that he had not won at all. He couldn't beat or drag what he wanted out of her.

"You might have been a handsome man," she told him. "Your ugliness, my lord, lies within."

He walked around her, his lips pursing. "Thank God that it is not my face! Because you will watch it tonight when I make love to you."

"When you rape me, you mean," she said flatly.

His hand lashed out, and he struck her. Tears stung her eyes, and she fell forward, just catching herself on the edge of the bed. She shook the tears from her eyes and started suddenly, looking at the linen bedding that stretched before her.

A rose lay on the bed. Between the down pillows, just touching the linen sheets. A single rose.

Perhaps it had been there. Perhaps Marie had set it there.

Perhaps . . .

A rose.

The scent of roses was on the air.

Damian! He had to be there. He had to be with her somewhere! Somehow, she found new courage.

De la Ville jerked her back to her feet. He spun her around. "I meant to be gentle, my lady. Why? Because you were different. I coveted you. I coveted this castle. Richard would hear none of my case, but John was willing to sell. Well, Richard is gone, and John will be King! And the castle will be mine. I had meant this to be different. You would have been my wife; you would have borne my children."

"And you have taken maidens in the woods to use so violently, as you enjoy?" she interrupted on a bitter breath.

"Have it as you will!" he retorted. He reached out, his powerful fingers coming to rest on the bodice of her tunic. Kat lashed out with a fury, gouging his face with her nails.

The tunic gave anyway, shearing from her body, leaving her clad in her soft pale blue underdress. "It will be as you will have it, bitch!" de la Ville raged, his hand flying to his face, and the marks she had left upon it.

He reached out for her again. Caught her arm, and slung her around with such fury that she went flying backward upon the bed.

Beside the rose. She smelled the sweet scent of it. Saw the bloodred petals.

And then she saw Raymond's face as he started to lower himself upon her.

But even as he began to smile, and even as a scream formed deep within her throat, he was suddenly and violently wrenched back.

His smile was swept cleanly from his face.

Damian was there. Aye, he had been in the room since they had come to it, and now his hands were upon de la Ville. He scarce saw Kat as she leaped to her feet, for his fury was all upon the man who had invaded his home. He had wrenched de la Ville with such force, by the shoulders, that the massive knight had actually flown across the room, crashed against the wall, and slunk down to the floor.

But de la Ville did not remain stunned. "You!" he

roared, rising. "You should be dead already!"

"You will die, de la Ville."

"But not by your hand!" de la Ville responded. "Guard!" he called out.

Damian was unarmed. His sword and knife had been stripped from him when he had been taken.

His fury had been such that he might well have taken de la Ville with his bare hands. But if the guards rushed in with swords . . .

Kat rolled to the edge and leaped from the bed, staring across the room. Aye, it was there! Her father's sword! Put back upon the wall after that night when she had defended herself with it from de la Ville's henchmen once before. She hurried to it, even as a pounding sounded on the door, even as the door burst open and de la Ville's two men rushed in.

"Seize him! Seize Montjoy!" de la Ville ordered. He pushed himself up and flung himself toward Kat.

She screamed. His hand just caught her foot, bearing her down to the floor. She looked up and saw Damian, ably ducking and leaping, avoiding the deadly blows aimed his way. She kicked furiously, evading de la Ville's hand, and managing to set her foot squarely against his nose.

He bellowed with pain and fury. She gave him no heed, leaping up, climbing the hard wood chair for the sword and spinning to see Damian still dodging and ducking.

"Damian!" she cried. He saw her there and smiled briefly. She tossed him the sword. It flew across the room in a beautiful silver arc and clattered to the floor in front of Damian. He seized it, and the men fell back.

It had become a different game for them. A deadly game. One thrust forward. Too easily Damian stepped aside, then parried with his own thrust, catching his opponent through the heart. With a gurgle, the man fell. The second man, Rothwell, paled, then stepped forward.

"Drop your sword!" Damian ordered.

"Do so and you die a traitor's death!" de la Ville countered. "Guards!" he yelled, shouting at the top of his voice.

But who would come?

De la Ville's men?

Or Kat's own castle guard?

"Give me your sword, coward!" de la Ville shouted to his man.

The blade was tossed his way. Kat dived for it, but de la Ville, his face bloodied, was quicker. With the blade in his hand, he lunged for her.

"Nay!" Damian roared, rushing forward. De la Ville fell back, forced to do so. They could all hear the clatter on the stairway now: men coming up from below. De la Ville made a wild swing at Damian. Damian ducked it, then caught hold of Kat's hand, throwing her behind him. "Get out into the hallway. Up the stairs, and to the parapets! Quickly!"

She had played this scene before, she thought, in a different life. Nay, the same life, and not so long ago.

Then she had tried to battle Damian for her life.

Now she battled with Damian, because her life would mean nothing without him in it.

"Damian!"

"Go! I am behind you!"

And he was. She pushed out into the hallway. Her eyes widened. "Damian, hurry, they're coming! De la Ville guards are coming!"

"Make it to the parapets!" he ordered.

She started to the stairs. Damian followed, his back to her as he and de la Ville engaged in vicious swordplay. More men were clattering up the stairs. Damian dueled with de la Ville from one side, and with one of his armored men from the other. Kat, so nervous her breath was coming in short pants, managed to burst the door ajar behind her.

They were out in the open. Out on the parapets. The rain had stopped. Curiously, it had ceased altogether.

While the lightning still streaked across the sky. Swiftly, viciously, brilliantly. And thunder would follow. Follow in loud crashes and explosions.

One jag of lightning suddenly seemed to make the sky as brilliant as day. Kat could see Damian there on the parapets, poised to do battle. Three swordsmen now fought to take them, one of them de la Ville.

The lightning passed. Darkness seized the parapets.

Thunder cracked and rumbled.

Lightning burst upon them again.

And it was just in time for Kat to see Damian triumphant at last. The blade of his sword skewered through de la Ville.

De la Ville caught hold of the blade, eternal surprise captured in his eyes.

Damian pulled back his sword. De la Ville fell against the wall, then crumpled to the floor.

It was a strange victory, for even as de la Ville fell, more men pressed through the door.

Damian could not take them all. He turned to Kat, a wry grin upon his lips. He offered her his hand, leaping to the rim of the parapets.

Ready to dive down into the stygian darkness of the moat beneath.

"My lady?" he offered.

And she smiled in return, accepting his hand.

"Don't be afraid!" he urged her softly.

"I am not," she replied. "I am not afraid. Not with you."

And together they plunged down, down, down into the darkness far below.

The cold water swallowed Kat. It covered her head, and it sucked her under. Her limbs seemed to freeze, her lungs to burst.

But her hand was still in his, and he was pulling her back up. When she thought she would die and stay forever in the gray-green blackness of the moat, she suddenly broke the surface of the water and breathed in desperately, choking, inhaling, gasping, choking once again.

"Kat, we must swim. The men on the parapets—"

"Hello, down there!" a voice suddenly rang out. A familiar voice. Kat and Damian both cast back their heads, looking up.

And Robin was there. A jaunty grin on his face, he looked down at them while a certain amount of swordplay still went on atop the parapets.

"Well, I do like this!" Robin called down. "The two of you off for a swim, right in the middle of the battle."

"Robin!" Kat cried. "How—"

"Marie and Ari brought us back through the tunnel!" Robin shouted down. "We've a man now seeing that the drawbridge is lowered again—and your men are waiting to ride in just as Kat's are doing their best to take over once again."

"Jesu, then it is done!" Damian gasped.

Robin sobered. "Not quite. There are more forces aligned against the King in John's behalf. You'll need to take charge of your men, cousin. But do come up first. You've time to change."

Kat's teeth were chattering. She was waterlogged and freezing and treading water. She didn't care. She turned, throwing her arms around Damian, sending them both back to the bottom as she kissed him soundly.

His strong kick brought them to the surface a second time. Still freezing but heedless of it, Kat found that she needed to talk. "Oh, Damian, I love you. I love you and

I love the Silver Sword. I never betrayed you, I swear it. They used Affa, and the poor girl is dead now. I'm so sorry, Damian, I really am, she did not deserve that, but still, I tell you, I love you, I'd never have betrayed you, I—"

"Kat, Katherine, I know," he said. She was going to start speaking again. He shushed her the best way he knew how, with another hungry, very wet kiss. When they broke apart, they were both breathless. Even his muscles were wearying from keeping them afloat. "I love you," he said softly.

"You were supposed to have run! I didn't want your life risked, then I saw the rose. Oh, Damian, I knew you were there!"

"It was the only sure way I knew to let you know that I was near," he whispered.

"Come after a damsel in distress once again," she told him, her eyes shining magnificently. "Bare-handed! Oh, Damian!"

"Come after the woman I love," he returned. "And the one to carry my name, my children, and my heart."

Once again, she kissed him. A deep, searing kiss that sent them both into heaven—and spiraling deeper into the chilling depths once again.

They surfaced.

"Hello, down there!" Robin cried. "Pardon me, my lord, my lady, we are awaiting your pleasure up here."

"And I'm quite freezing near to death," Kat said regally. "Next time you rescue me, my lord, perhaps we could avoid the exit through the moat?"

"A brash and willful vixen is what you are!" Damian retorted. "And I've a fair mind to leave you here, right in the midst of it!"

"You wouldn't!"

"Quite right, my love. There are many places I would leave you to await me, and this is not one!"

"Perhaps a place with a bed of roses," she said softly.

"Aye, a place with a bed of roses," he said soberly. He touched her forehead with his lips, then swam strongly, bringing them both from the water.

Marie had come to the soft earth embankment, ready to greet them with heavy wool towels. The castle was safe once again.

Kat did not know how safe until she and Damian ventured across the drawbridge arm in arm.

And the cheers went up. Cheers from Damian's men, and cheers from her own.

And cheers from Robin's men. His fine group of fellows who had come in their forest browns and greens, unarmored, and poorly armed with their staffs and salvaged swords and whittled arrows.

All of them greeted Kat and Damian. All of them cheered. And all of them raised a cry and hooted and hollered when Damian kissed Kat again, in the hall before the heat of the fire.

But the laughter and the cheers could only be shortlived. De la Ville was dead, but Prince John's quest was not. And on this night, the men had to fight again.

Waiting was hard for Kat.

And the waiting seemed to go on and on.

Damian and Robin and their combined forces did come back that night.

And Kat was ready to greet him, bathed and wrapped in the scent of roses.

And with roses strewn upon the bed.

And still, he told her when he returned, worn and weary, there was no rose in truth more beautiful than she, no bud to have bloomed more elegantly. There was no petal softer than her flesh, sweeter than her hair . . .

And surely no rose held such vivid colors as those

that graced her hair, her eyes, her ivory flesh, the rouge of her nipples or the ivory of her breasts.

With a blush she told him that she had quite decided that he was an excellent gardener.

He could, she dared say, make any rose bloom.

It was a wondrous night for them. One in which they made love again and again.

Made love . . .

And whispered love. The words spewed freely from them. About the things they had feared, the things they had expected, the things they had both believed in. The night was full of a rare, fine magic, for they had not only discovered each other, but they had done so in time, while love and life lay before them.

Or so they hoped.

By the morning, Damian rode again, as did Robin and the others.

The battles went on. Fighting flared here and there around England. Damian was gone far more often than he was home.

But on one green-shaded afternoon while Kat rode alone in the forest, she was startled to hear a low whistle. She turned and saw him there. He was Lord Montjoy now, but mounted on the favorite of his two black horses, the one he called Lucifer, the one who had been ridden by the Silver Sword.

He wore a tunic with his colors. With his wonderful lions. Beneath it he was clad in a vibrant blue undershirt and dark-hued chausses. He wore no armor, though his sword was in the scabbard at his side. His head was uncovered, and his hair was ebony-dark, lifting just slightly around the bronze-toned, rugged planes and angles of his face. He and the horse both stood so quietly.

Almost as if she dreamed them there.

As if they were memory. Myth. Magic.

Legend.

Then he smiled slowly, and she called out his name and spurred her mare to race toward Lucifer. Even as she neared him, she was leaping out of her saddle, just as he was doing.

"Oh, Damian!" she cried as he took her in his arms. He held her face between his hands. He kissed her lips, her forehead, her cheeks, her lips again. "It's over!" he murmured between kisses.

"Over?"

"John's forces have been defeated. The ransom for Richard has been raised."

"Oh, Jesu!" Kat breathed. She touched Damian's face, wondering at the worry that still seemed to remain on it. "Damian, you've said that it is over—"

"Aye." He paused again. "I know Richard. From what he said to me in the Holy Land I know he will pardon Robin and all of his men. And, of course, the Silver Sword and the Lady Greensleeves, but then, they haven't been heard from in quite some time."

"And things are right with Robin?"

"That they are."

"Then . . ."

He slipped his arm around her, and they walked down a pine-strewn trail. It was so beautiful here. So peaceful. The sun barely made its way through the branches. The green light was just as magical as her husband's appearance. The air was fresh and sweet, and seemed softly to caress them.

"I went to see John, Kat. He was very bitter against me."

"There is nothing to be done about that. And Richard will be home soon—"

"And things should be well." He paused, then pointed ahead mischievously. "The cottage lies ahead, Kat. Let's hurry to it."

"Aye," she agreed solemnly, and started to walk with him. But he suddenly swept her up into his arms. He pretended to stagger. "Alas! You grow so heavy!"

"Not so heavy!" she protested, but his eyes were twinkling, and he held her easily with one arm, running his fingers over the rounding expansion of her belly.

"I like heavy!" he told her, laughing, and held her close as he walked the trail the rest of the way to the cottage. Once inside, he set her down upon the pallet of furs, and poured them a mug of wine to share.

His eyes were grave once again as he spoke. "I needed to see John, just as John needed to see me."

"I don't understand—" Kat murmured, disturbed by his distress.

"In case, after he is released Richard still insists that John will be his heir. No one seems to realize this, but mark my words. Richard will not stay in England. He is already talking about war to keep his hands on his Angevin possessions. His life is ever precarious."

Kat was silent for a minute, her eyes on her husband. "So what did you say to the Prince?" she asked softly.

"I told him that if and when the time came that he was duly crowned king, I would be his servant, as I have been Richard's. But I warned him, too, that he would need to take care with his barons, for many of us know him well, and will still fight him if he will not rule justly."

"And then?"

"Well, we are at a truce, so it seems."

Kat smiled slowly. She brought the mug of wine to her own lips, then offered some to her husband. He still seemed thoughtful. She took the mug from him.

"At this moment, my Lord Montjoy, we are at peace."

"Aye."

"And you will have no immediate need to ride away again."

"No, my love."

Her smile broadened, and she pressed him back upon the furs.

"Then for now, I am grateful. I think that I would like to show you just how grateful."

"Oh?"

The worried look had left his eyes. For now. She wished suddenly that she was in their own chamber. That she had a bath of rose-scented water awaiting her. That the linen sheets had been strewn with the flowers.

That she had more to give.

She pressed her lips to his, then to his throat. Then she was smiling, and murmured against her lips as she spoke.

"We should have been home, before the hearthy. I should have bathed with roses. We should be upon very soft down—"

He lifted her above him suddenly. "Should we? After all, my lady, this is where the Silver Sword was first seduced—"

"Nay, it is where the Silver Sword first did his seducing!"

"Does it matter?" he asked, smiling.

She shook her head, clad in the muscled warmth of his body as he brought her down upon him, even if the growing life within her did cause them a curious separation.

None of it mattered. His hands were suddenly on her. Beneath the fabric of her sleeves. His lips were against her throat, tender upon the pulse there.

"Perhaps the forest is best," she agreed huskily. "Even if I am heavy—"

"Delightfully rounded," he protested, his fingers having found the curve of her breast.

"And even . . . even if we have no roses," she whispered.

He suddenly had her down beneath him. Silver eyes shone with passion and love into her own.

"My dear Lady Greensleeves, you are the only rose I shall require," he told her. And his lips came close to hers. "So bloom for me now, my love. Flower, and bloom."

Her arms outstretched to him like petals opening to the sun.

And curiously, to them both, it suddenly seemed that the scent of roses did fill the air around them.

Then love encompassed all.

Epilogue

Spring 1198
The Forest

It was a good life, the young lord Michael Damian Montjoy decided, in a very wise and thoughtful way. He had a beautiful home—in fact, he had two that he knew well, and his mother had told him that his father had more holdings, too, in other places. He wasn't quite sure why they needed so many homes, but the fact that they had them made his father a very great baron, and he knew that well.

He knew, too, in his very wise almost-five-year-old way, that it was far more than his homes that made him happy. The people in his homes made him the happiest. There was Ari, mysterious, funny, and there to teach him things like language and history and astrology and chemistry. There was Marie, always ready to cradle him if he fell, or slip him a piece of fresh-baked bread or honeyed cake when he was sad. There was Sir James, that valiant fellow, to teach him the rudiments of sword-play, and there was, now and then, his cousin Robin to teach him what he knew of archery. Robin had been pardoned by the King—the good King Richard who had come at last—but Robin still lived something of a secret existence, because the same good King who had returned had so quickly decided to go back to France, to wage more war against King Phillip. The King of England, it seemed, did not like the King of France very much. Nor did he seem to want to stay in England very long.

But such things really didn't bother Michael greatly. As he had thought to begin with, life was very good. Because along with all the other wonderful people in his life, he had his parents.

There was his father, the tallest, most magnificent knight ever. He sometimes served the King on his campaigns, but more frequently he kept guard in the north country, ever keeping a careful watch on the Prince, who wanted to be the King. Michael was always happy when his father was home. His mother was the most vivacious at those times; her eyes seemed to sparkle the most, her laughter to softly caress them all the most. And next to his father, Michael adored his mother more than anyone on earth. She smelled deliciously of roses all the time, and she had the most beautiful eyes, and she was never too busy for him. More than anything, he loved to come for a ride here with his mother and his father, on a day like today.

They would travel the deep forest trails, trails that few men knew. Trails where the sunlight would just barely filter through the canopy created by the branches and the leaves of the high oaks, birch trees, pines, and hemlocks that interlaced and interlocked high above their heads.

It was spring, a beautiful day. The air itself around them seemed to be soft, and the scent of it was fragrant. The earth beneath their horses' hooves as they rode was redolent and rich, and it seemed that everything was touched by the green, everything that they saw, everything that they touched, even everything that they breathed. Green darkness, green light. It was beautiful.

"This is where Robin Hood and the Silver Sword—and even you, Father!—gave the Prince his comeuppance!" he announced suddenly out loud.

His father, riding ahead, pulled back and glanced over his head, smiling to his mother. "And even me? So this is the place, eh? And where did you hear that?"

"Sir Godfrey said so, and Sir Godfrey knows! He says that he rode with you, Father. Didn't he?"

"Oh, aye, Sir Godfrey rode with me. Many times," Damian agreed.

"I would be wondrous proud to be a knight," Michael said. Then he grinned. "But then I would be even more wondrous proud to be a bandit!"

"A bandit! Hush, Michael, you mustn't say such things!" his mother remonstrated.

He turned in his saddle. "Oh, but Mother! It is true. Our cousin Robin is still somewhat a bandit, isn't he? Cousin Robin is the famous Robin Hood, right?"

She looked uncomfortably over his head in turn, seeking an answer from his father. Their eyes met with both amusement and tenderness, and he wondered then if life was so good because they loved each other so much, and that love just naturally spilled over him, and over his sister, little Elyse. Elyse was just three, and she wasn't riding her own horse. She was seated before his mother on his mother's mare. Elyse was watching him with big turquoise eyes, very much like his mother's.

"The King pardoned Robin," Michael's father told him. "But the King is seldom here, you see. So Robin prefers to live a very quiet life with Marian, and so keep his distance from the King's brother—"

"John," Michael said, wrinkling his nose.

"Who may very well be King John one day," his mother said softly, "and so we must take care with him."

"But you would never bow down to him, Father?" Michael asked.

"If John becomes the rightful King of England," Damian said somewhat bitterly, "aye, then I'll help to defend England for him. But bow down before him . . ." He paused for a moment, then shook his head. "Never!"

"I'm so glad!" Michael said, his silver-gray eyes sparkling like his father's. Then he said, lying just a little, "You are as wonderful as any of them, Father, I swear it! You're as wonderful as Robin Hood, as noble as the Silver Sword, as valiant!"

"Well, I thank you, young sir!" his father said. His father was gazing back at his mother once more, amusement making his eyes shine like silver.

Michael turned quickly to involve his mother in his compliment, "And you, my lady mother, are truly as brave and beautiful as the Lady Greensleeves ever might have been!"

She arched a delicate brow to him, hugged Elyse against her in the saddle, and laughed. "I thank you, too, young sir!"

They had come to the cottage in the woods. Unassisted, Michael leaped down from his pony. He had a wooden sword at his side—the only type he was allowed to carry at the moment when he wasn't in training. He pulled it from his small leather scabbard.

"I shall see that all is safe!" he told his parents.

"Aye, and thank you, sir!" Katherine told him.

She watched as Michael disappeared through the cottage door. "He's a quite remarkable child," Damian said.

She looked down, for Damian had dismounted from his horse and reached up now to take their sleepy daughter from her perch forward on the saddle.

Elyse perked up as Damian took her, pressing against his shoulders. "Elyse get down!" she commanded. "Please, Papa! I go with Michael."

He laughed and set her down. She grabbed his face before he could rise from her, and kissed him loudly on the cheek, then raced off to join her brother.

Damian, his eyes dancing, looked up to his wife. "Sad, isn't it, my love? But children will love their stories more than they might their sire or their mother!"

"Alas!" she agreed with a soft sigh, her aquamarine eyes alight. "'Tis a sorry thing, isn't it?"

He lifted his arms to her, and she slipped easily into his hold. He kissed her nose. Then he seemed to sober for a moment. "Richard said it again, before I left him last. He and Queen Berengaria have produced no children—"

"Has he even seen his Queen?" Kat asked.

Damian shook his head. "Not that I know of. It is said that Berengaria lies languishing, awaiting his call. And Richard does not summon her. Richard reiterates—after all that has happened!—that John must be his heir. So we must all be prepared. John will quite possibly be King one day, and the way that Richard wages war, it may come much sooner than we expect."

"And a way of life will be over," Katherine said softly.

"A time for legends once again," Damian murmured.

"Our children will grow to live in this time of legends," Katherine said. "Oh, Damian! I do worry so about the future!"

Damian shrugged. He worried about it enough himself.

He wondered why.

Like his son, he thought that life was good.

He was more in love with his wife than ever. He had one wonderful son, and a beautiful, stubborn little daughter. At three, she was already every bit as willful as Kat had ever been. And she had her mother's glorious and radiant coloring . . . aye, her mother's beauty. One day, she would take some poor lord upon a wearying ride, he thought.

Ah, but that was distant. For now . . .

For now, it was a time of peace. A precious, rare time. He looked down into his wife's beautiful eyes, and felt the silk of her hair tumble about his fingers.

He grinned suddenly, wickedly. He swept her up into his arms. "Jesu! I smell roses on the air!"

"Damian!" she cried in protest, laughing. "The children—"

"Look around, my love, 'tis nearly night. The little ones will sleep. You needn't worry about the future!"

"And why is that?" she queried boldly, her fingers falling lightly on his chest.

"Night is the time for legends, my love. For knights in shining armor, for damsels in distress. Let's have the night, for no matter what the future brings, we will survive. Didn't you know? Legends—"

She pressed a finger against his lips. "Legends last forever!" she whispered softly.

"Legends and love," he agreed, smiling as he gazed tenderly into the blue-green beauty of her eyes. "Legends—and love!—live forever."

She smiled in turn, echoing the promise. "Aye!" she vowed. "Legends and love! So here they began—and so here they shall live forever!"

Now that you've enjoyed
Shannon Drake's
DAMSEL IN DISTRESS,
sample one of Avon Books'
Romantic Treasures—
FIRE ON THE WIND
by Barbara Dawson Smith

*As the flames of revolution sweep through their world,
two yearning hearts—free-thinking Sarah Faulkner and
the handsome but tormented Damien Coleridge—seek
sanctuary from the chaos . . .*

She held out the pitcher to him. "Then fetch your own
water, *burra* sahib. Your slave just quit."

His expression infuriatingly cool, he regarded her.
"You're no slave. I pay you a huge salary. And in
case you've forgotten," he said with elaborate patience,
"there's a reason behind our masquerade."

"Hah! You're using that as an excuse to treat me like
your personal drudge."

"Shush," he said, casting a quick glance around. "God
help us if the wrong person were to overhear you. You're

supposed to behave like a Hindu woman."

"I'll lower my voice," Sarah murmured, "but don't expect me to meekly accept my role. We should be setting a good example for the others. We could show them how a husband and wife can work together. We might better the lives of the Hindu women."

"So you've found a new crusade. I might have known you couldn't leave well enough alone."

"The way these women work isn't 'well enough.' I'm merely trying to make the world more equitable to all people."

"Well, my philosophy is to respect the local customs. Now quit complaining and fetch me the damned water."

His constant profanities and arrogant attitude set her teeth on edge. "You might at least make an effort to be civil."

He stood perfectly still, feet planted apart, hands on his hips. His dark features might have been carved from teak. Yet she had the impression of a tempest raging inside him.

"Is it help you want?" he said. "All right, then." He lunged at her and grabbed the jar. Stomping over the sand to the river, he bent and sloshed the pitcher into the muddy water. Then he returned and shoved the dripping container back into her arms. "Say thank you, Miss Priss."

The heavy vessel dampened the front of her sari, but Sarah clutched it as tightly as her temper. "Now you keep *your* voice down. I'm asking you for a little cooperation, that's all."

"Just what the hell do you expect me to do?"

"Show the men that women aren't beasts of burden and inferior beings."

"No, thanks. I'll leave the reforming to do-gooders like you." His insulting gaze swept her, lingering for a moment on her bosom. "Hell, maybe some women *are* inferior."

He turned toward the camp. A great surge of rage broke inside her, drowning her judgment in a hot red mist.

"Mr. Coleridge."

He swung back. "Miss Faulkner?"

"You've forgotten your bath."

She hurled the contents of the pitcher at him. He leaped back, but water slapped him in the face and drenched his tunic and dhoti.

The soaked cotton adhered to his torso, outlining every sleek curve and hard muscle. The sight abruptly struck her as comical. Clasping the clay container, she swallowed hard, but a burst of merriment pushed past her lips.

"Damn you," he sputtered, shaking the sodden leaves of his tunic. "What the hell are you laughing at?"

"You look ridiculous," she said between giggles. "Like a wet heron flapping its wings."

He glowered for a moment. Then his bad-tempered expression eased into something halfway between a scowl and a smile. He snatched up a piece of driftwood.

"You're bloody lucky I'm not a true Hindu husband, else I'd take this rod to your prim little arse."

Stick in hand, he strolled closer. Was that a twinkle in his eyes or a trick of the sunlight?

Her heart tripping, she left the temple step and backed away, the sand hot beneath her feet. "You can't be angry over that trifling amount of water."

"Oh?" He slapped the stick against the flat of his scarred palm. "If I were you, I wouldn't be quite so certain."

Her feet splashed into the warmth of the river. She barely noticed the sting of her blisters. Damien Coleridge had no sense of humor.

Or did he?

Daringly she taunted, "Ganges water is supposed to wash away sin. Are you feeling the least bit redeemed?"

"No."

"Then perhaps you should have been completely submerged."

"Go ahead and try," he said. "By God, I'll pull you in with me."

"You'll have to catch me first."

She spun around and ran. Hot wind rushed past her cheeks. His footsteps pounded behind her. At some deep level, she was shocked at her rash behavior, but an inexplicable caprice drove her on.

Nearing a bend in the river, Sarah risked a glance backward.

Damien grasped her arm and brought her to a skidding halt. His rough-hewn features loomed over her. His warm palm cupped the softness of her breast through the thin sari. Gasping, she felt her belly twist with the same stunning urge she'd felt that night in the garden. The urge to feel him touch her naked skin, to press her body to his, to drown in the warmth of his lips . . .